The Way We Live Now

The Way We Live Now

MARIAN THURM

Bantam Books

New York   London   Toronto   Sydney   Auckland

THE WAY WE LIVE NOW

A Bantam Book / October 1991

Grateful acknowledgment is made for permission to reprint
the following:

"Isn't It Romantic" by Lorenz Hart and Richard Rodgers copyright © 1932 by Famous Music Corporation. Copyright re-
newed 1959 by Famous Music Corporation.

BOOK DESIGN BY GRETCHEN ACHILLES

Library of Congress Cataloging-in-Publication Data:
Thurm, Marian.
The way we live now / Marian Thurm.
    p.   cm.
    ISBN 0-553-07604-3
    I. Title.
PS3570.H83W36   1991
813'.54—dc20   91-3167
                                                   CIP

Published simultaneously in the United States and
Canada

Bantam Books are published by Bantam Books, a di-
vision of Bantam Doubleday Dell Publishing Group,
Inc. Its trademark, consisting of the words "Bantam
Books" and the portrayal of a rooster, is Registered in
U. S. Patent and Trademark Office and in other
countries. Marca Registrada. Bantam Books,
666 Fifth Avenue, New York, New York 10103.

PRINTED IN THE UNITED STATES OF AMERICA

FFG   0 9 8 7 6 5 4 3 2 1

For my daughter Kate.

*And with thanks to Deb Futter for
the many pleasures of our work together.*

Chapter

1

Lounging in bed in the middle of a steamy summer afternoon, watching, mesmerized, as his wife nursed their three-week-old son, Spike Goldman felt utterly at peace, content to stay forever just as he was. The foot of the bed was littered with the clothing they'd worn the day before, a sloppy collection of magazines, a pair of matching terry-cloth bathrobes; on the night tables at either side were empty 7-Up cans, a pitcher of water, an assortment of partially filled glasses and plastic mugs. Both Spike and Leora were topless, dressed only in their underwear. Benjamin, the baby, nursed in his sleep, tiny mouth pulsing soundlessly.

They had been married less than two years, had known each other only a few months when they decided to marry. A blind date had brought them together, and both of them had been wary and slightly embarrassed, swearing to each other that this was the first time they'd ever "sunk so low," as Leora laughingly put it. Almost immediately, Spike was won over by her easy, good-natured response to everything that went wrong that night—the projector breaking down for almost half an hour at the movie theater, the dry, overcooked fish at the seafood restaurant he'd chosen, the unexpected shower that filled Leora's new shoes with icy rainwater. He liked her pale, faintly freckled skin, her long wild ginger-colored hair that looked as if it had been permed but had not. She was delicate-boned, with thin arms and legs, but was soft and fleshy everywhere else. Each time he saw her she was wearing a necklace of brightly colored glass beads that she fingered as she talked, the beads making a rustling sound as they rubbed against each other. The sound was a comfort to her, she confessed, and so was the feel of the frosted glass between her fingers. The first time they made love, he'd unhooked the necklace dreamily, touching the soft skin of her throat with excitement, as if it were a secret place he never expected he might explore.

Leora was thirty-two when they met, a year younger than Spike, and from the beginning she had let him know that marriage and a family were what she was after. (Twice she had come perilously close to marrying the wrong man, she said, one a plastic surgeon who treated her like a second-class citizen, the other a jewelry maker whose chronic moodiness she had not been able to cure.) He liked her openness, her willingness to talk freely about anything at all. She held strong opinions about books and movies, music and contemporary art, and sometimes they fell into discussions that nearly slipped into arguments, but he enjoyed this too. He knew that he loved her when, one morning, he accidentally used the toothbrush she began keeping in the ceramic holder in his bathroom: instead of casting it into the sink as soon as he realized his mistake, he continued brushing his teeth with it, savoring the thought that it was hers. Hearing this, Leora laughed, saying for her, love had nothing to do with toothbrushes but with the tiny square fingernails of his pinkies. They look like they belong on the hands of a little boy, she told him, delighted. She kissed them almost reverently, unembarrassed. Then she smiled at him, saying, And incidentally, stay away from my toothbrush, okay?

She was exceptionally even-tempered and, unlike Spike, always expected things to go right. It was Spike who had been seeing a shrink for years, who'd occasionally suffered from episodes of deeply felt anxiety. Leora had described herself to him as someone from the "Snap-Out-Of-It School of Psychology"—someone who believed that therapy was usually a self-indulgence and that most problems could be cured by telling yourself to snap out of it. Spike laughed when he heard this. He admired her optimism, loved her for it, but went on seeing his shrink every Thursday night anyway.

Married to her, Leora predicted, he'd soon see that his Thursday nights could be better spent at home.

It was the only thing of any importance they couldn't agree on; gratefully, they acknowledged that everything else in their life together was nearly perfect.

"Hungry?" Spike said from his side of the bed now. "I think lunch time came and went without us."

"I might be," Leora said. "Let me think about it." Abruptly, the buzzer squawked in the foyer; Leora looked over at Spike with a rueful expression, then shut her eyes. "You're going to kill me," she said. "I completely forgot we were having company."

"Who?" Spike pulled a T-shirt over his head and got into an old bathing suit that he mistook for a pair of shorts.

"It's Suzanne. She called yesterday to say she had a present for the baby. I had to ask her over, Spike. There was no way out of it, believe me."

"Why would my ex-wife buy a present for *our* baby?" said Spike. "It seems a little bizarre, doesn't it?"

"Why are you wearing a bathing suit?"

"This is very creepy, Leora," Spike said as the buzzer sounded again. "What could she possibly be thinking?"

"I get the feeling she's nosy, just like me," said Leora. "She probably wants to check out the baby, see what the three of us look like together as a family, you know. I'm not bothered by her. Really. She's probably the last woman in the world I'd expect you to run off with."

"Very creepy," said Spike, and pretended to shiver.

Suzanne stood in the doorway of the apartment with an armload of yellow-and-white freesia, and smiled at Spike, who frowned at her uncertainly for a long while and said absolutely nothing. He and Suzanne had known each other forever, it seemed, and had a habit of running into each other every now and then on the street. But this, he told himself, was different: this was his home, his family's home, and the sight of her standing there so casually and self-possessed absolutely unnerved him.

"What's with the bathing suit?" Suzanne said finally. "And are you going to invite me in or not?"

"Come on in," he said, without enthusiasm.

"I heard rumors from friends about an alleged baby and just had to see for myself," said Suzanne. "But I'm sorry, Spike, really. I wasn't expecting you to be so cold and unfriendly."

After seven years of marriage she had left him for someone named Jim O'Connor, a chemistry teacher/soccer coach who taught at the same city high school where Suzanne taught French and Spanish. Jim was a soft-spoken, likable guy whom Spike would have loved to hate but could not, no matter how hard he tried.

"How's Jim?" Spike asked as Suzanne moved past him and walked through the living room toward the baby, who was now sleeping on the couch in his mother's arms. "Hello there, you little cutie," Suzanne said. She propped the freesia against a corner of the couch, then rubbed her index finger delicately up and down the length of the baby's terry-cloth sleeve. The baby was almost entirely bald and was dressed in a one-piece outfit that had once been a rosy pink but now had a decidedly grayish cast to it. "Benjamin, right?" she said. "So what's he doing all in pink?"

Leora looked down into her lap. "All of his good things are in the laundry," she said. "You just happened to catch him in the worst of his hand-me-downs." Her voice sounded a little trembly, and Spike's heart went out to her. He squinted at Suzanne without a word, willing her to simply vanish.

"Well, congratulations to one and all," Suzanne said. "I think this baby business is just terrific." She began her survey of the room, examining a collection of ceramic pieces arranged on a glass-and-teak étagère, then moving to the bookcase that occupied nearly a whole wall and which Spike had designed and built during the first year of his marriage to Suzanne. In fact, this dark, high-ceilinged apartment way up on Broadway was the same one she and Spike had shared for seven years. She moved about the living room like a real-estate broker, Spike thought—with an appraising eye that made him stiffen. He could imagine her wandering from room to room, opening and closing kitchen cabinets and closet doors, checking the bathroom plumbing, raising and lowering windows, peering into the freezer to see if it were frost-free.

"Do we pass inspection or what?" he said.

A tiny enameled piece shaped like a top sat in the center of her palm; she spun it a few times and then replaced it on the bookcase. "You wanted to know about Jim?" she said. "What can I tell you? He's married, with a baby, just like you."

"Did I ask about Jim?" Spike said. "I thought you were assessing our apartment."

"You know," Suzanne said, "I hated to move out of this place. But of course, under the circumstances, staying here wasn't an option." At this, the baby burped raucously.

"Good boy!" Leora cheered. She rose from the couch with Benjamin against her shoulder, her hand set protectively at the back of his neck. "And thanks for the flowers," she said. Absently, she stroked the baby's back, and then her eyes began to close and she swayed daintily on her feet.

"You're falling asleep on your feet," Spike pointed out.

"You're right, I am," said Leora. "Even though I've been

dozing on and off all afternoon, I'm still exhausted." A blue Persian cat slithered between her ankles, his tail straight up in the air.

"And who's *this* handsome fellow?" Suzanne said.

"Oh, that's Harold," said Spike. "He's highly neurotic but exceptionally loyal to those he loves."

"Sounds like a guy I used to date."

"Sorry to hear it." As Leora settled back down on the couch Spike gave Suzanne a quick once-over and decided that she still had that slightly undernourished look about her that he had once found attractive, but now her chest seemed shrunken, her wrists extravagantly scrawny. And yet she was still seductive in her way, with her prominent cheekbones and her mouth painted in darkish lipstick, her eyes decorated with very dark shadow. Studying her, it came to him again that he had never truly gotten to the heart of her, that she was, in fact, unknowable. She was not an intimate person, but someone who always held back an essential part of herself, he felt. During the years of their marriage, and before that, in college, he had tried hard to see through to her, but had always come up short. He considered this now with a fresh, stinging sadness that surprised him. He didn't know what to make of this sorrow, which seemed inappropriate, senseless, something that had no place in his life. He remembered that he had loved her, but couldn't recall what it had been like, the exhilaration, the passion, the heat. Perhaps, he thought now, every bit of it had only been imagined.

"Can I hold him?" Suzanne was saying.

"What?"

"Your son."

"Oh," he said. "Sure. But what for?"

"What *for?*" She looked at him and then at Leora, and laughed. "Because I like the feel of a baby in my arms. The sweetness of it, I mean."

"Good enough," Leora said. "But go and wash your hands first. With soap," she added as Suzanne went off to the kitchen.

Spike lowered his head to rub his cheek against the baby's.

"What's she *doing* here?" he whispered to Leora. It had been four years since his divorce and what he remembered with the greatest clarity was, predictably, the night she'd broken the news about Jim. He'd been completely dumbfounded by the anxious, heartfelt little speech she'd delivered as they stood side by side at the open refrigerator in their kitchen, trying to settle on what to have for dinner. He held a small head of Boston lettuce in one hand and a plastic box of beautiful white mushrooms in the other. The refrigerator door had slammed shut, startling him, and the lettuce rolled off his palm and under the table, where it remained for the next day or two until he happened to see it.

"I thought we had a pretty fair marriage," he'd said. "Jesus!" He dropped the mushrooms onto the table and began to clench and unclench his fists, over and over again.

"We did," Suzanne said, nodding. "But the truth is, we were never able to make each other happy."

"We weren't? I don't get it," he said, and rubbed his eyes, as if to clear his blindness.

"And anyway, this thing with Jim was kismet. It was unavoidable; it had to be."

"Kismet?" Spike said. "What do I care? I'll break his fucking head."

"I still really *like* you, Spike," Suzanne told him. "Our time together as a romantic pair is up, that's all."

"What kind of person are you?" Spike said, growling in a stranger's voice. "I mean, who are you?"

"Just someone who fell deeply in love with my long-lost spiritual twin," Suzanne said in a reverent whisper. "My soul mate," she breathed. "The one person in all the world who was meant to share my life."

And so he had let her go, unable to argue persuasively with a wife who had convinced herself that she'd found her spiritual twin right there in the chemistry department of Washington Irving High School. Except for the loneliness that hit him hardest around dinnertime every night and did not abate until after the eleven o'clock news, when his eyes began to burn with exhaustion, his life seemed, after a few months, to go on much as it had before, pleasantly enough. He enjoyed his work, teaching legal writing and research methods at Columbia Law School, and there were always piles of papers to grade and student conferences to fill up his time outside the classroom. He began to miss Suzanne less and less, and was no longer jolted by the silence that awaited him at home after school each day. The sound of her voice, the feel of her hands trailing along the length of his body, the soft place behind her ear that he loved to stroke—all of these seemed to vanish from memory. He missed the pleasures of a shared life, of human company, but not *her* particular company. To have come this far seemed a triumph. And then, in the spring, not long after their divorce had come through, he was held up on a Sunday afternoon in the courtyard of his apartment building. "What are you, crazy?" he asked the teenage hoodlums who wanted his wallet. "You can't hold someone up in broad daylight like this!" One of the muggers, who had the hood of a red sweatshirt drawn over his head, stared at Spike with a mixture of fear and contempt, and then groaned. "It's happening, baby, and you better believe it!" he informed Spike. Afterward, he found himself riding, in a trance, a series of subways all the way downtown to the apartment Suzanne shared with Jim O'Connor near Gramercy Park. She listened to his story sympathetically and gave him a drink that went straight to his head. Jim was out for the afternoon playing softball, she told him casually. Spike's hands shook, but he smiled at her.

"You're going to be all right," she said.

He embraced her, wanting her warmth and also something to hold on to. He remembered when they had lived together long ago in college, off campus in a cheap apartment they'd rented in an unkempt Victorian house. Their bedroom was enormous, and hot with afternoon sunlight, their bed a second-hand mattress they kept on the floor near a large bay window. Suzanne's clothing hung next to his in the single small closet; looking at her long Indian-print dresses intermingled with his jeans and sweatshirts gave him a thrill. As they shopped for

8

their meals together in the supermarket every week, arms slung low around each other's waist, hands tucked in each other's back pocket, they felt entirely grown up and settled in their lives. And unimaginably lucky to have found each other. He felt nostalgic, lifetimes later, for their innocence, their easy happiness.

He and Suzanne made love sweetly, slowly, in Jim O'Connor's bed, taking their time, exploring each other as if they had just met, as if there were a chance they might soon fall in love. When it was over, Spike was astonished at the tears that glittered for an instant in Suzanne's eyes.

"I have to go," he said.

She offered, uncertainly, her fingers playing with the soft ends of his hair that hung past his collar, to drop by and visit him one night.

"Not a good idea," he heard himself telling her. She looked hurt and also relieved, and he saw then just how needy he must have appeared to her when he'd arrived, a man who'd lost his wallet and also all his good sense. Falling into her arms, into her bed, had been a step backward, something to be regretted and quickly forgotten. "I'm sorry," he said out loud. "There won't be a next time, but if there is, don't let me past the front door."

Suzanne laughed, and hugged him in a friendly way. "Get out of here and don't come back," she said, smiling.

Leaving her then, he understood that he had been cured of her; he walked past her and out the door without even the slightest urge to gaze over his shoulder for one last lingering look.

The next time he saw her, on line outside a movie theater on Fifty-ninth Street, he and Leora were newly married. While they talked Suzanne kept her head on Jim's shoulder, as if to offer proof of their intimacy. If she'd had her way, the four of them would have gone for coffee together after the movie. But shamelessly and without hesitation, Spike offered his lie, saying they already had plans with another couple. Suzanne had seemed genuinely disappointed and told Leora more than once how terrific it had been to meet her. Just what was it that was so terrific? Spike wondered as they took their place on line miles behind Suzanne and Jim. Inside the theater, he was able to concentrate on the movie without any trouble at all, but Leora shifted about uneasily beside him. He held on to her hand until both their palms grew sweaty. She's nothing to me, he whispered, but it wasn't what Leora wanted. What she wanted, it turned out, was to catch up with Suzanne after the movie.

"Out of the question," Spike said.

"Why?" Leora wanted to know.

"Because it's inappropriate, that's why. And absolutely unnecessary."

"What are you so afraid of?" Leora asked.

"I'm not afraid of anything. Can we please just watch the movie?"

"Yeah, great idea," a man behind them hissed.

Leora fell silent and Spike turned his attention back to the screen, where a sensuous and womanly Kathleen Turner was doing her best to impersonate a high-school girl. Spike smiled at Leora in the darkened theater, smiled at the thought that he could ever be afraid of Suzanne. When the movie ended, he took Leora's arm and steered her out of the theater. Don't even think of trying to find her, he warned Leora, who sulked all the way home, and then, seeing she was getting nowhere, finally gave up. But he suspected that in Leora's mind Suzanne had assumed the stature of a celebrity; that, once seen, she was now a source of infinite curiosity. Let it go, he soothed her. Just let it go.

And it seemed that Leora had; she rarely spoke of Suzanne at all. But when they bumped into her on the street, as they did from time to time, Leora stared at her hungrily, eager to absorb whatever she could from these briefest of encounters in front of museums, department stores, and movie theaters. Mostly, she kept her thoughts to herself, though occasionally she offered up a comment on Suzanne's appearance ("sort of glamorous"), her voice ("kind of sexy"), her manner ("pretty self-confident"). That sounds about right, Spike always said, and then shrugged, letting her know he had no particular interest in pursuing the subject.

And here was Suzanne in his living room now, holding out her freshly scrubbed hands to receive his tiny son.

"There you go," Spike said, and eased Benjamin into his ex-wife's arms. "But you can only hold him for a second."

"Sweet sweet baby," Suzanne murmured, lowering herself onto the couch next to Leora. "He looks just like you, Spike."

"Really? We think he looks like Charlie Brown," said Leora.

"Now that you mention it, I do see a striking resemblance. It's the bald head and that big broad face, I guess."

"We're going to keep him anyway," said Spike. "Hand him over, please."

"I wonder why *we* never had a baby," said Suzanne as Spike leaned toward her to retrieve his son. "We never even contemplated the subject."

Glancing at Leora apologetically, Spike mumbled, "Sure we did."

"We did not."

"It was just about the time you met your spiritual twin," Spike said, "but of course I didn't know that. I remember the moment so well be—"

Leora got their attention by clearing her throat theatrically. "Do you really want to be talking about this?" she said. "Because part of me wants to sit here listening to every detail, and part of me just wants to run from the room. Do you believe I actually thought Suzanne only wanted to see the baby?"

"Oh, I did bring a present," Suzanne said. "Don't think for a minute that I came here for any other reason. I really did want to see this baby." She took a small unwrapped box from her bag and handed it to Leora.

"Why?" said Spike.

"We've known each other forever," said Suzanne. "What's the big deal about my taking a look at your baby?"

"It's not such a big deal," Leora said. In her palm she held a tiny unadorned silver bracelet. "It's lovely," she said. "Thank you."

"Babies don't wear bracelets," said Spike. "But thanks anyway."

"Sure they do," Leora said.

"Not in this family they don't."

"The consensus seems to be that you're wrong, Spike." Suzanne cast a smile in Leora's direction, and it was as if it were a net swiftly drawing her in, pointedly leaving Spike behind.

"You're making me crazy!" Spike yelled, startling the baby, who crossed and uncrossed his hands jerkily in front of his face and then began his newborn cry, a pathetic bleating that was painful to listen to. "Look at this, you're making *him* crazy too," said Spike.

"I came here," Suzanne announced, "bearing freesia and good wishes. I had nothing to do with making you crazy. That's your own doing, *chéri.*"

"Oh, forget it," Spike said, and tried his best to soothe the baby, jiggling him gently against his shoulder, murmuring endearments that failed to impress Benjamin at all.

"She's right," Leora offered. Annoyed at him, she let Spike struggle with the baby a few moments longer.

"Don't you know any children's songs?" Suzanne said. "Or a lullaby?"

"Here's a song," Spike said, and sang a few lines from "Yellow Submarine." Benjamin's eyes widened and his bleating faded to a whimper and then at last he fell silent. Just at that moment the cat meowed in a peculiar, nasal voice. Turning himself in a slow circle as the meowing ceased, Harold let out a series of desperate choking sounds. He moved in a faster circle now, and then took a few steps backward.

"What *is* this?" said Suzanne. "Some kind of pagan cat ritual?"

"Newspaper!" Spike said urgently.

"What?"

"Get a newspaper and open it up right in front of him. He's going to—"

"He's going to read a newspaper?" Suzanne said. "I wouldn't miss this for the world!" She hurried to a stack of papers piled up high in a V-shaped stand on the floor, pulled out a section of the *Times,* and placed it next to the cat, who immediately vomited on it and then slunk away.

"Why didn't you tell me he had an upset stomach?" Suzanne said.

Spike slipped Benjamin into his swing, a metal-and-plastic contraption that stood on four legs in the middle of the room, and cranked it up so that the baby drifted back and forth at a steady pace. He rolled up the newspaper and dumped it into the compactor in the hallway outside the apartment. When he returned, Leora was standing guard beside the baby, looking formidable, arms crossed over her chest. Suzanne sat slumped exhaustedly in a director's chair.

"God, I feel like I've been through a lot," she said.

Leora nodded. "I ought to apologize for Harold," she said. "He's very rude."

"The cat?"

"He can't tolerate guests for more than half an hour; that's why he vomited like that."

"He got sick to his stomach because he wanted me to go home?" Suzanne said.

"Don't take it personally—he does this to everyone who comes to visit for the first time." Leora flashed her a smile and shrugged her shoulders. "Would you like a drink? What can I offer you?"

"If the cat wants me to leave, maybe I should go."

"Stay as long as you like," Leora heard herself say. "Do you think I care what Harold thinks about anything?"

"What about what *I* think?" Spike said. "I think I've had about enough for one day."

Rising, dropping her hands to her hips, Suzanne rolled her eyes. "Oh, honestly," she said. She grabbed the sides of Benjamin's seat as he swung toward her, halting him in his tracks. She planted a kiss at the top of his head. "See you around, *chéri.*"

"You seem a little put out," said Spike.

"Can you blame me?" Suzanne said. "You do, however, have a lovely family, and I wish them well."

"Did I thank you for the bracelet?" Leora called out as Suzanne headed for the door. "And I'm sorry things were so hectic."

"Don't worry about it," Suzanne said over her shoulder. "I hope . . ."

Leora listened for the rest, but there was nothing except the sound of Suzanne's rapid footfalls against the worn tiles in the hallway outside.

"Well, that was fun," Spike said after a while. "Almost like getting a couple of impacted wisdom teeth pulled." He slipped the silver bracelet over two of his fingers, twirling it intently. "You all right?" he asked Leora.

"Just a little dizzy watching the baby swing back and forth."

"Something tells me," said Spike, "that she's washed her hands of us." Coming up behind Leora, he draped his arms over her shoulders, leaned his head against her neck. "Forever," he said cheerfully.

Leora could not imagine why, but what she felt was the briefest pang of disappointment. The feeling was purely physical, a momentary ache in her chest, a heaviness that lifted almost instantly. She wondered if Suzanne would give her a second thought, or if she had already dismissed her, as you would a movie that left no impression at all, that vanished once the theater was again filled with light.

On her way home following her visit with Leora and Spike, Suzanne wandered into a multiplex theater and sat through two movies one after the other, then stopped at a convenience market to buy a pack of cigarettes, something she did only when she was feeling particularly bleak. (She liked to brood with a lit cigarette in hand, to watch the smoke emerging from her mouth in a slow or quick white stream and then lingering under the light of a bright lamp before disappearing.) In fact, her visit had left Suzanne mildly depressed and also a little shaken; she now seemed, to herself, someone whose life had gone sadly and stupidly wrong.

With a pack of Parliaments and three fragrant peaches crowded into a small paper bag, she returned to her month-to-month sublet in Chelsea, a studio apartment that would never feel like home and wasn't meant to—really, for her, just a way station that happened to belong to a married friend of her father's who lived in the suburbs and liked to entertain various women in the city. Harv, her father's friend, was in Europe for the summer with his wife, and he'd asked Suzanne to keep a careful record of everyone who called. A couple of these women phoned Suzanne more than once, accusing her of lying when she insisted she was only a subtenant and that Harv was out of town until September. One of the stubborn ones, a woman named Grace, had been in the habit of calling at two or three in the morning, a little drunk, and begging Suzanne to let her know where Harv *really* was. Sensing Grace was poised close to the edge, Suzanne struggled to be patient with her, speaking into the phone in a low, soothing voice, trying to reassure her that Harv would be calling as soon as he got back into town. *Do you think he still loves me?* Grace asked her one night. *Or am I just being a big fool, as usual. Of course he does,* Suzanne told her, too exhausted to hold up her end of a tiresome conversation. She never heard from Grace after that, and found herself worrying from time to time, almost wishing she could call and check up on her.

She had forgotten to leave the air conditioner running, and the apartment, just below the building's tin roof, was suffocatingly hot. There were piles of clean laundry oddly scattered about—on the corduroy arms and cushions of a wood-frame couch, on the shaky card table she ate at outside the kitchen, on the counter above the miniature-sized dishwasher. Nightgowns, unpaired socks, a soft mountain of badly wrinkled sheets, a half-dozen black T-shirts. Ignoring all of it, she lay on her side along the floor in front of the air conditioner and went through three bottles of beer and a couple of cigarettes listening to a recording of Vladimir Horowitz playing his favorite Beethoven sonatas. Awakening several hours later, her face and arms ice-cold, and with an urgent need to pee, she got out of her clothes and slipped bewilderedly into the shower, as if it were six in the morning and she'd had a lousy night's sleep on the floor. It was, surprisingly, only dinnertime. She had a peach and a few more cigarettes and then called her older sister in Baltimore and her younger one in Arlington, Virginia, and was met with a pair of amiable invitations to leave her message after the tone. Julie, the younger sister, had borrowed a thousand dollars from her a few years ago and was too embarrassed to admit that she had no intention of ever repaying it; Suzanne knew the loan had been a mistake when Julie began avoiding her phone calls and ignoring her occasional letters, none of which even mentioned the money. Her older sister, Nancy, was a gay feminist who had hardened over the years—it seemed incredible that she and Suzanne had once lingered over *Seventeen* together for hours every month, that in their adolescence they had patiently set each other's hair on orange juice cans, shared clothing and shoes and Judy Collins albums, along with a great many small secrets. (The big secret was revealed just after Nancy's marriage failed, and it was then that she seemed to have lost her sense of humor and turned preachy and strident, Suzanne thought mournfully.) In recent years, they had all gathered together at Christmastime at their parents' house in San Diego, the three of them uneasy and wary of one another, talking too much about nothing at all, smiling falsely for their father and his camera. Suzanne, at least, grieved for the loss of their shared childhood, of their natural proximity to one another as they awakened under the same roof year after year, their lives overlapping endlessly, it seemed.

She read the newspaper now with the TV news turned on and in the background, the radio playing Chopin. "Sensory overload," she murmured out loud, but was too lazy to get up and turn anything off. In the newspaper she read that short hemlines were back and that the incidence of domestic violence was up. She thought idly of Spike and Leora, of Leora's shyness giving way as she asked her to wash her hands before holding the baby. It was clear that Spike was onto a good thing, and Suzanne allowed herself a moment of envy for the sweet simple path his life had taken. She had hurt him, without apology, but he had made a full recovery; that much was certain. Leora seemed nurturing and firmly fixed in place, someone who would not fail you. Suzanne could envision opening herself up, without fear, to someone like that. But what did she know—she who had known for sure that Jim O'Connor was her fate, her perfect soul mate she could not live without.

That night she dreamed that she was a guest at a birthday party Leora had thrown for Spike, that she and Leora sprang from a crepe paper-draped cardboard cake six feet high, the two of them dressed in black leotards, feathery red boas draped flamboyantly around their necks, a long-stemmed rose for each of them between their gleaming teeth. Spike had looked on in amazement, absolutely motionless, his shoulders turning to stone as she and Leora arranged their boas loosely around him in an awkward embrace.

Chapter 2

Alexander Fine, Spike's father-in-law and favorite confidant, is out on one of his disastrous blind dates again, waiting to be seated at a table for two in a restaurant of his date's choosing. This time around, the woman is named Paulette Wolfson, and she gets down to the nitty-gritty of things so fast that Alexander doesn't know what hit him.

"And do you own or rent in Florida?" Paulette asks. She is platinum-haired and narrow-eyed, and Alexander doesn't like the looks of her.

"Pardon me?" he says. The hostess is approaching them now, signaling with a victory sign that their table is finally ready.

"Florida," Paulette says hopefully. "I was told you have a second home there."

"Florida? God's Waiting Room?" says Alexander. "Hate the place. Too hot, and too many old people. I haven't been near the place in years—I'd guess about five years before my wife died. All those old people being taken away in ambulances left and right," he says, and shudders. "The thought of spending my golden years in a place like that gives me the willies."

Hearing this, Paulette takes out a little notebook and a short gold pencil and draws a horizontal line across the page. She snaps the notebook shut sharply. "Well," she says, "we can still have dinner, I suppose."

"Uh-oh," the hostess says. "Was that smoking or nonsmoking?"

"One moment, please," says Alexander, and nods in Paulette's direction. "Did you just draw a line through my name?"

"Only in the column marked 'Second Homes.' "

He makes a grab for the notebook, but Paulette instantly swings it around behind her back. "Nothing doing," she says, and, oddly, gives him a flirtatious smile.

"I'm afraid I've got you in the smoking section," the hostess says. "Can you handle it?"

Alexander's stomach growls in response. He peeks at his watch—it's already an hour past his dinnertime. Since his wife's death last spring, just nine months ago, he'd become rigid in his ways: breakfast at nine (two slices of unadorned rye bread and a coffee cup full of Swiss Miss hot chocolate), lunch at 12:30 (half a can of tuna fish mixed with a tablespoon of mayonnaise in a turquoise Melmac bowl), dinner at six (a plate of pasta in a sauce of melted I Can't Believe It's Not Butter).

"What a life!" he says out loud. But he knows that without his schedule he would be lost, an unshaven, emaciated old man in a stained bathrobe that would swirl around his bony ankles and trip him whenever he tried to stand on his feet. A lost soul. Like the homeless woman he keeps encountering at the library every morning, where he goes to read his copy of the *Times* from cover to cover in a fake-leather chair positioned near a display of videotapes and record albums. The woman is usually asleep, with her head down on a table and her hand-lettered cardboard

sign propped up against a pile of books. The sign says PREG-
NANT & DYING OF A POPULAR DISEASE, but according to the librar-
ians, she's just a drunk who likes the warmth and silence of the
library. One morning a few weeks ago she lifted her head from
the table and turned on Alexander in a fury. "Stop breathing so
loud!" she shrieked at him while people seated at tables nearby
stared in astonishment. "Keep it down, for Chrissake!" she'd hol-
lered. "Have some consideration for those of us who need a
little extra sleep." He'd responded with an embarrassed smile
and nothing more, but under his shirt, under his skin, his heart
raced noisily. When he finished with the newspaper and got up
to leave, his favorite librarian, a cheery young woman who always dressed in black, winked at him and said, "You have a nice
day, now, okay?" He winked back at her, though he was still
feeling a little shaky. He walked the ten blocks home along
Madison Avenue, hands jammed into the pockets of his cashmere overcoat, shoulders held back, a man with nothing to fear
in all the world. In front of his building, a handful of women,
all of them sixtyish and dressed in mink coats, gathered in a
crowd around one of their friends, who had gotten gum caught
on the bottom of her shoe. Clucking in extravagant sympathy,
they watched as the woman stood on one foot and struggled to
pull the gum from her heel. A couple of them looked Alexander
up and down as he passed them and nodded their approval.
It was the cashmere, he knew, and also his excellent posture,
which had fooled them into thinking that here was a man
you could count on, a man who knew which end was up. In
truth, he was still reeling from his wife's death, still waiting for
the end of the earthquake that had rocked his life and sent him
flying.

The hostess, apologizing all the way, leads Alexander and
his blind date to their seats in the smoking section, not far from
the piano, where a man in a dark turtleneck, his eyes shut tight
in passion, is singing "Glad to Be Unhappy."

"How many names do you have in that little book of yours,
anyway?" Alexander asks Paulette.

"Oh, dozens."

"Dozens? If that little book is all filled up, what are you doing here with me?"

Paulette sighs. "The world," she announces, "is full of losers."

"Define your terms," Alexander says, and arranges his napkin in his lap.

Another sigh. "Oh, you know, married men looking for a little action on the side, widowers who only want to sit around and talk about the good old days when their wives were alive and kicking and making dinner every night . . . you know. You'd be surprised at the number of men who get all weepy remembering their wives' stuffed peppers and sweet-and-sour meatballs. First they get all choked up, then their shoulders start to shake, and before you know it, the tears are flowing like mad. I'll tell you, it's so depressing I can barely stand it sometimes. Wake up and smell the coffee, I want to say. Your beloved Rose or Roz or whoever is gone! Forever! And so are her sweet-and-sour meatballs!"

"Don't yell at *me*," Alexander says. "My wife wasn't even all that much of a cook. To be perfectly honest, Margot was competent, but not particularly inspired. Her brownies were terrific, though," he says, and feels a lump rising dangerously in his throat. How he misses her! Not the way she was toward the end, sick of the pain and anxious to come to the end of it all, cranky and impatient with everyone, her face skeletal, eyes blackened, her skin greenish. The woman he misses was full-faced, and rounded in all the right places, usually sweet-tempered, almost always generous in her assessment of people. She had loved their daughter fiercely, loyally, and had kept track of Leora with brief, daily phone calls that left her satisfied that her love was returned. He remembers her faults with difficulty, always, resisting at this moment the memory of a bedroom door slammed in his face, the sound of her yelling, "You want to know what I think? I think that men are just plain dumb, that they were brought up to be dumb by their mothers and just don't know any other way!" Waiting for her to simmer down, to put aside whatever it was he'd said or done to inflame her, he'd watch a few minutes of TV, listen to some Vivaldi on the stereo. And when, perhaps a half hour later, she would emerge from the bedroom, it would be with a sheepish half smile and a mumbled apology and then she would kiss him, saying, "You're still as dumb as ever, but I've decided there are worse things a man can be." And then they would both have to laugh, because it was all so utterly predictable, so sweetly comforting, really.

"See what I mean?" Paulette is saying now. "Your wife's brownies have gotten to you in a big way. You men are all alike, I'm telling you."

"She was my number-one blessing in this life," Alexander says. "A lovely, lovely woman."

"I don't doubt it," Paulette says, surprising him with her sympathy. "I don't doubt it for a minute. But the fact remains that I've heard it all before. I can't go on like this, spending all my energy consoling every Tom, Dick, and Harry who can't let go of the past. I mean, what about *me?*"

"What you've got to do," Alexander says, "is find yourself a guy who had a miserable marriage and doesn't even want to think about his wife."

Paulette smiles. "Got anyone in mind? The thing is, those are the ones who tend to be bitter and distrustful—they want an accounting of your every waking hour. You can't even run out to the supermarket at midnight without having to explain your whereabouts the next day."

"You've really seen it all, haven't you?"

"You bet," says Paulette. "My little notebook and I could tell you stories that would make your hair stand on end. My husband flew the coop eighteen months ago and I haven't been idle for a minute. I'm absolutely determined to find someone who's going to make me happy. And believe me, I will. He's out there somewhere, and when I find him, I'll recognize him in an instant."

"Some enchanted evening," Alexander says. His stomach rumbles, reminding him again that he's off schedule tonight. But listening to Paulette has robbed him of his appetite; contemplating all she's said, he doubts he'll ever eat again.

"What?" says Paulette.

"You know, a stranger across a crowded room, and all that."

"Are you making fun of me?" Paulette asks.

Alexander shakes his head. "I'm just surprised that a woman who keeps a notebook filled with names and vital statistics could actually have a . . . romantic vision, I guess you'd call it."

"You think I'm cold-blooded, is that it?" Paulette says, reaching across the table and grabbing his fingertips with her icy hands. "Is that it?"

"Cold hands!" he says, and laughs uneasily. He tries to pull away, but she won't let go of him. Even in the restaurant's muted light, he notices, her elegant, polished nails are luminous, dazzling.

"I'm well organized, that's all," she says, and releases him. "I was an office manager for nearly my whole working life."

"Okay," says Alexander. He flips open the menu, which is enclosed in maroon leatherette and feels like a burden in his hands. One look at all the possibilities, and his head begins to ache. "What do you know about the blackened swordfish?" he asks Paulette, simply to make conversation.

"Tell me about your wife," Paulette says softly.

"What?"

"Tell me about her." She raises her elbows onto the table, sinks her chin into her palms. "Go ahead," she urges. "It's all right, really. I'm listening."

He smiles at her gratefully. "I won't bore you," he promises. He tells her only the most surprising things he can think of; that Margot was born in Czechoslovakia and spent the last years of the war hidden in a barn, thanks to a Gentile family who risked their necks to shelter her and her parents, to give them two meals every day; that she wept when she explained to him what it was like not to have seen sunlight in three years; that once she arrived in America, she never got over her fear of the sound of firecrackers on the Fourth of July, sure that they

signaled the start of war. He does not tell Paulette of the softness of his wife's fine blond hair, of the pale freckles that ornamented her limbs, the perfect delicate tapering of her ankles and
wrists.

"Tell me more," Paulette says when he falls silent.

"It's your turn," he says. "What happened to your husband?"

Sitting back in her seat, Paulette gives him an insincere
smile so broad, her narrow eyes seem to disappear entirely. "You're
going to laugh," she says, and her smile vanishes.

"I won't."

"You will," Paulette insists. "But what the hell, you look
like you could use a good laugh."

"The suspense is killing me," he says, already beginning to
smile.

"Well, here it is: the love of my life, that human slime, ran
off with my daughter-in-law." Paulette is looking at him in surprise, incredulous that she has not gotten a laugh out of him.
"What's wrong?" she says. "Are you all right?"

"I know you!" Alexander cries.

"What?"

"I saw you on one of the talk shows—*Oprah*, I think it was—
a couple of months ago."

"Are you crazy? What would I be doing on TV?"

"Talking about how your husband ran off with your daughter-in-law, of course. There were four of you, I remember, all
women who had been left by their husbands, and then there
were a couple of psychologists who were—"

"Are you *crazy?*" Paulette interrupts. "What do you think,
I'd go on national TV and spill my insides out to the whole
world? Listen, it nearly killed me when the two of them ran off
to their love nest in Marlborough, New Jersey, to start their
new life together. Talking about it to an audience of fifty million people wouldn't have made me feel any better, believe
me."

Alexander presses on, sure that the woman he heard that
day had to have been Paulette. "It's nothing to be ashamed of,"

he says soothingly. "There you were, up there in front of the audience, the little microphone clipped onto the collar of your shirt, your—"

"Will you stop it!" Paulette hollers. "I was never on *Oprah* or any other talk show blabbing the story of my life. Now get that through your head or you'll be dining solo tonight!"

"Shh," Alexander hisses, but it is already too late—the hostess is striding toward them now with a look of alarm.

"Is there a problem?" she asks politely.

"You bet there is," says Paulette. "This gentleman is insisting that I was a guest on the *Oprah Winfrey Show*, but the fact of the matter is that it's simply a case of mistaken identity."

"Ah," says the hostess, and matches her palms together in front of her.

"Thank you for your concern," Alexander says. "And everything is going to be just fine."

The hostess nods. "I'm sure it will be. Enjoy your dinner."

"I'm sorry," says Alexander as the woman walks off. "I guess I just couldn't quite believe that there could have been *two* women whose husbands left them for their daughters-in-law."

"Oh, for crying out loud," Paulette says in exasperation. "Don't you know there's nothing new under the sun?"

"Nothing?"

"That's about the size of it," she says breezily. She seems to have recovered from her anger, and opens her menu with a flourish. She decides on the lobster, the only item on the menu that doesn't have a price next to it.

Silently, Alexander curses his friend Sydney Packer—his best friend in all the world and a first-class troublemaker. *You ever get any big ideas about arranging another date for me,* Alexander tells him, *and I'll come after you and knock out every one of your beautiful, expensively capped teeth. Every last one of them, Sydney.*

Arriving home at the evening's end, after having graciously accepted the single kiss Paulette deposited on his cheek in the taxi they shared, Alexander hops into his black-and-white plaid flannel pajamas and switches on the TV. He watches in fascination as a group of female impersonators swap beauty secrets. There are four of them in all—men dressed up to look like Cher, Barbra Streisand, Marilyn Monroe, and someone with an extraordinary hairdo whom Alexander doesn't recognize but who is later identified as Diana Ross. The men are glamorous creatures, all of them, but their deep voices put a damper on things for Alexander. He finds himself feeling sorry for them, imagining each at the moment he removes his makeup and is faced with the real thing.

Just as the man dressed as Diana Ross rises to sing "Baby Love" in a shocking falsetto, the phone rings.

"Sydney," Alexander says. "Sydney Sydney Sydney."

"You struck out, I suppose," says Sydney. "I'm sorry to hear that, of course. But listen, Allie, I can't talk about your date with what's-her-name now. I've got terrible news; Ginger is missing," he says excitedly.

Alexander snaps off the TV with the remote control and stretches out flat on his stomach across the bed. He truly loves Sydney, whom he has known from childhood, but since recovering from his stroke several months ago, Sydney has turned weepy and fearful, and insists on involving Alexander in every one of his small crises. Sydney, a certified public accountant by profession, no longer remembers the number seven. It seems to have slipped permanently from his memory, along with a dozen or so simple words. And often he has to stop in the middle of a sentence, unable to recall at that moment the one word, temporarily lost, that he needs to get him through to the end of his thought. Alexander is as patient as he can be, but sometimes, like Sydney, he simply wants to give up.

"First of all," Alexander says now, "you know Ginger isn't missing, not really."

"We've been married forty years. Don't you think I'd know if she were missing or not? She told me she was going to a neighbor's apartment and then out to a coffee shop. She promised she'd be home by midnight and it's already twelve-fifteen. What am I going to do? Do you think I should call the . . . the men in those uniforms . . . the fire department?"

"The police," Alexander says gently. "No, I don't think you should call the police. She's fifteen minutes late, Sydney. Not exactly what I'd call a missing person. I'm sure she'll be home any minute."

"But what if she's not? What if she never comes home? I can't take care of myself the way I used to. I've been sick; I'm not the same anymore. I've never even been to the laundry room downstairs, I don't know the first thing about it. I'll have to keep wearing the same dirty clothes over and over again!" Sydney wails.

"Get a hold of yourself," says Alexander. "I'm telling you she's coming back."

"She is not," Sydney says, his voice high-pitched and unsteady. "She doesn't like the way I've been since the stroke. All she wants is to get away from me. She wants to go to Grand Bahama Island with her canasta buddies and never come back. And she'll do it too, believe me. She'll—"

"I'll tell you what," Alexander says, "if she does, you can move in with me. We'll spend our days doing laundry together and be as happy as clams."

"We will?" Sydney says doubtfully. "I'm on a very strict diet, you know. And there's all this medication I have to take. Do you think you can manage all that? It's not going to be easy."

Life with Sydney. Alexander can just see the two of them strolling down the supermarket aisles in search of salt-free this and salt-free that, taking cabs to doctors' offices all over town, spending hours in their waiting rooms, flipping through ancient magazines. And then, at home, arguing over whose turn it is to load the dishwasher, whose to unload, whose to dump the garbage down the chute, whose to make sure the towels hanging in the bathroom are clean.

He thinks of all the endless hours he'll be available to listen to Sydney alternately mourning and vilifying his lost love, his beloved Ginger, the selfish bitch who left him for a Caribbean paradise.

"Truly a nightmare," he says out loud, shaking his head.

"My oldest and dearest friend on this earth," Sydney says. "How can I ever repay you for everything you're going to do for me?"

"Don't mention it," Alexander says. "And anyway, Ginger's on her way home even as we speak, I guarantee it."

"She's twenty minutes late," Sydney moans. "You have to help me. Please, Allie. You have to come over."

"I'm in my pajamas, Sydney." He takes this a step further. "My teeth are brushed, my head is on the pillow. I'm just about asleep, in fact." Alexander sighs. "Here's the deal," he says. "Let's give Ginger another half hour. If she's not back by then, call me and I'll come over. What do you say?"

"I don't know if I can wait that long."

"You're a big boy, Sydney," Alexander reminds him. "You can do it."

"I suppose so," Sydney says, and hangs up.

Alexander goes to bed and falls into an uneasy sleep. He dreams the same dream he's had perhaps a dozen times since Margot's death—that the two of them are making love tirelessly, over and over again, as if there were no tomorrow. Beneath him, Margot's body is soft and generous, and he sinks into it with the deepest pleasure he has known. He is circling her navel with his mouth, savoring the slightly salty flavor of her skin, when the phone begins to ring.

"Margot?" he says eagerly. He doesn't know if he is asleep or awake, only that under his flannel pajamas he is painfully hard.

"She's never coming back," a voice says gloomily.

"Who?"

"My wife of forty years, that's who."

"Sydney?"

"You promised, Allie. I know how late it is, but we had a deal. And I just can't manage without you, buddy."

"All right." His erection is fading fast, for which he is grateful. When he hangs up the phone, there are tears in his eyes, and he talks to himself urgently as he throws off his pajamas and gets into his clothes. "Stop it," he says. "Stop it stop it stop it."

Standing in front of his door now, triple-locking it, he is surprised to see Mrs. Fish, his eighty-year-old neighbor, coming down the hallway in her slippers, her head lowered into the V of her woolen bathrobe. She is holding a plastic tray in her hands; on it is a single place setting of china and silverware, and a can of pineapple rings with a can opener hooked onto the rim.

"How are you?" he says.

"About the same," Mrs. Fish says. "My back is killing me and my chiropractor's been on vacation for three weeks. Three weeks! Can you believe it?"

"I'm sorry to hear it."

Mrs. Fish shrugs. "Listen, can you do me a favor and open this can of pineapple for me? I was down at the other end of the hall intending to have a little midnight snack with my friend Mrs. Maginsky, and wouldn't you know it, neither one of us could get the can open. Not that it's any great loss, having to cancel our little party. Truthfully, friends like her I could do without. She's the reason my back is in such terrible shape."

"Really," says Alexander. Leaving the pineapple on the tray in Mrs. Fish's hands, he bends slightly to open the can for her, inhaling the smell of medicated powder that rises from the V of her robe.

"She fell on me in the elevator last month and knocked me over and onto the floor. I landed in the hospital for two days. And I'm sure you know that a woman like me doesn't need that kind of trouble."

"Terrible," says Alexander. "Enjoy your pineapple."

"She's the kind of friend who wants everything from a person. It's take take take and frankly I'm sick of it. Would you like a pineapple ring?"

"Maybe another time," Alexander says, and makes his escape down the hall and into the elevator. In the lobby the doorman is dead to the world, a copy of *TV Guide* open facedown in his lap.

"Sweet dreams," Alexander calls out, but Gilbert sleeps on.

He walks half a block to Park Avenue and waits impatiently for a cab to come his way. The streets are hushed and brightly lit, nearly empty of traffic. As he steps off the curb, positioning himself in the middle of the street for a better shot at a cab, a man in a ski jacket and a halo of frizzy hair approaches, carrying a carton with holes punched in the top. Plaintive meows emanate from the box, and the man shakes it roughly.

"Shut up, you," he says. "I don't want to hear another word out of you."

"Pardon me?" says Alexander.

"Shut *up*," says the man. "You've been nothing but trouble since day one."

"Please don't shake the box like that," Alexander calls out, and slips into the cab that has pulled up beside him.

"What a night," the driver says, but does not elaborate. He whizzes down the street through an unbroken series of green lights. "I hate everybody and everything," he announces as the cab finally comes to a halt. "Ever feel that way about life?"

"Never," says Alexander.

"Yeah, well, check this out. A pickpocket got me in Macy's yesterday—in the basement, in the housewares department—and then I go home and my girlfriend tells me she's leaving me because, get this, I don't make enough money. 'You're never going to make enough,' she tells me. 'You're a loser, Bobby—it's in your eyes, your teeth, your hair, everywhere.' 'What are you *talking* about?' I say to her, and I run to the mirror. And you want to know what I see? A perfectly decent-looking guy, a guy you wouldn't be ashamed to be seen with out on the street. I point this out to my girlfriend, but she's not changing her mind. And then I come home today and my furniture's gone. I open up the door to my apartment and it's empty! *Empty!* Cleaned out except for the clock on the wall in the kitchen and the toaster oven. There's a note from my girlfriend and you want to know what it says? It—"

"I just don't think I can take much more of this," Alexander says. "I'm sorry." He hands the driver a ten-dollar bill. "I'm sorry," he says again, and asks to be let off at the nearest corner, several blocks short of his destination. He walks the distance to Sydney's building as quickly as he can manage it and tells the doorman which apartment to buzz. The doorman rolls his eyes when he hears the name.

"I don't think your friend Mrs. Packer is in the mood for company right now," he says.

Alexander sighs. "Really?"

The doorman, a slightly built young guy wearing a uniform and a cap that are a size too large for him, laughs cheerlessly. "She's plastered, is what I mean. And nasty too. I tried to help her into the elevator and she gave me a shove like you wouldn't believe. Lucky for her I'm such a nice guy. Somebody else would have been thinking assault and battery, let me tell you. My advice to you is stay out of her way."

"Sounds like good advice."

"You bet," the doorman says.

After a ride up in the empty elevator car, Alexander walks along the carpeted hallway to Sydney's apartment. The hallway looks astonishingly drab, he notices, then realizes the wallpaper is gone and that what he is looking at is bare, unpainted plaster. Just before he reaches Sydney's apartment, he fishes a pen from his pants pocket and writes his name on the wall, along with Margot's, and encircles them in a small heart. He steps back and admires his work for a moment, and then moves on.

"What's with the walls?" he asks, when Sydney opens the door.

Sydney is barefoot and is wearing a baggy maroon sweatsuit. His eyes are pinkish and glassy, as if he has been crying. "What?" he says. "Oh yeah, they're putting up new wallpaper one of these days. The building's going co-op."

"You buying?" Alexander says, and steps inside. The living room is decorated in what he thinks of as Contemporary Florida—a couch and matching armchairs upholstered in big pastel flowers, and a table and chairs and a breakfront, all stained avocado green. There are several large brandy snifters filled with seashells, and wind chimes hanging from the terrace door.

"I'm tearing my heart out over this woman," Sydney says.
"What?"

"I mean, tearing my hair out."

"That's better," Alexander says, and smiles.

"You miserable bastard," Ginger calls out from the bedroom. "You told me I could sleep alone tonight, but I can tell
you never meant a word of it. You're going to keep me company
all night, aren't you? Lucky me!"

"I told you she'd be back," says Alexander.

"And I feel a lot better, don't I," Sydney says darkly.

"Just put her to bed and she'll be fine in the morning. Well,
maybe not fine, but at least you know it's nothing serious." He
slings an arm along Sydney's shoulders and squeezes him. "Come
on, buddy, don't stand there looking like it's the end of the
world."

"She *will* be fine," Sydney says. "That's the problem. She
never gets . . . you know, what everyone else gets, and then
they have to drink a raw egg and some of that brown sauce all
mixed together, you know." He taps his bare foot in frustration.
"You know . . ."

"A hangover."

"Thank you."

"I have to go," Alexander says. "Want me to help you make
up the couch? If that's where you're planning on sleeping, I mean.
And after that I really have to go."

Sydney tips his head downward, covers his face with one
hand. "I hate her," he says into his hand. "And she hates me."

"No, you don't," says Alexander. "And neither does she.
Think how lucky you are to have each other all these years.
You wouldn't want to be alone, believe me. It's not a great al-
ternative." *Margot*, he thinks. Like a child who simply cannot
grasp the absolute, absurd finality of death, he keeps expecting
her to reappear at his side. In his bed. In his life. He had been
home alone with her when she died, and had waited an hour or
so before making the phone call that would bring the body bag
and the stretcher and the death certificate. He had talked to her
during that hour, telling her all his fears, apologizing for any-

thing that required an apology, pretending that she was taking every bit of it in lovingly and sympathetically. He had talked a blue streak, already half-mad with grief and able to recognize it. By the time the doctor arrived to pronounce her dead, Alexander's throat was hoarse, his lips dry, his eyes wild. He could not recognize himself in the mirror that hung in the foyer, and wept, at last, at the sight of the lunatic who looked only vaguely familiar. Leora and Spike got there just as the body was heading out the door. Alexander opened his mouth to say something to them, but he had lost the power of speech. It was three or four days before he was able to talk again. Just before the funeral service, his mother, eighty-four years old and going strong, took him aside and told him to shape up. People are expecting things of you, she explained. They certainly weren't expecting *this*. Talk to me, she insisted, as if he were some sullen teenager who was deliberately holding back. But the truth was, he had nothing to say that anybody wanted to hear. He mouthed the words "thank you" when people approached him before and after the service, and it was the best he could offer. At the cemetery, he held on to Spike and Leora and watched with eyes wide open as Margot descended into the earth. He understood that she was entirely unapproachable now, that she had vanished and would never reappear, but the thing that made him weep was the knowing that she would always be without sunlight, just as she had been during the war.

"I didn't say I wanted to be alone," Sydney says now. "I just don't want to be with *her*."

Alexander resists the impulse to strike him, to knock him to the floor and leave him there, without a word of explanation. Instead, he withdraws his arm from Sydney's shoulders and says, "I can't stay anymore."

"I wish," says Sydney, and then stops, shaking his head.

"What?"

"I wish that we were kids again, playing stickball in the schoolyard and getting beat up by the Irish and Italian kids on our way home." Sydney closes his eyes. "Doesn't that sound wonderful?"

They listen to Ginger's voice sailing powerfully all the way from the bedroom and past them. "I'm bombed out of my mind!" she boasts exuberantly. "And boy oh boy, does it feel great!"

"Wonderful," Alexander says in a whisper.

3

Although Spike would never have guessed it, for several months now, since Suzanne had moved uptown and back into the neighborhood, she had been baby-sitting for Benjamin nearly every week—usually for a half hour here or there on an afternoon when the weather was bad and Leora needed to run out to the supermarket or the drugstore or the nearest vegetable stand. Suzanne had made the offer in person, first calling Leora and confessing that she had been thinking of her.

"Me?" Leora had said, her face burning with pleasure and surprise.

"Of course I barely know you," Suzanne said. "But I'm interested in you, interested in your life. Is that okay, or does it sound too weird?"

Leora had to laugh at this. She couldn't imagine why anyone would find her of interest at this point in her life, when all she was, in her estimation, was a household drudge and a slave to her child. The reviews and essays she wrote for a smart-ass weekly paper aimed at a young and presumably hip audience had dwindled in the months following Benjamin's birth. Sometimes she felt the loss deeply, this loss of a seriousness of purpose, but most often she could not manage to focus on anything much beyond the endless laundry her child seemed to generate, and all the exhausting nights when he demanded to be held every hour on the hour for no particular reason at all. Days and weeks and months of her life had vanished, it seemed, time she could not account for. She was ashamed of this, ashamed of herself. But she had loved her child every inch of the way, even when, momentarily, she had hated him for taking everything from her, her strength, composure, her solitude. There was something to be said for that love, she thought, for such blind, instinctive, unfailing love.

"I'm not sure that I'm anyone to be interested in," Leora said. "I used to be, but I'm not anymore."

"Stop that," said Suzanne. "Is that self-pity I'm hearing?"

"Could be," Leora said. "I'm feeling very bereft today."

"Bereft of what?"

"Friends, family, you name it."

"So where is everybody?" Suzanne said.

"All my real friends," Leora told her, "seem to have moved their families out to the suburbs. And my mother, who I sometimes think really was my very best friend, is gone. She died last spring."

"I'm sorry."

"Yes." Leora could see her mother as she lay in her casket, her bald head wrapped in a beautiful silk scarf, her lips painted a vivid red, her wrists crossed neatly over her middle. She did not look at peace—her mouth was set in a severe expression, one of anger, almost. Bending over the casket for one final look, Leora had had the impulse to shake her mother hard, to yell,

"Get up, get up, get up, get out of there, come *on!*" There was something unfamiliar about her mother's face, she'd realized as she
closed the coffin's lid—something more than just the forbidding
look about her mouth. "Eyebrows!" Leora had said out loud to
no one at all, and the small cluster of cousins and aunts and
uncles had looked at her in surprise. The chemotherapy treatments had taken every bit of her mother's hair, even her lashes
and eyebrows. A makeup artist at the funeral home had given
her a new pair—two badly drawn crescents far too dark and
heavy for her mother's face and coloring.

Remembering this, Leora could not talk, then could not
breathe. She understood that she was going to die of grief, like
someone in a melodrama. Her wheezing made a whistling sound
that terrified her. And then, miraculously, air filled her lungs.

"I'll be okay," she whispered. "Really, it isn't anything."

But Suzanne had not been convinced, had heard the sad,
panicked wheezing, had insisted on coming over to see for herself that Leora was, in fact, all right. Unexpectedly, Benjamin
slept through her visit; she stayed for several hours, drinking
wine coolers straight from their bottles and murmuring sympathetically in the presence of Leora's grief. When at last Suzanne
stood up to leave, Leora found herself hugging her, as if they
had come a great distance together, traveled over miles of har-
rowing terrain. Suzanne smelled faintly of perfume and expensive makeup; her hair swung delicately against Leora's cheek as
they embraced.

"I didn't give you a chance to talk at all," said Leora, and
it was true that Suzanne had revealed little of herself that afternoon. "I've never been in therapy," Leora went on, "but it seems
like we've just finished a session together. I'm the one who gave
myself away and you're the wise one who sat taking notes."

"Next time I'll do my share of the talking," Suzanne said,
and smiled at her.

It hadn't occurred to Leora that there would be a next time.
A friendship between them seemed unlikely, if not inappropriate. And also, somehow, dangerous. Oddly, the thought of

it thrilled her. She knew Spike would think the two of them were crazy to pursue it. The certainty that she would keep it from Spike gave her a rush, a pleasing buzz, as if she had just smoked half a joint. She had no idea why this was so, why the thought of a secret life seemed so tempting. But then she realized what this was at least partly about—Spike's weekly visits to his shrink. Now *there* was a secret life! It pained her that Spike went there Thursday night after Thursday night, years' worth of Thursday nights, filling all those expensive hours with carefully arranged words that she would surely never hear. How was it? she would ask him every week, trying to sound casual, as if she were inquiring about his trip home on the subway, his day at the law school, lunch with his colleagues. Fine, Spike would say, and shrug his shoulders slightly, and that would be the end of it. She knew he discussed his childhood, his father (whom he had never been able to please), his mother (who thought he was the cat's pajamas), and, of course, her. He had gone into therapy after his father's death some years earlier—before Leora's time—and would, Leora suspected, stay with it until he found perfect happiness. At first, he'd let her in on a few not-very-startling revelations, but as soon as the shrink got wind of it he had counseled Spike to keep his business to himself. "You're my husband, for crying out loud," Leora objected. "Don't I deserve to know *anything* that goes on there?" She'd learned to live with it, this feeling of being shut out, but every Thursday night she was cold to Spike for a long while, refusing to take an interest in anything he said. She warmed to him gradually, eventually allowing herself to be held and kissed, though refusing to kiss him back with any ardor. In the end he always managed to win her over, but she would never make it easy for him. She understood that she was being childish, and there was a perverse satisfaction in that. She was being selfish, and there was satisfaction in that too. It was always a losing battle she was fighting, but she fought it anyway, week after week.

She stared at Suzanne in her black leather jacket, black jeans, and pointy-toed cowboy boots. She looked like an outlaw, and Leora found herself admiring her.

"Come back soon," she'd urged Suzanne.

"Sure. I'll come back and baby-sit for you."

"What?"

"I know you could use some time for yourself, Leora. Listen, please don't be offended, but you have that kind of desperate look that new mothers always seem to have. Desperate and defeated," Suzanne said, smiling. "Don't deny it. And besides, I like it over here—I always liked it here. I spent seven years of my life in this place and there's still something warm and soothing for me here; it's in the air, I think."

Leora nodded. "But I'm not sure I could ask you for anything. For help, I mean."

"Sure you can. And you will."

"I will?"

"Do yourself a favor and call me," Suzanne said. "And whatever you do, don't discuss it with Spike."

"I wouldn't dream of it," said Leora.

As the months went by it became clear to Leora that Suzanne was the only improbable element in her life and that she savored their friendship all the more for it. Having Suzanne in the secret center of her life was a little like having a boyfriend whom she suspected everyone disapproved of. As a teenager, Leora had dated a handsome, disagreeable, pot-smoking hippie whose favorite word was "plastic." Your parents are so plastic, man, Cliff would say contemptuously, scowling at her father in his three-piece suits and polished wing tips, her mother in an array of expensive outfits, each with matching shoes and handbag, and their apartment that was furnished with velvet couches and Persian rugs. Eventually he found Leora "plastic" too, and rudely dumped her for someone who smoked pot even more avidly than he did, but until then Leora got a kick from being in his company, from being seen in his company. Attaching herself to someone like Cliff satisfied a certain impulse she had to be perverse, and so it was with Suzanne, she understood. But she was tied to Suzanne in ways that transcended all that, and that sweetened her life. Suzanne had proved utterly dependable, always eager for a lengthy, late-afternoon telephone conversation, always willing to listen to every large and small thing on Leora's mind. And her affection for the baby was an extra gift that even Spike (if only he'd been given the opportunity) would not have failed to recognize. Suzanne was endlessly patient with Benjamin, waiting out his obstinate moments with good humor, forgiving him his crankiness, his ceaseless demands, calling to check on his progress when he was down with a fever, bringing him all the right toys and books whenever she visited after work. If, at first, it was curiosity and, perhaps, loneliness that had motivated her, her affection for the baby, and for Leora too, had grown and deepened over the past few months into something lovely and strong.

Why, Leora thought, would she ever want to step back from this, give up even the slightest bit of it?

At nine months, Benjamin was still almost entirely bald, with a fringe of fine light hair at his collar. Today he was dressed in a purple-and-green checked flannel shirt and green corduroy overalls. Suzanne watched as he slithered happily along the living-room floor on his belly, making remarkably swift progress.

"Today's the day I'm going to teach you how to crawl, my boy," said Suzanne, and got down on her hands and knees. "Think how proud your mother will be when she gets back from having her hair cut. Now pay attention, okay?"

Benjamin offered her a blindingly bright smile, and slithered off in the opposite direction.

"You don't care, do you?" Suzanne said. "You'll never get into a distinguished preschool with an attitude like that. Come on, Ben, this is serious business."

Making his way down the hallway and then into the master bedroom, Benjamin made small talk as Suzanne walked beside him.

"Buh-buh-buh to you too," said Suzanne. "What else can you tell me?" Hopping onto the Exercycle that stood near the window, she rode a leisurely quarter mile in silence. Outside the window, two floors below, a pigeon was pecking at what looked like an English muffin. A little girl in a down jacket and cat whiskers drawn across her face walked by holding hands with a tall teenage boy. Suzanne smiled at her and came down from the Exercycle. She walked around the perimeter of the room; all at once her heart was going furiously. Flopping down on Spike and Leora's bed, she flung one arm across her eyes and took a few deep, slow breaths. She could tell from the hard feel of the mattress beneath her that this wasn't the bed she'd shared with Spike, the bed she'd left behind when she'd run so swiftly, and as it turned out, so mistakenly, into the strong sweet arms of her lover. This new bed was positioned directly across the room from where the old one had stood. The ratty Berber carpet they'd had had been replaced with a pretty, rose-colored one, and the heavy mahogany bureaus she and Spike had inherited from his parents were gone too, exchanged for a large blond-wood armoire and matching dresser.

She slid off the bed and ran her fingertips across the polished surface of the armoire. Benjamin sat on the carpet and stared at her, watchful, his fist in his mouth. She opened the doors to the armoire, her heart racing even faster now, as if she were about to discover something absolutely electrifying. Pulling the top drawer toward her, she sorted through a jumble of loose, unpaired socks belonging to Spike. At the front of the drawer were several pairs of wire-rim prescription sunglasses. She slipped on a pair with purple lenses, and instantly shut her eyes against the dizzying, distorted world they brought to her. She put them back where she had found them and went on to the next drawer, which was stuffed with Jockey shorts and V-neck undershirts, all of them folded carelessly. She found a couple of ten-dollar bills and a strawberry Tootsie Roll lollipop, which she unwrapped and stuck into her mouth. Benjamin began to cry; she lifted him up and put the lollipop to his lips.

Going through Leora's dresser she eventually found her way into the underwear drawer and examined a silk camisole, and a cotton one patterned with little teddy bears. Everything in the drawer had the sweetish smell of fabric softener, or perhaps it was the sweetness of Leora herself. At the bottom of a pile of neatly folded panties, Suzanne came to the hard plastic case containing Leora's diaphragm, and next to it the half-empty tube of contraceptive jelly. She framed the plastic case between the fingertips of both hands and stared, as if it were a photograph and she were mesmerized by the sight of it.

There was something wet on her arm; looking down, she saw a ribbon of pink drool suspended from the baby's mouth. She lowered him to the carpet, wiping his chin delicately with the back of her hand. She closed the drawer and backed away from the dresser, her whole body drooping with exhaustion, and also relief. It was over; she would never have to do this again. She might return to this room, this apartment, a hundred times, a thousand times, and continue to be drawn to its mysteries—the secrets of Spike and Leora's marriage, their love, their life together. But, disappointingly, very little of it was palpable here. If Spike and Leora were happy together—and she understood that they were—then good for them. They were no threat to her happiness, just as she was no threat to theirs. She longed to remain attached to Spike's family; it was a longing like homesickness, she thought, something melancholy and also sweet. She couldn't put her finger on it, couldn't explain even to herself just what it was all about. Except, of course, neediness. In Leora, she'd found someone to nurture her, someone who knew how to listen with more than half an ear, even as the baby pulled at her, wanting to eat, to rest in her arms, wanting everything.

She loved the intimacy between them, something she had not shared with a friend in a long while, it seemed. The certainty that there was one person she would always call immediately with any news at all, the knowing that there was such a person in her life, was a wonderful comfort. There was no one she loved now, no man who had a passion for her. Lacking this, she was uneasy in the world; it was Leora's friendship, she knew, that made her less of a solitary creature, that gave her substance and validity.

Benjamin had disappeared. For an instant she panicked, and then she saw his bare feet sticking out from the bottom of the bedspread, two little, shockingly dirty feet. She went in under the bed after him and touched her nose to the tip of his.

"Listen," she said, "this is unacceptable. If your mother comes home and finds you like this, I could lose my job here. And then where would we be?"

Benjamin giggled joyously; for a moment or two she savored the sound of his happiness, and then she pulled him carefully out from under the bed.

"Remember," she told him in a whisper, "I'm counting on your loyalty. Anything you witnessed here today is strictly between us. Got it?"

Sitting upright now, the baby began to laugh again, was soon doubled over with the force of his laughter.

"Get a hold of yourself, *chéri*," Suzanne said, and all she heard was the sound of her own laughter.

Chapter

4

Like the rent bill, the package from Spike's mother arrived without fail at the beginning of every month. There was always a half-hour-long tape-recorded message inside the small brown mailer, and if Spike had given in to his baser instincts, the tape would have gone straight from the mailbox into the trash. It was Leora who insisted that they listen to it at dinnertime tonight, and Leora who always kept a pad and pencil at her place setting so that she could take notes on anything of particular importance. The fact that she had never once been inspired to write down a single word made no difference to her—she still liked to have things ready. Just in case.

"Just in case she happens to have a brilliant plan for easing the national debt? The crisis in the Mideast? Just in case *what?*"

Spike said irritably. He captured a few strands of cold Chinese noodles between his chopsticks and held them up to Benjamin's mouth.

"Behave yourself," Leora said. "She's your mother. She loves you. She wants you to feel close to her even though she's a million miles away in Leisure World. What's so awful about that?"

"The fact of the matter is," said Spike, "I wouldn't feel close to her if she were standing right next to me, breathing hot air down my neck. We weren't meant for each other, and that's that."

Leora sighed, and he knew that of course she was thinking about her own mother, whom she still missed terribly. Spike missed her as well. He and Margot hadn't started off on the right foot—because Spike had been divorced, his mother-in-law had told him, she would never be able to trust him. "I've got my eye on you, sir," she liked to say, and Spike knew she meant it, that he was always being watched. It made no difference that Suzanne had been responsible for the failure of his first marriage: in Margot's eyes he simply wasn't to be trusted. But once Leora became pregnant, Margot had finally warmed to him, as if the fact that they were soon to be what she considered a real family ensured Spike's loyalty. It pained him that she hadn't lived to see Benjamin, and he still grieved for her loss. But that didn't make it any easier for him to love his own mother, whose voice emerged brightly now from the tape deck and caused goose bumps of displeasure to rise along his arms and legs.

"Hello, my little chickadees.

"This is your mother speaking to you from beautiful sunny Florida. The temperature is a lovely eighty-two degrees, the winds are mild, the sky a perfect blue.

"So tell me, what could be better?

"I had lunch today with Harriet Rothman at a very lovely place in North Miami Beach. It was her treat since I had treated her last time, and I ordered a wonderful cold seafood platter and a small salad with the house dressing, which was something like Creamy Italian, only better. At first we

said we weren't going to have any dessert, because we're both trying to watch our weight, but then we decided to share the lemon mousse, which was just perfect, not too sweet and very light.

"Harriet sent her best regards and hopes that you remember her, Spike. I believe you only met her once, and that was at Dad's funeral. She's really a remarkable lady—all three of her sons are doctors, and she recently started her own little business baking oatbran muffins and selling them to various local stores. She's a little on the bossy side, but I find myself liking her anyway. Incidentally, did you happen to write her a thank-you note for the gift she sent the baby when he was born? She mentioned that she hadn't heard from you and wondered if you had ever received the gift. If you haven't written to her, please drop her a line, which would certainly be the polite thing to do."

"Who the hell is Harriet Rothman?" said Spike.
"Shh," said Leora.

"I also wish you would call Howard," Lucille's voice went on. "He told Uncle Eddie that he left three messages on your answering machine and that you never responded. I believe he has been accepted at a number of the top law schools and would like some advice from you on that subject. I don't need to tell you that our family is small enough as it is—to alienate your first cousin would be unforgivable. He happens to be a very sweet young man and his wife is a gorgeous girl and very sweet too. She teaches deaf children and is very highly regarded in her field, according to Uncle Eddie. It occurred to me that the four of you might get together for dinner sometime."

Spike rolled his eyes at this. "She never gives up, does she?" he said.
"Let her finish," Leora said. "Quiet!"

"It's six o'clock Tuesday morning now and I'm lying here in bed, so if my voice sounds a little strange, don't be alarmed." Lucille cleared her throat a few times and excused herself. "I don't need to tell you, Spike, that in the years since your father passed away I've had plenty of *time to think about him and our marriage, which, as you know, was far from perfect. Your father was a very difficult man, and plenty of times I said to myself, 'What do I need this for?' I told myself I deserved better, and God knows I probably did. But I loved him and I know he loved me. And I miss that, being the center of somebody's life. It's all very well and good that I've got a thousand and one friends down here, that I'm busy every minute of the day. I'm very popular down here, my phone rings day and night. I rush around like a crazy person from one meeting to the next. Did you know I'm tenth-floor fire captain this year? That's in addition to being a member of the condo board and the decorating committee. We're redoing the lobby this summer, and you can't believe the nutty ideas some of these people have. Mirrors everywhere and velvet wallpaper—kind of like a bordello, if you want to know the truth. Sometimes I feel like this building is filled with lunatics. Jack Rosenman, a very lovely divorced gentleman on the fourth floor who took me out a few times, called last night to say he was breaking up with me. I had to laugh when I heard that, because I never even knew we'd been going together. According to Jack, we can't go out anymore because his best friend, Arnie Weiss, who's also on the decorating committee, was very insulted at the way I criticized his suggestions for renovating the lobby. Arnie claimed that I was just plain nasty to him at the last meeting— which incidentally I was not—and that if Jack continued to see me, he would be forced to terminate their friendship. That was the word he used— 'terminate.'"* Lucille's voice grew trembly. *"Do you believe that?"* she said.

Abruptly, the tape went dead.

Spike let his chopsticks fall with a clatter onto his plate. He tipped his chair back on two legs and closed his eyes. "Why does she have to do this to me while I'm eating dinner?"

"Call her," Leora said.

He thought of his mother weeping in her bed as the sun rose over an endless series of beautifully tiled turquoise swimming pools. He watched as a breeze gently disturbed the surface of one pool after another, heard the rustle of the palm trees that lined both sides of the street where his mother lived. He saw himself sitting at the edge of her bed, holding her hand in his. His mother's head bent toward his shoulder and his hand rose automatically to her cap of soft gray hair, stroking it over and over again.

He tried to convince himself that he loved her for what she was. That he was the son she believed him to be—generous and compassionate, unfailingly loyal.

"You call her," he told Leora, and at that moment all of them were caught off guard by an electrifying explosion of music from the tape deck—the overture to *West Side Story*. Halfway through, the music disappeared and Lucille took over.

"Sorry about that," she said, breezy and self-possessed once more. *"Sometimes, early in the morning when I'm still in bed, things seem to be at their worst. And then I take a nice long shower, have my tea, watch a little bit of* Good Morning America, *and life seems good again.*

"So, what else can I tell you? I went to Dr. Harvey Coopersmith for my semiannual checkup a few days ago, and he informed me that I'm in perfect health. He wasn't much impressed with all my little aches and pains and hustled me out of his office in nothing flat. All things considered, I really am entitled to better treatment than that. I felt like telling him so, and may in fact write him a letter. Or not. We'll see.

"Well, my little chickadees, I'm off to my low-impact aerobics class. Picture your old mother in a leotard hopping up and down with a bunch of other old fatties. A sight for sore eyes, to be sure." Lucille paused here, and sighed deeply. *"They say these are my golden years, but I don't know. I just don't know. The older I get, the less sure I am of anything. What am I looking for? I ask myself what's missing from my day-to-day life, and the answer, of course, is you. I'd love to put my arms across the twelve hundred miles between us and gather all of you to me for a big hug. But please don't think I'm lonely, because I'm not. I repeat, I'm not lonely. How could I be lonely when my friend Pearl Pearlman from down the hall is coming by in a few minutes to pick me up for aerobics? And after that, a whole group of us are going to adult ed for our French class. So how could I be lonely? I don't have the time for it, I'm just too busy."*

Lucille's voice simply faded away; an instant later the tape clicked off.

"Spike," said Leora quietly.

"Please. Not so loud," said Spike. "I have a headache."

"Take two Excedrin and call your mother."

"The worst of it all is that I resent her for sending the tape. What kind of a person would send something like that in the mail, tell me."

"A desperate one?" Leora leaned across the table and wiped off the grains of rice that clung to the baby's cheeks. She opened his fists and removed the dark slivers of sesame noodle inside them. "I'm worried," she said. "That didn't sound like your mother. The chitchatty parts did, but the other . . . it sounded like someone I didn't know, a complete stranger, really."

"I wish," said Spike with an extravagant sigh, "that I were a full-fledged member of the Me Generation. You know, someone who wouldn't even listen to the goddamn tapes, someone who'd throw them out in the garbage without even a twinge of guilt and then be on his merry way."

Leora smiled. "There's a telephone in the bedroom just waiting for your hot little hands to fall upon it."

"I have to psych myself up for it first," said Spike. He lifted Benjamin from his high chair and tossed him into the air a few times, listening gratefully to his squeals of pure pleasure.

"Not after he just ate!" Leora shrieked.

"This boy is tough stuff," Spike said. "Trust me." He threw the baby up one last time and then waltzed him around the room with Leora struggling to stay at their side.

"What happened to your headache?" she asked. She tried to take the baby as Spike flopped down into the cushions of the couch with him, refusing to give him up, tightening his hold resolutely around Benjamin's waist.

"Gone but not forgotten," Spike said. "And hands off my child, please. He's got an important phone call to make."

"Still trying to pass the buck, huh?"

Spike stood the baby up against his thighs and regarded him soberly. "You're old enough to make a phone call, aren't you, my man? The question is whether you want to or not. I'll tell you what, make the call and I'll raise your allowance to a buck fifty. That's fifty cents more than you're currently getting, am I correct?"

The baby's eyes widened at this but he was silent.

"He doesn't want to do business with you," Leora said.

"Two bucks a week and that's my final offer. Two bucks a week!" Spike said with enthusiasm. "We're talking four packs of gum, or a *Mad* magazine, who knows how many packs of base-ball cards. . . . It's a good deal, baby boy, and I urge you to accept it immediately."

"This child has got to take a bath," Leora announced, and without warning whisked the baby away from Spike. "Send my love to your mother," she said, disappearing from the room so swiftly that Spike imagined wisps of dust rose in her wake.

He dragged himself to the phone in the bedroom and punched in his mother's number. After three rings the answering machine switched on and his mother's voice, sounding a trifle self-conscious, slowly and carefully informed him that she was unable to come to the phone at the moment. "Thank you, Lord," Spike said into the phone, just before the beep signaled it was time for him to leave his message. "Hi, Mom," he chirped, in a high-pitched voice belonging to a cartoon character. The relief he felt at her absence sent him soaring, and he chatted on about nothing at all effortlessly. But after he'd hung up, he had to acknowledge that there was something unsettling about being let off so easy. His body had gone limp with relief but now he could feel his fingers and toes, the backs of his knees, the bones of his shoulders, stiffening. What do you *want?* he heard himself whisper.

He slipped out of his clothes and left them lying on the floor. In the bathroom he smiled at the look of surprise on Leora's face as he eased himself past her and into the tub half-filled with lukewarm water. His son flapped his arms in greeting and let out a shriek. The baby's belly was astonishingly white and round, and Spike could not resist giving it a kiss before arranging Benjamin in his lap. The feel of the baby's warm flesh against his own was heavenly; the best that life had to offer.

Leora was kneeling at the side of the tub now, idly trailing her fingertips across the water. His hand went out to hers and he hung on to it fiercely, as if it were a lifeline that might, at any moment, have been in danger of slipping away.

Chapter 5

Alexander lets himself into his apartment one Friday night, instantly recognizing the fruity scent of furniture polish. From the doorway he can see that the dining-room table gleams, that the leather couch cushions have been plumped, the pile of magazines on the coffee table thinned out and straightened. Now he hears a murmuring sound, or perhaps a muted weeping, he thinks, and edges cautiously into the room.

"Ionie?" he says, approaching the figure standing at the living-room window, her elbows balanced on the sill, her shoulders hunched in obvious sorrow. Ionie Lewis has been his twice-a-week housekeeper for a dozen years or maybe longer; somewhere along the way he's lost count. She's a big bosomy black woman perched on a pair of beautiful slender legs. Her hair, which is dyed a reddish brown, glistens with drops of styling gel. Ionie's life has been one crisis after another, as he understands it, and yet there is always that splendid deep joyful laugh of hers that takes you by surprise every time and lets you know that she is nowhere near the end of her rope.

"Ionie," Alexander says again. He touches her elbow lightly, waits for her to turn around, but she does not. "What's the matter?" he says.

"There's something on my mind."

"What is it?"

"I don't know," says Ionie. "It's just on my mind to cry."

"It's the children," he guesses. He knows them all by name, the two who have come to grief, the two who have brought her pleasure. There are only three of them now: Willie, her youngest, had drowned one night a couple of years ago in a swimming pool in North Carolina. Alexander and Margot attended the funeral in a Brooklyn church, and what he'd witnessed there was unforgettable. Just as the service was to begin Ionie had announced that she wanted to hold her son one last time, then had proceeded to the open coffin and lifted Willie to a sitting position and draped her arms around him in an extraordinary embrace. Alexander had been horrified, had thought there was something unseemly, even ghoulish, about what she'd done, but later, after he had lost Margot, he fully understood Ionie's impulse and almost envied her for having given in to it. Ionie had returned to work only a week after the funeral, insisting she was all right. Once, shortly afterward, he had found her in Margot's walk-in closet off the bedroom, utterly overwhelmed by her grief. He tiptoed away, not knowing what else to do. It was the same closet where, following Margot's death, he too had come entirely undone, caressing Margot's things, searching for Margot herself, a sense of her physical presence, which had, incredibly, already begun to evaporate from memory. *I'm losing you,* he'd shouted. *I'm losing you, goddammit.* He remembers falling to the floor of the closet, rocking himself back and forth, his head resting on his knees. He'd understood then that he had been scarred for life, that he would never be entirely whole again.

Oddly, the revelation calmed him, and he had drifted easily into sleep on the floor of the closet, awakening hours later with a stiff neck and a mild headache. But there was also the feeling that he had reached bottom and was now headed upward, propelled back toward light, toward a place where he could see himself vividly again.

Ionie has turned her face to him now, a round face with a sheen of tears and perspiration. "It's Shavonne," she says. "That girl has gone and had herself a baby. Fourteen years old and she lets some boy go and do a thing like that to her. First her mother and now her. And I didn't even know a thing about it. All this time I thought that girl was just a little bit bigger and fatter than usual. Oh Jesus. Oh Lord," she says, and whacks herself on the forehead.

"What will happen to the baby?"

"I'm taking it. Don't have a choice, do I?" Ionie says. "Come September, I'm going to march that grandchild of mine straight back to junior high where she belongs. And she's never going to even *kiss* a boy again, not until she's eighteen."

Alexander smiles at this. "Sure sure sure," he says.

"Don't you laugh at me," Ionie says. "This time I'm putting my foot down. Hard."

"Fine. But tell me this: how's it feel to be a great-grandma?"

"It feels like bad news, is how it feels."

"No, really."

Softening, Ionie offers him a half smile. "She's a cute little thing, that baby. Sweet little fingers and toes, good enough to eat. No way I could give her up to foster care, like they want Shavonne to do. I'll take her in and raise her as my own, just like I took Shavonne when her mother ran off. I'm strong and healthy and Lord knows I'm not afraid of responsibility. That's all I got, is responsibilities. It's nothing new to me. In North Carolina, I was the oldest and always got to take care of the smaller ones. I got everyone, girls and boys, all together into a basketball team and nobody could beat us. I was team captain and we were the best around."

Alexander imagines her resplendent in a satiny uniform, her

perfectly shaped legs in knee socks, her big bosom rising and falling as she leaps to sink a basket. A beautiful seductive teenager, exuberant on a makeshift court of dust and scraggly grass. He is excited by what he sees, amazed by the absolute clarity of his vision.

"What are you looking at?" Ionie says.

"Me?"

"That look," Ionie hoots. "That look! Don't you lie to me."

He believes she has read his mind, that he has unwittingly shared everything with her. He rubs his clammy hands together and lowers his gaze. "I don't want to talk about it," he says.

"Sure you do," Ionie says. "But I got work to do, so you better hurry it up."

"You're going to need money," he says, eager to change the subject.

"What?"

"For the baby," he says. "And how are you going to work if you've got to stay home and take care of a baby?"

"Don't worry about me; I'll do fine," Ionie says. "I'm not going to starve."

"Let me help you."

"Maybe," Ionie says. "We'll see."

He reaches behind him and into his back pocket for his wallet, and pulls out a couple of twenties, everything he has. "Better yet, let me write you a check for something substantial," he says.

"We'll see about that later," says Ionie. "But thank you."

"We go back a long way, you and I," he tells her. "Let's not play games."

Ionie yanks her head back and lets out her deep, deep laugh, a bountiful gift that cannot be refused. "You are something funny," she wheezes.

"What's that supposed to mean?"

She squeezes his shoulder, and he winces in pain.

"Watch it, that's my bad shoulder. That's my bursitis you just squeezed."

"Poor old man," Ionie says. She rubs his shoulder gently, maternally, and he sighs out loud in gratitude. "We got to get you a lady friend," says Ionie. "Someone to watch out for you and your bursitis."

"I don't know that I'm ready," Alexander says. "That I'll ever be ready." He thinks of Margot in the pitch-darkness of her coffin, and is stricken hard with loneliness and longing. He remembers how he used to tease her, saying, Don't even *think* about divorcing me; wherever you're going, I'm going with you. Margot always rolled her eyes at this and said, Just my luck. *Just her luck.* When she had first fallen ill, they simply could not believe the diagnosis. But she had survived the war; of course she would survive this illness. In fact, she recovered swiftly from the surgery that went on endlessly, fifteen hours long. They moved to Boston for two months of exceptionally powerful radiation that was meant to better her odds. At the university physics lab where the treatments were given, they met patients with stories that struck them as sadder and more desperate than their own—women in their thirties with young children, teenagers who looked ancient, the half-dead and the dying. Miraculously, the radiation had no side effects, and so their time together in Boston was a honeymoon of sorts—he and Margot went almost every night to the theater or to movies or concerts, the two of them trying their best to forget the reason they were there at all. Looking back now, he wants to weep for their mistaken optimism, their absolute faith in a complex piece of machinery in a physics lab. But of course there had been no choice—without that optimism they would have been lost. *Lost.* And where is he now? He doesn't have a clue. Margot has been gone for a year, and so has he. His feet touch the ground, he eats and sleeps, gets dressed every morning, undressed every night, but where *is* he?

He crosses his arms on top of his head and breathes a couple of painful breaths.

"Want to take me to the movies or something?" Ionie asks.

"What?"

"I haven't been to the movies since about 1962," Ionie says. "*Ben-Hur*, it was. Chariot races and a whole lot of blood. The theater was like an oven, and my kids had to strip down to their underwear. It was real bad."

"What kind of movie would I take you to?" he asks. He feels impossibly stupid and slow, someone who has no idea what is expected of him. "Help me out here, Ionie," he begs.

She explodes into laughter at this, laughs and laughs as Alexander stares at her, amused and also embarrassed. "You don't know what movie?" she says. "Now listen, you can take me to any old kind of movie you want. It isn't the movie, see, that counts."

"It isn't?"

"Uh-uh, no. It's the getting out there, the not being alone."

"The not-being-alone," he says, trying out the words. "I like the sound of that."

"Sure you do," Ionie says. "Now, first we have to get you to eat some dinner."

"What for?"

"A person has to eat," says Ionie firmly. "Especially someone like you, who eats out of tuna-fish cans day after day."

"I do not."

"Tuna fish and spaghetti. I've seen your garbage. Lord, it's sad to see what's in your trash."

"I don't care," he says. "I don't care *what* I eat. It's just food, after all."

"Now, that is one of the saddest things I've ever heard." Ionie takes him by the elbow and ushers him into his own kitchen, where she fixes them both platefuls of scrambled eggs and salad. It's a warm night early in June, and they set themselves up on a wrought-iron table out on the terrace. Occasionally, soot flies overhead and comes to a landing on their plates; exhaust fumes from the traffic below drift toward them. But Alexander, a glass of wine in hand, has other things on his mind. Laughing away at something Ionie has told him about Boopsie, her favorite grandchild, he suddenly feels and then hears a small popping sound inside him and then a lightening, a physical sensation of having lost something. But it's a loss of something he can do without, is better off without, he knows this for certain. And he believes that Ionie is in large measure responsible for this lightening—a phenomenon he could not explain without sounding like a madman, he decides. So all he does is smile at her from across the table, a goofy smile that he holds in place without effort.

"What's this now?" Ionie says, immediately suspicious. "What kind of ideas you got cooking there?"

"Your scrambled eggs were delicious," he says, "cholesterol and all."

"No man ever smiled at my scrambled eggs like *that*, you liar," she says mildly. "Must be something else."

"The truth is, I feel good," he confesses. "It may not sound like much, but it feels like a miracle."

Ionie nods. "When Willie passed on, I wanted to die. I couldn't think straight, but the one thing I knew was that I wanted to die. There wasn't any point in going on, that's all. Everyone said, 'Don't talk stupid—*of course* you don't want to die.' 'What do *you* know?' I told them. 'What do *you* know about anything?'"

"But here you are," Alexander says in a whisper. "Sitting here at the table with me, helping me get by, like no one else."

"I'm real good at helping people get by," Ionie says, "because of all that's happened to *me*. I wasn't born under a lucky star, so I have to work twice as hard as everyone else. It tires me out sometimes, all that hard work. So I go to church every Sunday and ask Jesus to give me strength, like vitamins or something. And he must be listening, because I wake up real early every Monday morning and fly around the house like nothing you've ever seen. Three loads of laundry done before I even leave to go to work."

"I believe it."

Narrowing her eyes at him, Ionie says, "You don't go to that Jewish church of yours, do you?"

"Nope."

"Well, you should."

"I take vitamins instead."

Ionie shakes with laughter, stamps her sneakers on the tiled floor of the terrace. He loves the way she throws herself into her laughter like that, how she gives herself over to it with a full heart. Watching Ionie, he savors the richness of her, her fullness, and all at once he is seized by a fierce yearning to be enfolded in her embrace. He wants to feel her heat, to be warmed by her. He is ready but knows that she is not, that he will simply have to settle for a seat beside her in a dark movie theater where anything at all can happen.

"There you go again," Ionie says good-naturedly. "There's that look of yours. What am I going to do with you?" She leans across the table and grabs him by the wrists.

"Quit reading my mind." His heart is beating so loud he can barely hear himself speak; he feels pleasantly light-headed, and absolutely out of control. Eyes closed, he bends toward Ionie and kisses her, an awkward, timid kiss that soon gives way to something fuller. Her grip on his wrists tightens and she does not resist him. He is the one who pulls back finally, needing air. He is unable to speak, unable to choose appropriate words. It has been almost forty years since he's kissed a woman other than Margot. Forty years! No wonder he can neither speak nor move; sitting motionless in his uncomfortable wrought-iron chair, he decides he will remain there forever.

"You are some fine kisser," Ionie announces, sinking with a sigh all the way back into her chair. "I appreciate that. My husband always kissed like he was in a big hurry—I think he thought it was just a waste of time, anyway."

"And that's why you divorced him?" Alexander teases.

"I divorced him," says Ionie, "because he liked women too much. You know the kind of man I'm talking about." She seems tired and gloomy all of a sudden, very much unlike herself, and he sees that the conversation is headed in the wrong direction.

"Let's pick out a movie," he says. "A comedy."

"You kissed me," Ionie says, rubbing her finger slowly along her lower lip, "but I bet you're not sure why."

"Of course I'm sure."

"No way."

"I kissed you because I wanted to. And also because I needed to." Two good solid reasons, he thinks, nothing to be ashamed of. He looks to Ionie to see if she approves of his answers, but her mouth is set in a simple straight line and tells him nothing. "And I may just kiss you again," he warns. "So don't be too surprised."

"I got the biggest surprise of my life today," Ionie says, smiling, sending a warm wave of relief over him.

"So it wasn't a mistake, was it?"

"No, indeed. No, sir."

"So you'll go out with me to the movies?"

"Got to clean up the dishes first."

"You sit still," he says. "Let me do it. You have to let me do it."

"Don't start thinking you're going to take my job away," Ionie says sharply.

His face reddens, as if he has just been accused of any number of sins, none of them venial. He clears the table in two quick trips to the kitchen and returns to Ionie. "I just don't know," he says. "I just don't know what would be right."

"Soon as I get baby Deneece into day care I'm coming directly back to work. Here and to my other two jobs. I *have* to work."

"Not at this job," he hears himself say. "Not for me. I'll find you something just as good," he promises. "Same hours, same pay." He can see she doesn't like this idea, and he thrusts his arms into the air, saying, "How can I let you clean my apartment? Nothing's the same as it was half an hour ago, Ionie. Everything is entirely different." He plays with her fingers on the table, caressing each fingertip one by one. There are tears in Ionie's eyes and he has to look away.

"You kissed me and I kissed you back," Ionie says. "There

was something there, but what's that got to do with my cleaning your bathtub with a little Soft Scrub? You're dumb, real dumb, just like every other man I've ever known. I know you were a big lawyer on Park Avenue, but you're still dumb." Ionie finishes up with a short dry "hah!" and glares at him.

"You sound like my wife," he starts to say, but thinks better of it and decides to keep silent and out of further trouble.

Ionie shakes her head slowly from side to side. "I'm going," she reports. "I'll be back when I'm ready. But don't you sit waiting by the door for me."

"Can I call you?" he asks.

"No way! I'm mad at you, baby. Real mad!"

They rise from the table at the same moment and he kisses her cautiously, his hands at her shoulders for balance.

"Dumb," she pronounces, and marches out, leaving him with a sink full of dishes and a headache that flashes intermittently, like a vulgar neon sign, over the thin gray strip of his eyebrows.

Chapter 6

" 'Attractive and cerebral male seeks blond female with a warped sense of humor,' " Suzanne read out loud to Leora from the back page of the magazine she held against her knees. "What exactly do you think he means by 'warped sense of humor'?"

"Unless you're contemplating dyeing your hair," said Leora, "I think you'd better forget that guy." The two of them were seated at Leora's kitchen table, a white Formica disk that was littered with the day's mail, a couple of sections of last Sunday's paper, and an open jar of peanut butter with a knife plunged deep into its center. At their feet Benjamin sat sucking on the heel of a French bread, perfectly content.

"Here's one," said Suzanne. " 'Non-neurotic, intense guy seeks blond Ph.D. female for hand-holding and more.' Isn't it depressing that everyone wants blondes?"

"Besides your brown hair, there's also the small matter of the missing doctorate," Leora reminded her. "That's two strikes against you right there." She leaned over and took the magazine from Suzanne. "I'll find you someone suitable," she said. "Here we go: 'Married white male with emerald eyes seeks love slave. No neurotics, please.' "

"Thanks a lot," Suzanne said. Absently, she dipped a finger into the peanut butter and licked it clean. "Why am I doing this?" she said.

"Because you've dated and discarded every available teacher at Washington Irving? Because your thirty-fifth birthday is approaching and you don't want to spend it with your mother and father in a Chinese restaurant in the suburbs, where the waiters will put a candle in your lichee nuts and sing 'Happy Birthday' to you?"

"I *know* why I'm reading the personals. What I don't know is why I'm eating peanut butter off my finger."

"You're ill-bred, I guess. Now how's this: 'Good-looking MBA WASP male seeks humble blue-collar nonsmoking female who knows the score.' " Winking theatrically at Suzanne, Leora said, "I'll bet you know the score, all right."

"True, but I'm neither humble nor blue-collar."

" 'Stop here!' " Leora read, and held up one hand in front of her. " 'Sexy male paralegal seeks devilish divorcée; American Express card a must.' "

"I've only got MasterCard and Visa," Suzanne said mournfully. "We have to face facts—I'm totally unequipped to deal with these people."

"Let's not jump to conclusions." Flipping the page, Leora scanned four columns of ads. "Bingo!" she said at last. " 'Mentally stable male seeks nearly perfect female with short straight hair. If you'd like to know more about me, I'm only a phone call away at extension 472.' " Leora patted the top of Suzanne's head affectionately. "Let me be the first to compliment you on the straightest hair I've ever seen."

"And we all know I'm as close to perfect as they come, of course."

"Without question," said Leora.

Dipping her finger back into the peanut butter, Suzanne said, "I don't know. There's this cute little elf of a world-history teacher at school who has tickets to a Rod Stewart concert for next weekend. He's much younger than I am, and a little bit of a pothead, but maybe I ought to consider going out with him one more time. And I certainly wouldn't mind seeing Rod Stewart."

"Extension 472," said Leora. "If you won't call, I will." As she rose from her seat Benjamin grabbed her by the knees and pulled himself up expertly. Standing on his own now, he flapped his hands open and shut a few times, letting Leora know he wanted to be picked up. She slung him across her hip and went to the phone. "Come and listen," she said, waiting for Suzanne to join her, and then holding the receiver between them.

"Hi, this is George," the tape-recorded voice said uncertainly. "I'm thirty-something and graduated from Harvard a couple of centuries ago. I was a psychiatric social worker at New York Hospital for a long while, and then one day I simply walked away, with the hopes of making it as an actor. I was Henry Higgins in *My Fair Lady*, Tony in *West Side Story*, and in the choruses of *Brigadoon* and *Pajama Game*. This is all regional theater I'm talking about, of course. Anyway, I'm about to give it all up and go back to my old profession," the voice said, sighing. "It's a long story and not a particularly happy one, but never mind. The bottom line is I'm a nice guy. Even my ex-wife will attest to that. So if you're still interested, leave your name and number, and a little something of yourself, and I'll get back to you."

"Hurry up!" Leora whispered, handing the phone to Suzanne.

"Can't," said Suzanne. "I'm frozen with terror."

Unhooking the baby from her hip, Leora passed him over to Suzanne. "Hi, George," she said into the receiver. "This is Suzanne. I'm frozen with fear at the sound of your voice, but fluent in French and Spanish. Please call me at 972–9589. P.S. I don't do windows and I don't do drugs."

"That was truly pitiful," Suzanne said when Leora had hung up. "I could have done a better job myself."

"Well, I didn't have much time to prepare. Next time we'll write out a little speech and I'll deliver it with great passion and style, okay?"

"Shut up," Suzanne said mildly.

"You know," Leora said, "when I was about five or so, my mother washed my mouth out with soap for saying those very words to her."

"Ah, the fifties. We were a kinder, gentler nation then, weren't we?"

Leora laughed. She looked at Suzanne holding Benjamin so comfortably in her arms and was struck by the utterly simple thought that this was her husband's ex-wife she was gazing at fondly—a woman Spike had presumably loved and then lost, very much against his will. Where were the traces of resentment she and Suzanne might have harbored, so predictably, against each other? What had happened between them was something like falling in love, she thought. There had been a hunger to find out everything about each other, a need to know the tiniest, most inconsequential things. It was as if once she knew Suzanne liked lemon in her tuna salad or reading the last page of a novel first or waking up to classical music turned up loud on her radio every morning, she was that much closer to possessing her. Not in a selfish, greedy way, but in a generous one.

Years ago, when Spike had first spoken of his divorce and the circumstances surrounding it, she had listened carefully and concluded that Suzanne had been nothing more than a shallow fool, a flake who believed in kismet and spiritual twins. She had asked to see a photograph of Suzanne, and Spike had handed over an album full of pictures, a history of a doomed marriage. Leora couldn't take her eyes off them, turning the pages so slowly that eventually Spike had become exasperated and left the room, going off to the kitchen, where he mixed the batter for a German chocolate cake and then abandoned the project entirely.

What Leora had seen was Suzanne in a half-dozen different hairstyles, always thin, always well dressed, her eyes ringed with makeup; Suzanne aging imperceptibly over the years, her head set against Spike's shoulder, their hands linked, or their arms laced around each other. And there was Spike, with or without beard or mustache, hair reaching his shoulders or cut short, he and Suzanne undeniably an adoring couple as they posed, squinting against the sun, in front of the Grand Canyon, the Canadian Rockies, the entrance to Disneyland. This, of course, was before the shadow of Jim O'Connor, the chemistry teacher/ soccer coach, had fallen resolutely across the bright face of their marriage, altering it forever.

"So how come Spike never really made you happy?" Leora heard herself saying out loud. "I guess I finally feel close enough to you to ask that."

Suzanne brushed away the bread crumbs that Benjamin had left on her shoulder and deposited him gently on the floor. She went to the freezer and chose two frozen juice bars from an open carton, then handed one to Leora. "You really ought to defrost this stupid thing once every two or three years," she said. "Or at least take a hammer to it and smash away the ice every now and then. I used to do it when I was furious at Spike about something or other. It was very therapeutic, actually."

"Furious about what?"

"Oh, any number of things. They're family secrets, which I'm not about to reveal, of course. Not when I'm sober, anyway."

"Care for a pitcherful of martinis?" said Leora. "Not that I know what a martini is."

"Gin and dry vermouth," said Suzanne. "None for me, thanks."

"All right, we'll get to the things that made you furious some other time. Just tell me why he never made you happy."

Suzanne snapped off the top of her juice bar and chewed it slowly. She said nothing at all for a long while and then narrowed her eyes at Leora. "You love the guy, right?"

Leora nodded. "Your teeth are bright purple. From the ice pop," she said, laughing. "You look sort of hideous."

"Take a look at yourself in the mirror, sweetie."

With Benjamin in tow, they raced off to the bathroom and entertained themselves effortlessly in the mirror, the two of them making an inspired assortment of faces, each one more ludicrous and exaggerated than the next. This was how Spike found them, crowded together in the tiny bathroom, carried away by their own laughter.

"Hi there," he said, looking about in astonishment. He dropped his attaché case heavily to the floor. "So what's the story here, girls?"

"Daddy's home!" Leora said with false enthusiasm, and thrust Benjamin into Spike's arms. "A good hour and a half early, I might add." She felt herself slipping over into panic, felt the dryness inside her mouth, the dampness that was spreading under her arms and the backs of her knees, the galloping heartbeat that she could not control.

"Your teeth are purple," said Spike. He kissed Leora on the forehead and backed out through the narrow doorway and into the hall.

"What, no kiss for *me*?" said Suzanne as she and Leora filed out after Spike into the living room.

"I thought you and I were finished," said Spike. "That I had fallen in love with someone else, married her, started a family. . . ."

"True."

"So what are you doing trespassing?"

"Trespassing? *I* thought I was visiting friends."

"Great," said Spike, in the same flattened-out voice he customarily used to greet bad news. "Terrific."

Tentatively, Leora touched the warm, soft-skinned stem of his neck, but he shook her off in an instant. "It's not what you think," she said. She imagined that this was what it felt like to be discovered in bed with your lover, imagined that her words sounded just as foolish and dishonest as they would have rising from a tangle of bed sheets. "It really isn't," she said.

"How do you know what I think about anything?" said Spike.

"Frankly," said Suzanne, "I don't see what the big deal is."

"Fuck you," said Spike, and slammed out of the apartment, Benjamin still in his arms. A moment later he was back. "Take your kid," he ordered, and then was gone again.

Leora held the baby in silence, comforted by the feel of his legs clamped so fiercely around her waist. Her panic had subsided now that Spike was gone, and she simply stood and waited for Suzanne to say something reassuring. "He'll get over it, don't you think?" Leora said finally.

"You want to know why he never made me happy?"

"Maybe another time," Leora said.

"I'll tell you why," said Suzanne. "You know what I always wanted? A husband who would come up and goose me while I was standing at the kitchen sink doing the dishes. A guy who would casually stick his hand into the opening of my bathrobe while we were sitting on the living-room couch watching TV." Suzanne stared resolutely in Leora's direction. "Do you understand what I'm telling you? He wasn't impulsive enough—he's just too careful a person, someone who has to think things through a hundred times before he gets moving, and by then it's too—"

"Don't tell me these things," Leora said. "Don't betray him like that."

"This can't be news to you, the things I'm telling you."

In fact, Leora was startled by what she had heard. She could not deny that Spike was cautious, taking forever to choose something from a menu in a restaurant, trying on a half-dozen pairs of jeans in a store before settling on the one perfect pair, reading up on everything he could find on a variety of VCRs or stereo receivers until at last he felt secure in his decision. But she knew him to be spontaneous in other ways, quick to anger when he felt provoked, and just as quick and easy to express affection when he felt the impulse. This morning, while she was in the bathroom brushing her teeth, he'd sneaked up on her, slid his hand between two buttons of her blouse, and gone straight for the hollow under her arm where her breast began. Laughing, she had pushed him away, and he'd groaned in complaint. "You're late for work," she pointed out, but he had shrugged "Who cares?" and returned his warm hand to the inside of her blouse. That he had never shown this side of himself to Suzanne puzzled her, and she considered for an instant the possibility that Suzanne might have been lying. But to what end? It was senseless, and she knew it.

"Maybe it was you," she told Suzanne.

"What?"

"Maybe he saw you as unapproachable in that way, someone who just didn't want to be goosed in the middle of cleaning up the kitchen."

"That's crazy," said Suzanne. "It wasn't me; it was him. And I have to tell you there was never a whole lot of intimacy between us, and I'm not talking about sex. I'm talking about a closeness that's got to be there, or else. He wouldn't let me up close, close enough to read his mind, to hear his secrets. I was always opening myself up to him in a way that he never could. I felt like a jackass, giving so much of myself away and never getting anything in return."

"It sounds to me," Leora said, "as if you spent your married life with someone I don't even know."

"You're kidding."

"I *know* him," said Leora. "And I couldn't be married to him if he didn't allow that. What kind of marriage would it be without that?"

"I know the answer to that one," Suzanne said.

"It's clear that he's changed since you were married to him."

"Never," said Suzanne. "People don't."

"People don't change?"

"They only become more so of whatever it is they are."

Leora laughed. "Where'd you learn all this?"

"I read it in a book once," said Suzanne. "Or else I made it up, I forget which."

The door swung open now, and a grease-stained, flat cardboard box appeared, followed by Spike himself. "I got hungry," he said, "and a large pizza with extra cheese came to me in a vision. Fortunately, there's a pizzeria on every corner on Broadway." He settled the box on the dining-room table and flipped the ends of his longish hair back with both hands. "It's hot out there," he said. "I always forget just how much I hate summer."

Suzanne sauntered to the table, opened the box, and pinched her fingers together, seizing a mouthful of rubbery mozzarella for herself. "Now that we're done talking about the weather, I'd say an apology was in order."

"Absolutely," said Spike. "I'm all ears."

"No no no," said Suzanne. "The apology we're talking about was supposed to come from *you*."

"Me?" Spike said, and laughed unpleasantly. "You must be joking."

"On the contrary, I'm dead serious."

"Don't push him," Leora said in warning, but got no further.

"Listen, Leora," Suzanne told her, "I can handle this on my own. And anyway, he's not half as angry at you as he is at me. I'm the one he'd like to get his hands on, you can be sure of it."

"It's tempting," Spike confessed. "Lucky for you I'm such a gentleman. My rule of thumb is never to fight anyone under a hundred and ten pounds." He gestured toward Leora. "Or anyone with a baby in her arms."

"So we're safe," said Leora. She smiled hopefully in Spike's direction, but the withering look he gave her made her turn away.

"I don't need this," he said. "Life is complicated enough."

"You're really being childish," Suzanne said. "So Leora and I are friends. We're just two women who happened to have fallen into something together. And I'm a terrific baby-sitter—Benjamin and I are great buddies. Just ask him."

"You baby-sit for my kid?" Spike's face had turned a deep, unhealthy-looking red, and he was already striding toward the door again. "What the hell is the matter with you, Leora?" he said. "What the hell is the matter with the two of you?"

"Don't you dare leave this apartment!" Leora howled. "You have to talk to me."

"Talk to your best friend over there," Spike said as he flung the door open. "Tell her every goddamn secret of our marriage. What do I care, right?"

Leora ran to the doorway and stepped beyond the threshold. "Get back here!" she yelled into the hallway. A neighbor who was throwing her garbage down the compactor, a woman dressed in a short terry-cloth robe and rubber thongs, stopped what she was doing and looked at Leora with contempt. "Oh, honestly," Leora said, and kicked the door shut with her foot.

"You don't understand," she told Suzanne. "I don't *have* this kind of marriage."

"Well, I guess you do now," Suzanne said. "But he'll be back, don't worry. And I don't mean to be insensitive, but I'm starving." She disappeared into the kitchen and returned with plates and glasses and a half-empty bottle of red wine. She put Benjamin in his high chair and cut up a slice of pizza into tiny bits. "Come and sit down," she coaxed Leora, but Leora remained motionless at the door, staring out beyond the window to the street below, where she imagined Spike hurriedly weaving his way through the early-evening crowds, colliding into people left and right and murmuring not a single apology, oblivious of everyone's pain but his own. She imagined the crease across his forehead filled with perspiration, his hard, bony, nearly hairless chest damp and cool, his hands clammy. Inside him, a whirlpool of anger churned miserably. She focused her gaze now on Suzanne, elegantly eating her slice of pizza with a knife and fork, her appetite undiminished, as if the evening were as ordinary and unremarkable as any other.

"Sit down and have something to eat," Suzanne said once more, and this time Leora obeyed, drawn to Suzanne bewilderedly, feeling as if she were falling in slow motion under some kind of spell, benign or wicked, she had no idea which.

Just at the moment Spike stepped off the crosstown bus a young black guy on the street came his way, thrusting a brightly colored promotional brochure into his hands. "Check it out," he said encouragingly. "This beautiful sixty-piece microwave cookware can be yours for only thirty-nine-ninety-five." When Spike shook his head no, the black guy said, "How about your wife, man. She must need dinnerware."

"My wife's in jail," Spike heard himself say. "She's got all the dinnerware she needs." The satisfaction he felt in saying this brought a smile to his lips, and he continued onward to his father-in-law's apartment, his footfalls jaunty, lighter than air.

The doorman ushered him in with a half smile of recognition and asked about the baby as Spike started to disappear into the elevator.

"He's doing beautifully."

"And the wife?"

Spike grunted unintelligibly.

"That's good." The doorman beamed.

When the elevator door opened onto Alexander's floor, Spike could see his father-in-law out in the hallway, standing beside a little old lady in a flowered housecoat and backless leather slippers.

"Sammy, my boy!" Alexander called. Then: "Is everything all right?"

"Sure."

"Have an olive," the old lady said, offering a tall jar of black olives to Spike, who declined instantly.

"Mrs. Fish, my son-in-law, Samuel Goldman," Alexander said.

"I was just telling Mr. Fine here how terrible it is to get old," Mrs. Fish reported. "I said, 'Mr. Fine, whatever you do, don't get old. It's just about the worst thing there is in this world.' " She nodded toward Spike. "You're better off shooting yourself in the head, that's my recommendation."

Spike smiled. "I'll have to remember that," he said.

"See that you do," said Mrs. Fish. "Nice meeting you, Mr. Goldman."

They watched in silence as she vanished inside her apartment, and then Spike said, "What was that all about?"

"Oh, nothing special. Her best friend down at the other end of the hall accused her of cheating at Scrabble and then put a curse on her."

"Things are tough all over," Spike said with a sigh.

"You look terrible," Alexander said as they sat down in the living room. "Want a multiple vitamin or something?"

"Not right now, thanks."

"You hungry? You want some dinner?"

"Nope."

Alexander eased himself lower along his seat on the couch. He folded his arms behind his head and crossed his skinny ankles on the coffee table. "What's on your mind, Sammy?" he said.

"Wives," said Spike. "Wives and ex-wives, I should say."

"How many of each?" Alexander said, smiling. "Sounds like quite a harem you've got there."

"I'm ticked off at both of them. They've been palling around together behind my back for months now, apparently."

"You're kidding. That's a new one. Something tells me you're just the slightest bit jealous, Sammy."

"Not me," said Spike. "Pissed off maybe, but not jealous." He wondered if this were a lie, if, in fact, there were more to it than simply anger at having been deceived for so long by the two of them, but especially by Leora. Walking in on them today, hearing their wild, inexplicable laughter that left him feeling excluded and at a loss, he had wanted more than anything to seize them by their delicate wrists and dig his fingers into their flesh, to cause them, for only a moment, a flash of startling pain, pain so vivid it would leave them breathless. The impulse had shamed him, and so he had gone toward Leora and dusted her forehead with a barely perceptible kiss. A kiss! And there was Suzanne, clamoring for one of her own, as if it were her due.

"Well, whatever it is, you'll learn to live with it," said Alexander.

"I will?"

"You bet. A man who breaks up a friendship between two

women always lives to regret it. I did that to your mother-in-law once, and believe me, I never heard the end of it."

"This isn't just an ordinary friendship we're talking about, this is a friendship that goes against the laws of nature," said Spike.

"Whose nature? Yours?"

"I just want a little of your sympathy, Pop," Spike said, and closed his eyes. He could hear the whispery sound of Leora and Suzanne exchanging secrets, the sound of his name being uttered over and over again, like a litany. He heard a baby crying nearby, its voice becoming louder and more urgent. And still the whispering continued; how long were they going to ignore the baby? he wondered. So this was the way it was—poor Ben crying himself hoarse and sick while his mother and Suzanne endlessly traded confidences, unwilling to tear themselves away long enough to console a weeping baby.

Opening his eyes, Spike heard himself say, "*Somebody's* got to get that baby."

"I guess that somebody is me," said Alexander, and looked at his watch. "Two hours on the nose."

"That's not Ben," said Spike in amazement as the baby's cries grew even more insistent.

"Ben? It certainly isn't."

"Well then, who is it?"

"Be back in a minute," Alexander said, and when he returned there was an infant in his arms, a tiny black baby in a pink shirt and little gold earrings, and a single pink plastic barrette in her abundant hair. "This is Deneece," said Alexander, as if this were all the explanation that were required.

"Whose baby is this?" Spike said, rising from his seat and putting his finger into her hand.

"Should I feed her first and then change her, or the other way around?"

"Will you tell me who she is, for crying out loud!" Looking down, Spike saw that he was stamping his foot in exasperation. "Sorry," he said.

"She's Ionie's," said Alexander. "Hold her while I go heat up a bottle. And watch her neck; she's only five weeks old."

Following him into the kitchen, Spike said, "What do you mean, she's Ionie's? Ionie's got to be pushing fifty, at the very least."

"True," said Alexander.

"Listen, are you going to talk to me or what?" Spike said.

"Sure I'll talk to you," Alexander said. "This little girl we have here is Ionie's great-granddaughter. Her mother's in junior high and so Ionie just happens to be Deneece's legal guardian."

"So what's the baby doing *here?*"

"I was elected baby-sitter today." Alexander took the bottle from the microwave, tested the temperature of the milk against his wrist, and passed the bottle to Spike. "*You* feed her," he said. "I've got to make a phone call."

"No problem," said Spike. "I'm a pro at this." He lingered in the kitchen as Alexander made the call. The baby felt like nothing at all in his arms, and he marveled at her smooth dark skin, her thick curly hair that gave her the look of a tiny, perfect doll.

"Hi, sweetie," Alexander said into the phone. He kept his voice soft and conspiratorial, and Spike had to strain to hear every word. "Everything's great. Yup yup yup," said Alexander, nodding his head. "Burp her after every two ounces? Gotcha. I know, sweetie, I know you do. Me too, Ionie," he said. "See you in a couple of minutes." He stood holding the receiver in his hand, in midair, and then catching Spike staring at him, he hung it back on the wall. "Our instructions are to burp her every two ounces," he said.

"I know," said Spike. He stared with affection at Alexander's narrow, unlined face, set now in an expression of pure contentment. "Don't mind me," Spike said. "I'm just standing around eavesdropping on your happiness."

"Am I smiling?"

"You're radiant."

Alexander laughed. "Can you say that about a man?"

"I didn't say you were a radiant young bride, I only said you were radiant."

"So what do you think? I've got a girlfriend!" Alexander said joyously.

"Do you think she'll go to the prom with you?"

"She already has," said Alexander, and winked at Spike. "Many times, in fact."

"No fooling. Is this something serious?"

"We'll live, I think."

"So it's not serious?"

"It is what it is," said Alexander. "Whatever *that* is."

"Okay."

"Listen," Alexander said, "it's one day at a time in this house. I learned all about that after your mother-in-law died. At first everything seemed too much, eating a meal, going out for the paper, saying hello to people in the supermarket. And then little by little you ease your way back into the world. And I *am* back in the world, believe me. But I'm still taking it slow—I don't have any long-range plans. I go from Monday to Tuesday to Wednesday and I'm satisfied. Ionie understands this, because she's the same way. So we're a good team, she and I, grateful to have each other and not too worried about what's going to be three years from Thursday."

"My arms are breaking," said Spike.

"What? From that little bit of a thing? Give me that baby," said Alexander. He buried the tip of his nose in her hair as Deneece was transferred to his arms. "Are you going to tell Leora?" he said after a while.

"Tell her what?"

"About me and Ionie, of course."

"We're not on speaking terms," said Spike. "I stormed out of the apartment and left Leora and her pal alone with a nice hot pizza."

"Well, when you're on speaking terms again, you might want to mention this business to her in kind of a casual way.

79

Don't make it sound like too much of anything, though. I wouldn't want to scare her."

"She may be a little . . . surprised, that's all," said Spike carefully.

"I'm a little surprised myself," Alexander admitted. "We don't have a whole lot in common, after all. But somehow that doesn't seem to matter much. We found each other at just the right moment, I guess, and all the rest just followed naturally."

Spike nodded. He tried to envision Alexander and Ionie cuddled up on the couch together, or gazing at each other, love-struck, across a candle-lit table for two, but the only images that came to him were of Ionie bent over the kitchen sink, sponging down the bathroom floor, tossing a load of laundry into the washing machine. He had never seen her motionless, he realized, never seen her at rest. "She's not working for you anymore, is she?" he asked Alexander.

"Absolutely not, but it's a sore subject around here, so don't ever ask her about it. I found her another job, and it seems to be working out, but the baby's been shuttled around a lot among relatives, and I hate that. I'd arrange things to make all of this a lot easier, if only Ionie would let me." He bent his head toward the baby's face, and his voice softened to a coo. "Your great-grandma's a proud and stubborn woman, you know that?" he said. "Proud is good, and stubborn is sometimes good, but together they're an impossible combination." Raising his head, he looked up at Spike. "So, have we learned anything here today?"

"Me?" said Spike.

"Don't be so stubborn, you," Alexander said. "You can't let yourself get hassled by things that aren't a matter of life and death. It just doesn't pay."

"I'm just supposed to go with the flow, is that it?"

"That's it," said Alexander. "So go on home and get back to your two lovely ladies. Who knows, maybe they baked a cake or something in your honor."

"Why do I get the feeling you're trying to get rid of me?" Spike said, smiling.

"No, no," said Alexander. "Well, actually, I am."

The key turned sharply in the lock at the front door, and then Ionie was walking toward them, ornamenting the air with her perfume, which Spike found a little too sweet and strong. She was wearing a satiny dark pink dress, and stockings and sneakers; over the stockings were thick, ankle-length white cotton socks. She kissed the baby first, and then Alexander, and waved hello to Spike.

"How you-all doin', Spike?" she said softly, sounding a little shy.

"Pretty good." He watched as she took the baby from Alexander, and the swiftness with which his father-in-law draped his arm along her shoulders. He felt warmed by the sight of the two of them and understood in an instant that he was in the presence of lovers who would not fail each other. He wondered if Leora would weep when he told her what he had seen, and hoped that she would not, that she would put aside her loyalty to her mother and savor the undeniable fact of her father's happiness.

"Oh sure," he murmured out loud.

"Pardon?" said Ionie.

"I've got to get home," Spike said. "You know, dinner and all that."

"You want me to fix you a sandwich before you go? How about some fruit?"

"You're such a Jewish mother, Ionie," said Spike. "Really."

Ionie laughed her big generous laugh. "I'm doing my best," she said.

"This lady," Alexander announced proudly, "happens to be absolutely perfect."

"And you're out of your head," said Ionie.

Spike and Leora made love quickly and urgently, and without exchanging a single word. Afterward, Spike sighed a long, leisurely sigh and listened for the sound of Leora's voice in the darkness. "I'm sorry," he said finally, and dropped a kiss into the tangle of her hair before rolling over onto his back and his side of the bed.

"You ever disappear like that again," said Leora, "and you're history. And incidentally, I'm sorry too." She outlined the curve of his ear with her finger. "And Suzanne wanted you to know how awful she felt about—"

"Never," interrupted Spike, "ever mention that name in the sanctity of our marriage bed."

"She's my friend," said Leora. "I just want you to understand that."

"I *don't* understand it. In fact, I'm never going to understand it. And I think you're crazy for making room for her in your life. And that's all I'm going to say about it, at least for now."

"Are you sure?" Leora said in surprise. "I was expecting you to tell me how disappointed you were in me for—"

"Nope. It's time to move on to bigger and better things."

"Like the fabulous mink you're getting me for my birthday?" Leora teased.

"Dream on," said Spike. "But don't you want to know where I went after I slammed out of here?"

"Absolutely," Leora said. "So where were you?"

"At your father's. He was baby-sitting for a newborn baby with pierced ears named Deneece."

"Ionie's granddaughter's baby," said Leora.

"How come you never mentioned her?"

"The baby? I don't know, I guess it was one of those things that struck me as interesting the moment I heard it, but then I forgot all about it."

"Ionie's a lovely person," Spike said casually. He lifted Leora's hand and arranged it on his chest. He traced the contour of each of her fingers, taking his time.

"She's terrific."

"She and your father have gotten to be great friends."

"That's nice," said Leora. "It's always good to have a sympathetic ear."

Spike brushed the smooth surface of each of Leora's fingernails one by one, as if he were polishing them. "Actually, there's more to it than that."

"What do you mean?"

"They're lovers, honey," said Spike, and felt her hand harden into a fist against his chest.

"Don't call me 'honey,' " Leora said in a trembly voice. "And don't worry about me."

"Are you all right?"

"I *said*, don't worry about me." But she had turned over onto her side and was already weeping quietly into the crook of her arm.

Spike stroked her hair, starting at the top of her head and following the trail of her hair all the way down past her shoulders. "Do you want something to drink?" he said.

"It isn't Ionie," Leora said. "It isn't Ionie at all. It's my mother, shut away in the darkness, entirely alone. Every time it rains I think of her there, of the rain beating down on her coffin. I can hear the sound of it—I don't want to, but it's so loud and distinct I can't ignore it."

"The rain's not beating down on her coffin, Leora. You know that's not possible."

"I don't care!" Leora cried. "It's what I hear."

"Can I tell you something?" Spike said.

"No."

His mouth was at the side of her neck now, his voice whispery. "There's going to be a time when you're not going to feel this way," he promised. "Your mother will be a good strong vivid memory, something you can reach for in the middle of the night and be comforted by."

"When?" Leora said. "When is this great miracle supposed to happen?"

Chapter 7

Driving along the Strip in Las Vegas in a rented Chevy Cavalier, Alexander makes the mistake of rolling down his window halfway, bravely testing the air outside. It is 110 degrees at 5:00 in the afternoon; the air against his elbow is utterly astonishing, fiery and mean, he thinks. Beside him, Ionie fiddles with the air-conditioning and shakes her head.

"Will you close the goddamn window," Sydney barks from the backseat. "Please," he adds, more softly.

"You're very cranky today, you know that?" says Ginger.

It is Alexander who has planned this weekend trip, his first with Ionie. He has never been to Las Vegas before, primarily because Margot wouldn't have dreamed of setting foot here, claiming the city's reputation for vulgarity didn't intrigue her in the least. But Alexander had always suspected they were missing out on something—something that had to do with romance and brilliant lights and the heart-stopping sound of a thousand silvery quarters cascading down a slot machine's chute. Against his better judgment, he has allowed Sydney and Ginger to come along, knowing just how desperately his friends need the company of other people. On the flight from New York, the two of them had argued fiercely over the little bag of salted peanuts that the stewardess had placed on Sydney's snack tray; according to Sydney, all that salt would be the end of him, a notion Ginger pooh-poohed in her loudest voice. She'd torn open the little Mylar bag and dumped the nuts on Sydney's tray, urging him to enjoy them. "What are you trying to do, kill me?" Sydney complained, and swept the nuts into Ginger's lap. After she struck him once, lightly, across the face, Ginger had ordered three miniature bottles of Canadian Club, one right after the other, and had given Sydney the silent treatment for the rest of the flight. Watching uneasily from across the aisle, Alexander and Ionie held hands and said nothing, grateful for the cease-fire that had followed the arrival of Ginger's first drink.

"Lord, it's hot," Ionie says. "Even with the air-conditioning on. How do people live out here, I wonder?"

"Funny," says Ginger, "it would never occur to me to wonder about something like that."

"That's because you have very little interest in other people," Sydney explains. "You never did and you never will."

"Oh, you think I'm insensitive, is that it?"

"That's it, all right."

Leaning forward in her seat, Ginger brings her face up to Ionie's. "Ionie, what do you think? Do you think I'm insensitive?"

"I don't really know you, hon," Ionie says pleasantly, turning around to pat Ginger's manicured hand resting on top of the seat. "Maybe you ought to ask Alexander. He knows you from way back."

"Thanks a lot," Alexander says.

"Good idea," says Ginger. "What about it, Allie?"

"Just look at all this!" Alexander whoops. "Have you ever seen so many winking and blinking lights in your life? The electric bills around here must be phenomenal." It's true that the hotels that line both sides of the Strip are lit up spectacularly, beckoning and luring and boasting in broad daylight, inviting tourists out of the heat and into their icy, darkened casinos. Alexander feels a sudden sharp prickle of excitement and reaches out for Ionie's hand. He has forgotten all about Ginger, waiting impatiently for him to pass judgment upon her. "This is going to be great!" he sings out.

"You're such a child, Allie," Ginger informs him. "This town was made for people like you. And let me tell you, Margot would have hated the place. She was much too refined to stand around feeding change into a slot machine. She—"

"Talk about insensitivity!" says Sydney.

"Oh, Allie doesn't mind if we mention Margot's name like that. After all, it's been over a year. It's not like it happened yesterday. And look, he's already got himself a very nice girlfriend he's taking away for the weekend. I'd say he's in pretty good shape, wouldn't you?"

"She's drunk," Sydney explains. "I ought to know—I'm sitting right next to her."

"Maybe I am," says Ginger, sounding surprised. "If I weren't, I wouldn't be able to tell the truth like this. Alcohol makes you very uninhibited, you know. You wouldn't believe the things a person can say when he's drunk. Like, I could start telling you what a pain Sydney's been since he had his medical problems. He worries about everything—if the sun is out, he worries it's going to rain; if he's feeling good, he worries he's going to start feeling lousy. Sometimes I come home the tiniest bit late from wherever it is I've been, and I find him in the kitchen with his head down on the table, crying like a big baby. And I think to myself, this is the man who swept me off my feet in 1948, the first and only man ever to get inside my brassiere in a movie theater? What a transformation! Jesus Christ almighty!"

"Sydney," Alexander calls, at the moment Ginger falls silent. "Sydney, look, there's Caesar's Palace—see that guy they've got dressed up as a gladiator standing on top of the steps over there? Is that funny or what?"

"She's going to do something to me," Sydney says.

"Drive you crazy?" says Alexander.

"No."

"Raise your blood pressure sky-high?"

"Yes, but that's not it, it's something else."

"You're sure?"

"Destroy me!" Sydney says excitedly. "She's going to destroy me!" Ginger has dozed off with her head on his shoulder, and Alexander watches in the rearview mirror as Sydney's arm rises and lingers in the air for an instant before falling gently across his wife.

"Strangle her," Alexander whispers.

Ionie slaps his thigh for this. "It's just words," she says. "It doesn't have to be anything more than that."

"I'd strangle her myself if I thought it would make him happy."

"No way!" says Ionie. "He loves her, even if he wishes he didn't."

In the backseat Sydney sits motionless. He looks shrunken, Alexander thinks, as if he had lost part of himself somewhere along the way. His wrists seem poignantly narrow and delicate, and Alexander has to look away, back toward the Strip, where one hotel after another clamors insistently for his attention.

The hotel's casino is a cool and vast carpeted space filled with endless rows of one-armed bandits. In the center are blackjack and "21" tables, where unsmiling croupiers in white shirts and black bow ties keep their hands moving as gracefully as magicians. The room is noisy with the sharp metallic clatter of coins flowing and the occasional roar of celebration when someone wins big.

"Let me at 'em," Ginger says, flexing her fingers while Sydney stands at her side, hands loaded with rolls of quarters and nickels. She wins fifty nickels her first time at bat and immediately sends Sydney off to the bar for a drink.

"Go easy on him," Alexander warns her. "You embarrass him one more time and I'll personally put you on a plane back to New York, do you understand me?" He squeezes her plump little arm for emphasis, and instantly regrets it.

Ginger rubs her arm extravagantly, then surprises him with a smile. "You're a good friend to him, Allie, and I appreciate that. But just remember who you are."

"Who am I?" he says.

"You're not a partner in this marriage, okay? So stop acting as if you were, or you'll be sorry."

"What are you going to do to me?"

"I'll make your life a living hell," she promises, smiling sweetly. "Now, go find yourself a friendly slot machine and make some money to add to your retirement fund."

"Just remember what I said."

"A living hell, Allie, remember those words," says Ginger. She tears the paper off the top of a new roll of coins, drops a nickel into the machine, yanks back the lever, and wins a hundred nickels this time. "See, I don't fool around!" she says gleefully.

"Wow!" says Ionie, and helps Ginger scoop up the handfuls of coins, collecting them in a disposable plastic cup that looks like an empty cottage-cheese container. "Seems like an easier way to make a living than housekeeping," she says.

Alexander steers her to a slot machine down the line and sets her up with a roll of quarters. "Go to it, sweetie," he says. Turning his back, he studies a middle-aged woman in a wheelchair stationed behind a slot machine. Her face is impassive as an endless flow of coins comes her way; dipping into the pile, she deposits one coin after another into the slot machine, as mechanically as if she were in a trance. Nearby, a man with a little dog peeking out of the canvas bookbag that's slung over his shoulder gives his machine a nasty kick and moves over to the next one, where he swiftly loses an entire roll of coins. "You goddamn son of a bitch," the man tells the slot machine, and storms off.

Checking up on Ionie, Alexander discovers she has lost everything. "I'm no good at this," she says mournfully. "I won seventy-five cents a while back, but then I lost that too."

"You know it's just pure dumb luck," he says, and reaches to embrace her. Gazing idly over her shoulder, he sees something that brings goose bumps to his flesh—the lovely heart-rending profile of a woman's face, a profile so reminiscent of Margot's that for a fraction of an instant he is convinced she has returned to life. Then the woman swivels her head in his direction and he sees that she only vaguely resembles Margot after all. His hands are shaking as he lifts them from Ionie's shoulders, and his face is on fire. It is the most bitterly disappointing moment of his life, he thinks, and waits for the vigorous thumping of his heart to subside. He feels foolish and utterly defeated, as if he had fallen for the most transparent of deceptions. It is the first time since Margot's death that he has been deceived like this, and he doubts it will be the last. Next time around, he tells himself, he'll be able to shrug it off as if it were nothing. But the pain of his disappointment is so acute now that he can barely stand up, and suddenly he is holding on to Ionie for balance.

"You're sick," she says, and feels his face with her cool, steady hands.

He points rudely at the woman, whose face is in profile again. "Look," he says.

"Margot," Ionie breathes.

He stares hungrily in the woman's direction and then shuts his eyes. Go away, he tells the woman silently. Go away and let me be.

Ionie leads him away from the slot machines to an area behind a metal railing where he can see a long row of cushioned seats shaped like huge replicas of NFL football helmets. He sinks into an orange-and-blue one that says "Denver Broncos" across the back. In front of him, thirty feet in the distance, are a dozen large-screen TV sets mounted on an enormous wall, all of them tuned to the same channel, where the Mets are getting creamed by the Dodgers. The sound has been turned off, and the fans in Dodger Stadium roar silently as a home run is belted out of the ballpark, across the wide screens of the dozen TVs all going at once. Slouched in his Denver Broncos' helmet, still unnerved by the woman's profile, Alexander finds himself thinking of the Sunday afternoon a few weeks following Margot's death, when he'd forced himself to change the message on his answering machine, altered it from "We're not home right now" to "I'm not home right now." He'd recorded the message four or five times, his voice shivery and timid, as if the task were too much for him. The breezy, confident tone he was after seemed out of reach, and he'd wept in frustration. In the end he recorded his message in the inexpressive voice of a dullard, a voice belonging to someone who could barely comprehend his own words. The grief counselor he began going to a month or so later loved this story and repeated it several times to the group that assembled every Monday night for their two hours of therapy. "That's it in a nutshell, isn't it?" she said enthusiastically. "The 'we' has become an 'I.' As painful as this transition is to accept, none of you here has a choice; all of you must acknowledge that you are now simply an 'I.' "

"How many times do we have to hear the same goddamn stupid story about the goddamn stupid answering machine?" a man sitting next to Alexander complained. Chick was in his early thirties and had recently lost his wife in a motorcycle accident. It had been obvious from the first session that he had little patience for all the precise details, tearfully rendered, of everyone else's losses, for all the outbursts and vigorous sobbing and impulsive confessions that went on in the room each week. "Why can't we just cut through all the bullshit for once?" he said.

Johanna, the young social worker who led the group, looked offended. Her lower lip quivered for an instant and then she said, "Fine. Let's cut through the bullshit. You first, Chick." She sat back in her chair at the center of the U-shaped arrangement of seats and folded her arms behind her head. "Let's hear it."

"I don't know, how about 'life sucks'?"

"That's it?" said Johanna. She stared at him with a mixture of amusement and frustration. "That's all you have to say?"

"That, and my father-in-law's a pain in the ass. He keeps inviting me over for dinner, and when I turn him down, he goes wild. So I go over there and all I hear is, 'If I lose you, I've lost Sherry completely. Promise me I won't lose you too.' "

Around the room people were nodding their heads in sympathy with Chick's father-in-law. "And how do you respond to him?" Johanna said.

"How the hell do I know where I'll be in two years? I could be out in L.A. or on the other side of the world, for all I know. For all I know, I could be dead. We could all be dead." Chick flopped his head down on the Formica table and fell silent.

"Anyone?" Johanna said, looking to the group for a response. "Come on, you guys."

Alexander touched Chick's shoulder lightly. "Wake up and hear the good news," he said. "You're not going to die young in a motorcycle crash. You're going to get married again, have some kids, and live happily ever after."

"I am?" said Chick. He seemed surprised by the prophecy but perfectly receptive to it. "What are you, a fortune cookie?" He lifted his head from the table and smiled at Alexander. "How come you're such an optimist?"

"I don't know," Alexander said. "I'm sitting here looking at you and that's the message I'm getting." In fact, he was making it up as he went along, and growing bolder by the minute. "You'll be happily married within two years, Chick, trust me."

"What about me?" a woman at the opposite end of the table called out. "Do you have any good vibes about me?"

"Absolutely." He remembered that the woman's husband had died on the spot, of a heart attack at the age of thirty-nine, just as they were about to leave for the airport for a vacation in France. She had told the story a number of times, breaking down at the same point each time, the point where she had to unpack the suitcases she'd so carefully packed the night before. "I even used tissue paper between each layer of clothing!" she'd cried in outrage to the group. "Tissue paper! The joke was on me, wasn't it?"

"Okay, Marcy, this is it," Alexander said. He shut his eyes tightly and kept them closed as he spoke. "You're going to be on vacation in Italy when you meet the love of your life."

"A native?" Marcy said excitedly.

"Could be," said Alexander. "Or it could be a fellow tourist, I don't know."

"Let's have coffee after the group breaks," Marcy suggested, and then her face reddened. "I can't believe I just said that."

"I'd be delighted," said Alexander.

Johanna cleared her throat disapprovingly. "What are you trying to do here, Alexander?"

"It's nothing," he said. "It's just that sometimes I have this sixth sense about people and their lives, that's all." He had no idea where this was coming from, but it seemed reasonable enough, and so he continued on, surprised at how utterly confident he sounded. "In fact, I've been proven right on many occasions."

Marcy and Chick exchanged knowing smiles and sat up straighter in their seats.

"From now on," Johanna said, shooting Alexander a furious look, "please keep this sixth sense of yours to yourself, okay?"

Chastened, Alexander stared into his lap. "Come to think of it, I've been proven wrong on an equal number of occasions."

"No way!" said Chick. "This guy's on the level," he announced to the room. "If he tells you you're headed for happiness, you better believe it."

"That's enough!" said Johanna.

After the session ended, Alexander found himself encircled by a half-dozen women wanting to know what was in store for them; he had become a minor celebrity that evening when all he had wanted was to comfort Chick, to lift him out from under his burden of sorrow. He could not give them what they wanted, he told the women, but offered instead to take them all out for coffee. All but one accepted, and as they filed out of the room in a noisy group he had to laugh at the thought of himself surrounded by five widows; a widower's dream of an evening.

He laughs out loud now in Las Vegas, Nevada, where twelve extravagantly large TV sets are hawking new mesquite-flavor potato chips. Fortunately, he cannot hear a single word.

"Oh, baby," Ionie says, ignoring his laughter. "That lady looking like Margot gave me a scare, all right."

"But we're okay now, aren't we," he says. Standing over him is a tall young woman in a sexy outfit—hot pants, sheer black stockings, and high heels—selling cigarettes, and also yo-yos, rubber bracelets, and wristwatches, all of which glow in the dark. "I'll take a yo-yo," Alexander says, but only because the cigarette girl's legs are so long and beautiful.

With a smile, she selects a yo-yo and demonstrates how it works, swinging it back and forth in front of him, mesmerizing him with a brilliant green circle of light while in the near distance a million bright nickels and quarters are lost and won and then lost again.

Chapter 8

Suzanne's shoebox full of data on the various men she had met through the personals was organized into three sections: "Possibilities," "Beasts," "And Worse." The last two sections had grown so fat that they were soon to be moved into shoeboxes of their own, while the "Possibilities" seemed to look skimpier and skimpier from one day to the next.

"What do you *want* from these people?" Leora asked Suzanne over the phone. The two of them had for months now been in the habit of speaking to each other every day at five o'clock, reminding Leora of all the high-school friendships that had nourished her nearly twenty years earlier, friendships that were rock solid and shot through with love and envy both. Not that she envied Suzanne's troubled search for the love of her life, which struck Leora as poignant and depressing and sometimes very funny. Mostly, though, she savored the details that Suzanne shared so eagerly with her, as she savored the full blossoming of their friendship.

"If I hear about one more 'Beast' I'm going to hang up on you, and I mean it," she said firmly.

"This was a guy," Suzanne reported, "who takes me out for the worst Chinese-Cuban food in the world and then tells me he has a new policy of not dating anyone who makes less than fifty thousand dollars a year. 'Anything under that is problematic for me,' he says, and then asks if there's any possibility of New York City schoolteachers at my level getting a substantial raise in the near future."

"What a pig!" Leora said.

"Good reason to put him in the 'Beast' file." Suzanne paused; Leora could hear what sounded like a trio of fingernails tapping on a countertop. "Listen, Leora, I need to ask a favor of you. The thing is, it's not a small favor."

"Why is it I sense this isn't something Spike's going to be wild about?"

"Actually, you're right. I need you to invite me, and a companion of my choosing, for dinner."

"Anyone I know?"

"It's George. Remember—'Mentally stable male seeks nearly perfect female with short straight hair'?"

"I thought he was dating his ex-wife."

"That turned out to be a terrible mistake."

"Big surprise," said Leora.

"Don't be so hard on him. He's sort of a lovely person, actually."

"You don't sound too sure about that."

"Well, you know, I sometimes get the feeling my perspective on men is all fucked up. So you have to invite us over and tell me what you think."

"All right," said Leora. "But Spike will have to run it by his shrink first and then I'll get back to you."

"You're kidding." Suzanne sounded shocked. "I had no idea Spike couldn't make the slightest move without consulting the guy."

"Of course I'm kidding," Leora said. "What kind of a man do you think I'm married to?"

It was, Spike tried to convince himself, a privilege to have front-row seats at his ex-wife's date with another man. But he didn't feel privileged; what he felt was exasperated and put-upon as he mixed the two of them exotic drinks in a blender and set out a crowded tray of napkins, plates, and dip. Presenting his offerings before them on the coffee table, he leaned over and patted the pinkish, gleaming surface of George's balding head. "For good luck," he explained, and sat down on the love seat facing them.

"I don't get it," said George. "The connection between the bald spot and the good luck, I mean." He was a nicely built guy with strong, handsome features, and Spike had no trouble envisioning him on the stage, confidently belting out a Broadway showtune.

"Oh, it's one of the rules I've always lived by," he said. "Pat a bald spot for good luck, never wear rubber boots indoors."

"Why not?"

"Headaches," said Spike. "If you wear your rubber boots inside, you'll always get a headache. At least that's what my grandmother always told me."

"Interesting theory," said George. "I'll have to test it sometime." He turned his gaze toward Benjamin, who was tooling around the bare floor in his G.I. Joe jeep. "Nice robust baby you've got there," he said.

Spike nodded. "We like him," he said. "When he's bad we have to lock him up in the linen closet, but generally speaking he's pretty well behaved."

"Cut it out, Spike," said Leora, and moved deeper into her corner of the love seat. "Quit joking around like that."

"What? You're upset because I gave away a family secret?"

"Don't worry," said George, smiling. "I know a joke when I hear one. But my question for you, Spike, is why you would say something like that in the first place. I gather that sometimes when the baby's being difficult you *would* like to lock him away in the closet, am I correct?"

"Are you crazy?" said Spike. He imagined himself out of his seat, standing over George, his hands at the man's throat. He could feel ligament and muscle beneath his fingers, the wild beating of George's pulse.

"Not at all," George said. "I'm a psychiatric social worker."

"Well, I'm not one of your patients. I'm just your standard loving father and husband who happens to be entertaining his ex-wife and her date for the evening, okay?"

"What?" George was staring at Spike in amazement.

"It's true, actually," said Suzanne. She looked slightly embarrassed, as if she had been caught rearranging her underwear or picking at a stray crumb between her teeth.

Rubbing his hands together excitedly, George said, "This is fabulous. I love the family dynamics here. I'm dying to hear about this."

"Wait a minute," said Spike. "I thought I remembered hearing you were an actor. Didn't Suzanne go to see you at Westbury Music Fair a few weeks ago?"

"My final performance," George said quickly. "My swan song, as it were. But never mind about that. What about you and Suzanne?" He gestured to Leora. "And what about *you* and Suzanne?"

"Have some dip," Leora offered. She shoved a small white ceramic bowl into George's hands. "Sour cream and dill," she said. "Very delicate."

"Talk to me, Leora," George said. "Suzanne?" He sat with the bowl of dip cradled in his lap. "You're not going to tell me anything, are you?" he said.

"Of *course* we're not," said Leora. "It's out of the question."

"Don't look so sad," said Suzanne. "I happen to know there's a wonderful chicken dish with shallots on the menu." She patted

George's knee a few times. "I know it's a disappointment, but you're going to be fine." In a moment he had shot up out of his seat and was pacing the room, hands deep in his pockets. "Come on back here," Suzanne called.

"This is such a wonderful professional opportunity for me," George said. "Don't you think it's killing me that you're all being so reticent?"

"Get a hold of yourself," Suzanne warned. "Why don't you sing just one song from *West Side Story* or something."

"That part of my life is over," George said impatiently. "And please stop trying to distract me."

Spike felt himself growing dizzy as he watched George pacing the floor, but he couldn't take his eyes off him. He resented the sight of this stranger in his living room, trying to make all of them feel guilty for keeping their lives to themselves. Suddenly he was imagining George on the stage of the Music Fair, dying a quick, violent death in *West Side Story* with a knife plunged between his ribs. The image was a peculiarly satisfying one, and it cheered him enormously.

"Come into the kitchen with me," he told George. "I need some help with my chicken and shallots. And I want to talk to you."

"You do?" George said eagerly. "That's great." In the kitchen he got down to business immediately. "So what's the lowdown on this woman?" he asked Spike, and winked.

"I beg your pardon?" Spike pulled the baking tray forward out of the oven and concentrated on spooning melted butter over the chicken fillets. The heat from the oven burned his face but he ignored it.

"The inside dope," said George. "I mean, what's she all about?"

"I never did find out, to tell you the truth."

"Is that why your marriage broke up?"

"I'd really rather not get into that, okay?"

George sighed. "I thought you wanted to talk to me, Spike. I thought you and I were going to have a breakthrough here."

Nodding, Spike said, "Here's what I wanted to tell you: if you don't lay off the personal stuff, I'm going to throw you out on your ear."

"I see," said George evenly. "I guess in my line of work, I get so used to people opening up to me that I can't quite believe it when I run into someone who for one reason or another won't talk about anything more intimate than sports or the weather." Folding his arms across his chest, he said, "Tell me, Spike, do you find me threatening?"

Spike slammed the oven door shut vigorously; the small stack of salad plates on the countertop trembled. "Not in the least," he said. "But I do find you kind of obnoxious."

"You're very hostile," George announced. "And depressed too, I think."

Spike studied himself in the mirrored surface above the stove. He saw the broad pleasing face of a man who loved his wife and child, who endured his ex-wife, but who would not endure the infuriating presence of a lunatic.

"Here," he said, and thrust a spatula into George's hands. "You can start serving in three minutes. There's rice in that pot over there and the salad's already on the table. Have a nice evening."

"Wait a minute," George said, alarmed. "Where are you going?"

"Out for dinner," said Spike. "See you."

"Wait!" George called. "Wait. I'm going to lose Suzanne over this, aren't I?" He followed Spike out the service entrance, which led from the kitchen into the rear hallway of the building.

"Lose her?" said Spike. "I didn't know you had her."

"I don't," said George. "But I'd like to, believe me." Running alongside Spike to the elevator, he began to sweat. "You can't believe the kind of women who responded to my ad. Nymphos, a lesbian couple, bisexuals, cross-dressers . . . Suzanne was the only one who was even a remote possibility."

The elevator arrived with a thump. "I'm sorry," said Spike,

and stepped into the waiting car. He pressed a button and the door snapped rudely in George's face. Outside, the summer night was steamy, but he breathed deeply and with pleasure. He walked a few blocks south and stopped in a store called Organizers' Paradise, where he sifted absently through small bins of plastic paperclips and brightly colored ballpoint pens. He examined Lucite staplers and tape dispensers without interest, and smiled at a salesman who had been watching him. The man had a dark, waist-length ponytail and a reddish beard.

"How's it going, man?" he asked Spike.

"Pretty good."

"Can I help you?"

"I was looking for something for my son," said Spike.

"How old is he?"

"How old is he?" Spike repeated. "He's kind of young, a baby, I guess you'd call him."

The man swung his ponytail all the way around his neck like a noose and stared at Spike. "This is a stationery store," he said at last.

"I guess it is," said Spike, and laughed nervously. "It seems like I'm in the wrong place, doesn't it?"

"Not necessarily." The salesman reached into a bin at his side and withdrew a roll of Scotch tape. He tore off a long strip and pulled it tightly under his nostrils, distorting his face comically. "Kids love this stuff," he said. Wrenching the tape upward, he rearranged his features so hideously that Spike could hardly bear to look at him. "You can have hours of fun with this stuff, believe me," the salesman said earnestly.

"Oh, I believe you," said Spike, and struggled not to laugh. Not wanting to disappoint the salesman, he bought a roll of tape and thanked him with excessive enthusiasm. He left the store and continued walking south along Broadway, past fruit-and-vegetable stands, pizzerias, and junk stores that sold sunglasses, plastic jewelry, and T-shirts and buttons with obscene phrases printed on them. In front of a Gothic-looking church, a man with Rastafarian braids played "Für Elise" expertly on the steel drums, and Spike stopped to listen, tossing a handful of change into the musician's open cigar box. He transplanted himself, along with the musician, to a Caribbean beach, where the man played the "Moonlight Sonata" on his drums as Spike stood waist-deep in the tranquil sea.

He folded a dollar bill into the cigar box and moved on, looking for a restaurant that appealed to him. He was hungry, but had no yearning for anything in particular. "I'm *dying* for some hot and sour soup," he heard a woman walking in front of him announce, and followed her and her companion into the nearest Chinese restaurant. He ordered a container of fried rice and a can of Pepsi to go, and was out on the street again moments later. Halfway across the street, set on the grassy median that divided Broadway, were benches filled with a mix of elderly people and winos. He spotted an empty space at the end of one of the benches and sprinted across the street to claim it. He drank his Pepsi in small contemplative sips and barely touched the container of rice balanced in his lap. He thought of Leora and their dinner guests eating, in air-conditioned luxury, the chicken breasts he had cleaned and pounded and prepared with considerable effort an hour ago. "Jerk," he said out loud, and heard the condescension in George's voice as he said, *Tell me, Spike, do you find me threatening?*

"Asshole," he murmured.

"You talking to me?" the old man next to him said. Despite the heat, he was dressed in a ratty suit and vest and a gray felt hat. A soiled-looking white muffler was wrapped loosely around his neck.

Spike put the container of rice back into the paper bag and rolled down the top. "Sorry, no," he said. "Don't pay any attention to me—I was just talking to myself."

"Oh, I do it all the time," the man confided. "But of course when you get to be my age, you're entitled. The fact of the matter is, I was born in 1896, same as F. Scott Fitzgerald."

"Really," said Spike. "I'm impressed."

"Yup. Funny thing—he dies in 1940 and I'm still here. Of course he drank too much and wrecked his health, and there you have it. But listen, you planning on eating any of that food you got in that bag there? Because if you're not, I thought I might try some of it."

"Take it," said Spike. "With my compliments." He watched the man open the bag and peer inside it for what seemed to be a long while.

"What, no chopsticks?" the man said finally.

"Sorry." Spike handed him a white plastic fork. "This is all they gave me."

"I can't eat Chinese food without chopsticks," the man complained, and slipped the fork between the slats of the bench. "And that's that."

Turning to stare into the man's nearly colorless eyes, hoping to shame him, Spike waited. But the man sat unmoving and silent on the bench and at last Spike gave up.

"Not even a good-bye?" the man called after him.

Cruising homeward along well-lighted, sweltering streets, he made himself laugh, whispering "What, no chopsticks?" over and over again, savoring it as if it were a hilarious punch line. He thought of what he must have looked like to anyone who happened to notice him—a madman in jeans and expensive sneakers enjoying the simple pleasure of his own company.

Leora greeted him quietly in the doorway, without asking where he had been. She seemed distracted, saying nothing as the baby drove his jeep straight into the coffee table. "Your mother called," she reported.

"Okay. But what happened to our distinguished guests?" Spike pulled the jeep away from the table and gave it a small push toward the center of the room. "Have a good trip, buddy," he told the baby.

"Gone," Leora said, dismissing even the mention of them with an impatient wave of her hand. "Listen, Spike, I didn't actually speak to your mother. It was one of her doctors who called."

"And?" Instantly, he began clenching and unclenching his fingers and toes. "What about it?"

"She's in the hospital, but she's all right. Apparently," Leora said softly, "she almost OD'd on some tranquilizers he'd given her. He seemed to think it was deliberate, Spike."

"This is my mother we're talking about?" Leora came toward him and he stumbled into her arms, eyes closed. He felt the tires of the G.I. Joe jeep graze his heels and then a satisfying flash of pain as the baby went into reverse and backed into him, nearly knocking him over and onto his knees.

Chapter

9

Alexander awakens, at 6:15 in the morning, to the sound of
Ionie hissing furiously into the telephone on the night table next
to her. Turning over onto his side, he reaches out and strokes
her broad back, then traces the ridges of her spine with his
fingertip. She ignores him, and continues harassing whoever's
on the other end of the line.

"Girl, I be fixing to come on over there and slap you silly!"
she threatens, and then hangs up.

It always amuses him to hear her talk like this, mostly to
members of her family, and then switch back to ordinary
English, effortlessly and at will. He likes the spirited sound of
that talk, its stubborn refusal to pay any attention to the rules
of what he has come to think of as middle-class grammar.

"You be fixing to *what?*" he teases her.

"I said I'd slap her silly and I will. That Shavonne says no way is she going back to school next month, and I say no way she's not."

"She had to call you at six in the morning to tell you this?"

"The girl's got no sense. It's like she's been sitting out in the hot sun all her life and just baked her brains away."

"Well, like it or not, she *has* to go to school. She's only fourteen."

"Ha!" says Ionie. "Shows how much *you* know. This is the city of New York, baby. Those people don't have time to go chasing around after one more truant like her. They've got more important business to attend to."

"Maybe I could talk to her," Alexander says. "Give her a little incentive to stay in school."

"Like what?" Ionie wraps herself around him and lets out a noisy sigh.

"I don't know, what's something that would make her happy?"

"Cable TV. She likes that MTV, all those music videos."

"Okay. But now that she's staying with your brother and sister-in-law, we'd have to clear it with them first."

"Shavonne thinks they're going to throw her out," Ionie tells him. "She'd like that, you know, to get thrown out of there and then come on over here and make our lives a misery."

"I'm too old to live with teenagers," Alexander says, and smiles. "All that music and sex is just too much for me." He puts his lips against Ionie's, circles them with the tip of his tongue. In the bedroom next door the baby begins to howl.

"How do those babies *know?*" Ionie says, already starting to rise from the bed. "Every one of them knows from the day it's born just when to wake up and spoil things."

"Radar," says Alexander. He trails after Ionie in his bare feet and pajamas and goes out to get the newspaper that's waiting just beyond his front door.

"*You're* up nice and early," says his neighbor Mrs. Fish as she bends down to get her own paper. "How are you?"

"Very well."

"Not me," Mrs. Fish tells him. "I lost my sense of taste from this blood thinner my doctor's making me take. Nothing tastes like anything to me. I try to force myself to eat to keep my strength up, you know, but it's very hard."

"Sounds awful." He sneaks a look at the sports pages as she continues talking.

". . . and I hear that little baby crying in your apartment and I think to myself, isn't that nice, that at his age he can go and—"

"She's not mine," Alexander says without looking up. "She belongs to a friend."

"That lovely black lady I always see? She's been coming here for quite a few years, hasn't she? I always thought she was your housekeeper."

"Look, do you have any cans that need opening? Otherwise I've got to get going."

"I understand," says Mrs. Fish. "I understand perfectly. But if you could take a quick look at my television set, I'd be very grateful. The sound keeps fading and it's terribly upsetting."

Inside her apartment, a single room cluttered with ornate, old-fashioned furniture, he heads straight for the TV. It has been switched on to a talk show; three heavyset women are seated on a platform, all of them looking grim. The camera focuses now on the one who appears to be the youngest of the three, perhaps in her late twenties. Beneath her, on the screen, flash the words "SAYS HER LIFE IS MISERABLE." Alexander's first impulse is to laugh out loud, but his eyes open wide as the woman, who is named Darlene, begins her litany of misfortune. This is a woman who has never been able to hold a job, who has been dumped by one man after another, whose extensive medical history is filled with botched surgeries and cavalier doctors. The audience gasps with horror and sympathy; Darlene does not acknowledge them, but continues on in her soft-spoken monotone until at last the show's host holds up his hand and announces apologetically, "Back in a flash after these messages." As the camera pulls away, his hand falls on Darlene's shoulder and he bends to whisper something in her ear. Alexander is stupefied. He grieves for Darlene's multitude of troubles, for the loss of her self-respect. He wants to burst through the TV screen, seize her by the shoulders and say, *Why can't you keep all this to yourself, young lady? Why? Why does the whole world have to hear this from you?* But Darlene is gone, replaced by a close-up of two eggs being seat-belted into a little wooden car. The commercial is for a foreign-car manufacturer and seems to suggest that human life is fragile, as fragile as a couple of soft-boiled eggs out for a bumpy ride along a dangerous road. *Yes,* Alexander nods. *Yes yes yes.*

He shuts off the TV. "The set's working perfectly," he says.

"That's what the repairman told me," Mrs. Fish confesses. She grabs Alexander's pajama sleeve. "Do you think it could be me?"

"You?"

"My hearing," she says. "Maybe I'm going deaf."

"Maybe," Alexander says sadly, and gently removes her little hand from his sleeve. He backs away from her and edges toward the door.

Mrs. Fish is smiling at him now. "My whole life, Mr. Fine, I've always had a policy of minding my own business. Be that as it may, I just want you to know that it makes me smile every time I think of you and that nice black lady finding each other. You know, she always holds the elevator door for me when she sees me coming down the hallway, and once she helped me open my mailbox when I was having trouble with the key. So if you ever need me to baby-sit for that cute little baby you've got there, just give a holler. I wouldn't want you to go too far, of course, in case something terrible happened, like the baby stopped breathing or something, but if you just wanted to go to one of the movies they have here on Eighty-sixth Street, that would be fine."

"Thanks very much," says Alexander, and opens the door.

"Wait a minute, Mr. Fine." He stops, and looks back over his shoulder. "I just wanted to remind you that grapes, peanut butter, and hot dogs are the three leading causes of choking in young children."

"Thanks so much for telling me."

"Oh, don't be silly, you," says Mrs. Fish, waving him on. "I do what I can for my neighbors."

Alexander triple-locks himself inside his apartment and settles down at the kitchen table with his newspaper. From the other end of the apartment, he hears Ionie's voice singing "Splish Splash" and then the sound of the bathroom door opening. Soon Ionie appears with the baby, who blinks at Alexander with dark round eyes. She's wrapped in a hooded blue towel, the hood up over her head, framing her tiny face.

"You're too much, Deneece," Alexander croons. "Tooooo much."

"Where were you?" Ionie asks.

"Your friend Mrs. Fish lured me into her apartment to check on her TV."

"You went over there like that, in your pajamas?" Ionie says, amused.

"She's about a hundred years old, Ionie. I don't think she noticed."

"Next time wear your bathrobe."

"You're jealous of a hundred-year-old woman!" Alexander says.

"No way, baby," says Ionie, and begins to laugh. "You got a telephone call from your mama while you were over there. I got to tell you, she sounds real mean."

"She *is* mean," Alexander says. "When she wants to be, that is."

"I don't think she likes you very much, Alexander."

"She doesn't."

"Well, if I were you, I'd get out of town real quick. She's hiring a service car over there in Brooklyn and coming out here this afternoon for a visit."

"That can't be," says Alexander. "She never goes anywhere except around the block to the grocery store. She hasn't been here in ages, not since Margot died." He slams his fist against the table. "Goddammit," he says.

"So why's she so mean?" Ionie asks. "Does she have a good excuse, at least?"

"She got off to a bad start," says Alexander, trying to be generous. He tells Ionie what he has heard a thousand times from his mother, that she came to America as a young child and was held at Ellis Island because of a contagious illness while the rest of the family went off to Baltimore without her. *My father and stepmother left me there!* he hears his mother crying in outrage. *Left me there, for God's sake, as if I were just an extra suitcase they were leaving behind!* Eventually, they'd sent a pair of stepbrothers to retrieve her, but, Alexander knows, she was never able to forgive her father, never able to let go of that image of herself as an abandoned child. It was an image she summoned up, again and again: *What they did to me! You can't imagine it, as hard as you try.* Hearing the story when he was very young, Alexander wept for the desolate child who, grown up, had somehow managed to become his mother. Sometimes he and his mother had wept together in each other's arms until his mother pulled away, pulled herself together, saying, *Enough!* But at some point in his adolescence, the story lost its charm for him; he had heard it too many times and it lost its resonance. He saw that his mother was playing it for all it was worth, using it to manipulate him and his younger brother whenever she wanted something of them, usually something unreasonable. When they refused her, fifty years ago, or just last week, her response was the same: *If only I'd had daughters! One daughter is worth a dozen sons and there's no one who can deny that!* How could you respond to something like that? David, his brother, had responded by moving to Arizona at the first opportunity, building a small hotel on a picturesque man-made lake and returning east only for weddings and funerals. Alexander thinks of him now with envy and some resentment, as he has for years. The man was no fool, Alexander has to give him that. As for himself, he's endured a lifetime of exasperating encounters and phone calls he's learned to live with

as best he can. When Margot was alive, he had in her a sympathetic audience willing to hear him out, to listen, astonished,
to his recital of insults his mother had cast his way. *She's not like
the rest of us*, Margot always concluded. *The woman's a lunatic.* There
was no arguing with that. But sometimes, inexplicably, his mother
was sweet and pliant, yielding without protest last month to
Alexander's suggestion that he come by and drive her into the
city for an afternoon with Leora and the baby. Just as often,
though, she would greet him coldly over the phone and the
conversation would deteriorate almost instantly.

"Oh, it's *you*," he heard her say, her disappointment so obvious he nearly hung up right there.

"How are you?" he said.

"Never ask an old lady how she is, unless you really want
to know."

"I *do* really want to know."

"Well, I don't want to tell you, how's that? But I *will* tell
you one thing: I'm very disappointed in you and your brother
both. *Very* disappointed."

He stretched the silvery plastic telephone wire to its limit
and went to the refrigerator, where he discovered a stalk of
celery that was just beginning to go limp and brownish. He
rinsed a length of it at the sink and embellished it with cream
cheese.

"What are you doing?" Mary said sharply.

"Listening to *you*."

"You're not."

"Yes, I am."

"Well, you're not listening hard enough," Mary said.

"Want to bet?" He kicked the refrigerator shut with the toe
of his sneaker and bit down daintily on his celery stick. "You're
disappointed in me and in David and I'm waiting to find out
why."

"Why? Because I asked you both for pictures of your grandchildren and you didn't send me any."

"I don't know about David, but I know *I* certainly did."

"If you did, they weren't *nice* pictures. I'm looking at them right now and I don't like what I see. Benjamin's in Leora's lap and neither of them looks happy. And in the other one, he's in some kind of a little car or a truck, maybe, and he's not smiling in that one either. Why do you send me pictures like that where nobody looks happy?"

"It must be because I'm such a miserable son of a bitch," he mumbled, crunching his celery extravagantly.

"What's that static on the line?"

"Celery," said Alexander.

"What? I can't hear a word you're saying. This is a terrible connection. Call me back some other time, why don't you. And next time don't be so nasty. I deserve better than this from you. Not that I expect it, after all these years. You are what you are, Alexander, and that's that."

"What am I?" he asked, but she had already hung up.

"She's angry at the world," he tells Ionie now. "She's always been angry."

"Well," says Ionie, "she can come over here and be as angry as she wants. She doesn't scare *me*."

"She doesn't scare me either. She's only my mother."

Ionie rolls her eyes at this. "Only your mama? Baby, you're scared of that lady. I bet your heart's beating real fast just thinking about her."

Taking her hand and placing it under his pajama top and over his heart, Alexander says, "I'm cool as a cucumber, see?"

But Ionie isn't convinced. "You can't fool me," is all she says.

When the doorman buzzes from downstairs in the middle of the afternoon, Alexander races to a mirror to inspect himself one last time, as if, he thinks, he were a teenage girl awaiting the date of her dreams. Examining the worried face he sees in the mirror, he forces his mouth into a shockingly insincere smile, the best he can manage.

"Ionie!" he yells.

Answering the doorbell, he is suddenly face-to-face with a stranger, an overweight black teenager whose hair is meticulously arranged in dozens of braids, some of them ornamented with thin gold medallions. He nearly reaches out to finger the gold and stops himself just in time.

"Where's Ionie?" the girl says in an unfriendly way.

"Shavonne?" he says.

"Where's my baby?" says Shavonne, and marches fiercely through the living room in her high white sneakers and tight blue jeans, clearly a figure to be reckoned with.

"Oh Lord," says Ionie as she approaches from the bedroom. "Oh Jesus."

"I want my baby back," Shavonne announces. She starts to move past her grandmother toward the bedrooms, but Ionie blocks her way. She steers Shavonne back into the living room and forces her onto the couch.

"Want a Coke or something?" she says.

Shavonne glares at her. "Diet Pepsi."

"You'll take whatever we got and Coke is what we got," Ionie says severely.

"I want my baby back," says Shavonne when she gets her drink. She inches away from Ionie on the couch. "Where is she?"

"She's asleep," says Ionie. "And anyway, you can't have her."

"She's mine," Shavonne says. "I gave birth to her and she's mine."

"What do you know about what it takes to care for a baby? You can barely change a diaper, girl."

"Me and my boyfriend's going away and we got to take Deneece with us."

"Boyfriend?" says Ionie, and slaps Shavonne sharply across her cheek.

At his seat at the dining-room table, Alexander sucks in his breath. He half expects Shavonne to slap Ionie back, but what he hears is the sound of angry weeping. He watches as Shavonne leans into Ionie's embrace, watches as Ionie plays absently with the gold coins in her granddaughter's elaborately decorated hair.

"Go on and see the baby, but don't you dare wake her up,"

Ionie says, and in an instant Shavonne is flying from the room and out of sight.

Alexander plays with the all-in-one salt-and-pepper shaker on the table, twisting it so that a fine powder of black pepper falls across the table's gleaming surface.

"You're making a mess," Ionie says, and joins him at the table. "Shavonne's a little bit disturbed," she says after a while.

"Who wouldn't be? It *is* her baby, after all."

"That's not it," Ionie says. "In school they had her in a special class. They told me she was a little bit disturbed. E-motionally disturbed. They had a psychologist studying her, but I never did find out anything. They just told me she's not quite right and that she'll always need some special attention. Of course, I told them that myself before they ever even started in studying her."

"Not quite right," Alexander repeats. "So what are you supposed to do about it?"

"Pray," says Ionie as the intercom buzzes. "And then pray some more, I guess."

"My mother," says Alexander, "falls in love with strangers at the drop of a hat. So don't get all nervous. It's only her family she finds intolerable." He kisses Ionie hurriedly and pushes back his seat. "If things start getting nasty, take cover under the table. And dial 911 if you can get to a phone."

"How old is this mean old lady?" Ionie says, and laughs.

"Eighty-five," says Alexander, "but she's going to live forever."

It is Ionie who goes bravely to the door. "Come right on in," she tells Alexander's mother.

"I'm Mary Fine," his mother announces. "Who are you?"

"Ionie Lewis. How you-all doin'?"

"That's not what I meant, Mrs. Lewis. I meant, who *are* you?" Mary says as Alexander edges forward to greet her.

"Hi, Mom," Alexander says casually, and kisses his mother's fragrant, powdery cheek. She is a tiny woman in a dark blue spring coat and cotton gloves. Her long white hair is in its customary French knot, her thin mouth bright with crimson lipstick. Like him, she has a face that is almost entirely smooth and unlined, and he does not doubt for a minute that she will live forever.

"What are you doing with that coat on in this heat?" he says.

"Old people have a different kind of thermostat. You'll find that out soon enough," Mary says, removing her gloves. "If you live that long."

Ionie comes around behind her and helps her out of her coat.

"Thank you, Mrs. Lewis."

"Just Ionie."

"I still don't know who you are," Mary says. "Are you the maid? I'm sure I've heard your name over the years."

"I was," Ionie says, smiling, "but I got a promotion."

"Well, whoever you are, you're very nice, Mrs. Lewis. It used to be that colored people were always nice, and then a few years back, I think it was, they began calling themselves 'black people' and then all of a sudden they weren't so nice anymore, which was a shame for all of us, don't you think?"

Alexander is mortified, as embarrassed as he has ever been. His face blazes; under his arms, his deodorant turns to a thick paste. But Ionie is laughing, a deep, rich laugh that confuses him. "What's so funny?" he says.

"It's just on my mind to laugh. That okay with you?"

Shaking his head at the two of them, Alexander says, "That was a hideous thing to say, Mom. And utterly idiotic."

"It was?" his mother says mildly. "Well, then, I'm terribly sorry, Mrs. Lewis. I hope I haven't offended you, because that certainly wasn't my intention. It was just an observation, that's all."

"Let's just forget about it," Ionie says.

"Why are you letting her off so easy?" Alexander persists.

"People make mistakes," says Ionie. "You get my point, Alexander?"

"This Mrs. Lewis is a very refined woman," says Mary. "It's a pleasure to know her."

Alexander smiles and drapes an arm around Ionie. "That's good news, Mom," he says. "Because Ionie's very special to me."

"How do you mean?" Mary says slowly, staring at his arm that lingers across Ionie's shoulders. "Is she your wife?"

"Aren't you something!" Ionie whoops. "Isn't she something, Alexander?"

"Absolutely." He waves to Shavonne as she enters the room, the baby held awkwardly in her arms.

"Not like *that*," Ionie says in exasperation, rushing to arrange the baby properly. "And didn't I tell you to let her sleep?"

"Who's that white lady?" Shavonne says.

"Who are you?" says Mary.

"This is my baby," says Shavonne. "She's going upstate with me and my boyfriend."

"Is that so?" Mary says. "Well, have a safe trip."

"She is not going," Ionie says, taking the baby from Shavonne. "What kind of a great-grandmother do you think I am?"

Raising her eyebrows, Mary says, "Great-grandmother? We're just the same, you and I," she tells Ionie. "I'm a great-grandmother too. It's nice, isn't it, the way families go on and on and on. It sometimes warms me up inside just thinking about it. Of course, I always hope for girls when anyone in the family is expecting. Sons are just about useless; anything they do for you is done grudgingly. In my opinion, one daughter is worth a dozen sons, and that's a fact. Am I right, Mrs. Lewis?"

Ionie's eyes are suddenly bright with tears. "I lost a son a while back. He was a beautiful boy, handsome and good. It just about killed me when he passed on. So you can't talk to me like that about sons, I just can't take it."

"Oh my," says Mary, and puts her hands to her face. "It's a pitiful thing to lose a child. Please forgive me, Mrs. Lewis. I'm saying all the wrong things to you today, aren't I?"

Ionie shrugs. "It's like I said, sometimes you make a mistake. Like Shavonne here. She makes a mistake and goes ahead and has a baby anyway. That's mistake number two. And now she wants to go on to mistake number three, which is to take her baby out of this beautiful home and—"

"What beautiful home?" Mary says.

"This one right here."

"The baby lives here?"

"Come and sit down, Mom," Alexander says, and leads her to a seat on the couch. "How about a cup of tea?"

"The world is a different place now," says Mary, sounding dazed. "I understand that. I read about it in the paper and hear about it on the news. Drug-related killings every day of the week. The ozone layer's not what it used to be. And then there's the greenhouse effect and nuclear winter and syringes washing up on the beaches. It's enough to make you give up hope, isn't it."

"Does this mean she's not happy about us living together?" Ionie asks.

"There's more," says Mary. "Teenagers murdering their parents after a disagreement about a girlfriend or something; a nice churchgoing man killing off his whole family for the insurance money . . . And let's see, what else?"

"We get the picture, Mom," Alexander says wearily. "We've heard enough."

"I don't know what else to say. I'm just a confused old lady, I think."

"Why did you come here?" Alexander says softly. "What's this visit all about?"

"Well, to be truthful, I can't balance my checkbook anymore. I brought it with me so you could fix it up."

"You came all the way over here for that?"

"I think so, yes." Mary touches Alexander's wrist. "Tell me that you and this very refined lady Mrs. Lewis are just good friends."

Alexander glances toward Ionie, who opens her eyes wide

and nods her head once, gently. "Just good friends," he hears himself murmur.

"Thank God for that," his mother says in a whisper. "Thank God for that."

Shavonne lets out a low wail. "How come *she* gets what *she* wants but I don't get my baby?" she complains.

"Let me tell you a little secret," Alexander says, and gestures for her to approach him. "She's not getting *anything*," he says into Shavonne's ear. "Do you understand what I'm telling you?"

"Uh-uh, no," says Shavonne. "But you can keep my baby, okay, because I've changed my mind and I don't care."

"What?" says Ionie in astonishment. "What you talking about, girl? I know you do care *some*. You come way over here from Staten Island and then you say you don't care? You got to be feeling real bad now, hon, and what I want you to know is I understand that. Anybody would."

"I'm *mad*," says Shavonne. "At you and *him*." Dropping the baby into Ionie's arms, she says, "I don't want to take care of no damn baby anyway. Me and my boyfriend going to be too busy."

"Too busy going to school, you mean. But you can come over and see the baby whenever you want."

Shavonne kisses the top of Deneece's head. "Bye, baby," she murmurs.

"You think you're going away, girl?" Ionie says. "Come next month you're back in school."

Shavonne puts her hands on her hips and faces Ionie with a scowl. "I DON'T LIKE PEOPLE!" she announces. "Okay?"

"That's right," says Mary admiringly. "That's exactly right."

Chapter 10

All the way at the back of a crowded DC-10, on an early-evening flight to Fort Lauderdale, Spike arranged a blanket over his head like a tent, trying to keep away the bluish cigarette smoke that swirled about him in poisonous clouds. The chain-smoker seated next to him, an attractive woman in a mannish-looking business suit, punched away at a tiny calculator with the eraser end of her pencil and ignored him. Under his blanket, Spike dozed on and off and thought of his mother, who had been released from the hospital after forty-eight hours and who was none too eager to have him make the trip down to see her, or so she claimed. He didn't believe a word of it, and sensed that she was embarrassed by the whole affair, embarrassed and humiliated at having been discovered and brought back to life by strangers in uni-

forms who knew not the slightest thing about her. Talking to
Spike on the phone from her hospital room, she had at first
insisted that she was actually in pretty good shape and that it
had all been a misunderstanding. "A mistake, I mean."

"What kind of mistake?" Spike had said.

"An accident," said Lucille impatiently. "You don't really
think I had any intention of doing myself in, do you?"

Spike was silent. He knew only that he had to tread delicately, that his mother had touched bottom and was, quite possibly, planning another go at it just as soon as she were able. "I
don't know," he murmured.

"What?" Lucille said.

"I think we shouldn't be talking about these things over the
phone. I think we need to see each other."

"Come down at Christmas like you always do. I'll rent a
crib for Ben and get a baby-sitter, and you and Leora and I can
go out and do the town. Any restaurants you want me to make
reservations at?"

"Christmas is four months away, Ma. I don't want to wait
that long."

"I'm flattered, Spike, really," said Lucille. "But truthfully,
I'm not looking too terrific and I don't want anyone seeing me
until I have the chance to fix myself up a little."

"It's going to take you four months to have your hair done?"

"Something's happened to me, Spike," his mother whispered. "I'm not the same anymore."

"You're frightened," he said.

"No! I didn't mean that. I'm just the same as I always was.
I'm still tenth-floor fire captain and still on the decorating committee and all that. And I still have everything to live for, do
you understand what I'm telling you?"

"Sure," Spike said. "Absolutely." His hands were ice cold
and clammy, and he felt like weeping. "I'll see you soon," he
said, and went off to the bathroom, where he leaned over the
sink and toward the mirror, dipping his head and searching for
gray hairs. He pulled out half a dozen and immediately felt
better, as if he had just completed an arduous and painful task.

"Knock knock," an unfamiliar voice was saying now, and through the thin wool airline blanket he felt the weight of what turned out to be a small, well-manicured hand. He pulled the blanket from his head and greeted the chain-smoker sitting beside him.

"Do we know each other?" he said.

"Caroline Hirschfeld-Diaz," said the chain-smoker, and put out her cigarette.

"Spike Goldman."

"Listen, I'm sorry I drove you all the way under your blanket, but frankly, if you're going to sit in the smoking section, you've got to be prepared for a little smoke, you know?"

Spike shrugged. "It's not as if I had a choice—it was the last available seat on the plane."

"Well, carpe diem, as they say."

"Are you sure that's what you mean?" said Spike, and laughed. He noticed that her streaked blond hair was beautifully blow-dried, with perfect, symmetrical wings folded back against each ear. He thought of Leora's wild hair, always looking as if she had just come out of the wind, and felt a pang of homesickness and longing.

"Did I say 'carpe diem'? I think I meant c'est la vie."

"I think you did too," said Spike.

"Oh well, what do you expect from an accountant?"

"You're going to Florida on business?"

"Not exactly," Caroline said.

"Pleasure?"

A look of melancholy crossed Caroline's face, and she stroked one of her blond wings. "I'm going down to clear out my father's apartment before the new owners move in. He died a few months ago."

"I'm sorry," said Spike.

"Don't be. He had four wives and a terrific life."

"Four wives!" said Spike. "He must have been pretty hot stuff."

"I had three stepmothers at my wedding," said Caroline. "One in pink, one in silver, and one in black. Nancy, the one in silver, is meeting me at the airport. We're going to sort through everything together, separate the wheat from the chaff, you know." She nodded at Spike. "Did I get that right?"

"You're doing okay," said Spike, and smiled.

"*You're* not here on business, I can see that."

"How do you know I don't have an attaché case hidden up my sleeve?"

"You look like someone who threw a few things into an overnight bag and hopped on the first flight he could get."

"Something like that," said Spike.

"Well?"

He wasn't one to confide in strangers, an act in which he could only see reflected desperation and neediness and a lack of self-control. He confided in his shrink, of course, who had, after all, once been a stranger. He didn't mind seeming needy behind the closed doors of his therapist's office, and yet the thought of exposing himself to a perfect stranger struck him as unseemly.

"So, Sparky, what brings you to Florida?" said Caroline.

"Spike," he said.

"Come on, Spike."

"You don't even know my name."

"I do now. It's kind of an interesting name for a grown-up, don't you think?"

"Actually, I christened myself 'Spike' when I was about five. It seemed like a terrific name at the time."

"So why don't you tell me about your trip to Disney World, or wherever it is you're off to."

"I'm going down to Fort Lauderdale to check up on my mother," Spike heard himself say, and knew that he was sunk, that the rest would follow effortlessly. Caroline fooled with her calculator, playing it with the fingers of one hand like a keyboard, feigning a sudden disinterest in Spike and anything he might tell her. He waited a few moments and then he said, "Neat calculator. Very high-tech looking."

"Is she sick?" Caroline said.

"She tried to kill herself."

"Oh God," Caroline said, her hand flying from the calculator to her throat. "Is she all right?"

"I'm not sure."

"Poor thing."

"She doesn't want to see me," said Spike. "For all I know, I'll never even get a foot in the door."

"You're a good son, Sparky. Very devoted, I can tell."

"Not really. But I've been known to do the right thing and that counts for something, I guess."

"It counts for a lot, Sparky." Caroline smiled. She took a business card from her attaché case, printed something across the bottom, and then handed it to Spike. "That's my stepmother's phone number. Call me if you need me."

"Need you?"

"If your mother won't talk to you, I will."

"I'm married," said Spike, and tucked the business card into his shirt pocket.

"So am I," Caroline said. "And I didn't say I'd sleep with you, Spike, I just said I'd talk to you."

Feeling foolish, Spike looked away. He watched as a man across the aisle with headphones on rocked in time with the music he was listening to; beside him, a little boy colored furiously in a coloring book, head bent over his work. A pair of middle-aged women in bejeweled sweatsuits stood on line outside the rest room talking eagerly. Five miles in the sky, everyone seemed busy and content, and Spike had to envy them. He didn't know which would be worse: seeing his mother, or exhausting himself in an unsuccessful effort to talk his way past her front door.

"I'm planning on taking my father over to the Temple for Hearing-Impaired Jews," one of the women on line for the rest room said. "I think he'd enjoy it."

"What?" her companion said.

"The Temple for Hearing-Impaired—"

"I'm teasing you, silly."

Spike laughed. "What's so funny?" said the stewardess who approached him now with a steel cart loaded with dinner trays.

"Nothing much."

"Okay. How about some dinner, then. Lasagna or meat?" she offered.

"What kind of meat?"

"Don't tell anyone," the stewardess whispered, "but I have to say it looks like Alpo."

"I appreciate your candor," said Spike, and waved her on. Caroline lit a cigarette then, and he disappeared under his blanket and drifted off. When he awakened, the landing gear was in place and the plane was already in its descent.

"Want to meet my stepmother?" Caroline said as they stood waiting at the baggage carousel. "She's a real hot ticket. That's her over there, the chick in the white leather skirt who's smiling at me."

Spike could see that the chick in question wasn't much older than forty. "Your father must have been quite a guy," he said, shaking his head in astonishment.

"He lived the good life and then died in his sleep of a heart attack. I like to think he never knew what hit him."

Spike could imagine it perfectly: "He Never Knew What Hit Him" engraved on the old man's tombstone in solemn Gothic letters.

"I've got to go," he told Caroline. "Take care of yourself."

"Call me," she said, and slipped casually into her stepmother's suntanned, outstretched arms.

Slinging his bag over his shoulder, Spike hurried through several pairs of electric doors and picked out a cab from the fleet waiting out front. Twenty minutes later he was in the lobby of his mother's building, which smelled strongly of a perfumed disinfectant that almost made him swoon. He sat down on a pink vinyl bench and immediately attracted the attention of a quartet of silver-haired men who were hanging around the elevator bank, each of them wearing white shoes and a different pastel-colored polyester outfit.

"I know you," one of them said, and pointed at Spike accusingly. "You're Isidore Marx's son."

"I don't think so," Spike said.

"Sure you are," the man insisted. "You work for one of those big advertising agencies in Chicago. Your father is *so* proud of you, I can't tell you. Talks about you all day long. Frankly, it gets a little tiresome sometimes, not that we would ever let him know it."

"You seem to have me confused with someone else," said Spike. "I'm from New York. I teach at Columbia, actually."

"Get out of here!" the man said exuberantly. "I know who you are. I know you got a big fat raise this summer and bought a beautiful house on Lake Shore Drive."

"It looks like things are really going my way, aren't they?" said Spike, and stood up as the elevator arrived.

"You bet," the man said. "Make sure you enjoy every bit of it."

"Oh, I will," said Spike, and sailed up to his mother on the tenth floor. "Isidore Marx," he said out loud, and smiled. He walked past his mother's apartment and all the way to the end of the air-conditioned hallway to a large oval window that looked out over the pool, lit up now in the late-summer darkness. Beyond it, the lights of a thousand restaurants and shopping malls glittered elegantly. He tried to focus on a single point of light, which soon went blurry under his gaze. He did not want to see his mother, did not want to feel the texture of her sorrow, to run his fingertips across the prickly surface of her fear. He knew he was neither heartless nor extravagantly self-absorbed, but thought perhaps it was the thinnest gauze of selfishness that kept him back, kept him from wanting to plunge straight into the heart of someone else's life.

Beneath his fingers, the cool oval of glass grew smudged and warm. He took a step backward and then another, and presently found himself at his mother's door. He rang the bell, and after a while the door swung open.

"Spike, darling," Lucille said warmly, without expressing

much surprise. "I really am sorry, but you just can't see me like this," she told him, and then the door slammed shut.

"It's not you," said Spike, for the glimpse he had gotten of her showed a gaunt, birdlike woman with sharpened features and pure white hair.

"I've shrunk a bit, but it's me all right," Lucille called from the other side of the door. "Who else would it be?"

"Let me in," said Spike. "Let me see."

"Come back at Christmas. I'll take you out to some nice restaurants," Lucille promised.

"I'm here now," said Spike. "And I'm hungry. Let's go out to dinner."

"Didn't they feed you on the plane?"

"Dog food."

Lucille clucked in sympathy. "Well, maybe you'll have better luck on the return flight."

"I'm not going back until Sunday night."

"Really. What kind of plans did you have for the next two days?"

"Oh, I don't know, I thought we'd lie around by the pool together and talk a little bit. Or we can do whatever *you* want to do."

"I love you dearly, but what I want to do is be alone."

"I don't believe that for a minute," said Spike.

"Ask my neighbors. They've come by in droves to check up on me and I wouldn't let a single one of them in. They finally got the hint and started leaving food at my door. Homemade coleslaw, a roasted chicken, a banana bread . . . enough food to feed an army."

"The chicken sounds good," said Spike. "Is there any white meat left?"

"Sure. If you don't have any objection to eating out in the hallway."

"You're kidding."

"I kid you not, darling. Anything to drink?"

"Whatever you have," said Spike, and smiled at the thought

of catching her off guard, at the possibility of slipping gracefully through the open door before she had the chance to shut him out. But his mother was on to him and wasn't about to give him any such opportunity.

"I'm going to open up the door now," she announced a few minutes later. "You go across the hall and wait in front of the Michaelsons' apartment until I've got the door closed. You might want to add a little salt and pepper to the coleslaw, by the way."

"You don't trust me," Spike said shamelessly. "How do you think that makes me feel?"

"I'm not stupid, darling. I may be many things, but stupid isn't one of them. Now go stand in front of the Michaelsons, please."

Across the hall, Spike watched as his mother stooped down in her pink suede slippers and housedress to place his dinner on the floor. The tray of food was neatly arranged, and there was even a bud vase with a single silk flower. It was the vase and the purple-and-white iris that gave him hope; no one who was entirely off her rocker would ever have cared so much about the appearance of things, he thought.

"Thank you," he called as the door swung shut in his face.

"Enjoy," said Lucille, and thumped down against the inside of the door. "Want me to keep you company while you're eating?"

"Good coleslaw," said Spike, with a mouth full of food. "But you were right about the salt and pepper."

"What?"

"I was just praising the coleslaw," Spike yelled, pressing his lips almost against the doorjamb.

"Don't yell, please."

"I wouldn't have to if you'd let me inside."

"It isn't that I don't want to," said Lucille. "It's simply that I can't. You'll just have to forgive me, darling."

Spike tipped his chin upward, raising a wineglass of club soda to his lips, and was startled to see the talkative silver-haired man staring down at him.

"Hey, Izzy's boy," the man said. "What are you doing out in the hallway with that picnic lunch? Don't you know it's against the house rules?"

"My mother prefers to keep me at a distance," Spike said loudly. "She won't let me into her apartment."

"Your mother's on the fourth floor," the man said, looking confused. "Why are you camping out all the way up here on the tenth?"

"I'm Lucille Goldman's son, that's why."

"You told me you were Isidore Marx's son!" the man whispered furiously. "You were pulling my leg, weren't you?" He thought this over for a few moments, then said, "Lucille Goldman, what do you know. I heard she was in the loony bin for a couple of days. How's she doing?"

"She was in the hospital, having a few things taken care of. And keep your voice down—she's right on the other side of the door."

"Well, listen, whoever you are, you can't eat out in the hall. I'll have to report you to the condo board if you don't get rid of all that food. Nothing personal, but it reflects badly on the building to have weirdos camping out like this."

Lucille pushed the door open slightly. "I'll have you know that weirdo happens to be a graduate of Yale Law School," she said. "So leave him be, Leon, or I'll report *you* to the board for harassing my son."

"How are you, Lucille?" Leon said politely. "Word has it you've been under the weather, which is why I'm going to forget that you just threatened me. Now be a sweetie and let your big handsome son into the apartment, please."

"He *is* handsome, isn't he? But that's no reason to let him in."

Seizing the doorjamb with both hands, Leon said, "Believe me, whatever's between you can be worked out. My own son and I were strangers for eight years while he was married to that horrible girl who wouldn't even let me see my grandchildren. And then he gets a divorce and custody of the kids and it's like old times again—the two of us talking on the phone every Sunday night like there's no tomorrow. And let me tell you, when we kissed and made up, it was the sweetest moment of my life. Really," he said, turning to Spike and gripping his elbow, "it was a wonderful, wonderful thing. So don't be stubborn. Make your mother happy and do what she wants."

"She wants me to spend the weekend out in the hallway," said Spike.

"That's out of the question," said Leon. "The board won't allow it."

"Oh *please*," Lucille said. "That's a lot of baloney, Leon, and you know it. I happen to be on the board, and if I say he stays out in the hallway, that's where he stays."

"You're off the board!" Leon said excitedly. "I'm holding an emergency meeting tonight and after we take a vote you'll be out so fast it'll make your head spin!"

Lucille threw open the door at this, in time to see Leon begin his strut down the hallway, his white shoes rising and falling stiffly against the carpet, his arms absolutely rigid. "You don't think anyone in this building is going to take your little kangaroo court seriously, do you, you self-important jackass?" she yelled after him. Spike flew past her and into the apartment, his dinner tray balanced on one palm. Lucille watched his flight with amusement, making no attempt to stop him. "Pretty tricky footwork," she said. "I'm impressed."

Spike came toward her in the living room, just a bit uncertainly, and embraced her. In his arms she seemed to be nothing more than an arrangement of hard bones, as if she had lost her bosom, all her softness. "Where are you?" he whispered.

"Don't sound so frightened. I'm right here."

"Are you sure?" He nudged her head down along his shoulder and smoothed her hair, which had gone from frosted gray to white since he had last seen her. Pressed up close against him, she was slipping away, withdrawing to someplace beyond his reach. "Don't go," he said.

"Where would I be going?" she said, and laughed. "Of course, if they throw me off the board, I just might move out."

"Why?"

"The shame would be too much, I think. You know, they've never thrown anyone off the board in all the years I've been living here, not even Miltie Simon, who went to jail for six months and came back just as obnoxious as ever. Every time the board had to vote on something, they let him cast his ballot from his prison cell. When he got sprung, they made him a big party in the TGIF Lounge." Spike looked at her curiously. "The Thank God It's Friday Lounge," she said. "It's right here in the building, you know, across from the pool. The site of many a wild party."

"I'll bet. But listen, they're not going to throw you off the board," he said as Lucille eased herself away from him. "Where are you going?"

"If you think you're not going to let me out of your sight, you're mistaken, darling. But rest assured I'm not going to hurl myself off the roof the minute your back is turned."

"We have to talk about that," said Spike. He opened the sliding-glass doors that led to the terrace and stepped onto the ceramic-tiled floor. Below, the pitch-dark waterway was nearly motionless; in daylight, an occasional speedboat buzzed angrily across its surface. The long narrow terrace was cluttered with tall cactus plants and a couple of pieces of lawn furniture. When he and Leora came down for their yearly visit at Christmas, they had always made love on the padded chaise longue whose metal frame, he noticed now, had rusted over in the dampness. And once they had gone down to the pool after midnight, skinny-dipped in the water warm as a bath, and then made love in the shallow end, while above them a large sign posted on the side of the building listed all the activities forbidden in the pool: No Diving, No Splashing, No Spitting. They hadn't even come close to getting caught, though Leora was uneasy and kept looking back over her shoulder for spectators. Afterward, drowsy but also exhilarated, they tiptoed back inside the apartment, where Lucille lay dozing on the couch in front of the television set. Awakening at the sound of their return, squinting under the light of a single lamp, she asked how their swim had gone.

Leora had burst into nervous, uncontrollable laughter and had to leave the room, while his mother looked on in bewilderment and Spike simply shook his head, as if he knew nothing. He considered now the possibility that his mother, in the years since his father's death, had grown nostalgic for sex, for the sensation of being touched, even for the scent of it. What a loss! For only an instant, he perceived the profound sadness that marked her life, and he let out a little cry of astonishment.

"What's the matter?" his mother said. "Did you get pricked by a cactus out there?"

"In two different fingers," he lied, and sucked on them noisily.

"I can't seem to get rid of them. Daddy loved them, you know, and I guess that's why I can't bring myself to let go of them." She stepped over the metal track that held the sliding doors and joined him on the terrace. "Do you ever miss him?" she asked.

After a pause that lasted too long Spike said, "From time to time, I suppose."

"Like when?"

"I don't know, when I see Leora's father playing with Ben, see the bond between them—I'm warmed by it. And then I find myself wondering if Daddy ever could have had that with Ben, that loving, easy acceptance of him."

"Daddy would have envied your relationship with Alexander, I know that."

"He listens when I talk to him," said Spike. "He knows who I am."

"And Daddy didn't?"

"I don't want to get into it," Spike said. "Please."

"He meant to be a good father," Lucille said wistfully. "He bought you all those fish for your aquarium, started you on your stamp collection . . . he came in and kissed you every night while you slept. . . ."

"What?" said Spike. He did not believe that his father's arms had ever slipped around him, or that the briefest touch of his father's lips had ever fallen across his face. He remembered him, from childhood, as brusque and cool, a man who sat with him at the dinner table each night and talked past him to his mother. Their connection, his and his father's, was tenuous, seemingly empty of open affection; what they shared, in Spike's memory, was a meal every evening and an occasional obligatory half hour of catch in the backyard, an oddly quiet game where a softball was tossed back and forth endlessly and without much interest. Perhaps, he thought now, his memory was faulty, but he re-called no joyous moments between them, no solid evidence that his father had ever loved him or expressed any real interest in him. In later years they had always been cordial to each other, like business acquaintances making small talk. His father had never handed out compliments to him, not even when Spike graduated summa cum laude from college, or when he was ac-cepted at Yale, or when he married Suzanne, whom his father had described merely as "a nice enough girl." Spike could not help but assume that he had never been able to please his father, and was still, years after his father's death, trying to puzzle out why this was so.

"He did," said Lucille. "Every night before he went to sleep, he came into your room to kiss you. Even when you were a big boy, already in high school."

"It doesn't seem likely," said Spike. "In fact, it strikes me as one of the most unlikely things in the world."

"He was shy about that sort of thing. It was very hard for him to approach someone and touch them, even his own child. He wasn't a cold man, believe me. He was just too self-con-scious to relate to people like that. And it was a pity, really, because think how much he missed."

"Do you think about these things a lot?"

"I think about *him* a lot," Lucille said. "Sometimes it's as if I'm still angry at him for the ways in which he failed me. Other times I only remember the good parts, and can't, for the life of me, remember any of the thousand and one things he did that infuriated me. I talk to him sometimes, you know. I say, 'Irv, wherever you are, I'm selling all our Coca-Cola stock, which I know you told me never to do.' I feel better just getting something like that off my chest, that's all. And it's like we have this ongoing relationship, which makes a lot of sense, I think. Because how can you be married to someone for forty-three years and then just be cut off from him entirely? You can't, it's not natural. Not to me, anyway."

"I'm sorry you're alone," said Spike. Weak with sympathy and affection, he heard himself uttering words he had not ever imagined himself saying. "Come back to New York," he urged her. "Sell the condo and get something up north. You could see Ben whenever you wanted to. Not to mention your exceptionally wonderful son and daughter-in-law." He slung his arm around his mother and dropped a kiss that landed on her ear. "What do you think?"

"It was a great thrill for me to hear those words coming from you."

"But?"

"It was a sweet thought, but a terrible idea."

"The worst," Spike acknowledged.

"I've lived here for so long I wouldn't dream of going back."

"But what kind of a life is it?"

Lucille lowered her eyes. "I find myself feeling terribly depressed sometimes, but mostly it's a good life."

"What were you thinking," Spike said in a whisper, "when you emptied that bottle of Valium?" He looked at his mother, but she would not meet his eyes. "I have to know," he said.

"I can't tell you. I can't tell you because I honestly don't know. It's all confused in my mind. I wasn't feeling well all that day, and then in the middle of the afternoon the sun came through my bedroom window and lit up that bottle of Valium. I couldn't take my eyes off it; it seemed irresistible, just sitting there on my night table glowing in the sunlight." Lucille threw her hands in the air. "You know the rest."

"You're not making sense, Ma," Spike said, and heard his voice crackling irritably. "That's not a story I can take home with me and be comforted by."

"Who says I have to make sense all the time? What do you want from me?"

"I can't leave you like this, knowing you're like this." How can I *ever* leave you? he almost said.

"What's this all about? You think I'm a crazy person?" Lucille said, outraged. "How could you insult me like this?" She marched off the terrace and disappeared into her bedroom, kicking the door shut behind her as Spike trailed after her.

"Here I am again on the wrong side of the door," he called out. "Do you think there's any possibility we might have this conversation face-to-face?"

"Please leave me alone," said Lucille.

Sinking down onto the carpet, Spike lay on his side in front of the door, his chin propped up against his palm. He pulled at the tufts of carpeting for a while, waiting for a sign from his mother that all had been forgiven. But there was nothing but a stony silence from her and he understood that she was not going to give even the smallest fraction of an inch.

"Well, at least I'm making progress—at least I'm actually *inside* the apartment," he said loudly.

"Go home," his mother told him. "We've talked and now it's time for you to go home."

There was a gap between the bottom of the bedroom door and the carpeting—a gap wide enough to slip his hand through, Spike realized, and he wriggled his fingers now, waving to his mother. "I know you're in there, so there's no use pretending you're not," he teased her.

"Go home, Spike," Lucille said, sounding weary. "We'll talk some more over the phone when I'm not so angry at you."

"Are you armed?"

"Only with my wits," said Lucille, laughing slightly.

"Then I'm coming in after you," he warned, and thrust open the door. Lucille was seated at her desk, sorting through some papers, and paid no attention to him. The room was dominated by a king-sized bed, looking large enough for three, and was remarkably neat, except for the dresser, which was crowded with

an array of framed photographs, mostly of his father: in gradu-
ation robes, in his army uniform, in a pale blue leisure suit, in
a tuxedo and ruffled shirt at Spike's first wedding, dancing cheek
to cheek with Lucille. Spike ran a finger gently across his father's appealing face and sighed.

"What are you doing with all those papers?" he said.

"Revising my will," said Lucille. "I'm leaving all my money
to my beloved cat."

"You don't have a cat."

"Well then, I suppose I'll have to go out and get one."

"You're that angry at me, huh?"

"I'm not a child, Spike. And I'm not some whacked-out,
suicidal old lady who belongs in a straitjacket. I'm just someone
who had a little 'incident,' shall we say."

"That 'little incident' could have cost you your life."

"But it didn't," said Lucille. She stood up and, turning toward
him, slapped her hands against her hips. "Come on, Spike, give
me a break, will you?" she said.

There was a liveliness in her manner now, in her face now,
that convinced him she would go on, that she would return to
her life of condo meetings and classes and lunches with her
friends—an ordinary life worth holding on to.

"All right," he said. "I surrender. But isn't there anything I
can *do* for you?"

"You may be sorry you asked," Lucille said, smiling, and
immediately put him to work. He labored for hours, checking
light fixtures, repairing the toaster oven, tightening the handles
on frying pans, fixing a dresser drawer, a leaky faucet in the
shower, a pair of silver Levelors that would not open properly.

Afterward, exhausted, he fell into a deep, untroubled sleep
on the living-room couch. In the morning his mother gave him
an enthusiastic send-off, filling the pockets of his sport jacket
with individually wrapped breadsticks she had taken as souvenirs
from a slew of restaurants, and kissing him noisily on both cheeks,
her hands pressed a little too hard against his ears. She seemed
more robust than she had the day before, as if she had miracu-

lously gained weight and substance overnight now that the ordeal of having faced him was over. Buoyant at the prospect of his departure, she chattered on as they waited in the lobby for the taxi that would take him to the airport.

"It was wonderful to see you, Spike darling," she said for the third time. "I hate to admit it, but you were right to force yourself on me like that. And best of all, I can use my toaster oven again. I can't begin to tell you how many grilled-cheese sandwiches I ruined in the regular oven. My friend Cookie Shapiro can give you all the details—she was here the day I actually set one on fire and—"

"You'll have to tell me next time I come down," Spike interrupted. He signaled to the taxi as it pulled up noisily into the drive.

"What's the matter with your muffler?" Lucille asked the driver. She leaned into the front seat and gestured toward Spike in the rear. "This is my son," she said. "He's down from New York and now he's going back. He flew all the way down just for an overnight visit, isn't that something?"

"That's something, all right." Adjusting his mirrored sunglasses, the driver said, "In or out?"

"Me?" said Lucille. "I'm out." She came around to the backseat and kissed Spike one more time. "You're delicious," she said.

"Have a good flight," said Spike. "And don't forget to call when you get in."

"That's right," said Lucille. "And I love you to pieces."

This was more than the driver could bear. "Ever hear the expression 'All ashore that's going ashore'?" he said, and beeped his horn.

"You know what a Jewish Good-bye is?" Lucille asked him. "It's kind of a long-drawn-out—"

"I'm a Lutheran, what do you want from me?" the driver said as Lucille retreated and, at last, closed the door. "She really your mother?" he called out to Spike.

"All my life," Spike said.

At the airport, having time to spare, he wandered in and

out of souvenir shops and finally bought Ben a mesh sack filled with little rubber balls that were meant to look exactly like miniature oranges. He stopped at a bank of telephones and called Leora, but the line was busy and he gave up after three tries. Searching through his pockets for tissues, he came across the business card with the name "Caroline Hirschfeld-Diaz" printed across the front. His heartbeat picked up speed as he dialed her stepmother's number. As soon as the answering machine switched on it came to him that he had absolutely nothing to say to her, and he hung up the receiver with relief and gratitude, and the overwhelming feeling that he had narrowly avoided making an utter fool of himself.

Chapter 11

When Leora and Spike finally make their entrance, the birthday party Ionie has thrown for Alexander is in full swing. It is, Alexander realizes, the first time that he and Leora have seen each other since Ionie moved in with him nearly two months ago. He waits for Leora to step beyond the threshold and advance toward him and into the living room, but she hangs back, studying her toes and holding fast to the sleeve of Spike's sport jacket.

"Hello, stranger," Alexander says, and takes his daughter's hand. "I feel like you've been away at college or something."

"I know," she says darkly as Spike slips away into the crowd of thirty relatives and friends, most of whom have settled into the rented folding chairs and are balancing plates of food in their laps. The stereo is playing Cole Porter; occasional bursts of laughter can be heard over Ethel Merman's exuberant voice.

"Well, I'm thrilled to see you," says Alexander. "And are you going to wish me a happy birthday?"

"Happy birthday," Leora murmurs. She eases her hand from his, grips his wrist, and squeezes it so fiercely that his eyes fill with tears.

"What was that for?" he yelps.

"To make me feel better," says Leora.

"Do you feel better now?" He examines his wrist, which looks only slightly pink and bears no evidence of the force of Leora's anger.

"A little," Leora says, and reaches for his arm again, this time raising it to her lips and kissing it sweetly. "I'm sorry," she says in a whisper.

He nods and says nothing. Hearing Ionie's rich laugh from across the room, he turns to see her holding court at the buffet table, which is loaded with all the food she's prepared in his honor. "Come on over and say hello to Ionie," he suggests.

"I can't."

"Sure you can."

"This has nothing to do with her in particular," Leora says. "What I'm feeling, I mean."

"Time has passed, honey," he says. "Months and months. It's only natural that after a certain amount of time, a person begins to feel . . . open to possibilities."

"I hear you," Leora says. "Loud and clear."

"Well, that's a start, at least."

Leora shrugs her narrow shoulders, spins the bracelet of glass beads that ornaments her wrist. "I don't know that I'll ever be someone you can count on for support in this."

"You'll come around," Alexander predicts. "You'll take pleasure in my happiness—I feel sure of it."

"What makes you so optimistic?"

"Today's my birthday!" he whoops. "I feel optimistic about everything today, even about Shavonne."

"Ionie still hasn't heard from her?"

"This private detective we hired seems very sharp, but so far there's been nothing."

"Poor Ionie."

"Don't feel too sorry for her. She's got *me* to look after her, after all."

"Who'da thunk it," Leora says glumly.

"Come *on*, Leora!" he says. He feels impatient with her, as if she were a young child again and he were trying to teach her something fundamental, like simple addition or subtraction, and she just wasn't getting it, no matter how many different approaches he took. He snaps his fingers in front of her face and she blinks at him.

"What?" she says.

"I'm just trying to work some magic on you," he tells her. "Could you give me a little smile, do you think?"

Leora obliges, offering a smile that is skimpy and short-lived, not the generous one her father had in mind. Still, he smiles back at her gratefully.

Ginger and Sydney swoop down upon her without warning now, like two large dark birds, entirely in gray, and almost knock her over in their boisterous greeting. "How *are* you, Leora?" Ginger booms. "Have you got any pictures of that cute little baby of yours?"

"Of course she has pictures," says Sydney. "What kind of a mother goes anywhere without pictures of her baby?"

"I guess I'm not an exemplary mother, then. All I've got in my wallet are credit cards," Leora says apologetically.

"Shame on you," Ginger says. All of a sudden she is scowling at Alexander, waving a disapproving index finger at him. "And shame on you, Allie. What kind of a host are you, anyway? You're already running out of wine."

"What's so bad about being sober for a change?" Sydney says.

"Living with you, Sydney, anyone would need to get a buzz on now and then, do you understand what I'm telling you?"

"Not really, no."

"Listen, you," Ginger says, "want to hear a story you've heard before? When my mother moved into the nursing home where my father had been a patient for months and months, she asked to be assigned to a private room. 'Don't you want to be in the same room as your husband?' the administrators asked her. 'Nothing doing,' my mother says. 'I spent sixty-two years of my life with that man and he's been nothing but trouble. Why would I want to die with him too?' "

Alexander hears himself laugh out loud, sees a corner of Leora's mouth quivering. Sydney looks pained for a moment, then says, "You come from a long line of cranky old ladies, what can I tell you."

"Sydney," says Ginger, and claps herself on the forehead, "you are so dopey sometimes that it's beyond belief." She walks off to the buffet table, fills a plate with food, and returns to Sydney's side. "Eat," she orders, and walks off again.

"Try the fried chicken," Alexander says.

"You reach a point," says Sydney, "when enough of someone is enough. I myself have reached that point."

"The rice is excellent too. Try some," Alexander urges, but is ignored.

"When I fell in love with her, she was twenty years old. She was cute and funny and one day in the balcony of the Loew's Theater she let me slide my hand all the way up the inside of her leg. I mean *all* the way up. No girl had ever let me past her knee before. I was in heaven."

"Who wouldn't have been?" says Alexander.

"So those are the reasons I fell in love with her," says Sydney, and ticks them off on his fingers. "Number one, she was a looker, number two, she could make me laugh, and number three, last but by no means least, she let me put my hand in a heavenly place. And so we got married. Not for a minute did I ever imagine getting old and sick. I just imagined life going on and on, getting sweeter and sweeter."

"Young people *should* think that way," says Alexander. "It's their privilege to be utterly optimistic, to be ignorant of misfortune."

"But it's such a shock when things begin to go wrong. It just seems so unacceptable. When I had the stroke," Sydney says, "after I was able to understand what had happened to me, I couldn't get over the surprise of it. I wanted to talk, wanted to explain myself, but the words came out all cockeyed. One day, when I was still in the hospital, I needed Ginger to look for something that I knew was in my suitcase. I kept saying, 'It's in the violin case,' over and over again. And the more I insisted it was in the violin case, the angrier she got. She took the room apart, looking for whatever it was I wanted, and finally she just said, 'God, I hate this,' and went on home. I should have known right then that she had shown her true colors, that things were never going to be the same between us." Sydney gathers a forkful of rice with a shaky hand and chews for a long while. "The fact of the matter is, at least I'm still alive. But sometimes, when Ginger and I are really going at it, that fact doesn't seem like much of a consolation."

Alexander cannot recall, throughout the long history of his friendship with Sydney, a time when Ginger had ever been any different with him, had ever shown a softness, a sweetness, a patience that would have made their life together that much easier. It seems to Alexander that she had always been fond of chipping away at Sydney's self-esteem, that he had gradually learned how to retaliate, and that their marriage thrived on this trading of insults. He does not think that the marriage was ever in danger, or even that it might be in danger now. They will be together for life, bonded by their devotion to slugging it out, preferably in public. He can hear the sound of Margot's outrage now, hear her saying 'I will never, *ever*, go out to dinner with them again! I thought I would *die*, listening to them carry on like that in front of the whole world.' What he would give to hear the sound of her voice at this moment! His stomach suddenly feels queasy, as if he had eaten too much or not at all. He looks at his daughter, still battling her grief, and thinks, if only he could free her of her painful attachment to Margot. What a ludicrous thought, he tells himself, when he too feels the pain of his own attachment, a pain that he suspects will linger for the rest of his life, surfacing at odd moments, bringing tears to his eyes and a sick feeling to his stomach just when he is about to make love to Ionie, or when he wakes up beside her in early-morning half darkness and for an instant mistakes her sleeping form, her warm presence in his bed, for Margot's, or when he is filling out some endless paperwork at the bank and has to think twice or three times before checking off "widower" as his marital status. He would never dream of telling Ionie, but sometimes when they are lying together in bed, their mouths open to each other, his hands examining her breasts, he willfully imagines that it is Margot whose flesh is touching his. He does not know if this fantasy falls in the realm of the normal or acceptable, only that it is something he finds himself indulging in occasionally and not without a measure of guilt. He is in love with Ionie, of that he is sure, but now and then he aches for his wife, mourns her absence, which is still, at the worst of moments, so palpable.

"You're not being much of a help, Allie," Sydney moans.

It is Leora who turns on him angrily. "You still have your wife, Sydney, for God's sake," she says. "Why don't you go after her and *do* something?"

"Like what?" says Sydney. "What do you have in mind?"

"I'm not a marriage counselor, Sydney."

"Do you think Ginger and I should go to one?"

"Don't answer that," says Alexander quickly.

"Why not?" Leora and Sydney chorus.

"Because it's none of your business, Leora."

"You're absolutely right," Leora agrees. "Just like it's none of my business who you happen to share your bed with every night."

"Jesus Christ, Leora," says Alexander, and winces. "There's a roomful of people here. What are you trying to do?" He steers her away from Sydney and out of the room. He takes her into the master bedroom and quietly shuts the door. "Like it or not," he tells her, "your father has chosen to go on living. I've chosen to savor the happiness that's unexpectedly come my way. If that offends you, well then, you'll just have to bite the bullet."

"It doesn't offend me!" Leora cries. "What offends me is the thought of my mother sealed up in a satin-lined box in the darkness. And those terrible eyebrows they gave her! How am I going to forget those eyebrows?" She is weeping now, using Alexander's hard chest as a resting place. He touches his lips to the top of her head, gently fingers her hair, runs his thumb across the slender curve of her eyebrows, but does not say a word.

"I've got to let go," she tells him. "And I would, if only I knew how." She draws her head back, looks up at him for an answer. "What's your secret?" she asks.

"Ionie," he breathes, knowing this isn't the answer she wants to hear. But it's the only one he has. "Ionie," he says again.

"It's as simple as that, huh?"

"It isn't simple at all."

"I'm happy for you," Leora says, sounding so doubtful that both of them begin to laugh.

"Sure you are," says Alexander. "You're thrilled to death."

"I'm not?"

"Nope. You're confused and jealous, and sad, I think."

"I don't sound like much of a daughter, do I?" Leora observes.

"I love you more than anything in this world." Alexander sighs. "What can I do to help you?"

"You know what? I *am* jealous," says Leora. "Not of Ionie, or of you and Ionie, but just the fact that you've made such progress, that you're miles ahead of me. I'm still stumbling around in the dark, bumping into things that hurt, memories. . . ."

"Tell me," Alexander says.

Leora shakes her head. She cannot tell her father these things, but keeps them for herself: here is her mother, shaving delicately under Leora's arms for her for the first time, showing her what to do, the heat of the wet razor warming Leora's skin, the menthol fragrance of shaving cream suffusing the bathroom air even as Leora holds her breath, trusting her mother not to hurt her. *All done,* her mother calls at last. *See how nice?* A momentous occasion, her mother understands this. Another time in Leora's early adolescence: her mother shops with her for her first bra, a flimsy thing of plain white cotton with a tiny circle of plastic pearls at the center. Margot slips the straps across Leora's shoulders in the dressing room of a lingerie shop while a severe-looking saleswoman looks on. Then, growing bored, the saleswoman leaves the two of them alone so Leora can stare at herself in the full-length mirror for as long as she likes, Margot's smiling reflection visible behind Leora's own. *My big girl,* her mother says, sounding amazed and also a little bit sorrowful. Afterward, they sit at a luncheonette counter with their ice-cream sodas, and Leora keeps running her fingers down and over her shoulders, tracing the straps of her bra, wondering if anyone can possibly know that she is finally out of undershirts. Her mother drinks her soda in dainty sips. *You can't imagine how old I feel,* she tells Leora wistfully.

"Leora," her father is saying, "believe me, I understand how it is with certain memories that just can't be shared. But do me just one favor, please."

"What?"

"Say a quick hello to Ionie."

"I'm not in the mood to be gracious now."

"Do the best you can, honey."

"Wait," says Leora. "Do I look as if I've been crying? Maybe I'd better wash my face and put on a little makeup."

"You look great to me," Alexander says, and begins to push her gently out the door.

"Wait," Leora says again. "Who's that over there?" She points to a woman with a helmet of platinum hair, a nicely dressed woman who's balanced precariously on a pair of very high heels. "I thought I knew everyone."

"That," says Alexander, "is Paulette Wolfson. We had a blind date once and never saw each other again, and now it turns out she's here with my friend Bill Messina. I couldn't believe it when they showed up together. It was actually a little embarrassing when they first walked in, but it's fine, really."

"They're on opposite sides of the room," says Leora. "I guess it's not working out."

"She's on the prowl, I bet. But never mind about her. Where's Ionie?"

"Right behind you," Ionie says. "Where've you been, baby?"

She looks beautiful, he thinks, in the purple silk pants and yellow silk jacket he watched her put on a few hours ago. She's a big, graceful woman; she reminds him now of a butterfly with purple-and-yellow wings. He wants to tell her this and also to embrace her, but he doesn't want to scare away Leora, and so he keeps his arms at his sides and simply smiles at her. "Leora's been looking for you all night," he says.

"She has? Well, let me get a good look at you, baby. Tell me how you-all are doin'."

"I hear you're taking good care of my father," Leora says, and it's impossible to tell from the neutral tone of her voice whether or not this pleases her, whether she is ally or enemy.

"Well, he's been eating a whole lot better since I came along, I have to say that. You wouldn't believe the tuna-fish cans and all those cold wet noodles I used to find in his garbage. There's got to be a better way of staying alive, I told him. But you know men—they've got to have their habits or they're lost. Take my ex, for instance. He had to drink a great big bottle of Pepsi-Cola first thing every morning or he couldn't see straight. I kept telling him, 'Morris, you keep on drinking that stuff and you're going to lose every one of the teeth you still got left.' And you know what happened? He ended up with a mouthful of root canal, but he still had to have that bottle every morning. By the time I threw him out, he was spending more time in that dental clinic than he was with his girlfriends."

"So much for your ex," says Alexander. "He's history. I, on the other hand, haven't got a single bad habit to speak of."

Leora and Ionie exchange a look and shake their heads at one another. "You use too many towels every time you take a shower," Ionie informs him. "And then you leave them lying around on the floor. And you always dump the loose change out of your pockets anywhere you damn please."

"Any other complaints?"

"You always call just when we're sitting down to dinner," says Leora. "And then you say, 'Oh, were you having dinner? I'll just keep you a minute,' and then you go right on talking."

"Clearly, I'm a very annoying guy," says Alexander. He is stung, though only lightly, by their criticism, hating it that everything they have said is true. But looking at the two of them, identical half smiles arranged on their faces, he understands that this is the right moment to leave them alone together, two allies united against him and his annoying habits. "I'm going off to sulk," he announces, and abandons them with a wave of his hand overhead.

He runs into Spike at the buffet table and points out the reassuring sight of Ionie and Leora with their heads together, looking very intimate. "Isn't it great?" he says. "Look how well they're doing. All they needed to bring them together was the opportunity to criticize me."

Spike nods, impressed. "You have a visitor," he says. "Your little friend Mrs. Fish is here to wish you happy birthday. I asked her to come in, but she's still standing out in the hallway."

"Maybe we can set her up with my friend Bill over there. It looks like his date ditched him."

"Something tells me Mrs. Fish isn't into the dating scene," Spike says, smiling. "And anyway, she's not exactly dressed for the occasion—she's in her traditional housecoat and slippers."

"You never know," Alexander says. "She just may be in the market for a little romance." When he approaches her in the hallway a few moments later, she stands on her tiptoes and gives him a hug.

"Get dressed and come on over," says Alexander.

"I don't think so," says Mrs. Fish. "My hair's a mess and I haven't had my nails done in a month."

"No one's going to be looking at you," Alexander says, then immediately corrects himself. "I mean, there's no need to be self-conscious."

"Well," says Mrs. Fish, "I don't know. I don't go to too many parties anymore. Most of my friends are dead or in nurs-

THE WAY WE LIVE NOW

ing homes. It's very depressing, but the longer you live, the more you have to face these things. But, as my second husband, Dr. Murray Fish, used to say, 'If you can't stand the heat, get out of the frying pan.' "

"Kitchen," says Alexander.

"What?"

"What would you be doing in a frying pan?"

"I have no idea," says Mrs. Fish. "What do you think Murray meant by that? He was a podiatrist and a very smart man, but a lot of the things he said were very puzzling. Even so, I miss him terribly. When he died, there were over five hundred people at his funeral, you know. Standing room only. And over fifty carloads of people drove from the chapel to the cemetery. The procession was so long, we disrupted traffic for miles. And of course it rained and there I was standing in the mud in my very expensive Andrew Geller pumps and—"

"Stop!" Alexander yells. He has begun to sweat and feels a little light-headed. He sees himself in a casket of varnished pine, being lowered roughly into the earth as Ionie wails inconsolably, begging for one last look at him before he vanishes forever. "I don't want to talk about funerals and cemeteries on my birthday," he says.

"Why? How old are you?"

"Sixty-eight," says Alexander.

Mrs. Fish laughs. "You're a young man, Mr. Fine," she says. "You don't have to worry. When you're my age, it's another story."

"We *all* have to worry," he says.

"Well," says Mrs. Fish, "try and enjoy your party anyway."

As he steps back inside the apartment Ionie and Leora take him by the arm and march him over to the buffet table, where a large chocolate sheet cake blazing with candles awaits him. Most of the guests gather around him, though a few remain in their corners, absorbed in conversation.

"You're over the hill *now*," Ginger calls out. "How can you stand it?"

"Attention, everyone," says Leora, and shuts off the stereo.

"There's going to be a musical interlude," she announces. "Everyone settle down, please." A delicate-featured little boy in slicked-back hair and dressed in a blue blazer picks up his violin and plays an excruciating rendition of "Happy Birthday" that seems to go on forever. The boy, who is Alexander's brother's grandson, draws the bow across his instrument with exceptional grace each time, making the hideous squeaks he produces all the more shocking.

"Play the theme from the *New World* symphony, Spencer," his mother urges, when he is finally finished. "You always do a lot better with that one."

"Are you crazy?" Spencer says loudly. "I suck." He thrusts the violin at Alexander, confiding, "I'm the second worst in my whole class."

"Well, at least you're not the worst," Alexander consoles him.

"Yeah, right. That's supposed to make me feel better, right?"

Not knowing what else to do, Alexander fits his chin to the child-sized violin and tentatively plays a few notes. "You've got rosin buildup," he says, but Spencer has already disappeared. He plays a little bit of a Bach concerto, a fifty-year-old memory, and closes his eyes. He sounds far better than he has a right to, he thinks, and is overwhelmed with pleasure. He fingers all the right strings as the bow is drawn, as if by magic, back and forth, over and over again.

"What are you, Nero?" someone yells. "Blow out the candles before the whole building burns down."

It is Ionie and Leora who attend to the candles and then the cake, slicing it wide open with broad silver knives while Alexander plays on, celebrating something, he thinks—surely not his birthday, but perhaps just the simple bright happiness of the ordinary life that is his.

When the phone rings, disturbing his half sleep, his first thought is that it is Shavonne, tearful and penitent and in need of money. He's all set to hand the phone over to Ionie, but the voice on the other end is soft, somewhat apologetic, and entirely unfamiliar.

"You have a lovely apartment," the voice says, bolder now. "I meant to tell you that at the party tonight, but somehow I never got around to it."

"Who *is* this?" Alexander says, annoyed now that he knows the caller has nothing of any urgency to report. He gently presses Ionie's raised head back against her pillow, telling her in a whisper that it's all right, that nothing is wrong.

"It's Paulette," the voice says. "Paulette Wolfson."

"Do you know what time it is, Paulette?" he says. "Why aren't you asleep?"

"I didn't know you could play the violin. How come you never told me?"

"We had one date, Paulette," he reminds her. "There's a lot I didn't tell you." Hearing this, Ionie's head shoots up again, and this time he lets go of the phone. Kissing Ionie, stroking both smooth shoulders, he says, "There's nothing to worry about, believe me, honey."

"Did you say 'honey'?" Paulette asks, when he picks up the phone again. "Who's 'honey'?"

"Didn't Bill tell you I'm . . . seeing someone?" he says. "We're living together, in fact. Didn't you see her at the party?"

There is a brief silence as Paulette takes this in. "He may have said something, but it must have gone right over my head. God, you must think I'm crazy," says Paulette. "Please apologize to your honey for me."

"It's okay," Alexander says. "But I've got to get back to sleep. How about if we talk in the morning?"

"I need your help, Alexander."

"Why me?" he says.

"Because I need a man's help and you seem to be the only decent man I know." .

Alexander laughs when he hears this. "What about that little notebook of yours that's overflowing with names and numbers? There's not a single person you can turn to at two in the morning for help?"

"They're all losers in one way or another," says Paulette. "Like your friend Bill Messina. He took me to your party but all he really wanted was to give me a blow-by-blow account of his divorce and everything that led up to it. Now, why would I want to hear all that, tell me. I listened to as much of it as I could take and then I wandered away to mingle. At the end of the party he takes me home in a cab and tries to put his hands where they don't belong. This," Paulette sighs, "is the caliber of man that's out there."

"I see your predicament," says Alexander, trying not to sound too sympathetic. He yawns into the phone, then apologizes.

"Am I boring you?" says Paulette.

"Not at all. But it was a long day and I'm not as young as I used to be."

"Me either." Paulette pauses. "So what's it going to be, will you help me, or not?"

"With what?" he says, and holds his breath.

"I need you to come with me to Marlborough, New Jersey, for an afternoon."

"What's in Marlborough, New Jersey?"

"My ex-husband, my ex-daughter-in-law, and some of my jewelry."

"Ah-ha," says Alexander. "You want me to help you get your jewelry back."

"Please," she says, so simply and sweetly that he feels himself immediately weakening. But there's one last out for him and so he asks, "What about your son? Why can't *he* go with you?"

"Because he's a wimp," says Paulette. "And his therapist told him it would be too painful for him to set foot in the house where his ex-wife and his father are so busy creating happy memories."

"What about *your* pain?"

"That's over with," says Paulette. "I just want my jewelry back. After two years of wrangling, Victor finally admitted that one time when I was gone for the weekend he and Beth helped themselves to a few of the things he'd once given me. He told me to come and get it, figuring, I suppose, that I'd be too much of a coward to meet him on his own turf. In his little love nest, as it were."

"Bastard," says Alexander sleepily. Lying curled up on his side now, eyes shut, he hears but does not listen as Paulette goes on.

"Your honey can come with us," she says. "The more the merrier."

"Honey?" he murmurs.

"There's just one more thing I suppose I ought to mention. I happen to know Victor has a gun, though I'm sure he wouldn't dream of using it. But you never know," says Paulette. "He might turn mean and crazy at just the wrong moment, just when I'm slipping my long-lost charm bracelet over my wrist and heading out the door."

"No," says Alexander.

"Alexander, are you listening to me?"

"I can't hear you and I'm not listening," he says, and hangs up.

Chapter

12

The bumper sticker on the beat-up station wagon directly in front of Alexander on the New Jersey Turnpike reads, "Come Any Closer and I'll Kill You." An enormous truck hauling a fleet of brand-new cars begins to pass him, giving him a good look at a sticker that says, "Complaints About My Driving? Dial 1-800-EAT SHIT." Even with the windows fully closed, the air reeks of ammonia and other noxious chemicals he can't identify. Oil refineries and chemical processing plants ornament the landscape for as far as he can see; all at once he is shivering, feeling as if he is in the presence of evil. Beside him, Paulette sits patiently knitting an afghan of black wool threaded with metallic gold. The incessant clicking of her needles alternately soothes and annoys him, and he can't decide whether or not he wants to ask her to stop. And he misses Ionie, whom he dropped off, along with the baby, at a cousin's house on Staten Island about half an hour ago. What could he have been thinking, he wonders now, when he agreed to take Paulette all this way to reclaim her stolen jewelry? He hates to admit it, but it must have been her persistent flattery that got to him, her pronouncement that he was the only decent man she knew.

"Where do they come off calling New Jersey the Garden State?" he says, sounding crankier than he'd meant to.

"Just don't breathe too deeply and you'll be fine," Paulette advises.

"Are you nervous?" he asks her. "How long has it been since you've seen him?"

"Victor?" says Paulette. "Not long enough. Look, there's our exit."

"Years?"

"A little more than two years. We spent a night dividing up our things between us, down to the last grapefruit knife. I wouldn't speak to him at all, and that slowed everything down, of course. All I would do was shake my head yes or no or shrug my shoulders. It drove him so crazy he hardly knew what he was doing, and I ended up with a lot of heirlooms, his grandmother's silver and china, things he probably didn't even realize he wanted. He left finally, very late at night, kissing me on the forehead, which was very sad. I went to bed feeling as if someone had died, but of course it was only my marriage. In the morning I got up and went to work, dressed all in black, though I don't think it was deliberate. A couple of people in the office asked me if I was going to a funeral, and eventually I started to cry. I couldn't get ahold of myself, which isn't like me at all. But of course it isn't every day your husband leaves you for your daughter-in-law."

Alexander shakes his head. "And then comes sneaking back for your jewelry. Not to be believed," he says.

"I don't have trouble believing anything anymore. I saw a woman on TV the other day describing how her ex-husband broke into her house, raped and stabbed her, then went into the children's rooms and shot them to death. This was to punish her for divorcing him. The studio audience sat there in disbelief, but not me. I believed every word of it, especially when the woman described her husband as remorseless."

"Please tell me he's in prison," says Alexander, and makes the turn-off that leads them to a highway cluttered with every standard fast-food spot imaginable, and some he has never seen before, restaurants called Stuff Yer Face and Eat Your Heart Out, Baby.

"What are you laughing about?" says Paulette. "He's in prison, all right, but he'll be eligible for parole in ten years, which is why his wife is so worried, of course."

"Terrible," Alexander says. "Want to have lunch at Stuff Yer Face?"

"I'm not particularly hungry. In fact, the thought of seeing Victor and Beth turns my stomach."

"Me too," says Alexander.

"I think I scared Victor when I told him I was coming with my lawyer/bodyguard. So we probably don't have anything to worry about."

Smiling, Alexander imagines himself seven feet tall, a gun strapped to his hip, a set of brass knuckles hidden in each pocket of his pants. "Nobody messes with me and my client and lives to tell the tale," he growls. Following the directions Paulette reads off a bright pink index card, he takes them past an assortment of public schools, an administration building, and a library, all long, low structures of clean red brick. Then the housing developments begin to appear, one following another, seemingly without end. These are large, new houses on half-acre plots, with fancy swing sets, and, occasionally, belowground swimming pools, hot tubs, and tennis courts in their yards. For Alexander, a city dweller all his life, the landscape of suburbia in all its glory is numbing and slightly sad. He tries to envision himself a homeowner on this cool and bright October day, raking leaves, clearing out gutters, putting up storm doors, exchanging tips with his neighbors on how to keep crabgrass in check. And there is Ionie sliding out of the driver's seat of their station wagon, unloading a half-dozen supermarket bags from the back, a beautiful Shetland sheepdog circling excitedly at her feet. Enter a suburban version of Mrs. Fish, dressed in jeans and sneakers and a sweatshirt, trudging across their perfect lawn with a question about her new automatic garage-door opener, which she just can't seem to get the hang of, she complains.

"Sure sure sure," he says out loud.

"This is the street," Paulette announces, after consulting her index card. "Just follow the curve to the cul-de-sac." The tree-lined street is wide and free of traffic. On the sidewalk two little girls about kindergarten-age cruise slowly by in a pink plastic convertible.

"Hey, party dudes!" a slightly older boy on a two-wheeler shrieks. "What's happening?"

Alexander puts the car in "park" and yanks back the emergency brake. Silently he admires Victor's house, a gray-and-white Colonial set back on a broad expanse of manicured lawn. A small bright red BMW gleams in the driveway.

"You know," Paulette says, her voice trembly, "I was lying when I said I don't have trouble believing anything anymore. I don't believe *this*, that's for sure. The evidence is right here in front of my eyes, but somehow it's just not real." Alexander pats her hand awkwardly, but she ignores it. "I was thinking about my wedding a minute ago," she says. "Victor's father had died, very unexpectedly, about a month before, and his family insisted I couldn't wear my wedding gown, because technically we were all still in mourning. They had me go out and buy a midnight-blue dress that I hated. And then his mother proceeded to cry bitterly all through the ceremony and the reception. It was the gloomiest wedding in history, let me tell you. Who knows, maybe it was a sign from the heavens above that it was all going to end disastrously one day." Again Alexander pats her hand; this time, she responds with a quick light kiss that misses his mouth, but only because he turns away from her just in time.

"You're irresistible," Paulette informs him. "Are you sure you're taken?"

"Absolutely," he says. "I'm sorry."

"Well, if things don't work out with your honey . . ."

"Let's go in," he says.

"May I take your arm?" Paulette says as they cross Victor's lawn together. "These high heels of mine are murder."

"Of course," he says, and they walk up three concrete steps to the front door, which swings open before they even have a chance to ring the bell.

"Hey there!" Beth says cheerfully, as if they were welcome guests whom she couldn't wait to usher into her home.

You ought to be ashamed of yourself, Alexander wants to say, and instead finds himself staring at her shirt, a long-sleeved black T-shirt patterned with neat rows of death's-heads, each skull decorated with a pair of rhinestone eyes. Beth is nearly six feet tall, he guesses, and her dark straight hair hangs to her waist. All in all a threatening figure, except for her manner, which, oddly, is extravagantly friendly.

"Cheese and crackers?" she says, and leads them to a sun-lit room where a pink marble coffee table holds several trays of food, enough for a light lunch.

Paulette shakes her head. She has not let go of Alexander's arm since they arrived, and seems to have lost her voice. "Victor?" she squeaks finally.

"He's at the hardware store looking for some special kind of screwdriver," Beth volunteers. "But he should be back any minute." She flips her hair over her right shoulder, then her left. "So," she says. "What's up? How are things in the big city?"

Clearing her throat, Paulette says, "What do you think this is, a social call? Who do you think you're talking to?"

"There's no need to be hostile," Beth says. "Why don't we all sit down and have some cheese and crackers?"

"Hostile?" says Paulette. "Call me crazy, but for some strange reason I still think of you as the person who destroyed my marriage, not to mention my son's."

"I did not," Beth says mildly, as if she had been accused of leaving the cap off the toothpaste or the car windows open in the rain. She piles her hair on top of her head, then lets it fall. "Can't you at least try the goat cheese? You're really missing out on something."

"Stop offering me food!" Paulette hollers. "You were never such a great hostess when you were married to Michael—I could barely get a drink of water in your house. What's gotten into you all of a sudden?"

"Victor *told* me you were going to be this way," Beth says, furiously spreading some Brie on a cracker, then tossing the whole thing into her mouth. "But I said he was wrong, that you were above all that."

"What way? Above all what?"

"Hostile and bitter, you know."

Lunging for Beth, grabbing a fistful of her hair and yanking on it hard, Paulette says, "Get rid of some of that hair. It's too long for someone your age."

"I'm thirty-three years old," Beth says. "And you're hurting me. Let go."

"Let go, Paulette," Alexander orders, and uncurls her fingers from Beth's hair. "You're a grown woman," he hisses. "Behave yourself."

"I don't want to," says Paulette. "She ruined my life. The least I can do is ruin her afternoon."

"If I hurt you, it wasn't deliberate," Beth says.

"This isn't a court of law, sweetie. Intent or no intent, the fact is you might as well have driven a stake through my heart."

Beth smiles strangely at this. "Why? Are you a vampire?"

Just as Paulette is about to take a swing at her, Victor appears, his mouth falling open in surprise. "What the hell is going on here?" he booms. Paulette freezes, then wheels around to face him.

"Look at how low I've sunk! Look what you've done to me!" she cries.

"Me?" says Victor. He's a big, potbellied man in chartreuse corduroy pants, a pink button-down shirt, and polished loafers.

"Me?" he says again. "I've been at the hardware store all this time."

"Just give me my jewelry, Victor," Paulette says wearily. "I just want to go home."

"You're not staying for lunch?"

"She's not interested in lunch," Beth says. "She only came here to torment me."

"Hand over my things, Victor," says Paulette. "And if my beloved charm bracelet's missing, I'll see that your alimony payments go sky-high, get the picture?"

"The picture I'm getting is of a woman who's about to go off the deep end, who can't even be civil to her family anymore," Victor says.

"Family?" Paulette shrieks. "Is this your perverted idea of family?"

"Easy now," Alexander murmurs. He feels absolutely invisible, certain that he could do or say anything at all without being noticed. It's a surprisingly invigorating feeling, and suddenly he finds himself wandering out of the room and into the kitchen, then through a pair of sliding-glass doors and onto a wooden deck that overlooks a half acre or so of well-tended grass. On the deck there's a bar and a gas grill and a large redwood hot tub that can accommodate about ten people, he guesses; he imagines Beth and Victor and his potbelly and a partyful of people all slipping noisily into the scalding water on an icy day, while in the background Paulette stands at the grill, cooking up a storm, taking orders from the crowd in the tub.

Descending the steps that lead from the deck to the lawn, he wanders across the grass, all the way to the boundaries of the property, his hands held behind his back. He feels lost and alone, though in the yard to the left, children are playing on a swing set, the sound of their sweet high-pitched voices floating toward him like music from a distant radio. After a while, tired of walking, he seats himself on the steps of the deck and watches a neighbor at work in his vegetable garden next door. The neighbor, a gray-haired man on his knees among tomato plants, is whistling "Mack the Knife" over and over again, switching at last to a melancholy version of "Ode to Joy."

"Nice tomatoes," Alexander offers.

"I work hard," the man says in lightly accented English. "Come and have a look."

Alexander admires the garden and hears about the cucumbers and zucchini and beets that were harvested at the end of the summer, and all the gophers that the man has had to do battle with. He stares for too long at the series of dark blue numbers tattooed on the man's hairless forearm.

"I'm Rudy," the man says, and rolls down his shirtsleeves. "Are you Victor's brother?"

"Not exactly," Alexander says, and introduces himself.

"Are you Victor's friend?"

"I'm afraid not." Rudy is looking at him curiously, waiting for an explanation. "My wife," Alexander begins, pointing to Rudy's arm.

"Your wife is Victor's friend?"

"My wife was born in Czechoslovakia. . . ."

"She was in the camps?" Rudy says, instantly attentive. "Where?"

"No, no, she was one of the lucky ones. A Gentile family kept her hidden in their barn. Her parents too."

"Very good," says Rudy, though he seems a trifle disappointed at this, at hearing that he and Alexander's wife have nothing in common after all. "Very lucky." He hugs himself, rubs his arms in the chill air. "I was a young man in Poland," he says. "What they did to me . . ." He looks up at the sky, where a silver plane is spelling out the words ELITE USED CARS in smoky white letters. "They threw my baby daughter into the fire."

Alexander lets out a choked sound; his legs feel shaky. He can hear the commotion going on inside the house now, an unpleasant trio of raised voices that has nothing to do with him, with his life.

"And here I am in New Jersey," says Rudy. "In my beautiful yard, telling my nightmare to a perfect stranger."

"I'm honored," says Alexander. Heartbroken, his head suddenly aching, he imagines Margot as he had never seen her, a young girl in a darkened, ice-cold barn, talking with her parents in endless, careful whispers, waiting quietly for a miracle. He misses her so terribly at this moment that he cannot think straight, and when, an instant later, he sees Paulette rushing toward him, triumphant, her charm bracelet encircling her wrist, glimmering in bright sunlight, he gazes at her bewilderedly, unable to recall where he might have seen her before.

Chapter 13

Christmas shopping for his wife and mother close to deadline, Spike was about ready to throw in the towel. Every year he spent far too much time and effort searching for something spectacular for each of them, and every year he ultimately resorted to the old standbys—an expensive silk scarf or perfume for his mother, and what the stores called "intimate apparel" for Leora, insubstantial-looking satiny things that she rarely wore, claiming they made her look like a hooker. (Not the worst thing in the world, Spike had told her, half teasing.) In the department store's crowded elevator now, he eyed a tiny dog dressed in a fleece-lined jean jacket, and its owner, a man in sunglasses and a fur coat.

"And how does your little doggie feel when he sees all the

homeless dressed in their plastic bags for the winter?" said an elderly woman whose shoulders were touching Spike's.

"Pardon me?" said the man.

"What kind of a world are we living in?" the old lady persisted.

"Oh, blame it on the bossa nova," the man said airily as the elevator eased to a stop.

"Doesn't that fancy little dog jacket just make you want to go out and embrace communism?" said the woman. Someone in the elevator—Spike couldn't see who—began humming "God Bless America," and a few people laughed mildly.

"I see what you mean," Spike told the woman, knowing it wasn't enough but not in the mood to offer anything more. The one thing he was in the mood for, the chance to collapse on his living-room floor with headphones clamped to his ears while he listened to a new Dylan CD, was absolutely out of the question: in less than twenty minutes he was expected to meet Suzanne and Leora at a building on Eighty-sixth Street on the West Side, where Suzanne's shrink had his office. Spike was embarrassed at the thought of the three of them sitting around shooting the breeze with Suzanne's savior, and also the slightest bit anxious. It was Suzanne's proposed Christmas gift to them— a family portrait of him and Leora and Ben, a painting in oils to be done by Suzanne—that was the cause of the most recent trouble between them. Spike, who had no desire to be painted by Suzanne or anyone else (though especially not by Suzanne), had turned her down on the spot, politely but firmly. Why they had to exchange gifts at all was a mystery to him, and when he made the mistake of letting Suzanne know this, it was clear to him that he would never hear the end of it.

"You are *so* unfeeling, Spike," Leora had informed him. "I can't believe you."

"Really, Spike, I'm very insulted," said Suzanne. "There's a warmth here, you know, that can't be denied. A connection between all of us that's very special. Why do you keep fighting it?"

"Connection?" he said. "If there's a connection here, I'd have to say it's a very unnatural one." He couldn't look at either of them and busied himself gathering Ben's pale hair into a miniature ponytail. Ben soon broke free of him and raced off to the telephone, which he examined briefly and then hurled to the floor with both hands. "All I meant," said Spike, "was that generally speaking, after a divorce the two parties in question go their own way. That's the usual course of events, isn't it?"

"Still singing the same old tune," Suzanne said. "And what's so great about the usual course of events, anyway?"

The three of them argued away the rest of a Sunday afternoon, getting nowhere as the apartment darkened and the smoky odor of someone else's dinner filtered through the air, reminding them that they were hungry. In the end Spike was elected to go out in search of barbecued chicken, which he brought back for all of them, along with a Greek salad for Suzanne. He watched her pick out the black olives with her fingers, watched in discomfort as her fingertips took on an oily finish that she licked off inelegantly.

"How could you forget how much I hate black olives?" she scolded him. "It's the green ones I like."

They fell headlong into another argument, and it occurred to him that they had rarely fought during their marriage and that it was only since their divorce that they seemed unable to agree on anything. Suzanne laughed appreciatively when he pointed this out to her.

"I was just discussing this very subject with my shrink a couple of sessions ago," she reported.

"Did he laugh?" said Spike.

"Don't be ridiculous. He wants to meet you, Spike, and Leora too. He thinks it would be helpful for all of us."

"I'm game," said Leora, responding so swiftly that Spike knew this couldn't possibly have been the first she'd heard of it. "Though of course I've never been in therapy. Maybe I'll be terrible at it, who knows?"

"You can't be terrible at it," said Suzanne, smiling. "There's no such thing. And no one's going to grade you on your performance, *chérie.*"

"Why would I be interested in what Suzanne's shrink has to say about anything?" said Spike. "And besides, I can already guess what he's going to say about me, at least."

"You'd be surprised," said Suzanne. "I'm constantly surprised by the insight the man has into my life."

"He's going to say," Spike predicted, "that I feel threatened by your friendship with Leora."

Reaching across the dinner table, Suzanne stroked his cheek. "Please don't feel that way," she said.

"Don't look into my eyes like that, please," said Spike, and took her hand away.

"Like what?"

"Soulfully," said Spike. "Cut it out."

"Don't you see the sympathy there?" Leora said. "And besides, your eyes are so beautiful she can't help looking at them like that."

"It's true," said Suzanne. "Don't you think that's why I fell under your spell all those years ago?"

"Me too," said Leora, and the two of them giggled. "Those blue-green eyes were irresistible."

"Flatter me all you like," Spike told them. "But no way are you going to get me into group therapy with you guys."

As he left the store now, empty-handed, worn out from too many unproductive hours of shopping, Spike gave in to his weariness and took an expensive taxi ride to the West Side, where he found Leora and Suzanne waiting for him in front of a massive old building, both of them in boots and long tweed coats, both of them stamping their feet in the cold.

"This is going to work out beautifully, I promise you," Suzanne said as Leora greeted Spike with a kiss. "You'll be grateful to Dr. Formica forever."

"One session and that's as far as I go," said Spike. "And don't even think about the possibility of dragging me back here again, is that clear?"

"Of course," said Suzanne. "And incidentally, did I mention how grateful I am to you for showing up today?"

Shrugging his shoulders, Spike said, "Let's just say the holiday spirit got to me." He opened the door for the two women in their tweed coats and waited for Suzanne to give their names to what looked like a uniformed prison guard sitting on a folding chair, hands at his knees. The three of them rode up to the twenty-fifth floor in silence and followed Suzanne to one of the only two doors in sight. They stood there for barely an instant before a short man with thinning black curly hair and red plastic-framed glasses bounded toward them.

"Dr. Bobby Formica," he said briskly, shaking Spike's hand and then Leora's. "Let's get started, why don't we."

In his office, a large overheated room that smelled of steam heat, Spike and Leora arranged themselves on an old leather couch as Suzanne settled into a chair positioned near Dr. Formica's desk. A pair of windows that faced east offered a pretty view of the Central Park reservoir, the surface of which was dotted with bright white ducks drifting slowly by in a single straight line.

"It's nice, isn't it?" Dr. Formica said, gesturing toward the window behind his desk. "Not that I get to see much of it while I'm working." He was wearing a tie and a plaid shirt and faded dungarees, and Spike had quickly decided he was a mellow guy, someone he might place some faith in. He relaxed a little and draped his arm around Leora's shoulders.

Dr. Formica nodded at him. "So what's on your mind, sir?" he said.

"Me?" said Spike. "I'm just along for the ride."

"I see."

"No, really," said Spike, hating it that he was already on the defensive. "I'm here as a favor to Suzanne, but I'm sure you must know that."

"I only know what you tell me, Spike. Whatever Suzanne may have told me, well, that's reality as she sees it. You, no doubt, see a different reality, as does Leora. So don't assume

I know anything about you at all. Even though I may feel as if I know you, we both have to remember that I don't. And if I know how Suzanne sees you, what I don't know is how you see yourself."

"How I see myself . . ." said Spike.

"Good place to start."

"Okay, I see myself as a loving husband and father who just doesn't want his family portrait painted by his ex-wife."

"Excellent!" said Dr. Formica. "That tells us a great deal."

"Excellent?" said Suzanne. "The man is full of resentment. I offer him a lovely gift and he rejects it because he can't stand the thought of my having assumed a place in his family's life. And you want to know why? It's obviously because he's insecure. A secure person would have accepted my friendship and would have said, 'Hey, this is cool. Look how lucky we all are to have each other.' But not this guy. This guy wants to play it safe, to keep his little family all to himself, huddled under his paternal wing with no room to breathe."

"Wrong," said Spike, his face blazing. "I'm *not* insecure. And I don't resent you, Suzanne, I just don't like you very much anymore."

"That's a lie," said Suzanne. "You expect me to believe that you once loved me and now you don't even like me?" She rolled her eyes to show her disbelief, then said, "Get real, Spike."

"This is as real as I get. This is me telling the truth."

"Excuse me, is it my turn yet?" said Leora. "And whether it is or not, I have to say how absolutely ill at ease I feel sitting here. There's no way I can talk in front of you, doctor. I don't even know who you are. In any case, I'm not about to open up to you, so don't waste your time on me. I'm just going to sit here and listen."

"It's your turn whenever you want it to be," Dr. Formica told her. "And hold that thought, because that must be our pizza," he said as the buzzer sounded in the hallway. "I hope you all like mushroom and pepperoni."

Not knowing what was expected of him, Spike slipped his

hand into his back pocket in search of his wallet and offered Dr. Formica a ten-dollar bill.

"Forget it, it's on me. Just the cost of doing business, that's all."

"God, you're wonderful," Suzanne said, sounding awe-struck. "I'm so touched I can hardly speak, except to tell Leora that she just needs to relax a little."

"I can't," said Leora. "I hate being here and I'm pissed off at Spike. So everyone just pretend I'm not here, okay?"

The moment Dr. Formica was out of sight, Spike said, "So what do you think Freud would have thought about the pizza?" When no one responded, he understood that he was no longer among friends, that his honesty had been neither appreciated nor desired. What they had wanted to hear from him, he guessed, was a confession of doubt, a willingness to admit that perhaps there was, after all, something of value in Suzanne's friendship and affection. And now, of course, they were waiting for an apology, both of them with their arms folded across their chests, their mouths set resolutely in anger. It was as if he had two wives to account to and to satisfy, a double burden that was weighing down so heavily upon him that all he wanted was to be free of them both. But that wasn't right—he loved Leora and counted on their marriage as the centerpiece of his life. It was Suzanne who was poison, or at the very least a major pain in the neck, keeping Leora on the phone at all hours, playing with his child so lovingly, lingering at dinnertime waiting for the inevitable invitation to join them. Leora's fondness for her was genuine and deep, there was nothing he could do about that. All he could do was hope for a gradual falling away, a time when the two of them would simply begin to drift apart for whatever reasons friends might. And there was always the pos-sibility that Suzanne would suddenly recognize her true spiritual twin at the deli counter at the supermarket or browsing at the library and find that her life no longer had room for her ex-husband's wife.

Heartened by the thought of her vanishing forever, he suddenly felt generous. "Look, Suzy Q," he began, "I didn't mean to be so rough on you."

"Well, that's nice to hear but it's too late for apologies. The damage is done."

"You know," Leora pointed out quietly, "you were hard on him too. And that's all I'm saying."

"That's because he makes my life so difficult," said Suzanne.

Just as he was about to deny this Spike stopped himself short. "I have a terrific idea," he said. "Why don't we try a trial separation and see how that works out? It might be the answer to everything."

"You're a real comedian, you know that?" said Suzanne.

"Why stop at a separation? Why not go all out and get a divorce? And this time we could really make it stick."

Dr. Formica reappeared now with the pizza and a set of paper plates. "Who's getting a divorce?" he said.

"This isn't working out," said Suzanne. "Spike isn't taking any of this seriously. He doesn't want to compromise, he just wants me out of the picture."

"And how do you feel about that?" Dr. Formica said, dividing up the pizza and handing out each slice with a flourish, clearly enjoying himself.

"I'm outraged," said Suzanne. "I want to slam his head against the wall a few times."

"That's good," said Dr. Formica. "That's very good. Why don't you close your eyes and imagine it, experience it. Then report back to us and tell us how you feel." Obediently, Suzanne shut her eyes. Hands raised and clenched, she grunted ferociously. Dr. Formica smiled.

"I FEEL GREAT!" Suzanne roared.

"Excuse me," Spike said when Suzanne had quieted down. "Are you an MD or a Ph.D.?"

"Both, actually," said Dr. Formica. "And incidentally, you're next, Spike."

"No way. I'm not into this primal scream stuff." He stared at Suzanne, who looked sweaty and satisfied, as if she'd just had an orgasm. "And anyway, I have no desire to bang her head against the wall."

"Sure you do," said Dr. Formica. "You're not being honest with us, Spike."

"The point is, I'm not a violent guy."

"We all have the potential for violence, but most of us manage to keep it in check, that's all. So go ahead and beat her up, Spike. You'll feel better, believe me."

"Maybe in a little while," said Spike. "In the meantime I'm just going to sit here and enjoy my pizza."

"What about you, Leora?" Dr. Formica asked. "Want to give it a try? Or are you still feeling too uncomfortable?"

"The only people I want to do violence to are the doctors who failed my mother and let her die," Leora said. "But that doesn't relate to matters at hand, so let's just forget it."

"Do you want to talk about it?"

"Nope," said Leora. "I just want my husband and my best friend to cut the crap and give each other a break now and then."

"Ah, so you feel hostility toward both of them."

"Not hostility," Leora said, looking downward into her lap. "Disappointment."

She looked so desolate, so utterly forsaken, that all at once Spike felt an overwhelming need to please her. "You want your pal here to paint our portrait?" he said. "All right, then. Let's do it. Just don't expect a smile from me while we're posing."

"I knew it!" Suzanne cried. "I knew Dr. Formica could work wonders with you! I feel as if we've just entered into a new era of peace and cooperation."

"What are you, the secretary-general of the UN?" said Spike.

"You know what, Spike?" Suzanne said, smiling and shaking her head at him. "You remind me so much of my father. In any given situation he ultimately does the right thing, the good thing, but he always has to give my mother a hard time first, fighting it out with her before he gives in. It's a strange way to do business, don't you think so?"

"It *is* strange, isn't it?" said Leora, but she leaned across her seat to kiss him, her hair sweeping against Spike's face, tickling him, arousing him slightly.

Spike closed his eyes. He imagined himself in a boxing ring with Suzanne, the two of them circling each other endlessly, breathing hard, waiting for just the right moment to strike. Finally he pulls his punch and knocks Suzanne off her feet. She's down for the count; victory seems his. But then, out of nowhere, Leora appears. Kicking off her shoe, she jumps into the ring and hits him over the head with her black patent leather high heel, not once, but repeatedly, until at last she's knocked some sense into his thick, thick skull.

It was Ben who refused to cooperate. Dressed in a bright red cabled turtleneck that Ionie had knit for him, he stayed put in Leora's lap for exactly three minutes and then took off, unmoved by Suzanne's pleading. Paintbrush between her teeth, she went after him, promising him the world if he would climb back into his mother's warm lap. The perfection of the afternoon light did not impress him, nor did the tears of frustration that welled briefly in Suzanne's eyes. He wanted a ride in his G.I. Joe jeep, a handful of Cheerios, a look out his bedroom window. He was eighteen months old and intractable.

"I can't believe he would do this to me," Suzanne murmured, and packed up her paints and easel and went home. She painted their portrait from a recent five-by-seven glossy that Alexander had developed himself as part of a course he had taken at the Y. In the photograph Leora was smiling sweetly, Spike broadly, and Ben not at all. Held between his mother and father as they stood posed on a friend's spiral staircase, Ben seemed to be thrusting forward, as if he were about to bolt at any moment. His expression was one of pure dissatisfaction.

"Leave it to me," Suzanne promised.

Unveiling the painting a few weeks after Christmas had come and gone, she stood uncertainly in their living room, waiting for their reaction. She looked even more undernourished than usual, and Spike could almost believe she was frightened; if he touched her thin white fingers, they would feel like ice, he thought.

"It's wonderful," he said in astonishment. He had not known she was this good, that she could have given life to their eyes, their hands, the tilt of their chins. And she had delicately altered Ben's expression to a smile that matched Leora's. "You outdid yourself," Spike said, surprised to find himself planting a kiss at her cheek. And this was what he would never confess: that he had half expected her to paint herself into the picture, a vague, ghostly presence hovering poignantly above them in midair.

Chapter

14

Suitcase in hand, broad shoulders slumped forlornly, Sydney stands outside Alexander's door grinding his teeth to a rhythm only he can hear.

"Don't tell me," says Alexander.

"She's at Club Med in Santo Domingo with one of her canasta buddies, wearing a necklace made out of shells and a very small bathing suit," Sydney reports all in a rush. "She cleaned out a nice chunk of my savings account and she's not coming home anytime soon. Mind if I come in?"

Alexander focuses on the cuff of a pale pink shirtsleeve that droops from Sydney's suitcase. "Oh, Sydney," he says, and shifts Deneece from his right arm to his left.

"I brought my laundry with me," Sydney says, pulling a

large nylon bag out from behind him. "Dark and light, all mixed together. Do you think you can teach me what to do?"

"Is that what this is all about?" Alexander says lightly, hopefully. "Is that laundry you've got there in the suitcase too?"

Shaking his head, Sydney says, "I don't even know where Santo Domingo *is*, for crying out loud."

"I think it's the Dominican Republic, but come in and we'll check it out in the atlas."

"Atlas?" says Sydney, sounding bewildered. Thumping his bags down in the foyer, he sinks slowly to the floor.

"Actually," Alexander says, "I think I've even got a globe stuck away in a closet somewhere." Deneece begins to pull on his earlobe vigorously, and he sets her down, watching as she rises on all fours and rocks back and forth, threatening to crawl at any moment. He is the only one standing upright, the only able-bodied one among them, he realizes. The temptation to leave them both, to vanish without explanation or apology into another life, is almost irresistible. He remembers the thick, palpable silence that filled the rooms of his apartment in the days and weeks following Margot's death, the dull sluggish movements of his limbs as he dragged himself aimlessly from room to room, moving about simply because he had to, like an invalid turning in his bed to avoid bedsores. He could not have imagined then the fullness of his life now, the busyness, the noise, the large sound of Ionie's laughter, the insistent cries of the baby greeting them at dawn, signaling, without fail, the start of an inevitable cycle of activity that left him weary but also grateful. And here is Sydney, sitting on the floor among his bags, looking stupefied and absolutely at a loss, desperate to ease his way into the very heart of Alexander's life, a life so full that sometimes it feels as if it's nearly bursting at the seams.

"Maybe," Alexander suggests softly, "maybe you ought to fly down to Santo Domingo and try to win her back."

"What would I want to do that for? I'd rather stay here with you and be miserable. And anyway, Allie, you made a promise to me. You said you'd take me in and we'd do laundry together."

"I remember."

"You don't sound very happy. You want me out of here, don't you?" Sydney stretches out, leans back so that his head rests against the laundry bag, and crosses his ankles. All he needs, Alexander thinks, is a newspaper covering his face and a couple of empty whiskey bottles at his side.

"I wouldn't say that."

"What *would* you say?" Sydney asks.

"I love you, Sydney, I really do. . . ."

"Oh God, here it comes." Flinging an arm across his face, Sydney howls, "I can't listen to this!"

"You'll have to share a room with the baby," Alexander hears himself say. "She's up at the crack of dawn every morning and the room always reeks of pee before we get that overnight diaper off of her. Is that what you want for yourself, Sydney?"

"Yes!" Sydney says triumphantly. "Yes!"

Alexander smiles. "Let's plan on a few days and see how things go. Who knows, you might get homesick or even start yearning for a little privacy."

"I've already filled out a change-of-address card at the post office." Seeing the stricken look on Alexander's face, Sydney says, "Just kidding, buddy."

"In that case I'll need a month's security deposit, a credit check, and all your medical records."

"No problem," says Sydney. "And you can count on me to do the dishes every night, if Ionie will let me." He looks at Alexander worriedly. "Do you think she'll go through the roof when she sees me and my suitcase?"

"Nope. She's used to people coming and going. In her family they take people in without a moment's hesitation."

"She's a sweetheart. Does she have a twin sister she could set me up with?"

"What are you talking about? You're a married man, Sydney."

"Oh sure," says Sydney, and slaps his palm against the side of his head. "For some strange reason I keep forgetting that."

• • •

After dinner, Alexander sits Sydney down and encourages him to take a good look at the spot on the globe where his finger is now pointing. "Here's Haiti," he says, "and here's the Dominican Republic. And here's Ginger, warming her tootsies in the Caribbean."

"Not interested," says Sydney, and places his hand across Alexander's index finger, covering over the Caribbean, the Sargasso Sea, part of South America, and all of the U.S. eastern seaboard. "Big deal."

"You've got an attitude, baby," says Ionie, "and it's not a good one."

"Let's watch a little TV," Sydney says, ignoring her.

"No TV," says Alexander.

"Not even the news?"

"We've got to formulate a plan."

"Fine," Sydney says. "My plan is to watch some TV, read the newspaper from cover to cover, and then head off to bed."

"That's short-range," says Alexander. "I'm talking about long-range."

"I've been here for what, four or five hours, and you're already planning to evict me?"

"It isn't that," Alexander says. "I think you've got to confront Ginger, let her know that she's behaved badly, and demand to know what's on her mind. She owes you that much, at least."

"I'm too old for this," says Sydney, and gives the globe a vicious spin, so that it tips over Alexander's knees and falls to the floor. "Divorce is for young people," he announces. "And on that note, I'm going to bed."

"At eight o'clock?" Alexander puts out a hand to restrain him, but Sydney keeps right on going, out of the room and down the hallway and out of sight. Waiting for the sound of a door slamming, Alexander closes his eyes. He feels Ionie's lips sweep past his face, and he turns and his arms go out to her.

When the bathroom door finally bangs shut, he shudders, as if chilled.

"Just let him be," Ionie says, and it is as if Sydney were their child, still young or perhaps adolescent, in any case a child they have failed miserably.

Eyes still shut, Alexander imagines Sydney forty-five years earlier, sitting beside Ginger in a warm, darkened movie theater, his hand slipping past her knees and then making its slow careful way upward until at last there is impossibly soft flesh beneath his fingers. *That's right*, Ginger breathes, and like everything else she will tell him, it is a lie.

Reaching Ginger by phone is no easy trick, but after a half-hour battle with an assortment of operators and hotel clerks, Alexander tracks her down late at night in her room at the Paradise Beach Inn. He starts out politely enough, apologizing for calling so late.

"It's all right—I'm on vacation," she tells him, her voice echoing thinly and sounding vaguely unreal.

"You," he says, and stops. *You miserable unfeeling bitch.* "You've really gone too far this time, Ginger."

"I'm shaking in my boots at the sound of your voice, Allie."

"In addition to everything else, you're a thief."

"That was a joint savings account, in case he didn't tell you."

"Still. Sneaking around like that, leaving while he was still sleeping. Can you imagine what it's like to wake up to an empty apartment and find a note filled with nothing but bad news? Don't you have a conscience?"

"Don't lecture me, Allie. And at least I let him know where to find me. It's not as if I disappeared off the face of the earth. Though believe me, I was tempted."

"When are you coming home?" he says, teeth clenched, barely able to control his anger.

"Who knows?" says Ginger, and he can see her lifting a

pair of sunburned shoulders in an apathetic shrug. "When the money runs out. When the weather turns bad. When it feels right, I don't know. All I know is that we need a rest from each other."

"And then what?"

"I have no idea."

"Forty years of marriage and you have no idea?" Alexander yells into the phone.

"Butt out, or else," Ginger warns him, her voice bearing a threat all the way from paradise.

In the morning he delivers a slightly altered version of the conversation to Sydney, who goes right on eating his toast and imitation cream cheese, crumbs drifting downward into the wiry curls of his chest hair.

"She misses you," Alexander offers, and has to look away as more crumbs settle on Sydney's chest.

"Bullshit," says Sydney. "How stupid do you think I am?" A bit of cream cheese is smeared along the bridge of his nose like zinc oxide on a sunbather; at the sight of it, Alexander loses his cool entirely.

"You're a mess!" he shouts. "Crumbs and cream cheese in all the wrong places!"

"Here?" says Sydney, and wipes his mouth with his finger-tips. "What are you getting all hysterical about?"

Reaching across the table, knocking over a bowl of Sugar Twin, Alexander goes for the white spot between Sydney's eyebrows. As he retreats to his side of the table a tiny bright bubble of blood appears above the spot of cream cheese.

"That hurts," Sydney says.

"It must have been my fingernail. I'm sorry."

"What's with you, buddy?"

"Can I get you a Band-Aid?"

"It's Ginger. She wants a divorce, doesn't she?"

"Absolutely not," Alexander says, with such conviction that he almost believes it himself. "She didn't mention a word about it."

"That's strange," Sydney says coolly, reaching for another piece of toast. "I just assumed it was uppermost in her thoughts. All yesterday morning I kept expecting a letter or a phone call from a lawyer, but it never came. Incidentally, this is excellent bread. Where's it from?"

"A shelf in the supermarket. Don't you *care*, Sydney?"

"I do. Is it some kind of whole grain, or what?"

"Will you forget the stupid bread! I'm talking about your marriage."

"My marriage," says Sydney, his mouth full, "is over. Dead and gone. And to tell you the truth, it's . . . something good, but I can't think of the word."

"A blessing?" says Alexander.

Sydney puts his elbows upright on the table and his hands over his ears. He is working hard; his face has turned shiny with perspiration. "A relief!" he says at last. "A goddamn relief!"

"Are you sure?"

"You know her, Allie. You know what kind of woman she is."

"She's the woman you love," Alexander murmurs.

"What?"

"She's the woman you love," Alexander says again, more boldly this time. "You know that."

"Not anymore. Not after this."

"It's how you feel at this moment. Tomorrow you may feel differently."

"I think of her lying on the beach without a care in the world, dancing in a halter dress to a steel-drum band or whatever it is they have over there, with her moronic friend Honey Finkleman, and it comes to me that not only don't I love her, but I hate her."

"Hate's a very strong word, Sydney," Alexander says, and rises to clear the table. He tries to take Sydney's plate and silverware, but in an instant Sydney has grabbed him by the wrist.

"I'm not done. Do you think I could have an omelet?"

"Nope. Too much cholesterol."

"Come on, Allie, I'm starving. I'd do anything for a mushroom omelet."

"Forget it. A mushroom omelet today, a porterhouse steak tomorrow, and before you know it I'll be visiting you in the hospital again."

"A steak and a side order of greasy fries would be heaven," says Sydney dreamily.

"Do you want to live or do you want to die? Make up your mind, Sydney."

"I want to go home if you're going to treat me like this. You're no fun, Allie."

"Were you expecting to have fun here?"

Unaccountably, Sydney begins to weep, his face lowered onto the breakfast table, dangerously near a plateful of brittle toast. "I want to feel hopeful," he sobs. "I want to be sixteen years old."

"I know," Alexander says. He pushes away the plate of toast and comes behind Sydney and rubs the hard bones of his friend's shoulders. "Try not to be so afraid," he whispers. His palms are sweaty as he lifts them off of Sydney and examines them under the kitchen's fluorescent light, as if they held something worthy of contemplation. But they are only an ordinary pair of empty hands after all, pinkish and slightly unsteady, and he does not know what to do with them except to let them fall again across Sydney's broad heaving shoulders.

Bending over to lace up the pair of scuffed-looking ice skates he's just rented at an indoor rink near Madison Square Garden, Alexander lets out a slow leisurely groan. "The last time I went skating," he tells Sydney, "Margot fell and broke her wrist in two places. She was in a cast for eight weeks, poor thing, and her wrist was never the same after that."

"Please," says Sydney, and rises up on wobbly ankles. "You're sure this is like riding a bicycle? That you can't forget how to do it even if you haven't gone skating since the turn of the century?"

"Would I lie to you?"

"Possibly," says Sydney. Arms linked, they hobble off the rubber floor and onto the ice, where they immediately collide with a little boy about nine or ten who snarls at them and then whizzes off without a word.

"Let's just try and stay out of trouble," says Alexander, and hums the sweet sad movie music piped in through the speaker system. Leaving Sydney behind after a single cautious trip around the rink, Alexander begins to zip along confidently, casting his arms from side to side rhythmically, gathering speed, his face cool in the chilly air. He passes three Oriental teenage boys wearing false noses, mustaches, and glasses, and an elderly woman with bluish hair that matches her bulky ski sweater. He stays away from the center of the rink, where a couple of dazzling skaters have staked out a bit of territory for themselves, a small space where they can show off to their hearts' content, spinning on one leg in their tiny skirts. One of these show-offs is actually a woman in her sixties, Alexander realizes, and he pulls off to the side to watch her. Soon Sydney comes limping along, his face brightening at the sight of the woman. "That," he announces, "is the girl of my dreams."

"I'm getting dizzy just looking at her," says Alexander.

"Not me. Get a load of that body! You know anybody else that age who could look that good in a skirt like that?"

Alexander has to admit he doesn't.

"I lust after this woman," Sydney says earnestly. "Think she'd go out with me?"

"What?"

"Sure. Now that I'm single again, the world's my oyster, right?"

"I didn't know that having a wife on vacation qualified you as single."

"Some vacation," says Sydney. "I think the word 'vacation' here is just a polite euphemism."

"There she goes." Alexander points as the woman glides off the rink in her lavender leotard and purple skating skirt, and disappears behind the booth where the rental skates are given out. Soon an announcement is made for all skaters to clear the rink for a few minutes so that the ice can be cleaned.

"Want some hot chocolate?" Alexander says, the two of them negotiating their way back onto the rubber floor.

"Where's the girl of my dreams? What if she's gone forever?"

"Then I guess it wasn't meant to be," Alexander says with a shrug. "How about some coffee?"

A bright yellow vehicle resembling a tractor rumbles out onto the ice and slowly circles the perimeter of the rink, then makes smaller and smaller circles until it reaches the center. Behind the wheel, perched high above the ground, sits Sydney's dream girl.

"Do you believe this?" he says excitedly. "What a woman!"

"Multitalented," says Alexander.

"If she gives me the brush-off, I'll die," says Sydney.

"What are you going to do, climb up into the truck and pop the question?"

"I never knew you were such a romantic," Sydney says, giving him a playful shove in the ribs. "But I think I'll wait till she's done working first."

As the skaters drift back onto the ice again Sydney approaches the booth, where the lady in lavender is now manning the cash register. "Excuse me," he says. "May I speak to you, please?"

"Something wrong with your skates?"

"I was just admiring your perfect form out there," Sydney says. "Were you ever in the Ice Capades?"

"Are you kidding?" the woman says. Her face is a little hard looking, softened now by the smile she flashes Sydney's way. She runs a hand through her short bleached hair and shakes her head at Sydney. "I'm strictly an amateur," she says.

"You were wonderful. I couldn't keep my eyes off you."

"Stop right there," the woman says, her smile vanishing.

"Pardon me?"

"You were trying to pick me up, weren't you?"

"Not exactly," says Sydney, but his face reddens. "My friend and I were just . . ." Looking frantically over his shoulder at Alexander, Sydney appeals silently for help.

"That's right," Alexander says, stepping forward. "Sydney and I were so impressed with how gracefully you were spinning and twirling that we had to come by and tell you personally."

The woman leans over the counter in front of her. "Thank you," she says. "That's very sweet. But I want you gentlemen to know that I make it a policy never to date anyone I meet on the ice."

"Why?" says Sydney.

"It seems like a good policy, that's all."

"Do you ever make exceptions?" Sydney asks, suddenly fearless. "I'm sure that sometimes you happen to find yourself the slightest bit intrigued by someone and decide to bend the rules a little. I'm right, aren't I?"

"Okay, Sydney," the woman says. There's a half smile at her lips, and she winks at Alexander. "What's so special about you, anyway? You've got three minutes to fill me in."

"I don't need three minutes," Sydney says. "My life is a long story, like everyone else's, but I'm not going to get into that now. Let's just say I'm about to start over, and it would be a big thrill to spend a few hours with a woman like you."

"A woman like me?"

"A woman who can skate like that *and* drive a truck has got to be in a category all her own."

"I have to tell you, Sydney, that I think you're slightly insane," she says slowly. "But it's a sweet kind of insanity, so it's okay."

"Terrific!" says Alexander. He does not wait to hear their plans but makes a swift exit, soaring joyfully around the rink once, twice, three times, confident that Sydney won't be home for dinner. And perhaps, with any luck, he won't be around for breakfast, either. This seems like the best kind of news and effortlessly he embellishes it, imagining Sydney in a leotard of his own, a spangled cape flowing from his shoulders, dazzling light reflected from the silver blades under his feet. Holding the girl of his dreams aloft over his head, he spins her fast as the speed of light.

Chapter
15

Whispering had become a way of life for Leora and Spike ever since his mother arrived for what she'd planned as a two-week-long visit. They whispered in her presence when they thought she wasn't paying attention, and when she sat across from them at the dinner table and stared directly at them, and after she had gone to bed and could not possibly have heard them. At first Lucille said nothing, watching them curiously or with disapproval or sometimes with an injured look that shut them up immediately as soon as they were aware of it. Finally, when her visit was nearly half over, she let them have it.

"You people are unbelievable!" she cried, and threw down the sponge she was using to clean the inside of their refrigerator. "Everything is a big secret around here, and I'm so tired of it."

"What do you mean?" said Spike, rolling his eyes at Leora.

"*Please.* I sit here trying to read your lips all day and it's very hard work, believe me. Either include me in what's going on or I'm cutting this trip short and going back home."

"There's nothing going on around here," said Spike.

"It's like you're walking on eggshells around me, Spike. Do you know how insulting that is? I want you to treat me the way you always did—as if I were your mother and not some mental patient who could crack at any moment." Picking up the grayish-looking sponge, Lucille returned to the refrigerator, lifting a half-dozen bottles of salad dressing one by one, wiping their bottoms and slamming them back down onto the shelf.

"We're truly sorry," said Leora. "I don't think we were even aware of what we were doing. Really." She gestured to Spike to say something, but his fingers and toes clenched, and he could neither move nor speak. In his mother's presence he had turned anxious, moody, impatient. He could not sit comfortably in the same room with her, and it seemed to him now that it was as if he were allergic to her, as if his body could not tolerate her voice, her scent, her love, except at a distance of 1,200 miles. Worse, seeing her these past few days, he found himself returning to the image of a bottle of Valium incandescent in the Florida sunlight, his mother reaching for it in a trance, the plastic bottle nestled in her small pretty hands. He was still afraid for her, still resentful of that fear. Since Lucille's arrival, he'd drifted off to sleep at night thinking of these things, and awakened in the morning to the same familiar worry. He could not get past it, could not give it up.

"How could you do this to me?" he heard himself murmur.

"What?" said his mother.

"I mean, how could I do this to you?" He steered her away from the refrigerator and closed the door. "I'm sorry," he said.

"Fine," said Lucille coolly.

Leora shot him a pleading look, and after a moment he understood what she wanted. He kissed his mother on the forehead and waited for her to warm to him.

"I don't forgive so easily," she said.

"Try," said Spike.

Ben came through the kitchen, dragging a beloved, battered-looking doll in a discarded vegetable drawer from the refrigerator. Stepping on Lucille's toes, he walked blithely past her.

"Say you're sorry, sweetie," Leora instructed him.

"Sorry."

"Now that we've all apologized," said Spike, "is it safe to assume we've been forgiven?"

Lucille shrugged. "Why not? But just remember I'll be watching you like a hawk," she warned. "Every minute."

With Spike staying behind to baby-sit, Lucille and Leora took a cab downtown on Saturday to a theater on Forty-eighth Street, where Suzanne was waiting for them in the lobby in a low-cut dress that could not be ignored. A third friend had canceled at the last minute, and it was Suzanne who suggested that Lucille use the extra theater ticket. Spike's exasperated protests had been disregarded, and now, as Lucille returned Suzanne's wary smile, it struck her how easy it was to forgive someone you no longer cared about at all. Long ago, she'd told Suzanne she loved her as if she were her own daughter, but now she could not remember what had inspired her to say this, or even if the words had been heartfelt. Hearing the news, so many years ago, that Suzanne had betrayed her son, Lucille had broken out in a rash that resembled poison ivy, but which the dermatologist had diagnosed as a case of giant hives. "Stress," he said, frowning at the extraordinary-sized pink welts that covered her limbs and back. "Go home and relax and take it easy." Instead she worked on several drafts of a letter to Suzanne, each one colder and more sarcastic than the next. She made photocopies of each draft, and finally sent off the mildest of the bunch, which said, "You are garbage, sweetheart, and undeserving of happiness." She knew that there would be no response, but continued for weeks to check her mailbox, as though a letter of

outrage from Suzanne would officially mark the end of the entire business. Her own letter was returned to her nearly a month
later, postage due. So she had forgotten to put a stamp on it,
she told Spike in astonishment. She could not believe she hadn't
really meant to mail it, but Spike insisted there was no other
explanation. The letter went into the top drawer of her dresser,
where she kept her bankbooks and jewelry—as if it were some
sort of treasure, instead of the mean-spirited arrangement of words
that she knew it to be.

"It's been a long while," she said now as Suzanne's smooth
cheek brushed against her own. "Truthfully, I never expected to
see you again."

"It's nice that we can do this, you and Leora and I."

"Well, it's certainly a little peculiar under the circumstances. I have to tell you Spike was dead set against it."

"Oh, *Spike*," Suzanne said, dismissing him with a sigh. "He's
not happy with anything I do. I've nearly given up trying to
please him. You know how it is, there are some people you just
can't do business with."

"He's an angel," Lucille said. "As generous as can be. The
things he puts up with—me, you two girls . . ."

"Okay, so he's an angel," said Suzanne.

"Don't get snippy with me, cutie. Remember who you
are."

"Who am I?" Suzanne said with amusement. "You tell me."

Instinctively, Leora took her mother-in-law's arm, as if to
restrain her from swooping down upon Suzanne and knocking
her over. Feeling the muscles of her stomach contract painfully,
and then a flash of panic that intensified the pain, she let go of
Lucille. She was in over her head with these two, she thought—
both of them hard, bony, insistent women. She felt soft and
pliant, close to tears. Confrontation always made her uneasy,
and usually she faltered, unable to keep up with whatever angry
flow of words happened to be directed at her. It was marriage,
and especially motherhood, that had softened her, slowed her,
made her dreamy. Sometimes, since Ben's birth, she paid for her

THE WAY WE LIVE NOW

groceries at the supermarket and then simply walked off without them or without her change, only to be summoned back by an annoyed cashier who gave her a look that said, Get with it, lady. The world went on around her and she trailed behind, loaded down with a baby in a stroller and bags of groceries, her mind drifting from thought to thought, all of them slightly blurry. Ignoring Lucille and Suzanne now, she listened to a woman at her elbow in the overheated lobby, noisy and impossibly crowded with weekend tourists.

"So he gets her this Mercedes 560 SL, the sports-car model?" the woman said to her companion. They were both deeply tanned, and dressed in fringed suede jackets and cowboy boots.

"Yeah yeah yeah."

"And he leaves it downstairs in front of their town house for maybe three minutes while he goes up to get her? And they come back outside and she looks around and says, 'What birthday present? Where is it?' And of course he's having a major heart attack because the car cost sixty-five grand and where is it?"

"They stole the fucking car!" her companion said gleefully. "I love it."

"Before he even had a chance to show it to her." Glancing at her friend, the woman said, "I don't think you're supposed to be laughing, Bradley."

"I'm not?"

"You're a pig, Bradley," said the woman, and turned toward Leora, who immediately wheeled around and lowered her gaze, her heart thumping. "You think he's a pig, don't you?" Oddly, Leora's silence seemed to satisfy the woman, and she shrugged and turned away.

"Let's go find our seats," Leora urged Suzanne. "Right now." Hurrying inside, sinking thankfully into her seat between Suzanne and Lucille, she waited as her heartbeat slackened.

"The American musical theater isn't what it used to be," Lucille complained. "And the prices they charge for a ticket are out of this world."

"Maybe so," said Suzanne, "but let's just try and enjoy ourselves."

"I keep thinking Spike should have been the one to use the extra ticket."

"Spike hates musicals," said Suzanne. "It's a dumb, blind hatred too, like someone saying, 'I hate classical music' or 'I hate foreign films' or 'I hate opera.' It's just so ignorant."

"He loved *Bye Bye Birdie* when I took him to see it maybe thirty years ago," Lucille said. "And I'd appreciate it if you didn't badmouth him like that. It's very insulting to *me*. And to Leora. Leora," she said excitedly, "why do you let her talk like that? Don't you have any loyalty? What's the matter with you?"

"I *am* loyal," said Leora. "But Suzanne happens to be right."

"Listen," Lucille said, "please don't take offense at this, but the two of you are a bad combination together. I think there should be a parting of the ways."

"What are you talking about?" Suzanne said, leaning across Leora and waving a *Playbill* at Lucille. "Don't you think we adore Spike? I can't please him, of course, but the fondness I have for him runs deep. Tell her, Leora. Defend me."

"It's true," said Leora, but didn't elaborate. One of the few things she and Suzanne almost never discussed was Suzanne's feelings for Spike, which seemed to range from antagonism to affection, mostly hovering at either extreme. She was quick to criticize him and always took Leora's side when Spike disagreed with Leora about anything at all. But sometimes, Leora noticed, Suzanne rested her head briefly against his shoulder, or pushed his hair back from his face for him, or even dropped a single kiss on his cheek. Leora read these small simple displays of affection as a kind of friendliness that had nothing to do with desire, but she had seen the puzzled looks of her father and also a couple of her friends, the few times any of them happened to witness one of those moments. Once her father had taken her aside to say that perhaps Suzanne was too much a part of their lives, that perhaps Leora ought to step back a little, create a little distance between them, but Leora assured him, smiling patiently, that she was in no danger of losing Spike to his ex-wife. Maybe there were other dangers, her father suggested. Maybe if she can't have him, maybe she wants to see to it that *you* can't have him either. Don't be ridiculous, Leora told him, because, of course, it *was* ridiculous. The truth was, she was still excited by the prospect of a little danger.

"I don't know," Lucille was saying. "I just don't know." She tried to read the *Playbill* that sat in her lap, but could only concentrate enough to page through the ads for perfume and makeup and extravagant-looking jewelry. Sitting next to Leora, with Suzanne merely a pair of seats away, she had the absurd, distressing thought that her son was a bigamist, that both of the women belonged to him. And that he was in danger of them both. Leora surely didn't look the part, but who knew, really? Suzanne, her mouth severe in coffee-colored lipstick, her eyes ringed in dark shadow, appeared almost ghoulish, as if she were capable of sinister things. She thought she might warn Spike that he was in jeopardy, in danger of loss and pain. But she had nothing to offer up as evidence, only a vaguely disturbing feeling as she sat with his wife and former wife all in a row and listened to an overture that did not move her. *Who do you think you are, a fortune-teller?* she could hear Spike say. *You expect me to take you seriously?*

The evening before her flight back to Florida, he came into the little study she had taken over as her own, and watched her jam a hair dryer, a pair of walking shoes, and her makeup kit into what was already a very full suitcase.

"Are you sorry to be leaving?" he asked her, thumping himself down on the suitcase to shut it.

"Not really," Lucille said. "You and your family are delicious, but guests, like fish, begin to stink after a couple of days, you know."

"We were happy to have you," Spike said.

"Maybe you were and maybe you weren't."

"What's that supposed to mean?"

"I'm just one more person to worry about, aren't I?"

"The moment I became a parent," said Spike, "I became a

worrier. That's certainly true. But it goes with the territory, I think."

"But why do you have to worry about me? Don't you have anything better to do?"

"Like what?" Spike said.

"Oh, earning a living, keeping your wife and child happy, keeping your ex-wife happy . . . it seems to me you're plenty busy as it is."

"My ex-wife's happiness isn't high on my list of priorities. In fact, it's not on my list at all."

"Is it on Leora's list?" said Lucille. She smiled absently at Ben, who arrived with his doll lying facedown in the vegetable bin. He went immediately for Spike's shoes and pulled open the laces.

"Stop that," Spike said halfheartedly, swatting Ben's hands away. He bent over to tie his shoes and felt something warm and moist on his lips. It was Ben's small, juicy mouth, gleaming with saliva as he backed away, tripped over Lucille's feet, and fell into the vegetable bin.

"I have to tell you, Spike, that it seems to me Leora and Suzanne are just a little too close for comfort. I don't like seeing them together in the same room. It does something to my insides, seeing them together like that," said Lucille, and put her hand against her middle. "It makes me feel like I could use a swig from a bottle of Pepto-Bismol. And truthfully, I never liked Suzanne much. Not from the moment I set eyes on her in your dorm room all those years ago. She was always too skinny and her clothes were always black, which is very unbecoming on a young girl."

Spike laughed. "That's harsh criticism, all right. And I don't know what you're talking about. You were very happy with her while we were married. She wrote you letters and called you once a week and made you dinner whenever you came to visit. You thought she was wonderful."

"She loved you, Spike. And anyone who loves my son is good enough for me."

"And now that she doesn't love me . . ."

"That's right. Now she's just a skinny sexpot with makeup that makes her look like a witch."

"Sexpot?"

"That's right. The dress she was wearing at the theater was open to her belly button. It's terrible for Leora to be hanging around someone like that."

"Why? She might turn into a sexpot?"

"You're making fun of me, aren't you? You know what I'm talking about, and it has to do with a sweet loving wife and a not-so-sweet, not-so-loving ex-wife. The two of them together."

"And?" said Spike.

Lucille was losing patience fast. "Do I have to spell it out for you?" she whispered furiously. "What if there was something between them? Something unnatural. Wouldn't Suzanne just love to make a mockery of your marriage like that!" The idea had just now occurred to her and she seized it eagerly, detailing a scenario that she hoped would awaken Spike, alert him to the danger that might very well be looming just beyond him, over his shoulder, behind his back. She shivered with an unpleasant excitement and watched as Spike screwed up his face in what she at first mistook for horror or astonishment. But he was laughing uncontrollably now, sweeping Ben out of the vegetable bin and dancing him around the room, the baby's piercing, de-lighted squeals bringing Leora to the doorway, where she stood smiling and then laughing at the merry senseless swirl of activity. She smiled at Lucille, who did not smile back but stared at her darkly.

"I'm giving up," Lucille announced. She felt terribly worn-out, and as distant from her son as if she were on the moon, looking down at him from a quarter of a million miles away.

Slowing down now, Spike soon collapsed at her feet, Ben lying prone on top of him, small flushed face tilted upward. Leora, smiling still, shook her head at them both.

"I hope to God I'm wrong," said Lucille. "In all the world there's nothing that would please me more."

Chapter 16

Before 6:00 A.M., before anyone else in the household has awakened, Alexander slips out of bed and walks on tiptoe into the kitchen. He seats himself at the fake butcher-block table and composes on paper (as he has been dying to do for days now) a list of Sydney's most annoying habits:

> goes to bed depressingly early
> gets up depressingly late
> sits around until almost noon in bathrobe that has seen
>   better days
> leaves little puffs of shaving cream on bathroom mirror
> makes bed halfheartedly, leaving sheets trailing to the
>   floor

spits into toilet and then walks away without flushing it
uses handfuls of ice cubes for his Mountain Dew then
    forgets to refill tray in freezer
flosses teeth anywhere he pleases, in full view of others
expresses gratitude too frequently and too profusely

The list could go on forever if Alexander had the heart for it, which, he is surprised to realize, he does not. He fantasizes about easing the slip of paper under his friend's pillow, but can see the humiliation and pain in Sydney's face as he learns of his sins one by one. If only his date with Maureen the figure skater had gone well, Alexander thinks, Sydney might have had the confidence to return home. According to Sydney, the evening, just two weeks ago, had been a disaster, starting with the small chunk of glass Maureen discovered in a mouthful of the poached salmon she was enjoying at the Tail of the Whale, and ending with the knee she slammed into his crotch when he tried to burrow his way under her sweater.

"On the first date?" Alexander had said, amazed. "You tried to feel her up on the first date?"

"She's sixty-two years old," said Sydney. "She's got grand-children. You think she hasn't been felt up before?"

"You have to go slowly, Sydney. You have to take your time with women, talk to them sweetly, ask to see pictures of their grandchildren, take the glass out of their salmon for them. . . ."

"Her lip was already bleeding by the time I knew anything about it. And then, of course, when we got to the emergency room and she started to feel a little dizzy—"

"The emergency room? Oh God, Sydney!"

"No, no, it wasn't that bad. She only needed two little stitches. It was the shot of Novocain that did her in, actually. One look at that needle and she fainted dead away. But at least I caught her before she fell to the floor."

"Chivalry lives," said Alexander, then grabbed Sydney by the elbow. "You made sexual overtures to a woman who'd just had surgery? Are you out of your mind?"

"She was feeling much better by then. Of course, her lip was hideously swollen, but other than that she looked great. I think the Novocain was just beginning to wear off when I—" Sydney blushed deeply, and then went on. "Well, so we were in her apartment watching Johnny Carson after we left the hospital, and I was rubbing her ankles because they ached from all that skating and then all of a sudden my hands just began to move upward and . . . I guess it was a mistake."

In the two weeks since then, Maureen hasn't acknowledged a single one of the numerous flower arrangements Sydney has sent her way, and she's hung up on him each time he's called. Moping in his bathrobe and bare white feet, Sydney has been the picture of abject misery, utterly bereft. And he has rarely mentioned Ginger's name—a bad sign, Alexander thinks. He would like to pick a fight with Sydney and send him packing but cannot find the words to set things in motion. Sometimes, making love to Ionie as quietly as he can, he imagines that Sydney can hear every squeak of the box springs, every shift in position, every faint moan and sigh. That when Sydney hears water running in the bathroom after midnight, he knows it is Ionie, wiping away the milky semen that runs down the inside of her legs in a thin warm stream.

He beats his fists lightly against his thighs now, and then stops, hearing something at the door. Who else could it be at six in the morning but Mrs. Fish, he guesses, knocking in her tentative way.

"I went to get my newspaper and saw the light under your door," she whispers. "And I thought to myself, 'Gee, *he* can't sleep, either.' "

He ushers her in, notices that she is empty-handed. "Where's the can opener?" he teases. "Don't you have any work for me?"

"You look awful, Mr. Fine."

"I'm not a happy man this morning," Alexander admits.

"What a shame. Your lady friend giving you heartache?"

He smiles at this; saying, "Nope. No complaints in that department."

"That's nice. Who's this?" she says, pointing to Sydney as

he comes toward them, squinting in the bright artificial light, his thick curly hair standing out from his head clownishly.

"Go back to sleep, Sydney. It's way before your wake-up call," Alexander says. He looks at Sydney sharply, letting him know he's unwanted at this moment, but Sydney sits down next to him in his tartan plaid pajamas and yawns mournfully.

"I'm Rachel Fish," Mrs. Fish offers. "And you are . . ."

"I'm just poor old Sydney."

"Do you live here?"

"No," says Alexander. "He doesn't."

"I'm a guest," Sydney explains. "My wife left me and I haven't been the same since. I'm a mere shell of my former self."

"Well," says Mrs. Fish, "maybe some antidepressants would be in order. They were a great help to me when my second husband, Dr. Fish, passed away. They put me in kind of a fog, now that I think of it, but at least I wasn't so weepy anymore."

"Can't," Sydney says. "I'm already on a blood thinner that took away my sense of taste, and a couple of other drugs, as well."

"I'm on that blood thinner too," Mrs. Fish says. "Nothing tastes like anything to me, and my doctor isn't the least bit sympathetic. But maybe your wife will come back to you, and then you won't be needing any drugs at all."

"Fat chance," says Sydney, and his eyes fill with tears.

"Gee whiskers," Mrs. Fish says, patting his hand.

"I should have married Barbara-Rose Blanksteen when I had the opportunity. She didn't have much of a figure, but she was warm and sweet, and her baked apples were excellent. If I had married her, I would have had children and grandchildren and God knows what else by now."

"Just a minute," Mrs. Fish says excitedly. "I *know* this Barbara-Rose. She was married to a little cousin of mine, Jack Barnett. They had a wonderful little family—twin sons who both became accountants for the federal government."

"So much for Barbara-Rose," says Sydney, wiping his tears away with a pink paper napkin.

"She's dead," Mrs. Fish reports. "She had two strokes one after the other, went into a nursing home, and that was the end of her."

Slumping down over the table, Sydney circles his head in his arms. "Strokes!" he groans. "Nursing homes!"

"Well, I think I'll be going now," says Mrs. Fish. "It was a pleasure to meet you, Sydney." Over her shoulder she calls, "Give some thought to those antidepressants, all right?"

"Bye," says Alexander. He can hear the baby stirring and goes off to tend to her, but before leaving Sydney behind, he squeezes his friend's shoulders and murmurs, "Perk up, buddy." He is nearly overcome by the smell of ammonia as he enters the baby's room, where he finds Deneece on her back in the Port-O-Crib, smiling her toothless smile and kicking her legs under the blanket.

"Hello there, my stinky little doll," he says cheerfully. Her diaper is warm and heavy with fresh urine; he tosses it into the diaper pail, powders the baby back and front, and dresses her in a pink sweatsuit that says "Baby Jogger" across the chest in purple satin letters. His hands move swiftly, unfaltering, and it occurs to him once again that he had never done these things for his own child, and not even for Ben. Only for this baby who does not belong to him, who is thriving in his home on Ionie's love and his affection. What an odd, perfect household they are, he thinks with pleasure. Lifting the baby out of the crib, pressing her to him, he enjoys the tightening of her arms around his neck, her small solid weight fastened against him. He finds himself hoping that Shavonne stays out of sight forever, continuing to call in from time to time as she has over the past few months, requesting nothing but money. If Shavonne were *his* granddaughter, he would be sick with worry, but since she is not, and since Ionie seems content to hear from her only periodically, Alexander too is well satisfied with the arrangement. He is certain that if it ever came to it, Ionie would never give up the baby without a fight, and he can see himself standing beside her in court as she testifies what they both know to be the simple truth: that theirs is a family secure in its happiness.

"My sense of taste is coming back!" Sydney announces jubilantly as Alexander approaches him in the kitchen. Standing over a frying pan filled with a half-dozen strips of bacon smoking and spitting in the air, Sydney crunches on a small burned piece. "Want some?"

"That stuff is pure poison," says Alexander. "Fat and salt and chemicals that can kill you." He buckles the baby safely into her high chair, then turns the flame off under the frying pan, but Sydney instantly turns it back on again.

"Then why do you buy it?" Sydney asks.

"Ionie likes it."

"Okay, so do I."

"Ionie doesn't have medical problems. You do."

"You're a good friend, Allie, a wonderful friend. But you can't keep me away from bacon."

"Oh yes I can," says Alexander. "When you're under my roof you follow my rules."

"What rules are those?" Sydney says, and holds a strip of bacon up to Alexander's lips.

Brushing his hand away, Alexander says, "Rules that prevent lunatics like you from poisoning themselves."

"That's right, Allie, go ahead and take away my only remaining pleasure in life."

"Bacon is your only pleasure?" Alexander shouts. "Bacon?"

"Bacon," says Sydney, and flips a few strips expertly. "Now go away from here and stop bothering me."

"This is my kitchen," Alexander reminds him, "My *home.*"

"And a lovely home it is. Now beat it," says Sydney. Raising a red plastic spatula menacingly over his head, he yells, "Stay away from my breakfast, you understand me?"

"Don't you threaten me with my spatula!" Alexander says, and makes a grab for it, bending Sydney's wrist with all his force. But Sydney puts up a good fight, and the two of them do a grotesque dance away from the stove, dipping forward and back, over and over again, grunting like barnyard animals. It is suddenly clear to Alexander that he cares nothing about the spatula, that all he wants is the satisfaction of forcing Sydney to the floor and hearing the sound of his voice pleading, "I want to go home."

"Say it!" he growls, casting his leg behind Sydney's and bringing them both to the ground, where he sits on his friend triumphantly.

"What?"

"Say it!" They are both out of breath and panting, their chests rising and falling in synchronized rhythm, two old men gasping for air.

"What?" Sydney says, exasperated. "What are you trying to do to me, goddammit!"

"Tell me you want to go home."

"I only want you to get off of me, that's all I want."

Looking downward, Alexander stares at Ionie's large feet, at her toenails neatly painted with red polish. "Good morning," he says.

"What are you-all doin' on the kitchen floor? Lord, you look silly down there."

"Your boyfriend's trying to kill me," says Sydney. "Any minute now I'm going to be crushed to death."

"Is that true, Alexander?" Ionie says as she removes the bacon from the burner. "Looks to me like you were trying to set the apartment on fire."

"Of course it's not true. Do you think I'm the kind of man who's capable of murder?"

"I don't, but I once had a boyfriend—this goes back years and years, when I first came up from North Carolina—who killed his mother and father with a shotgun when he was about twelve or thirteen. They were both junkies and beat him all the time and one day he'd just had enough. He turned himself in and they sent him to some juvenile detention center for a while and then when he got out he went to live with some real nice foster parents."

"You dated a teenage killer?" Alexander says.

"This is all very interesting," says Sydney, "but I've got to go pee. You're putting all your weight on my bladder, I think."

"He had cause," says Ionie. "That mother and father were beating him day and night."

Arching his back, raising his legs from the ground, Sydney tries to throw Alexander off of him. "What were those magic words again?"

"I want to go home," says Alexander.

"I—WANT—TO—GO—HOME!" Sydney howls. "Now, get off of me, you big ape."

Alexander springs to his feet, a young man who's just been told the world is his. "Sure you do," he says. "Think what a pleasure it'll be to be back in your own bed again, your own shower, to sit in front of your own TV with your own remote control. . . ."

"We've been friends for sixty years," Sydney says as he struggles to get up. "And not once in those sixty years did you ever disappoint me. Until now. I'll tell you, you think you know a person, think you know what you can expect of them, and then it turns out you were dead wrong. And I'll tell you another thing, I would never have thrown *you* out, if you were the one who came to me. I would have taken you in and fed you and given you clean sheets and a soft pillow and let you stay until you felt strong enough to stand on your own two feet again."

"What a wonderful friend," Ionie murmurs.

"I *am* a wonderful friend," says Alexander.

Both Sydney and Ionie glare at him. "Not *you*. Him," Ionie says. "He's the wonderful friend."

"I've got to make a phone call," says Alexander, and shuts himself away in his bedroom, where he finds the scrap of paper with Ginger's number on it in his wallet, hidden between two blank checks. Incredibly, he gets through to the Paradise Beach Inn on the first try. His mind goes blank as the operator rings Ginger's room; the receiver feels slippery in his palm, something he can't hold on to.

"Yes?" says a thick, dazed voice.

"Ginger, you have to listen to me," he begins.

"This is Honey," the voice says, sounding more alert now. "Ginger's in the shower."

"Honey?"

"Honey Finkleman. Is this Sydney?"

He remembers her now, a small round-faced woman who had lost her husband at about the time of Margot's death. He vaguely recalls Ginger's attempts to get them together, but Sydney had protested so vehemently that she gave up without much of a fight. *Let's put it this way—this Honey is no rocket scientist*, he can hear Sydney saying.

"This is Sydney's friend Alexander," he explains. "You've got to get Ginger out of the shower for me."

"Hang on a minute, please," Honey says, and takes her time coming back to the phone. "She's conditioning her hair," she reports gravely. "Can you call back in half an hour?"

"I'm calling from New York," he says. "Please, Honey."

Giggling, Honey says, "That sounded so sweet, the way you said my name. My real name is Marilyn, you know."

"Please, Honey," he says again, more urgently this time. "I'm begging you, Marilyn."

"What will you do for me if I can get her to come out?"

"I'll be forever in your debt, that's certain."

"Okay, fine," Honey says, but the disappointment in her voice is unmistakable.

"You hear that, Allie?" Ginger says a few minutes later. "That's the sound of my hair crying out for the protein and vitamins that were washed away too soon because of *you*. This better be good, Allie."

"Come home," says Alexander. "We need you."

"We?" says Ginger, and laughs. "He's driving you crazy, is that it?"

"He's miserable without you."

"He's miserable *with* me," Ginger says.

True, Alexander thinks sadly, but decides to ignore this

fact, which can only weaken his case. "He's been at a loss, these past few weeks," he tells her. "He doesn't know whether he's coming or going."

"Not me," says Ginger. "I've been living it up in the sun, eating crab legs every night, flirting with the waiters. I even walked the high wire in the little circus the Club Med people put on at the hotel. It was the thrill of a lifetime," she sighs.

He thinks of Sydney pinned beneath him on the kitchen floor; high above them Ginger balances herself perfectly on the thinnest, most precarious of wires as he and Sydney raise their heads in astonishment.

"Come down from there," he says.

"What?"

"Come home," he says. "Back to earth, where you belong."

"I'm in paradise," she says. "Why would anyone leave paradise?"

"Okay, you got me on that one," he admits. "But how about if I send Sydney down to join you?"

"Then it wouldn't be paradise, would it?" Ginger says reasonably.

"Be generous," he says. "It won't kill you."

"It's not my forte, being generous. It doesn't come easily to me."

"I know," says Alexander. Moved by the artlessness of her confession, he feels himself soften. But still he waits for her surrender, tapping his finger almost soundlessly on the crystal of his watch.

"All right," she says at last. "Ship him down to me and we'll see how it goes. But he'll be bunking by himself. There's no way I'm making room for him in my bed."

"Come on, Ginger."

"Take it or leave it."

"I'll take it," he says, and savors the sweetness of partial victory.

Getting Sydney up and out is another thing entirely.

"She *wants* me there?" Sydney says for the third time, eyes wide open in disbelief. He takes a noisy sip from the pink-and-white coffee mug of Mountain Dew Ionie offers him, and leans back in his seat. "Really?" he says.

"Absolutely," says Alexander.

"I don't know about this," Sydney says. "I don't hate her anymore—that was only temporary—but I don't know that I trust her. What if I go all the way down there and it turns out she can't stand the sight of me?"

"You've got to trust her, baby," Ionie says. "She's all you've got."

"I wish we'd had children," says Sydney mournfully. "A nice sympathetic daughter with a house in the suburbs and an extra room over the garage with my name on it. I could have lived out my last remaining years in the bosom of my family, a grandchild on each knee, three hot meals a day. . . ." He smiles and shakes his head. "What a life!"

"Well, I'm calling my travel agent," Alexander announces, slapping his hands against the kitchen table and standing up enthusiastically.

"At seven A.M.?" Sydney says.

Alexander sinks back down into his seat in disappointment. He feels as if he has been awake forever, as if he has already expended a day's worth of energy arguing with Sydney and Ginger. He wants to relax, to fall into Ionie's embrace and feel her cool hands slip below the waistband of his pajamas. Here are the two of them lying together on his bed, their bed, Ionie tickling his bare stomach with her eyelashes, fluttering them against his warm flesh.

"I'll do a laundry for you," he hears her telling Sydney. "Then we'll go get a hat to keep the sun off your head."

"And a couple of new bathing suits," says Alexander. "My treat."

"It sounds like I'm going on a vacation," Sydney says doubtfully. "Against my will. And my better judgment."

"Take a chance, hon," Ionie says.

"I'm too old for taking that kind of chance. And I've been battered too long by that woman. I want a divorce."

"That's it," Alexander says. "A divorce or a Caribbean vacation: your choice."

Sydney turns on the TV, flipping past three news programs to a talk show, where a burly man in an ill-fitting suit informs the audience that the woman he had been married to for eleven years recently revealed that she had once been a man.

"Can you tell us what that was like for you?" the host says, barely concealing his excitement.

"Well, it *was* kind of a shock and all," the man drawls, and lowers his head.

"I'll take the divorce," says Sydney, eyes on the TV screen, "*and* the vacation. I mean, I'll definitely take the vacation. The divorce is a maybe. You know, I guess things could have been worse all these years. Ginger could have turned out to be someone who was once a man, for example. And then where would I be?"

"There's the attitude!" says Alexander. "Things can always be worse."

"What about . . . ah . . . sex?" the TV host asks. "Forgive us, but we're trying to understand this thing and we have to know."

Flipping his palms upward, shrugging his shoulders, the man says, "She told me she had female troubles and I couldn't touch her down there. So there was just a lot of hugging and kissing."

"For eleven years?"

The audience hoots at this; the man smiles sheepishly, shows his palms again.

"The man's a saint," Ionie says, impressed.

"He's a fool," says Alexander.

"Poor baby," says Ionie.

Sydney shuts off the TV with a stab of his index finger. "I suppose they're getting a divorce," he says sorrowfully.

At the airport a few afternoons later, Sydney has an anxiety attack that includes all the classic symptoms: rapid heartbeat, sweaty palms, difficulty breathing. Swallowing down half a Valium, along with water from a fountain in a pleated paper cup, he drops into a plastic chair and squeezes his eyes shut tight.

"My mouth is full of that soft stuff on the beach," he reports. "Sand. Or maybe it's dust. Anyway, I'm not getting on that plane."

Alexander considers falling to his knees and begging softly. And then perhaps loudly. He imagines himself on the waxed linoleum, looking up at his friend's stricken face, tempting him with offers of money, jewels, eternal happiness. Instead he simply says, "You *are* getting on that plane. A change of scenery and weather will do you good. And maybe it'll be a second honeymoon for you and Ginger, who knows?" And then he winces, remembering Ginger's stipulation that Sydney find a bed of his own.

"You mean a second honeymoon for Ginger and Honey and me?" Sydney says.

"You'll work it out." Alexander helps him out of his overcoat, arranges it deftly over Sydney's knees. With his handkerchief he blots away the sweat that runs past Sydney's ears in two narrow trails. He watches a woman in a warm-up suit eating a steamy baked potato wrapped in tinfoil. A uniformed maintenance man comes by, pushing a barrel of trash; the smooth pale severed leg of a mannequin sticks straight up out of the barrel, a spooky sight that Alexander has to turn away from.

"Well, my heartbeat's back to normal, at least," Sydney announces.

"Wonderful!" says Alexander, just in time to catch sight of Paulette Wolfson marching by on high heels with a mink coat thrown over one arm, her other arm linked through a young man's, a guy who's clearly dragging his heels.

"Hey, look who's there," Sydney says loudly, and calls out to them as Alexander clamps his teeth together in exasperation.

Smiling broadly, Paulette introduces them to her son Michael, who barely lifts his head to acknowledge the introductions. "Michael's going to Club Med in Santo Domingo, the lucky guy," she says with excessive cheerfulness. "He and his girlfriend just broke up over New Years, and I thought, what better antidote than ten days in the Caribbean?"

"Hiding out in my apartment with the blankets pulled up over my head and the telephone unplugged seemed pretty inviting too," says Michael.

"He's a little depressed," Paulette says in a stage whisper. "But he'll get over it. We all do, eventually." Seizing Alexander's hand, she says, "And where are you gentlemen off to?"

"To reclaim my wife," says Sydney. "Or not, depending on how things go."

"He and Michael are on the same flight." Alexander studies Paulette's son, a string bean of a guy with pale skin and a thin blond mustache. So this is the man who lost his wife to his father, he thinks, wishing he could comfort him, or at least put a little color in his cheeks.

"Terrific," Paulette says. "It's always nice to travel with friends. Or friends of friends. Maybe they can sit together."

"I'll be out cold as soon as we take off," says Michael. "I just took three Dramamine."

"Well, maybe you can sit together anyway."

An announcement is made informing them that the flight will be boarding in five minutes, and the words send a thrill through Alexander. "You're going to be fine," he whispers in Sydney's ear.

"Can I call you?" Sydney asks. "If it's a disaster, I mean."

"It's not going to be a disaster," Alexander says, and slings Sydney's carry-on bag over his friend's shoulder. "Think positive and stay away from the jellyfish." He watches as Paulette and her son embrace, as Paulette folds some money into the pocket of her son's bleached denim jacket.

"Let's get out of here," she says as the line of passengers begins to form. "He's such a pill," she whispers to Alexander.

"Pardon me?"

"Michael. He's a pill. Want to go for coffee?"

He looks at her in her tight suede pants and silk shirt, her platinum hair softer, less like a helmet this time, her eagerness for a few minutes of his company so evident that he cannot say no to her. The passengers are disappearing now through the tunnel that connects the boarding area with the plane, and as he sees Sydney glance back over his shoulder before vanishing, a weight of guilt and remorse mixes with his exhilaration, diluting it, until all he feels is an odd, surprising sense of loss.

"Coffee?" he says. "Sure."

They find themselves in one of the airport bars, darkened at two in the afternoon and nearly empty, except for some business travelers and a couple of off-duty stewardesses looking severe in short haircuts and navy-blue suits. Eating a dried-out, overcooked hamburger with his coffee, Alexander listens as Paulette talks and talks.

"You can't imagine what a relief it was to see him finally get on that plane," she says. "In some ways he's my greatest heartbreak. Everything he wants always seems to be out of reach. You know anyone like that?"

Alexander shakes his head. "It must be very difficult for you, having to worry about a grown child like that," he says, without thinking much about it. He pushes his watch up along his wrist, trying to see exactly what time it is. He wants to go home, to hear Ionie tell him, as he knows she will, that there's absolutely no reason for him to feel guilt-ridden about hustling Sydney out of their home and onto a plane headed for paradise.

"You're so compassionate," Paulette is saying. "It's one of your many charms." Even in the half darkness he can see that her smile is full of longing. "Does your girlfriend appreciate that in you?" she asks him.

"I appreciate that in *her*," he says. "After my wife died, it was Ionie who understood what I needed. She was the only one who knew exactly what to do with me."

"Ah," Paulette says. She leans toward him and rubs his bad shoulder. "Just a little lint on your jacket. And I have to say," she confesses, a smile still on her lips, "that I can't help thinking she's entirely wrong for you."

"Really," he says, feeling himself stiffen.

"For starters, of course, she's . . . you know, black," Paulette says, lowering her voice.

"She is?" says Alexander, and laughs. "Thanks for pointing that out to me."

"I don't mean it as a racist thing, I mean it as a people thing. A cultural thing. I keep trying to figure out what the two of you could possibly have in common and I keep drawing a blank. It's just a mystery to me."

"Love is often a mystery," he announces. He is enjoying himself now, enjoying the sound of his own voice, so confident, so decisive, so absolutely right on the money. Because if there's one thing in all the world he knows for sure, it's that Ionie is at the red-hot center of his life, nurturing him, inspiring his passion, keeping him alive. Deprived of her, he would simply wither.

"I suppose that's true," Paulette says slowly. "And what's also true is that I made a huge mistake. When we first met, I told you I was determined to find someone who would make me happy, that I would recognize him in an instant. Well, it took a bit more time than that, as these things usually do." Grabbing Alexander with both hands by the points of his shirt collar, she kisses him madly, grinding her lips into his, teeth clicking against his as she tries unsuccessfully to find her way into his mouth.

"Check please!" Alexander calls out in desperation.

"I'm so glad I did that," says Paulette, and settles back in her seat. "I had to let you know how serious I was. How serious I am."

"Don't ever do that to me again," Alexander says stupidly. *"Please."*

"In the fall, when you took me all the way to New Jersey, I thought, This man is one in a million. I had this fantasy about seeing you again, about making up excuses to see you again, but then I thought, *He* knows where to find me. And so I waited. It's been months, you know," Paulette says accusingly.

"I'm sorry."

"About what?"

"About disappointing you. About always having to disappoint you." He signals to their waitress, a middle-aged woman who's standing in a near corner smoking a cigarette, shamelessly eavesdropping. She arrives in a hurry, smelling of smoke, and immediately gives Paulette a sympathetic look.

"Men," she says, rudely snatching the check and twenty-dollar bill from Alexander's fingers. "As if life weren't hard enough."

Paulette nods, then looks away, waiting for her to disappear. Just before the waitress makes her way across the room to the cash register, she steps deliberately, and firmly, on Alexander's toes with the heel of her boot.

"Ow," he murmurs, and imagines that the inside of his shoe is slowly filling with blood. And then, strangely, he is fighting back the urge to laugh—at the thought of himself as someone who can inspire such animosity in a woman he doesn't even know. And he wants to share the joke with Margot, who, after all, knew him better, saw him more clearly, than anyone. *Look at me*, he yearns to tell her. *After thirty-eight years with you, I've got one woman in love with me, another who thinks she's in love with me, and a third who wants to break my toes for no good reason at all. Look at me!*

"Don't worry," Paulette says. "You'll come around."

"I will?" he says, then: "I won't."

"I have faith," Paulette says, and it sounds to Alexander like a threat he ought to take seriously. He watches her slowly and carefully outlining her mouth in scarlet lipstick now, an ordinary sight that at this moment gives him a serious case of the jitters.

Waiting for Ionie in front of the supermarket, Alexander crouches low on the sidewalk to chat with Deneece in her stroller. It's a clear spring afternoon, and the sun is high and strong. Against the supermarket window leans an old man in a yarmulke, sunning himself with a homemade reflector of cardboard and aluminum foil. A slender man wearing a long, filthy quilted coat, his age impossible to determine, stands just outside the door, asking for money from everyone who passes by. "Can you spare a hundred dollars?" he repeats over and over again. Most ignore him, some roll their eyes at him in annoyance, and some,

like Alexander, toss a handful of change into the soiled Styro-
foam cup he holds at his waist with both hands like a bouquet.

"Nice weather," the man says, smiling sweetly at Deneece.
"Can *she* give me a hundred dollars?"

"Sorry, no," Alexander mumbles, and moves farther away
from him.

The old man in the yarmulke says, "Strengers like that have
no right to be here."

Sighing, Alexander wheels the baby into the supermarket,
which is clean and attractively laid out but clogged, as usual,
with too many shopping carts manned mostly by old people in
no hurry to get moving and on with their lives. After circling
the store twice, he finally discovers Ionie gabbing with a white-
coated, elderly stock boy about the high price of orange juice.

"Hi, baby," she says, and gives him a brilliant smile, as if
she hasn't seen him in ages. "Four nineteen a half gallon, can
you believe it?"

"I don't care," Alexander says. "Buy it or not, and let's get
going."

"How come you're feeling brave enough to come in here
today, hon?" Ionie asks. "Got your lucky rabbit's foot with you?"

"Oh, this store's as safe as they come," the stock boy reassures them. "We haven't had an incident in maybe ten years,
not since the night manager was shot to death in a holdup."

"Oh, he's not afraid of being shot," Ionie says, "or anything
like that. He's just afraid of running into his old girlfriend, is
all."

"She's not my old girlfriend," Alexander grumbles. "And let's
get out of here, shall we?" It's been nearly three months since
he was kissed, so desperately, by Paulette Wolfson in the middle
of the afternoon, but less than a week since he last saw her here
in the supermarket, which is half a block from his apartment but
a half mile from Paulette's. She preferred the meat department
here at the Food Emporium, she'd told him, lying boldly and
with great enthusiasm.

"So how *are* you, Alexander?" she'd asked at the produce

counter as he wiped away her cool kiss from the side of his cheek. "You never called to thank me for the little pot of Persian violets I left with your doorman. He did deliver it, didn't he?"

"It's doing real nice," Ionie had said, laying her hand in a friendly way across Paulette's wrist. "Real nice. But don't you know you can't trust this man with any green thing at all? He'll kill it in no time. The man's got a black thumb."

"Really," Paulette said.

"Yes, he does, so if you want to send any more plants, you make sure they got my name on them and I promise you I'll take real good care of them. And now I'll leave you alone to talk over old times and all."

"What old times?" Alexander called after her as she sauntered with the baby stroller down the aisle to the junk-food corner, her posture beautifully straight, her head held high and proud. "Come back here, Ionie," he hissed, but she paid no attention to him, studying cellophane bags of taco chips and fluorescent orange Cheez Doodles, even putting on her reading glasses to show she meant business. Abandoned just when he needed her most, he watched as she removed her glasses and winked at him theatrically, then slid the glasses back on again.

"You've got to stop leaving those messages on my answering machine," he told Paulette.

"Why?"

"Because I can't respond to them, that's why."

"Why not?"

"Because it wouldn't be appropriate."

"Which ones were a problem?"

"All of them!" he said impatiently. " 'Call 766-3273 for a hot time; call 766-3273, day or night, and your call will be answered by one of our beautiful operators wearing nothing but what God gave her . . .' " *How can you face me?* he'd wanted to ask. *Why aren't you blushing even the slightest bit? Can't I even shop peacefully in my own supermarket, for crying out loud?*

"Did you happen to see that movie with Kirk Douglas's son and that blonde with the boy's name?" Paulette said. "You know the one I mean? It had kind of a frightening title, which I seem to have forgotten. Do you know which one I'm talking about?"

He didn't. "*Ruthless People?*" he said.

"It was all about love and it was really quite terrifying."

"*Endless Love?*"

"A woman scorned is a woman to be feared, remember that," said Paulette.

"*Fatal Attraction*," said a man next to them who was squeezing small green plums with a vengeance, one after the other. "And it was terrifying, all right."

"That's the one." Paulette nodded. "Thank you, sir." Patting Alexander's shoulder, she said, "Well, see you again soon, I hope. Do you shop here often?"

"You *know* this is my supermarket, Paulette."

"Well, now it's mine too."

"Don't do this to me, Paulette. Don't do this to yourself."

"Do what?"

"I'm in love with someone," he whispered fiercely. "I'm going to marry her, in fact."

"You really crack me up, you know that?" said Paulette, but she looked worried. "She's not going to marry you. Those people don't believe in marriage. They can't handle it. They believe in sex and having babies, but marriage isn't for them."

"What people?" said Alexander, foolishly (he knew) goading her on but unable to resist. And he could not resist either the fantasy of marriage to Ionie, an idea that had not seriously occurred to him until that moment, probably because he had spent so little effort, since Margot's death, thinking about the future at all. The possibility that Ionie could reject such an offer pained him deeply and he could already feel the humiliation, could hear Ionie's roar of good-natured laughter. *Now why would you want to go and do a thing like that when we're happy just the way we are?* he heard her say. And why would he? Simply to seal the bargain they had so easily, so naturally, struck between them? Like it or not, there *was* the future to consider. What if he had a fatal heart attack next week or next month and left Ionie with her grief and nothing else? Let her be his widow, then, with money and a place to live and all the documents to prove they were hers. If she laughed at him, he'd twist her arm a little or a lot, if necessary.

Why not?

"*What* people?" said Paulette. "Ne-groes," she mouthed.

"Think what you may, but I'm telling you this marriage is *on.*"

Paulette shrugged. "Well, good luck to you and yours. And I don't mean to scare you too much, but remember *Fatal Attraction.*"

"What about it?"

"Rabbit stew," Paulette had said mysteriously, and swept down the aisle toward the exit.

At the checkout counter now, Alexander thinks again of the marriage proposal he'd been contemplating so nervously for the past week. Each time he'd come close to delivering his little prepared speech, his nerve had failed him and he'd backed away, ashamed and also relieved. He'd told himself he was waiting for a sign from above—a bolt of brilliant lightning, an unexpected spring snowfall, a reassuring appearance by Margot in one of his dreams.

"Well, well, if it isn't the groom-to-be and his love child," Paulette says, taking her place in line behind him now, her shopping cart empty except for a newspaper and a single bottle of raspberry-flavored seltzer. "So when's the big day?"

"Soon," says Alexander. Pretending that Deneece wants something from him, he squats next to the stroller and gives her his hand to play with. "Go away," he says under his breath to Paulette.

"You didn't call me back yesterday. I left two very polite messages on your machine, you know."

"I'm never going to call you back."

"Never say 'never,' " Paulette advises. "Did you watch the movie I recommended?"

"Nope. I've been terribly busy."

"Better make room for it in your schedule, dearie. You really shouldn't miss it."

Arriving with a wire basket loaded with groceries, Ionie squeezes past Paulette to the baby, who's howling strenuously now for no apparent reason. "That other seltzer right there is·two for the price of one," she points out helpfully, lifting the baby from the stroller. "Canada Dry, not the one you've got there."

"I don't need two bottles," says Paulette. "I'm on my own, completely alone, as I'm sure you know."

Ionie shoots her a sympathetic look, then turns away. "Hush, you big fat girl," she tells the baby. "Oh, and the violets are blooming like crazy."

"I'm glad *someone* appreciates them." Paulette stabs Alexander in the back with her pointed elbow, but he doesn't respond.

"I do," Ionie says. "That's for sure."

"Wonderful," says Paulette.

Ionie has made popcorn in the microwave and is eagerly circling the living room now, methodically switching off all the lights. Cozying up to Alexander on the couch, she says, "Sometimes I like to scream at scary movies, so don't you be getting all worried—it's just me having fun."

"Ho-hum," says Alexander. He doesn't particularly enjoy watching movies at home; usually he finds himself getting too comfortable on the couch and dozing off at all the best moments. He suspects this will happen again tonight and that he will miss the point, Paulette's point, and have to get it second-hand from Ionie. But he is drawn into the movie immediately and looks on in horror halfway through as the beautiful rejected lover, Glenn Close, ceases to be an object of sympathy and goes off the deep end entirely.

"Oh Lord," he says, and in the same instant Ionie's shriek stings the inside of his ear like some furious flying insect. The camera focuses on a gruesome surprise, a pot bubbling in a suburban kitchen, a pot containing a little girl's beloved pet rabbit, dumped there, the audience knows, by the rejected lover. It is the little girl, belonging to Glenn Close's ex-lover, whose scream merges now with Ionie's, turning the back of Alexander's neck bumpy with gooseflesh.

"No!" he cries, because he cannot believe that this is what Paulette has been trying to tell him, that she is not simply a lonely divorcée, a persistent annoying voice on his answering machine, but someone to be feared—a psychopath bent on extinguishing the bright flame of his happiness.

This has got to be a joke, he tells himself, for of course Paulette is no psychopath, but still his heart is pulsing like crazy. "Ionie!" he cries, and leaps from the couch to stop the VCR. "Can we get married please?" Hurrying back to her in the pitch-darkness of his living room, he collides with the coffee table.

"Sure, baby," Ionie says warmly, "but how come you had to ask me in the dark? Too afraid to look me in the eye?"

"Just a coincidence," he says, but it's true that the darkness has emboldened him like magic, without his even realizing it. "Where are you, anyway?" he calls out.

"Right here," says Ionie, extending her hand out of nowhere to drag him back to shore, to the cool leather couch where she waits for him. "Ask me again," she says, "nice and proper this time, and let me look at your face." Turning on the reading lamp at her side, she says, "You're a sight, all right." She pushes his hair from his eyes and kisses him, her mouth tasting pleasantly of popcorn.

"Please marry me," he says, blinking in the startling light. "I love you like you wouldn't believe."

"You do, don't you?" says Ionie, and her dark eyes are lit with tears.

"No crying," Alexander says. "There's no time for it. We've got to start making plans."

"Can we finish watching the movie first?"

"You watch it. I've got a phone call to make."

"Going to call your mama with the news?" Ionie says slyly. "She'll be all excited, I bet."

"She'll survive," says Alexander. "And if not . . ." He shrugs, indifferent. "She's a tough little bird."

"And Leora?"

"She might even be pleased, who knows? And if not, she'll survive too."

"Well, my family's going to be real happy. They're going to show up all dressed up in their fanciest clothes." Grabbing Alexander by the shoulder, Ionie asks, "This a dream, baby?"

"It feels like one, doesn't it?" he says softly. He wishes he could offer a heartfelt explanation to Margot, see the slightest nod of her head as she murmurs, with only the slightest hesitation, "Yes." He imagines himself at her grave (which he has visited only once, just a year ago, on the first anniversary of her death), filling her in on everything she has missed, his voice falling uncertainly to a whisper when he gets to the subject of his love for Ionie. But the man he sees isn't him, it's someone else, a stranger who is drawn inevitably to his wife's grave, who finds solace there. But his solace is here, in Ionie, who is watching him now with affection and gratitude and also a trace of bewilderment.

"It's no dream," he says, his hands at her earlobes, tracing now the outline of the gleaming silver shells that are suspended gracefully beneath them on thin silvery wire.

"You sure?" Ionie says. "Then maybe I'll have one of those Jewish weddings like you see in the movies, in a big room with chandeliers and waiters in uniforms and all the guests doing the cha-cha, even the old ladies like your mother."

"We'll see," is all he says, but laughs at the unlikely picture of his mother dancing spiritedly at this wedding of his that he cannot yet even begin to imagine.

From the telephone in the bedroom he calls Paulette Wolfson and is met by her Ease-A-Phone Message Center, which plays a few bars of "The Girl from Ipanema" and then asks him to leave his name and message.

"This is Alexander Fine," he says, starting out stiffly. "My fiancée and I watched that movie and let me tell you how relieved we were that our own little pet rabbit happened to die of natural causes just a few days ago. Just kidding, Paulette," he says, warming up, "as I know you were too. I don't know if your machine is getting all this, but all kidding aside, I really am getting married . . . in June, in fact. So it's time to throw in the towel, Paulette, okay?" Hanging up the phone he whispers, "Okay?" An imprint of his perspiring palm remains behind on the receiver; picking it up again, he rubs the moisture into the black plastic with the cuff of his shirtsleeve.

"Women," he grumbles into the phone, brave as can be.

In the mail a few days later he finds a flowery card from Paulette congratulating him on his engagement. Toward the bottom of the card is a P.S., written in large generous letters: "If you happen to end up in divorce court, be sure and give me a call!!"

Chapter

17

Spike's recent impotence had been an on-again, off-again thing, made even more troubling by its very unpredictability. Sometimes, over the past few months, he'd been able to perform perfectly well, but sometimes there was simply nothing he or Leora could do to keep him in a state of arousal. Tonight, lying in bed, listening to her moving about in the bathroom, knowing, by the length of time she was in there, that she was fooling with her diaphragm, spraying her thighs lightly with perfume, softening her hands with scented lotion, he worked himself into such a state of anxiety that he was sure he would go deaf from the hammering sound of his heart. He plugged his headphones into the clock radio at his bedside, and turned up the volume until all he heard was Ray Davies of the Kinks, amiably urging him to come dancing.

Flat on his back, he stared at the ceiling and moved his fists in time with the music; he did not notice Leora standing naked in the bathroom doorway, her knees trembling slightly.

She had been patient with him throughout these months, but exasperated at his absolute unwillingness to talk whenever he experienced failure. His bewilderment and shame were overwhelming; the thought of discussing these things with her only heightened his anxiety. Several nights ago, feeling himself go soft inside her, he withdrew and turned his back to her, curling into a fetal position, ignoring her entirely. This had become his standard response, but even after a few such episodes Leora continued to seek him out, to sweetly stroke the back he had turned toward her, to thrust her feet between his ankles, to nuzzle the back of his neck.

"Please talk to me," she'd begun.

"Go to sleep," he'd said, not unreasonably—it was, after all, two in the morning, and both of them would be up at seven.

"Your shrink knows every detail, doesn't he? What's so special about him that he gets everything and I get nothing?"

His shrink had, in fact, gotten it out of him bit by bit, as if he were slowly removing a palmful of painful splinters. It was Spike's theory (confirmed by Dr. Kling) that Suzanne was at the very center of his misery, that his fears that she knew every last thing about his marriage—including details of his intimate relationship with Leora—were the probable cause of his sexual troubles. But isn't it too obvious, Spike asked Dr. Kling, too easy an explanation? And why, so many months after Suzanne's reappearance, would he suddenly be affected this way?

You tell me, was the answer he got. *You tell me.*

"Just go to sleep," Spike had said to Leora again, more gently this time. He'd wondered what Leora would think if he offered her the truth: that while they were attempting to make love moments earlier, he had envisioned Suzanne sitting cross-legged on Leora's dresser, filing her nails industriously, from time to time looking out over their bed with interest, a smile at her lips that he could not read, no matter how hard he tried. *Here's the thing*, he could hear himself saying to Leora: *I'm being visited by a phantom ex-wife who just doesn't know her place.*

"You can tell your shrink I said thanks for nothing," Leora said, and abandoning him, had stalked out to the kitchen. He found her there a few minutes later, furiously emptying the dishwasher, grabbing handfuls of silverware and flinging them onto the counter, ignoring the forks and spoons and butter knives that slipped from her grasp and landed with a metallic clatter at her bare feet.

Sweeping her hair away from her face, kissing her, he'd said, "If I could talk, I would. I just can't."

"It's the selfishness of it that I can't stand," she said. "You're not a selfish person, and that's why I can't accept this from you."

As he led her back to bed he'd tried to win her over with an assortment of apologies, all of them heartfelt, but none of them entirely satisfactory, it seemed.

"Yeah yeah yeah," Leora said. "Lucky for you I still love you."

One arm entangled in the wire from the headphones, Spike turned his head as Leora bent over him tonight, her nipples grazing his shoulder as she worked to free his arm.

"Ooh," he said appreciatively. "Nice."

Leora lifted his pajama top to his shoulders and played with the sparse straight hairs on his chest. He transferred the headphones to her and she sat up on her knees, dancing in place, her small breasts swinging freely above him. He enjoyed the sight of her, the sheer silliness of her naked dance.

"I love it when you're being undignified," Spike said, and slipped his arms around her, pulling her on top of him. Aware that his nervousness had evaporated, he made love to her easily, thankfully. Just before he came, he found himself thinking that he could do this forever, spend the rest of his life poised there at the edge of a steep place, waiting for that instant of perfect pleasure. It seemed a shockingly simple revelation, and then he remembered that of course it was nothing new, that of course he had felt this way before, but not, he realized sorrowfully, in a very long while. And then he willfully closed off his mind and allowed himself to slip over the edge, yelling "Yes!" like someone in a moment of hard-earned triumph.

"Quiet, you'll wake Ben," Leora said, laughing, and because he had forgotten her, he was startled by the sound of her voice.

"Was that really me?" he asked.

"OhGodOhGodOhGod," she said, mimicking someone, though he didn't know who.

"*That* wasn't me."

"That was *me*," Leora said.

"Didn't hear a word of it," said Spike. "I think I was someplace else." He pulled away from her, his stomach, damp and sweaty, making the sound of a suction cup against Leora's moist skin.

"In heaven?"

"Oh, higher than that," he boasted.

"Me too," Leora said drowsily, and that was the last he heard from her. He fell instantly into a deep warm sleep that was like sinking into bathwater. Awakening in a sweat against the sheets just as the alarm went off, he was thrust out of a dream that left his face burning with panic and shame. In the dream Suzanne had slipped down from her perch on the dresser and joined him and Leora in their bed, where, unasked, she helped to satisfy them both. He and Leora accepted her presence without protest, welcomed her even, and *this* was what he found most troubling of all. It sickened him to consider that the dream was simply wish fulfillment, an expression of suppressed desire. He could not remember what he had seen of Suzanne's body, or even if she had been naked or clothed: all he remembered was a silent shadowy presence that did its work and asked for nothing in return. Recalling this now, it came to him that what he had experienced was clearly a nightmare, something frightening and oppressive and not about desire at all. Limp with relief, he lay in his bed and breathed deeply.

"Out now!" he heard Ben call, and then the familiar rattle of the bars of his crib. "Out *now!*"

"Tell him to find his way to a good day-care center," Leora murmured. "And be sure to give him cab fare."

"It's okay—I've got to get up anyway," said Spike. "I've got student conferences scheduled back-to-back all day."

"Bless you," Leora said. "You're all a woman could ever hope for."

"And more."

"Let's not get carried away." Thrusting her hand underneath his pajama bottom, Leora squeezed his behind playfully. "Sweaty," she said, and took her hand back. "Are you all right?"

"Yup," he said, and went off to Ben's room, where he was greeted with a joyful "Hi!" Several months short of his second birthday, Ben was an exuberant being, a man of few words, but one who knew how to get his point across.

"So I hear you want to get out," Spike said.

Ben shook the bars eagerly.

"I can deal with that," said Spike, hoisting him high in the air so that Ben chirped "Out out out!" wildly flapping his arms.

"Am I the best dad who ever walked the face of the earth?"

"Yah!" Ben whooped.

"Promise me you'll still feel the same way ten years from now." In response, the baby grabbed Spike's nose and twisted it with enthusiasm, his miniature, razor-sharp nails sinking into the curve of his father's nostrils.

"Cool it," said Spike. "Who taught you to behave like that?" Seizing Ben's hand, he examined his nails, which Leora had cut straight across in a hurry. "Time for a manicure, my boy," he announced. With the baby on his lap, he filed away at the tiny pointed edges, his own hands seeming enormous and far too clumsy for the task. The top of his son's head smelled irresistibly of apricot-scented shampoo, and Spike lowered his face into it, seduced. Forgetting himself, he loosened the arm that was holding Ben in place, and in a moment his son was off and running.

• • •

Spike's office was a small, disorderly space that lacked a window, fresh air, and adequate room to stretch. Sitting at his desk, taking a final look at his least-favorite student's memorandum, he tried hard not to laugh. The student, a handsome, sleepy-eyed boy in a sweatshirt and jogging shorts, had just begun growing a beard, and his face appeared smudged and dirty in the harsh light of the desk lamp. Whenever Spike happened to glance at him in class, the boy looked either bored or exhausted, or possibly both, his head propped up in his palm, eyes cast downward, perhaps completely closed.

"How'm I doing, Mr. G?" he asked languidly.

"Pretty good," said Spike, "but the plaintiff's name is Myron, and not, as you seem to prefer calling him, Moron."

"What?" the student said, pained. "Where?"

"Here, there, and everywhere. Take a look for yourself, Mr. Witkin." Spike went back over the facts of the case, which involved poor Myron, the plaintiff, who was filing a complaint against his estranged wife, Angela, because her Labrador retriever had bitten him about the ankle and thigh when he returned to his former home to retrieve a favorite cardigan sweater he'd left in his closet. The complaint had been fabricated for the writing assignment by Roger Geraci, the head of Spike's program, but Spike knew that Roger's ex-wife's Lab had bitten him on the behind last year and that he had threatened to go to court over it. The thought of this now made him laugh out loud, and his student responded by slapping the memo on Spike's desk and flashing him a look of outrage.

"These are all stupid typos you've underlined," he said. "And it's not very professional of you to be laughing at me."

"I wasn't laughing at you, Mr. Witkin . . . Phil. It was something else. Really."

"Really?" said Phil in a thin voice. "Well, try this on for size: I don't think much of you as a teacher, I think your class is a big bore, and I don't want to be a lawyer."

"I see," said Spike, suddenly feeling more alert than he had all morning. After a half-dozen conferences with polite, all-too-eager-to-please students, he was ready for a confrontation, even if it meant having to hear what a lousy teacher he was. "Shoot," he said. "I'm all ears."

Leaning forward, Phil began to play with a pliant red rubber face that sat in a plastic cup on top of the desk. He squeezed its ear, pulled hard at its nose, dug two fingers into its eyes. "Sorry," he said, and sat on his hands.

"No no, that's what it's there for. Go ahead and poke out its eyes if you'd like."

"Okay, listen," said Phil after a moment. "It's like this—your class is a drag only because I don't want to be a lawyer."

"But I'm still not a very good teacher?" Spike braced himself for a string of adjectives that would hit him like an open palm against the side of his face.

"Actually, I like you. You've got . . . presence, and now and then you're pretty entertaining. But these writing assignments are bad news."

"I imagine they would be, if you have no desire to become a lawyer. So what *do* you want to be?"

"A stand-up comedian," said Phil mournfully.

"Sounds great. Are you funny?"

"Not funny enough, apparently. I get to work these clubs at one or two in the morning, and I don't hear too many people laughing out there." Plunging two fingers into the rubber face, sighing, Phil said, "It's such hard work, getting an audience to appreciate you. Sometimes, when I know I'm dying out there, I think to myself, evidence, torts, constitutional law—that's what's waiting for you, dude—and then I *really* want to die."

"Try your routine on me," said Spike. "I'm always up for a good laugh."

"What the hell," Phil said, and slowly rose out of his seat. Pacing the small room, he put his hand up over his brow like a visor, as if shielding his eyes from a spotlight. "Can we dim that just a little, Myron," he said, and then launched into the story of his childhood, gloomily portraying himself as "a wimp to end all wimps, a major dork if you know what I mean."

Soon lulled into a half-conscious state by what followed—

an endless accumulation of details that were neither funny nor poignant—Spike drifted helplessly back into his early-morning dream, watched as Suzanne came toward his bed, dressed in a dark satiny undershirt, which she removed dramatically with one hand as soon as she hit the sheets. She immediately went after Leora, dragging her long polished fingernails up and down the length of her, raising goose bumps along the way. It couldn't be that this was what Leora wanted, what he wanted, yet his arms and legs had turned to gooseflesh too, and he couldn't take his eyes from the sight of Suzanne's fingers trespassing so slowly across Leora's skin. *More,* he heard his wife cry urgently, and then Suzanne's mouth was pressing lightly against his, and her tongue was circling the outline of his lips.

Someone was rudely snapping two fingers together in front of his face, saying, "I put you to sleep, for Christ's sake, didn't I?"

Jerking his head back, Spike opened his eyes in time to catch the look of disgust and despair that crossed his student's face.

"I quit!" Phil announced, and clumsily seized his paper, tearing the cover page in two, letting the memorandum slip from his fingers and under the desk.

"Law school?"

"Everything."

"Hold it," Spike yelled, and raced after him down the corridor to the elevator. "Your memorandum was fine—well written, excellently reasoned, your logic was good. . . ." He was out of breath and out of compliments, overcome with guilt. "Look, let me take you to lunch, Phil. We can—"

"You didn't laugh once. You slept through the whole performance."

"I didn't sleep well last night." Spike hung his head. "If I nodded out for a minute just now, it had nothing to do with your routine, believe me."

Stepping into the elevator, about to disappear, Phil offered him a false smile that he seemed to hold in place forever. "How stupid do you think I am?" he said slowly, and then was gone.

Spike gave the elevator a few satisfying kicks and, for a moment, contemplated running down eight flights of stairs in an attempt to catch up with Phil, who probably didn't want to hear what he had to say anyway, he guessed. Kicking the door one last time, he went back to his office and waited for his next student, thinking, while he waited with clenched fists and jaw, that the only way to clear Suzanne from his dreams was to disengage her from his life entirely. It would be, he imagined, a great and satisfying relief, like throwing off a high persistent fever. And then he was envisioning his life as a soiled bed sheet that only needed to be shaken out strenuously and aired in blinding sunlight; he could see it billowing in a vigorous breeze, hear it snapping sharply under a perfectly cloudless sky. Exhilarated, he saw that of course he could reclaim his life. *Of course.*

"She's gotten into my dreams," he told Leora that night. "And I don't want her there or anywhere else in my life." They were seated at the dining-room table working together on their tax return; it was almost eleven and Spike was ready to abandon the calculator and the litter of sickening paperwork that fully covered the surface of the tabletop. It had been a terribly long day, he thought, but weary as he was, he just couldn't go to bed without asking Leora to hear him out.

"I barely made three thousand dollars this year," she wailed. "I managed to write a half-dozen pieces, using every minute of Ben's nap time and every other minute I could spare, and three thousand dollars is all I have to show for it."

"Forget about the money—you should be proud of yourself anyway," said Spike. "But we'll get to that later." Stretching across the table, brushing aside a jumble of receipts and a legal pad full of depressing calculations, he kissed the underside of her neck. "Just listen to me, okay?"

"You want to talk about Suzanne and I want to obsess about my halfhearted career. Why should I let you go first?"

"She's invaded our bedroom. Our bed. She's screwing me up, Leora."

"She's in our bed?" Leora raised both eyebrows comically,

exaggerating the gesture so that her forehead was patterned with wrinkles. "Funny that *I've* never seen her."

Looking away into a corner of the room, focusing on the dark dusty leaves of a rubber plant, he said, "Mostly she's just hanging around watching us, but this morning I dreamed that she actually joined us in bed."

"Am I really hearing this?" said Leora. "This is crazy stuff, Spike."

"I was counting on your being a little more sympathetic."

"What was she doing in our bed?"

"Use your imagination," said Spike.

"I'm feeling a little sick right now," Leora told him. "And also a little bit like laughing.'" She poked Spike's chest lightly. "Don't tell me you don't find this the slightest bit funny."

Spike shook his head. "She's taken away my confidence. I'm in bed with you and there she is in the audience, taking notes, passing judgment . . . and God knows what else."

"I guess you've really been suffering, haven't you?" Leora murmured. She would not look at him, though, and bent her head, playing with a handful of pencils that she balanced carefully one on top of the other against the table.

"She's got to go, Leora."

"No!" Leora said, as a single pencil, slightly off balance, rolled away and off the table, upsetting all of the rest, so that they too slid from the edge and then disappeared.

"Pay attention!" Enraged, Spike shoved his chair roughly against the wall, shot up out of his seat. "This isn't a joke. She's ruining our sex life, she's ruining *me! Us!* Don't you care?" He was breathing heavily, as if he had traveled many flights of stairs carrying a heavy burden. "Help me, Leora."

Leora's face was eggshell pale and she had drawn into herself, drawn her legs up onto her seat and under her chin. Arms clasped protectively around her knees, she looked shrunken and fearful, someone who had lost courage and perhaps a little blood. "You're scaring me," she told him.

Good, he almost said. You *should* be scared. "Don't be," he heard himself say. "It's not a complicated thing, really," he soothed her in a near whisper. "Just give her up, Leora. Don't see her, don't talk to her, don't think about her. Spend more time with your other friends and after a while you won't even miss her."

"What does the all-knowing Dr. Kling think?"

"*You* know it's the only thing to do, Leora."

Leora slowly uncurled herself and sat up perfectly straight in her seat. "Fine," she said. "You give him up, I'll give Suzanne up. It's not a complicated thing, really," she said, mimicking him exactly, stroking him with her whispery voice.

"You want me to stop seeing my shrink? That's completely unfair, Leora. I *need* him. I need the relationship."

"Aha," said Leora. "My point precisely. She's my best friend, Spike."

"Find another best friend. And this time make sure it's not someone I was once married to."

"I can't stand this!" Leora cried. "Just cancel the next goddamn appointment with your guy. Just do it!"

"I can't."

"What are you, enslaved to him?"

He hated it that she thought him weak, that she could not understand that weakness had nothing to do with it. Or if it did, it wasn't weakness of character, but merely a weakness for the cool, uninflected voice of Dr. Kling as he patiently helped him puzzle out the mysteries of his mother, his father, the tangle of his wife and ex-wife. It was that dispassionate voice that so calmly drew Spike out week after week, allowing him to unburden himself, to say the same things over and over again if he chose, or gently nudging him in the right direction, away from anxiety and toward a clarity of vision that sometimes amazed him.

"Oh come on! You think I don't know he's the keeper of your secrets? You think I don't hate that? Why can't you just dump him and come back to *me*?"

"Come *back* to you? I haven't gone anywhere."

"Spike," Leora said, and he read in her face an eagerness,

an anxiousness, that stirred his sympathy. "Just listen to me. There isn't anything in the world you can't tell me, anything that I can't help you with. And the best part," she said, smiling, "is that I'm free. I don't charge eighty-five bucks an hour like you-know-who."

Approaching Leora, he played with her lovely wild hair, grateful that she allowed it, worrying that she would shake him off at any moment.

"You'd think I was asking you to give up your mistress," she said.

"It almost seems like that's what this is all about."

"If you're asking me if I'm jealous, you know I am," Leora said.

"That's crazy."

"No crazier than your imagining Suzanne is spying on us in our bedroom."

"So where are we?" said Spike, and let go of her hair. Backing away from her, he bumped into the wall behind him, knocking his head hard against the plaster. "Great," he said.

"You didn't by any chance knock some sense into your head, did you?"

"Fuck you," said Spike. "That's very helpful, you know?"

"Saying 'fuck you' to me was very helpful too."

A small hard kernel of frustration planted like an irritant inside him quickly swelled into something unmanageable and he could no longer tolerate the sight of her, her pale, narrow face hardened with contempt for him. "I can't be here with you," he said.

"Fine," Leora said coldly. "I'll leave."

"You can't leave. I'm the one who's leaving."

"You're not leaving—I'm throwing you out!" Leora hurried toward him, hurling herself against him with surprising force. She tried to push him, toward the door, he thought, or perhaps anywhere at all, but he resisted her with little effort and she soon saw that she could not win. "Out!" she said, beating his chest with her fists.

"I'm not leaving if you're going to throw me out," he said.

Letting her fists fall to her sides, Leora said, "Then *I'm* out of here. I'm calling Suzanne to see if Ben and I can go and stay with her awhile."

"Hold it a second," Spike said, and was struck by a potent wave of nausea that sent him flying to the bathroom and then to bed, where he waited helplessly for his stomach to settle.

Without his asking, Leora brought him ginger ale and a wet washcloth, which she held up against his forehead with gentle hands. "I hate to leave you like this," she said as he bolted again for the bathroom. She stood in back of him as he retched, gathering his hair away from his face and safely behind him. "I feel awful," she murmured.

The sound of her voice, the sympathetic words she uttered, were lost upon him; all he wanted was to be put out of his misery. "I'm going to die," he announced.

"I don't think so," Leora said. "Tomorrow at this time you'll probably be up and around and furious at me."

"Make sure you sit in the front row at the funeral—otherwise people will think there was something wrong between us."

"There is," said Leora, "but let's not get into that now, okay?"

He closed his eyes, and when he opened them again, a half hour had passed and Leora was packed and ready to leave. She stood at his bedside, shifting her weight from one foot to the other, making his dizziness worse.

"Stand still," he said.

"I'm going to see if I can get Ben out of here without waking him," she said. "We'll be at Suzanne's, but we'll be happy to come home as soon as you've wised up."

"This is insanity," Spike said. "There's no other word for it." He was going to vomit again and ran to the bathroom on wobbly legs. His throat was sore and his mouth tasted of bile. Bits of undigested food splashed up in his face as he leaned over the toilet; the fact that his wife was leaving him seemed beside the point, something that he had neither the physical nor emotional resources to contemplate for more than an instant.

"Go," he told Leora. "Scram." When he was finished, she walked him back to bed; leaning on her, he felt like a scrawny old man weakened by age and disease, someone who needed help with the simplest things.

"You've got vomit on your T-shirt," said Leora, and burst into tears.

"Well then, upack your suitcase and stay awhile."

"Can't," Leora said, sniffling. "I'm too angry at you."

"Then go."

"Why do I have the feeling that you got sick deliberately, just to make me feel guilty?"

"Shut up, Leora."

"Let me put it this way: you don't think it's possible this is just your body's response to my leaving?"

"Go!" Spike croaked. "I *want* you to go!"

Leora rested her hand lightly at the top of his head as he turned away from her. "Don't get dehydrated," she warned. "The bottle of ginger ale's right here. Promise me you'll remember to drink some." He did not respond, and then she too was silent, still keeping her hand upon him. "This doesn't feel like us, like anything that could ever happen to us," she said after a moment. "It seems like our marriage is much too good for this."

Her confusion, her uncertainty, matched his own, and he could only say, "Just do as you damn please," mumbling the words miserably into his pillow. He heard her leave the room and go into Ben's, listened for the familiar but now oppressive sound of the front door shutting behind them.

He was overcome with nausea, and then slowly, miraculously, it seemed to him, it passed.

The following afternoon, awakening from a long nap, he washed away the sour taste in his mouth with a swig of ginger ale that he drank straight from the green plastic bottle. Turning away from the night table, trying not to be sickened by the movement of his head, he caught, out of the corner of his eye, a glimpse of a figure in the doorway.

"Leora?" he said.

"It's me," Alexander said. "How are you, Spike?"

"Rotten."

"I guess you are. Well, I brought you some soup from Ionie. It's in the refrigerator in a pink container. Want me to heat some up for you?"

"God, no," said Spike. "But thanks."

"Want me to open the blinds and let a little light in here?"

"Maybe later." Flat on his back, Spike threw his arm dramatically over his eyes. "Leora is sure it was the thought of her leaving that made me sick. I want you to know that's bullshit, plain and simple." He gestured for Alexander to come further into the room. "Really."

"She'll be back," Alexander promised. "Listen, don't be offended, but I'm going to keep my distance. Just in case whatever you've got *is* a virus after all."

"Of course it's a virus. It was just bad timing."

Dragging in a swivel chair from the study, Alexander planted himself back in the doorway. "I hear she's at Suzanne's," he said disapprovingly. "Not very smart, in my opinion."

"I'm not feeling up to this conversation," said Spike. "Not at all."

"Do you want me to leave?"

"Stay," said Spike. "And you're a sweet guy for coming."

"Well, it was Leora who sent me over. And the soup was Ionie's idea. I'm just the delivery boy, really."

A bus making its noisy way down Broadway wheezed to a stop outside the bedroom window, then took off with a roar. Someone carrying a ghetto blaster passed by three stories below, broadcasting rap music edgy and threatening. A single car horn shrieked insistently, was silent for a moment, then sounded again for what seemed like forever. Spike guessed at the scenario: a frustrated driver hemmed in by a car that was double-parked beside him.

"Did I mention I'm moving to the country next week?" he said as the horn was silenced and a pair of female voices traded obscenities.

"No, you didn't. Did I mention I'm getting married?" said Alexander.

Shoving his pillow along the wall behind him, Spike eased

himself up, groaning slightly at the effort. "Pop," he said. "Hey, that's great." The pleasure he felt at Alexander's news was tempered by a sharp prick of envy that shamed him, but there it was; he was jealous of an old man's happiness.

"When?" he said.

"Soon, in a couple of weeks. I'm not getting any younger, am I? It doesn't seem smart to wait."

"Right," said Spike absently. He had an urge to call Leora at Suzanne's, to hear exactly what she had to say on the subject. He supposed that she had wept at first, out of the most stubborn loyalty to her mother, and then had pulled herself together and offered her congratulations in a trembly voice.

He wondered what it would be like to see Leora settled in at Suzanne's, and who, eventually, would be the first to let go of the stubbornness that had set them apart. Clearly he was feeling better, he realized, for the anger he had felt at Leora's demands the night before was returning to him, and it was a tonic that strengthened him, pushing him out of bed now and toward the bathroom, where, with great effort, he washed his face and combed through his hair, grooming himself for a visit to Leora, for a head-on collision with her that would leave her reeling. Examining himself in the mirror, he saw that his skin was greenish, his eyes deep set and ringed with the same appalling green. He looked like someone who could be felled with a single ordinary slap or even a halfhearted shove.

Dizzy with exhaustion, he grabbed the sides of the sink with both hands and swayed, as if he were at some precarious height and in danger of plunging over the edge fast and far. He vomited into the sink and staggered back to bed. "She'll be back," he heard Alexander say, in a voice so bright it could only be disguising the worst sort of bad news.

Spike lingered three days before attempting to see his wife. He missed Ben terribly, ached for his noisy, bustling presence, but did not want Leora to think he was lacking for anything, and so he stayed away, catching up on the work he had missed during the day he was absent from school, cleaning the apartment with a thoroughness Leora had rarely matched, cooking dinners for himself that he sat down to eat at ten each night, only to find he had no appetite whatsoever. As busy as he was, the days seemed to pass in slow motion, and he was reminded of the time when Suzanne had left him, those first few weeks when he had felt slightly shell-shocked, aware that his life had been altered dramatically and yet unable to accept it as absolutely real. *Suzanne.* Occasionally he daydreamed of her death, though he never got as far as choosing a murder weapon; in his daydreams he simply willed her death and it was done. No blood was shed; it was only a matter of a phone call or a telegram announcing that she was gone, that he and Leora were free to resume the life they had enjoyed before her.

When he'd confessed this to his shrink yesterday, Dr. Kling had nodded approvingly, saying, "It's your anger, of course, and your frustration, a perfectly normal response, given the situation." He was a middle-aged man, precise and serious and yet not without a sense of humor. He was always immaculately groomed, and dressed in expensive sweaters and highly polished shoes. His fingernails gleamed with a coat of clear polish, which still, after so many years, fascinated and repelled Spike. He decided Dr. Kling was probably quite vain; it amused Spike to imagine him in a nail salon getting his weekly manicure, his hands attended to by some sexy woman in a lab coat who treated them with the reverence they deserved. But that was all right, Spike felt: everyone was entitled to his own nuttiness, even his shrink.

"So," Spike had asked, "can this marriage be saved?"

"A little bit of compromise can go a long way," said Dr. Kling.

"I can't give you up just because Leora wants me to. It's an outrageous demand."

"Perhaps. But not from her point of view."

"I don't care about her point of view."

"Aha," said Dr. Kling, slapping one hand down on his desk and gazing at it admiringly. "You *should* care."

"I have to keep coming here," said Spike. "I need to."

"You might think so. But it seems to me you're in pretty fair shape, Spike. You're far more confident than when I first started seeing you, your anxiety is under control . . . I'd say you'll do fine on your own. In fact, I'd been thinking for a while about cutting the cord, anyway."

"Are you firing me?" said Spike in disbelief.

Dr. Kling looked amused. "Relax," he said. "I'm not firing you. I'm just giving you a little push in the right direction."

"I'm not ready for this," Spike said. "My wife took my kid and left me and now you want to dump me in a lifeboat without oars or a compass and let me fend for myself? Forget it!"

"Care to explain the nautical metaphors? Did you and Leora buy a boat?"

"It's been forty-eight hours since I've seen my baby," Spike complained. "He's a few blocks up the street but he might as well be in Sri Lanka." Wringing his hands, he said, "I'm losing it, I am really losing it." He got up and circled the room, stopping in front of a framed Jackson Pollock detail on the wall. He stared at the large spidery blotches of black paint that seeped across the canvas, and was chilled to see the painting was entitled *Lucifer*.

"Great!" he said. "What are you doing with a painting called *Lucifer* in your office? Is this supposed to be a calming influence or something?"

"It's been hanging there for months," Dr. Kling pointed out. "It never bothered you before."

"That was before my life fell apart. Everything's different now."

"You're feeling out of control," said Dr. Kling. "Your well-ordered life has taken on a different shape and you need to get back in control of it. The first thing I want you to do is take a few deep breaths and tell me how you feel."

Spike did as he was told, but inside his shoes his toes were clenched, and he bent the fingers of both hands into tight fists. "I feel like a jerk," he said. "An asshole."

"So we've got to get that self-esteem back up to an acceptable level. You need to take charge of things. Go see Leora and tell her you're going to try and wean yourself from me."

"I am?"

"It's going to be gradual and painless, I promise. So your next appointment is two weeks from today."

"You're canceling next week's appointment?"

Nodding, Dr. Kling said, "And how does that make you feel?"

"Weirded out," said Spike.

"Well, try and think of it as a positive step."

"You're firing me," said Spike. "The handwriting's on the wall. I may as well start cleaning out my desk."

Walking up Broadway now on his way to Suzanne's, he stopped at a store called Roses R Us and bought a dozen dark red roses at a bargain price.

"For your girlfriend?" the Korean man behind the counter asked as he wrapped them in flimsy green paper.

"My wife."

"Anniversary?" When Spike shook his head, the man said, "Fight?"

"Something like that."

"Good luck, yeah?" the man said, and rolled his eyes.

On the stoop in front of Suzanne's building, a teenage girl was having her long black hair braided elaborately by a girl who closely resembled her. A joint burned in a plastic ashtray at their feet; the girl who was acting as hairdresser took a hit with her eyes closed, then released the smoke directly over the top of Spike's head as he climbed the steps.

"This is some real good shit here," she announced, and tugged at the leg of Spike's jeans. "Hey, you, want to get high for twelve dollars?"

"No, thank you," said Spike.

"How about a haircut for eleven dollars? I do a real nice job."

"I'm sure you do," Spike said, and yanked his leg away from her.

"Wait," the girl yelled after him, laughing. "You got two big white hairs in the back of your head. Want me and my sister to pull them out for you?"

He opened the outside door and waited impatiently to be buzzed in as the girl's thin shrieky laugh grew more raucous. In a few moments he was entering a darkened lobby, which smelled distinctly of cooking odors and was clearly overdue for a paint job. The interior of the elevator was decorated with a handful of messages that had been scratched into its painted surface: "Fuck the fucking super," "Fuck you, wise guy," "I fucked Andrea R. 12/31/89."

"Big deal," Spike murmured. Arriving at the top floor, he saw that Suzanne's door was cracked open in welcome; there was Ben hurtling along the hallway, calling "DaddyDaddyDaddy," his voice high-pitched and jubilant.

"Whose daddy is this?" Spike said, startled by the tears that sprang to his eyes as he scooped Ben up from the floor.

"*My* daddy," said Ben. He ran his hands through Spike's hair. "*My.*"

Leora waited in the doorway, smiling at the two of them, at the roses that Ben tossed at her in a limp, underhand throw, the same way he tossed a ball.

"We don't throw flowers, Ben," she said.

"We don't?" said Spike. Knocking on the open door, he said, "Is this the West Side Home for Wayward Young Mothers?"

"Come in," Leora offered; behind her stood Suzanne, who was wearing black leggings and a long T-shirt that said "WARNING: When I See You I Feel Pain."

"Nice shirt," said Spike. "Kind of makes me feel all warm and fuzzy inside."

"It was sort of a gag gift from a guy I'm dating—he's in the T-shirt business, actually."

"And are you in love with him?"

"As a matter of fact, I'm not, not that it's any of your business, I might add."

"Sure it is," said Spike. "But that's only because everything that goes on in my life seems to be *your* business."

"Come on, Spike. Just remember this is *my* home. My castle."

"Such as it is," Spike said. He stared at the refrigerator that stood out in the hallway opposite the tiniest of kitchens. On the countertop was one of Ben's baby bottles half-filled with juice; on the linoleum floor were his Wiffle ball and bat and a plastic Sesame Street book he liked to play with in the bath. It was unnerving to see his child's things lying about so casually in Suzanne's apartment—it seemed to reflect the impossible ease with which his family had been transplanted here. And yet moving into the small square living room where Leora and Ben had been camping out to sleep at night, where an opened futon was littered with blankets and pillows and an assortment of large plastic building blocks, he was cheered by the chaos that clearly must have reigned from the moment they arrived.

Uninvited, he sat at the edge of the futon and constructed a pair of twin towers from the blocks. "So how are things?" he said finally.

"Pretty good," said Leora, without hesitation. "A little hectic, but okay, really." She snapped a block across the tops of both towers, joining them, and positioned a little plastic man in a yellow hard hat above them.

"They've been the perfect houseguests," Suzanne said. "I'm writing them both glowing letters of recommendation."

Spike wandered over to the opened window, where he watched a bare-chested man in gym shorts doing jumping jacks on the roof of an apartment house across the street. Adjacent to it was a building where small children were playing in a caged-in roof-top playground. A child in a neon-green shirt cartwheeled along the roof; another child, dressed in shocking pink, hung by her heels from a set of monkey bars.

"So," said Spike, his back to Leora, "I hear your father's getting married."

For a few moments there was no response from Leora. "The

truth is," she began, "I'm convinced I'll never make it to the wedding in one piece. Or that if I actually get there, they'll have to carry me out on a stretcher." She fell silent, and Spike kept his eyes on the children in their bright clothing, at the flash of pink as the little girl rose in the air on a seesaw and then descended swiftly to the ground. "I know," Leora said slowly, "that Ionie is wonderful for him, that my mother's been gone for so long, and that I've still got a problem."

"I honestly don't mean to sound callous," Suzanne said, "but we've been over this a hundred times and my advice is still the same: either go into therapy and get some help, or force yourself to stop thinking about it."

"That's why I'm shutting up right now," said Leora halfheartedly.

"I wouldn't be so quick to take advice from *her*," said Spike.

"Why not?" Suzanne said. "I'm her best friend—don't you think I'm as understanding as anyone could possibly be? Why *shouldn't* she listen to me?"

"And you're always right, don't forget that."

"You're really beginning to bug me, Spike," said Suzanne. Kneeling on the floor next to Ben, she said, "Let's leave these two guys alone and go out for some ice cream. Would you like that, kiddo?"

"Yah," said Ben, beaming at Suzanne.

"Don't go," said Leora.

Hearing this, Spike froze. "Don't go?" he said. "Don't you think we need some time alone?"

"I'm not in the mood."

"I didn't ask you to get into bed with me," Spike said, and saw, a moment later, that he had embarrassed her, that she was fingering her glass necklace impatiently, anxiously. "I'm sorry," he offered.

Leora nodded. "Of course I was looking forward to seeing you," she admitted. "But now that you're here . . . all I'm feeling is a terrible uneasiness, as if you're expecting too much of me."

"I'm not expecting anything." He flapped his arms limply to his sides. "It's been a very long couple of days, that's all."

"I've missed you too."

"And?"

"I feel safe here," Leora said. "Contented. Suzanne's teaching me to play bridge. I get my lessons at night, after we've gotten Ben to sleep in the bedroom. So it's just the two of us sitting here with some old James Taylor albums playing in the background, the two of us talking away or not after my lesson, depending on our mood. It feels very cozy, like something I don't want to give up."

From her seat on the floor, her legs open in a wide V, Ben sitting comfortably between them, Suzanne smiled.

Do I have to spell it out for you? Spike could hear his mother saying. But her fears were wild and unfounded: there was no sexual heat between them, certainly not from Leora's end, anyway. As angry as she might have been with him, he knew, she would never betray him that way, never risk that kind of intimacy with another woman. She was simply too conventional, too much a married woman. Suzanne, he suspected, might risk it, though hesitantly, but Leora would never yield to her. He tried to read Leora now, to penetrate the dreaminess in her voice and in her eyes, but it was as if she were draped in layers of veil that allowed no light at all.

How can you be so selfish? he asked her silently, and then there was the sound of a fluttering of wings and in through the window flew a slender turquoise parakeet. It circled the room frantically and finally came to rest on a picture frame as Leora and Suzanne shrieked and clung to Spike, grabbing his arms with a fierceness that he found entirely gratifying. Laughing, Ben boldly approached the bird, terrifying it, sending it back into flight.

"Oh Jesus," Suzanne said, trying to bury her head under Spike's arm. "I'm all shook up."

"You and Elvis," said Leora. "And me too."

"It's a parakeet," said Spike, "not a vulture. It's obviously someone's pet."

"He's an intruder in my home," said Suzanne. "I feel violated somehow."

Returning to the picture frame, the bird began to chirp softly, then said, "What's your name?"

"Don't answer that!" Suzanne cried, and flung her arms around Spike's waist.

"What's your name?" the bird persisted.

"Ben?" said the baby shyly.

"Hello, Ben," the bird said twice, and then began to clean its feathers.

"Maybe he knows his telephone number," Leora said. "We could call his owner."

"Ask him, Spike," said Suzanne.

"Ask him yourself."

"I couldn't. He wouldn't answer, anyway. He senses my hostility, I'm sure."

"So do I, but *I* talk to you."

"I'm begging you, Spike."

"Do you have a shoe box?" he said. "I'm going to try and capture him, and then I'll take him downstairs and send him on his way."

"You're a braver man than I," said Suzanne. "And God, am I grateful."

"Let go of me, then, and get a shoe box."

"Couldn't we all go and look for one together?"

"You've got to let go of me," he said again. "You too, Leora." But neither of them would release their hold on him, and he shook them off as impatiently as if they were curls of dust attached to his shirtsleeves. "I never knew you felt this way about me, girls," he teased.

Suzanne found him a box and its lid, into which she thoughtfully punched a grid of air holes. "Get this guy and I'll be your slave forever," she said.

Trying a gentle approach, Spike spoke softly to the bird and offered his index finger for a perch. The parakeet responded by taking off in a panic, settling on the TV set only after it navigated the room three or four times, its flight sending Leora and Suzanne into a corner, where they huddled miserably.

"Take a couple of deep breaths," said Spike, "and you'll feel better." Obediently, Leora and Suzanne breathed in and out noisily. "I was talking to the bird," he said. "Do you think he was listening?"

The parakeet uttered a sound resembling a harsh little laugh. "Hello, Edward," it said. "Hello, Rob."

"Edward and Rob who? Don't they have last names?" Slowly Spike lowered the shoe box to the top of the TV set. "Are they the couple you live with?" he said in a whisper. Hearing this, the bird flew straight into the bulb of a tall narrow halogen lamp, which made a horrifying sizzling sound at impact but continued to burn brightly.

"He's going to fry!" Leora screamed, but the bird, apparently unharmed, was soaring again, a blur of turquoise beyond Spike's reach. At last it lighted on the windowsill and Spike tiptoed toward it.

"That's right," he murmured. "This is the way home."

"Push him out," said Suzanne.

Ignoring her, Spike made soothing little noises that failed to entice the bird, who headed resolutely back to the center of the room. "You want to play hardball?" said Spike. "Fine." He held the shoe box aloft over his head, pursuing the parakeet dizzily around the living room, knowing he had lost his cool, humiliated in the presence of his wife and ex-wife and even his little boy, all of whom crouched on the floor now observing his failure in utter silence.

Out of breath, his hair hanging damply in his eyes, he scaled the cardboard box through the air, hoping for the satisfying sound of something, anything at all, breaking irreparably. He had lost all sense of purpose, forgotten why he had come. All he wanted was to flee, and as he whirled across the room and out the door, he took no notice of the small colorful bird that sailed after him, as if in pursuit.

Chapter

18

Two weeks before the wedding, Alexander's mother falls getting out of the bathtub and breaks her leg in a big way—a spiral fracture that may require surgery in the future. "It seems I won't be coming to your wedding after all," she tells him cheerfully from her hospital bed, her long thick white hair hanging loose past her shoulders instead of in a French knot, so that to Alexander she looks a little wild and entirely unfamiliar. "And besides, you told me you two were just good friends. So what's this I hear about a wedding?"

"I only told you what you wanted to hear," Alexander confesses. "That was a mistake, of course."

"You never in all your life told me what I wanted to hear."

He helps himself to a piece of melba toast wrapped in plastic on his mother's lunch tray. "Well, tomorrow's the big day," he announces. "I'm taking you home, you know, and there's a very nice woman named Venus who's going to stay with you for a while and help you with all the things you can't do for yourself."

"Home?" Mary says, sounding panicky. "I'm too sick to go home. And if you think I'm going to that wedding in a wheelchair, you can forget it."

"You're not sick, Mom. Your leg is in a cast, but you're going to be fine."

"Are you a doctor? What do *you* know?"

"Not much. But I do know the orthopedist wants you out of here by tomorrow morning."

Mary begins to cry, though not very convincingly. "I'm eighty-seven years old," she complains.

"Eighty-six," says Alexander. "Don't exaggerate."

"The point is, I've lived long enough," Mary says. "If I die right here in this bed, that would be fine by me."

"Don't *talk* like that," Alexander says, squeezing his mother's hand. *"Please."*

"When *you* get to be eighty-seven, we'll see how you like it. You know, I don't even get dressed and go down in the street anymore. I stay in my housecoat all day and watch the news on the television. I've got arthritis in my toes, my glaucoma's getting worse, and I think the cataracts are coming back. I can't see well enough to read the paper anymore or wipe away the dust on my furniture. What have I got to look forward to, tell me."

"The wedding," says Alexander, and absently goes for another cracker, which is stale and no better than cardboard, he thinks.

"I want to be cremated," his mother says. "You can bury my ashes in the cemetery, right next to your father. And no funeral, remember that. Or," she says, "maybe just a small one."

"I'm too busy to think about all that right now. I'm getting married in a couple of weeks."

Mary smiles. "If I die tomorrow, you'll have to cancel the wedding. It wouldn't be right for you to be celebrating and carrying on when you just lost your mother."

"Come *on*," says Alexander. "Ionie's out looking for a dress for you even as we speak. I told her pink or rose are your best colors. You'll be at this wedding, trust me."

"Who's Ionie?" Mary says casually.

"Are you joking?"

"That's a very peculiar name. I'm certain I've never heard it before."

"You know who she is, Mom," Alexander says, but suddenly he isn't at all sure that she does. His mother's eyes are magnified by the lenses of her new glasses, giving her a bewildered, childlike look that he notices now for the first time. "Mom," he says softly. "Ionie's the woman I'm marrying. You've met her, remember?"

"I met a nice colored lady in your home once, a very refined woman who told me she lost her son a few years back. But I didn't know you were going to marry her. I thought she was the maid."

A middle-aged nurse wearing a blue cardigan sweater over her shoulders arrives to take Mary's temperature and check her blood pressure. "This is my son who's marrying the colored lady," Mary says, pulling the thermometer from her mouth. "The one I was telling you about."

"Get that thermometer back in there," the nurse says, and nods at Alexander. "Your mother's not going to the wedding," she whispers into his ear. "She says if the bride's not Jewish, she won't go."

"We can fix *that*," Alexander murmurs. "We can't make her white but we can certainly make her Jewish."

"Pardon me?" the nurse says.

"Is she all right?" he asks, taking the nurse aside to the metal wardrobe where his mother's few things droop mournfully from a row of heavy wooden hangers. "She seems a little confused now and then."

"That's the hardening of the arteries. It causes senility, of course. But most of the time she's right here on this planet, tuned in to everything." The nurse tilts her head and squints at him, as if trying to discover his secret. "I must say she's not very happy with you. I've never heard anyone complain so much."

"Par for the course," says Alexander, shrugging, but his face goes hot with embarrassment. "Did she tell you one daughter is worth a dozen sons?"

"Several times," the nurse says, and laughs. "In my family the opposite's true. My son happens to be a prince, but my daughter you can forget about. She's a doctor right here in the hospital, and let's just say that's the only positive thing I can tell you about her. The rest is all bad news."

"What's all that whispering?" Mary calls from her bed. "When are you going to do my nails for me, Mrs. Odell? You promised me yesterday and here it is today and I'm still waiting."

"I've just been so busy," the nurse says. "Maybe your son can fill in for me." Taking a bottle of coral-colored polish from a small cabinet next to the bed, she places it in Alexander's palm. "Ever polish anyone's nails before?"

"Never," he says warily.

"Well, there's nothing to be afraid of. Small even strokes from bottom to top, and keep your hands steady. And hers."

"Forget about him," Mary says. "He must be good for something, but nail polishing isn't it. I'll just wait for you, Mrs. Odell."

Alexander slips out of his jacket and rolls up his shirt-sleeves. "Have a little faith in me," he says, and is rewarded by a friendly pat on the shoulder from Mrs. Odell. "Put your hand on the table here," he instructs his mother, pushing aside the plastic tray holding her green-and-gray lunch.

"I don't know about this," Mary says, but extends her small fine hand with a smile. Her nails are whitish and ridged like

tiny shells, her fingers straight and slender, the ring finger ornamented with a narrow circle of emerald and gold, a treasure
left over from his father's time. Sam, his father, who died almost
forty years ago, had been a shoe salesman in department stores
all his life. Appealing in his exuberant way, he'd been the
one person to charm his wife into laughter, into occasionally
revealing a softer, easier self that did not seem like Mary
at all but some sweet unflappable distant relative whose visits
were all too brief and infrequent. Alexander had envied him
the magic he'd worked on his mother, the mysterious singular
talent that could not be learned or duplicated, it seemed. He
misses his father at this moment, longs for a little help from
him, a word or two to ease the way to his mother's buried
sweetness.

Diligently, he paints her nails in silence, slowly, one by
one, his hands deft and steady.

"This is nice," his mother tells him. "Just the two of us like
this."

"Yes," he says, reaching for her other hand, thinking this
is the closest she's come to a declaration of something like love
in a very long while.

"If only you weren't getting married," she sighs, "we could
do this all the time."

"I'll visit you more often," he promises. "My marriage has
nothing to do with it."

"I don't want you to visit more often," his mother says, and
bends her head to whistle a mouthful of air against the wet
polish. "And I don't want you to get married. What would Margot think, knowing you were marrying the maid?"

"She's not my housekeeper anymore. She's the person I love,"
he says, losing control for an instant and spreading polish way
down to the knuckle of her index finger. "As for Margot, don't
you think she'd want happiness for me?"

"A Gentile woman can't bring you happiness."

"She's going to convert," says Alexander, the lie coming
easily and painlessly to his lips. "She's already been to see the

rabbi." With a tissue he tries unsuccessfully to wipe away the polish that stains her finger a creamy orange.

"You're making a mess," his mother says disapprovingly. "But maybe one of these days, before I die, you'll surprise me and do something right."

On his way back to Manhattan he sees a skinny woman with a grimy face and neck lounging in a broken-down baby stroller just outside the entrance to the subway. Sipping a bottle of beer, her knees drawn up to her chin, she's simply not to be ignored. "God bless you and have a nice day," she says gravely, and takes his money in her warm and sticky hand. He is careful to keep the hand that has touched hers away from his body, and to wash it as soon as he walks in the door, not even stopping to speak to Ionie first. He does not know what he is afraid of—AIDS, TB, or just plain bad luck rubbing off on him. And he does not notice Shavonne, sitting impassively on his living-room couch, listening to a woman on TV who has been married thirteen times talking of her current love, saying this time she knows it's for real.

As he bends to kiss Ionie in the kitchen she gestures for him to lean out and have a look around the corner and into the living room. "I don't know *what* that girl wants," Ionie hisses. "She shows up here Lord knows why, plays with the baby, but not for long, and now she got herself parked in front of that TV set and isn't saying a word."

"Whatever it is, it isn't good," he says, and something in his middle pulls sharply, as if in confirmation.

"That's for sure," says Ionie.

"Did you find a dress for my mother?" he asks.

Ionie shakes her head. "Deneece wouldn't let me shop but for thirty minutes today. She fussed and fussed and I was getting all kinds of looks from the salesladies and finally we just had to leave. I'll go out again tomorrow, baby, if you'll watch her for me."

He listens to the woman with the twelve ex-husbands in-

sisting that marriage is the only way to go. "I still have faith,"
she says, and the audience applauds wildly.

"How's it going, Shavonne?" Alexander says, trying to sound
casual. "It's been a long time—since last summer, am I right?
The baby's doing so well, don't you think so?"

"Yeah."

"Are you still living in New Paltz with your boyfriend?"

"Yeah." Eyes focused on the TV screen, she seems to be in
a trance. When he shuts off the television set without warning,
she says, "Hey!" and gives him a withering look. Her hair has
been straightened, he notices, and in her ears hang heavy gold
triangles that just clear her shoulders. The coppery-colored snap
at the top of her jeans is undone—beneath it, her stomach bulges.
"What you looking at?" she says.

"Do you think you might be pregnant, Shavonne?" he says,
and holds his breath as Ionie gives out a yelp and comes flying
into the room on bare feet.

"Yeah." She gets up to turn the TV back on, but Ionie shuts
it off instantly.

"You goin' to make me old before my time, girl," Ionie
says, and grabs Shavonne by the shoulders. She shakes her hard
and then bursts into tears.

"You stop that," says Shavonne, but her face is absolutely
expressionless, as if Ionie's pain and even her own were beyond
her comprehension.

"I ain't takin' care of this baby and neither are you," says
Ionie, and shakes her some more. "I got a life of my own to
live, you hear me?"

Slipping out of her grasp, backing away and into the couch,
Shavonne falls heavily against the cushions. "You got any Diet
Pepsi?"

"Diet Pepsi?" Ionie cries. "Diet Pepsi?"

Stepping forward to embrace her, Alexander whispers, "I
know you don't believe this, but we'll manage. We'll manage
everything."

"Oh yeah," Ionie says. "That's for sure. If I hadn't stopped going to church, none of this would have happened. I got to start going again. Every Sunday, like I used to. I got to pray for a whole lot of help."

"Better pray that she starts using birth control," says Alexander.

"I got to get her co-mitted to some kind of institution, a residential school or something, like she used to be in," Ionie says in a whispery voice. "Got to lock that girl up so no boy can get to her."

"A boy can always get to a girl. And when he can't, he'll find a way."

"You're doing a real good job of cheering me up," Ionie says, and offers him a laugh that's a half sob. "The baby's up— want to go change her?"

"You go," he says. "I'll stay with Shavonne."

"I'll go," Shavonne says.

"How many diapers you changed in your life, girl?"

Alexander follows Shavonne into the bedroom, where the baby lies serenely on her back grinning at a black-and-white cardboard mobile. The moment Shavonne tries to pick her up, Deneece begins to wail, thumping her arms and legs against the mattress. "She doesn't know you well enough," Alexander says apologetically. He lifts the baby into his arms and Deneece gives him one of her spectacular smiles.

"Put my baby *down*," Shavonne tells him.

"She knows me, Shavonne. We're good friends." He wants to acknowledge that he understands it isn't supposed to be this way, that he's supposed to be the stranger here, the stranger whose face the baby cannot abide. But he doesn't know how. "I'm sorry," is all he says. "I'm terribly sorry."

Waving her fingers in front of the baby's hand, Shavonne says, "She thinks you're her father and that's just a lot of shit." The baby grabs Shavonne's finger and puts it into her mouth. "I got to get an abortion, don't I?"

"That's up to you and Ionie. It's none of my business, is it?"

"I'm scared," Shavonne says. "I want a Diet Pepsi."

He holds the baby's ankles together and lifts her legs with one hand as he slides a dry diaper under her bottom with the other. "You're fifteen years old," he says. "Of course you're scared."

"I did a lot of bad shit." Letting her fingers graze the baby's smooth rounded belly, Shavonne says, "You got a dog here I could play with? I like a big dog like Lassie."

"I'm sorry, we don't."

"You got a cat, then?"

Shaking his head, Alexander says, "What kind of bad things?"

"I don't get my period anymore and that's bad. Can you gimme some money for comics? I like Archie the best." Shavonne runs her hand slowly from the baby's toes to her thigh. "Cute baby, but dogs are cuter. Where's *your* dog?"

"We don't have one, but I can take you down to the store and get you those comics and your Diet Pepsi too, how would that be?"

"When I had the baby, it hurt so much I had to yell," Shavonne says. "The nurse was a mean white lady. I bit her hand and she hit me."

"That's over with now," Alexander says, and snaps the baby's overalls. "All done," he says. "Ready to go out?"

"You like Ionie?"

"I like her a lot," he says, and smiles.

"You and Ionie have sex?" Shavonne says mildly, as if she were asking "You and Ionie have lunch?"

Chickenhearted, his pulse racing, he says, "You'll have to talk to Ionie."

"You and Ionie have sex when Deneece is in the room?"

"Never!" Alexander shouts. "Never ever."

This pleases Shavonne: she smiles at him for the first time and he knows he's won her over. "I don't like people," she says, "but I like *you.*"

He feels sweaty and utterly exhausted, sinks down against the bars of the crib with the baby in his arms. He has passed safely through dangerous territory and can still feel the frightened beat of his heart.

"You sick?" Shavonne says, looking down at him with her arms crossed over her big, womanly bosom. " 'Cause I got to have my Archie comics *now*."

When Ionie comes to check on them, her eyes are pink-rimmed, and she's holding a sheet of paper toweling up over her nose. Blowing vigorously, she says, "What she do to you? She knock you down on the floor like that?"

"We're fine," he says. "Aren't we, Shavonne?"

"I want my comics."

"Hush up," says Ionie. "The first thing we're doing is going to the clinic over at the hospital and find out how far along you are. Let's just pray it's not too late."

"You're mad at me," Shavonne accuses her.

"Mad? No way! Why would I be mad? I'm happy," Ionie says, her voice growing more and more shrill, Shavonne shrinking back from her, eyes narrowing with suspicion. "I'm getting married next month and everything is beautiful."

"Who you marrying?" Shavonne says.

"That man over there, the one holding your baby."

Shavonne nods. "You have sex with him?"

Holding her hands to her chest, Ionie makes a worrisome choking sound that soon turns into laughter. Bending at the waist, she lurches about the room, stamping her feet now and then, wheezing noisily. None of them, not even the baby, can take his eyes off her; they follow her progress around the bedroom, not saying a word.

"Oh, you funny kid," Ionie says at last, and abruptly comes to a full stop.

Unable to sit still, Alexander straps Deneece into her stroller and goes out for a walk, heading nowhere in particular. It is an exceptionally raw spring day; an early-morning sun has vanished and there's a chill breeze that makes him long for his winter coat and a pair of gloves. Arranging an extra blanket over the baby, he apologizes for dragging her outside when they might just as well have stayed in and napped away the afternoon together. But the baby sucks on her orangey rubber pacifier and seems content. Alexander thinks of Shavonne on a cold metal table staring indifferently as the doctor prepares to vacuum away the clump of cells being nourished in her womb, or, perhaps, letting out an enraged shriek just before she rises up to bite the doctor's hand. Either seems possible: there's no telling which way she'll go. That she will be an official member of his family and a source of worry for the rest of his life he finds a little frightening. He would like to help her find her rightful place in the world but cannot imagine what or where that place might be. He has never known anyone so lost, so far from anything to hold on to at all.

Shivering in the icy air, he rubs his finger absently across the baby's warm cheek.

To his surprise he finds himself directly across the street from the white brick apartment house where Sydney and Ginger lived for so long together and where Sydney now lives alone. He has to admit he hasn't been the loving and endlessly sympathetic friend that Sydney has been in need of these past few months, seeing him infrequently and cutting short Sydney's phone calls, offering excuses that made him stammer with shame. When he asks himself why he has lost his patience (though not his affection), he can only think that he has grown lazy and selfish in his old age, keeping his reserves of sympathy for his family only.

"What's happened to me?" he asks Deneece, who spits out her pacifier at his feet but does not answer him.

In the window of the stationery store in the building next to Sydney's, a quartet of Coca-Cola cans dances to music that can only be imagined from outside. The soda cans are wearing dark glasses and headsets and they sway sinuously, ludicrously, in the window; in fact, the entire window is in motion, with an assortment of stuffed animals, noses pressed to the glass, swaying ceaselessly. Alexander and the baby stare in astonishment, mesmerized, Deneece stretching her arms forward, trying to reach beyond the glass.

"Forget it," Alexander advises, and goes into the store to buy a Coca-Cola can for Shavonne. Inside the window a tape deck is playing noisy rock music.

"You got a radio at home?" the teenage salesman asks, and Alexander buys a small transistor for Shavonne too. He finds a get-well-soon card and adds it to his purchases, which for no good reason at all transform him into someone jaunty.

Backing the stroller expertly out the door, he zips into Sydney's building and is greeted upstairs by a gaunt figure in baggy pants and red suspenders who smiles at him uncertainly.

"When did you stop eating?" Alexander says, and nearly weeps at what has become of his friend. "Does your doctor know about this?"

"Can't keep my pants up without these," says Sydney, thumbing his suspenders.

"Why didn't you tell me?"

"Tell you *what?*"

"That . . . . that your pants won't stay up without help."

"So I lost a little weight, so what? My speech is back to normal, my kitchen floor is clean enough to eat off, I iron all my own shirts like a pro. . . . I'd say I'm doing pretty well, thanks. And how's little Desirée," Sydney says, squatting on his heels to shake the baby's hand.

"Deneece," says Alexander.

"So you're getting married and I'm getting a divorce. Congratulations to both of us."

"May we come in and sit down?" Alexander says. "Or am I persona non grata around here?"

"I don't know, Allie, I just don't know," says Sydney, ushering them in with a broad sweep of his arm. "I was under the impression you and I were going through a divorce of our own. Do you still love me, or what?"

"Of course I still love you. What a question!" says Alexander, but he lowers his head, studying the slightly scuffed tips of his loafers rather than examine Sydney's open, vulnerable face. He busies himself with the mechanics of getting Deneece out of her stroller and her jacket and watches as she walks unsteadily toward the coffee table in the center of the room, where she immediately seizes a ceramic vase full of silk flowers. "No!" he says, and arrives at the table just as she raises the vase over her head triumphantly.

"I see your little friend's been keeping you on your toes," Sydney says. "No wonder you have no time for me."

"It's been a circus," says Alexander, clutching the vase against his chest. "And then there's my mother and Leora and Spike and Deneece's mother. . . . I'm tangled up in all these lives that seem to have gone wrong lately."

"I'm tangled up in no one's life but my own," Sydney says, "and believe me, it's enough. And you know, my analyst says it's important for me to be selfish now, to indulge myself in as many ways as I can."

"Your analyst?" Alexander says in surprise as Deneece goes for the bookcase, tossing hardcovers and paperbacks over her shoulder energetically.

"The whole world is in therapy. Why should I be any different? And this Dr. You knows how to work magic. The first day when I cried in her office she gave me her own personal monogrammed handkerchief to use and then she told me I could keep it. That's because I'd already finished off the box of tissues on her desk, but even so, what a woman! She's this little Chinese lady barely five feet tall, very beautiful, and she has this kind of porcelain look about her—hey, that's my first edition Somerset Maugham she's got there! Stop her!"

"Deneece!" cries Alexander, tripping over his own feet as he races to the bookcase. "Stay away from first editions," he warns, and carries the baby off to the couch. "Sounds like you might have fallen for her," he tells Sydney.

"Don't be ridiculous . . . well, maybe a little." Sydney smiles. "She's like this lovely petite doll and so smart, besides. You know what she told me? She said I stayed so long in that miserable marriage because it never occurred to me that maybe I deserved better. Isn't that amazing?"

"Amazing. But be careful, Sydney."

"Of what? Oh, that . . . that's pure fantasy. It's very common. Dr. You says it's nothing to worry about. And anyway, she's married."

"Are you sure?"

"Absolutely. She wears a diamond wedding band. Her husband's a psychoanalyst too."

"I meant, are you sure it's nothing to worry about?" says Alexander. Deneece has been playing with the remote control and has finally hit the right button: the TV comes loudly to life, its volume turned up painfully high.

"Jesus Christ!" Sydney roars, and grabs the remote. "She's one very annoying little pipsqueak. How can you stand it?"

Stung, Alexander pulls the baby into his lap. He kisses her fingertips, tickles her tummy, ignoring Sydney entirely. "She's a wonderful little girl," he announces.

"I see," says Sydney. "Well, each to his own, I suppose. You know, I sometimes wonder if Ginger and I would have been different together if we'd been able to have children. Maybe motherhood would have brought out something wonderful in her, something entirely loving and generous. . . . She's a very difficult woman, Allie. She treated me like nobody deserves to be treated and I didn't know how to stop it. But look," he says, thrusting out his left hand. "Just look."

"What am I looking at?"

"I've stopped wearing my wedding ring," Sydney says proudly.

"Congratulations," says Alexander. "Listen, I want you to be best man at my wedding."

"Just like last time. All those years ago when you and . . ."

"Yes," Alexander says, and a hot and salty lump burns way back in his throat, something that feels like fresh grief and that he struggles to swallow but cannot. *Margot*, he whispers. When she was lowered into the earth he did not look away; he had to know where she was going, had to see with his own eyes the proof that she had vanished. And so he had watched, not bravely, but simply because he needed to have the image fixed in his memory like a good sharp photograph taken in perfect light. And that is what he sees now as he stands in Sydney's living room, as his friend puts his skimpy arms around him and holds him fierce and tight against him.

Chapter 19

Spike brought Leora home with him after a dinner date and a leisurely walk along Columbus Avenue, which was brightly lit and flooded with couples set on romance. When he'd picked her up at Suzanne's a few hours earlier, Suzanne had said, "Now remember, I want this little girl back by midnight," and then fluffed out Leora's hair in such a motherly way that even Spike knew she had to be joking.

"Come on, Ma, don't be such a pain," Leora said, and all of them had laughed.

"This is just so *weird*," Spike had said as they rode down in the elevator. "I haven't been on a date in years."

"Me either," said Leora. Taking his arm, she confided, "If my husband ever found out, he'd shoot us both in the head."

"Ooh, nasty," said Spike, without missing a beat. "Sounds like a pretty scary guy."

"He is," Leora said. "He is—how shall I put this?—insanely jealous."

"I don't know about this," Spike said. "It seems awfully risky for both of us."

"It is, but that's the thrill of it, don't you think?"

"I guess."

The restaurant Spike had chosen meant to re-create the fifties with plenty of Formica, an enormous jukebox, and waitresses dressed in poodle skirts and saddle shoes. Waiting for their order to be taken, he and Leora had held hands under the table and smiled identical, goofy smiles at one another. "My son would just love you, I bet," said Leora. "And of course he desperately needs a father figure at this point in his life."

"You have a kid? Oh, Jesus," said Spike, and rolled his eyes. "I make it a point never to date anyone with kids."

"Why not?"

"It's just one more complication, that's all."

Leora squeezed his hand urgently. "Does this mean we won't be seeing each other again?"

At this moment a half-dozen waitresses lined up in front of the soda fountain and began to lip-synch to "Shake, Rattle and Roll," adding choreographed hand gestures and a bit of jumping around that was meant to pass for dancing. All of them appeared to be teenagers, their faces rosy and exuberant. When the song ended, they acknowledged the enthusiastic applause with solemn bows and sauntered back to work in their saddle shoes.

"Kid or no kid, I'd like to see you again," said Spike. He studied an autographed black-and-white picture of Howdy Doody and Buffalo Bob on the wall above their table and then turned toward their waitress, a girl with big freckled cheeks and a witless look that somehow mimicked Howdy's.

"I'm Giggles," she said.

"Not really," said Spike.

"Actually, I'm Diane, but I'm not supposed to tell you that."

"This is my girlfriend Mary Ellen. Her husband's over there in the back," Spike said, pointing to a gray-haired man seated alone, eating a hamburger from a turquoise cardboard Thunderbird.

"Oh my God," Giggles said, jaw dropping. "What are you going to do?"

"We're going to keep a low profile, of course," said Spike gravely. "Just bring us two bacon burgers in a Thunderbird."

"Good luck!" said Giggles, and shook her head. "I'll be back as fast as I can."

"Hurry!" Leora said.

Swinging open the door to his apartment now, Spike scooped Leora in his arms and carried her into the living room, where he dropped her on the carpet ceremoniously.

"I've never been carried over a threshold before," Leora said. "Not once in my whole life."

"There are many tricks up my sleeve," said Spike. "Just wait and see."

Leora sat back on her elbows. "Nice place you have here."

"Would you like to see the rest of the apartment?"

"I just love seeing other people's homes. They reveal so much about a person, don't you think so?" Following Spike out of the living room, Leora ran a fingertip across a shelf of the bookcase. "Like this, for instance," she said, showing Spike the dark oily film against her index finger. "The person who lives here clearly hasn't been dusting."

"I've been a little distracted since my wife left me. And I know about making beds and loading and unloading the dishwasher, but I didn't realize dusting was one of the things a person actually had to do."

"Your wife left you?" Leora said, peeking into the kitchen. "I'm sorry."

"Don't be," said Spike. "It was a ridiculous thing, actually. We were both stubborn as mules and—"

"Selfish?" Leora looked in the sink and sighed. "Does the word 'Ajax' have any meaning for you?"

"Ajax who fought so bravely in the Trojan War and then killed himself?"

Rummaging around in the cabinet under the sink, Leora found what she was looking for and began to scrub spiritedly at the scratched porcelain. Her hair swung forward over her shoulders, revealing an oval of pure white skin at the back of her neck.

"Hey, you don't have to do that," said Spike. "You're on a date, remember?" Seizing her by the waist, he slowly turned her around and kissed the corners of her mouth. Her fingers dripped water onto his shoes as he slid both hands under her silk T-shirt and unhooked her bra.

"Don't get any ideas," she said, smiling. "Just because you paid for my dinner doesn't necessarily mean you're entitled to"

"Quiet," Spike said. He raised her shirt over her head and her bra straps slid to her elbows; the rest of the bra hung precariously at her waist. He sighed noisily at the appearance of her breasts under the fluorescent lighting; it was as if they were something remarkable, an entirely unfamiliar sight. They were small and extremely, beautifully, pale and he could not imagine what it would be like to feel them beneath his fingers. Reaching for them, his hands shook. He felt needy and weak, but the feeling wasn't an unpleasant one.

"It's only me," Leora murmured.

He could not recall why she had left him or why he had so foolishly refused to submit to her, to sacrifice whatever it was she'd wanted from him.

He sank slowly to the shining tiles of the kitchen floor. Leora's skin, as she lowered herself on top of him, seemed to sizzle against his and he listened for a hissing sound but heard only the magnified voice of his own breathing, as if he were deep underwater. And then there was the sound of Leora unbuckling his belt, her fingers working diligently at his waist.

"On a first date!" he said. "When I was in high school, girls like you didn't go out with guys like me."

"Times have changed," Leora said, "and aren't you lucky." Tearing his shirt open, she laughed at the buttons that popped quietly and then scattered along the floor.

When he came, legs jerking outward, one foot kicked against something that felt like hard plastic, sending a wave of warm water across his knee. It was the cat's water bowl he'd knocked into; the cat himself appeared a moment later and went straight for Leora, burrowing his head under her arm.

"He seems to know you from somewhere," said Spike. "Are you sure you two haven't met before?"

"Maybe in another life," said Leora. "Who knows?" She mopped up the water he'd spilled with a dish towel, snapped her bra back together with her eyes closed.

"Want to spend the night?" said Spike.

"Maybe another time."

"Want to get married and bear my children?"

"Things are moving awfully fast, aren't they?" Leora said.

"It feels like we've been separated forever. Come on, Leora."

"A deal's a deal: kiss Dr. Kling good-bye and I'm yours for life."

"Actually," said Spike, stepping into his pants, "I'm almost weaned. A visit or two more and then it's my swan song."

"So you keep telling me."

"You don't believe me," Spike said. "You think I'm playing games, but I'm not."

"To tell you the truth, I'm tired of living out of a suitcase," said Leora. "And Suzanne and I have been stepping on each other's toes lately. Yesterday, I accidentally used some of her super duper thirty-dollar-a-bottle shampoo to wash Ben's hair and I thought she was going to evict me on the spot."

"Come home," said Spike. "You can use any shampoo you want here."

"What an inducement," Leora said, smiling. "But listen, the day you tell me you've seen the last of Dr. Kling is the day I'll see the last of Suzanne." Her smile gone, eyes suddenly teary, she said, "I feel sick whenever I think about what that's going to be like. I never even told her why I left you, you know. Not that she hasn't tried more than once to get it out of me, of course."

"What *did* you tell her?"

"Oh, something about envy, sloth, gluttony, pride. . . ."

"Everything but the kitchen sink, huh," said Spike. "Thanks a lot."

"Everything but the truth," Leora corrected him.

He returned her to Suzanne's reluctantly, kissed her with great urgency just outside the door, then left in a hurry without saying good-bye. If anyone had asked him, at that moment he would have said he knew nothing about women and even less about love. Or that he knew everything but simply could make no sense of it.

Chapter 20

Venus Jones, the woman Alexander hired as a live-in companion for his mother, has been trying determinedly for nearly half an hour now to get Mary out of bed, but Mary isn't budging. She's a small stubborn lump under the sheets, fighting a losing battle and aware of it, but entirely unwilling to surrender.

"Come on, lazybones," Venus says for the third time, but cheerfully. "I got your clothes all laid out for you. Let's go."

"Go away," says Mary. "Go back to the agency that sent you and let me die in peace."

"Shame on you," Venus says. "Here your son's getting married and you're talking about dying. That's not nice."

"*I'm* not nice," Mary says. "Just ask my son."

"Your son says you got to go to the wedding, and since he's the boss we got to listen."

Under the bed sheets Mary snorts, "Says who?"

"He's paying my salary, so he's the one I listen to."

"You *never* listen to me," Mary complains. "I ask you for Frosted Flakes in the morning, you give me Raisin Bran. I ask you to make coffee, you make tea. I ask you to put on Channel two news, you put on Channel four, just because you're hoping to get a look at that cute colored gentleman who does the weather."

"He's cute all right."

"Aha! So you finally admit it."

"What?" Venus says, trying a new tack. "I can't hear you under there. Come on out and talk to me like a normal person."

Pulling the sheets back grudgingly and with a sigh, Mary says, "My son's trying to trick me. He told me his lady friend was going to become a Jew just so I'd come to the wedding. Now, who's going to believe a story like that? And anyway, I told him to forget about it—converts don't count for much of anything in my book."

"Could be a true story," says Venus. She helps Mary to a sitting position and holds out the rose-colored chiffon dress that Ionie found for her in *The* Shop for Petites on Madison Avenue. "Sometimes people will go to a whole lot of trouble to please somebody else. Now, look at this pretty dress. And look what your son did to those big ugly shoes of yours." She shows Mary her black space shoes, which Alexander had carefully sprayed with silvery paint. "These are real glamorous now," Venus says, "though they kind of look like something out of a science-fiction movie, don't they?"

"Who cares? And why did he paint both of them? He knows I can only wear one shoe."

"Well, the cast will be gone in a couple of weeks and then both feet can look beautiful."

Mary stares at the cast that extends from her toes all the way to the bend in her knee. She wiggles her big toe, tries to remember how she has come to be in this heavy plaster thing that itches and makes her leg look so swollen and shapeless.

Not being able to remember makes her cry. Sometimes it seems she can remember everything that ever happened to her, but now and then she forgets if her hair has been combed, if she has had breakfast, or even something important like whether she has paid her rent bill for the month. She hates feeling stupid when all her life she has been so sharp. Tears roll past her jaw and under her neck and her shoulders shake.

"What?" says Venus, looking at her in surprise. "What's this all about?"

"Don't ever get old and stupid," Mary says, and then she recalls the moment she slipped in the bathtub, the pain and the terrifying thought that she would die right there in her bathroom, naked and absolutely alone. But she had managed to hoist herself over the side of the tub and drag herself to the phone on the night table in her bedroom, which she'd pulled down onto the floor and wept into like someone utterly out of control. I can't understand you, the 911 operator at the other end said impatiently. If you want help you have to make yourself understood. It was his impatience that enraged her, that helped her find her voice.

"I am *tough*!" she says now, giving a little whoop of pleasure.

"I think you're a little wacko today, that's what *I* think," Venus says, and raises Mary's thin little arms one at a time and smoothly slides a stick of deodorant under them.

"Not today," Mary says. "Today I've got it all straightened out. This party we're going to—"

"Wedding," says Venus.

"No no, you've got it all wrong! It's just some fancy party Alexander's throwing himself. And the best thing is," Mary says joyfully, "we don't even need to bring a present."

Spike's mother has flown in for the wedding, looking softer and less gaunt than she had during the winter, her hair no longer white but back to the frosted silver that Spike finds familiar and appealing. Dragging a mesh sack of grapefruit along with a small

suitcase and a garment bag, she drops everything in the center
of his living room and casts her arms around him.

"I love you to pieces," she says, "even if you didn't come to
pick me up at the airport."

"You told me not to," says Spike. "You told me it was easier
just to take a taxi from La Guardia, and I agreed with you because you were right."

"Still, it would have been a nice surprise. There aren't all
that many nice surprises in a person's lifetime, if you know what
I mean."

"I'm truly sorry," Spike says. Easing out of his mother's embrace, he tears open the sack of grapefruit and peels one, like
an orange. He does not offer any to his mother.

"*I'm* truly sorry about your marriage," says Lucille. "I told
you those two were up to no good. So how's the grapefruit?"

"Sour," Spike reports.

"Oh well."

"Listen," says Spike, "I want you to know Leora will be
home any day now. So there's nothing to be sorry about."

"And Suzanne's moving to the north pole, I suppose."

"That would be terrific," Spike says, smiling, "but I'm not
counting on it."

"What *are* you counting on?"

"The simple fact that Leora and I belong together. It's as
uncomplicated as that."

"Well, I wish you the best of luck," Lucille says in a per-
functory way. "And Alexander too. What a strange bird *he* is.
Under the circumstances, I thought it was awfully peculiar that
he chose to invite me to this wedding, but then I thought, Well,
it's actually a good excuse to come up north and see you, and
so here I am." She folds her hands in her lap, begins to whistle
tunelessly. "So your father-in-law's marrying the maid and your
wife left you for another woman, who happens to be your ex-
wife, who I never liked anyway. So what has all this got to do
with me? I'm happy. My friend Pearl Pearlman and I—"

"She did not leave me for another woman, Ma," Spike says.
"You know that's not true."

"Whatever," Lucille says. "*I'm* happy. My friend Pearl Pearlman and I are taking a fascinating class on Jewish mysticism with the rabbi of our temple. You know, the cabalists interpreted the scriptures in a very interesting way. May I tell you about it?"

"Not right now," says Spike. *Who are you?* he wants to ask. *And why are you here in my living room?* This is the woman who brought him into the world, but their connection seems tenuous. She loves him to pieces but something at his very core always stiffens in her presence. He feels his allergy to her kicking in full force now, feels his fingers and toes clenching fiercely as she moves on to a new subject: plumbing problems in her condominium. Her mouth is moving, but he hears nothing; she is a character in a silent film gesturing wildly, expressing outrage and disbelief, and he watches her closely, comprehending nothing, feeling light-headed and drunk with power.

"What are you smiling at?" Lucille says, and grabs him by the arm. "I'm telling you it was beyond belief—these people were throwing feminine-hygiene products down the toilet for years and then they're surprised when the whole plumbing system breaks down and floods the hallway to the tune of eight thousand dollars in repairs."

"What people?" he says.

She looks at him sorrowfully. "You don't *care*," she tells him. "Your marriage is clearly in disastrous shape, despite what you tell me, and you know what—you *shouldn't* care about an eight-thousand-dollar bill from Roto-Rooter. It must have been something, watching Leora and the baby pack up their things and desert you like that. It breaks my heart to think about it." Whistling again, she soon cuts herself off in the middle and says, "I bought them a microwave, for which I received no thank-you note, incidentally. Which really burns me up, to be honest."

"Who?"

"Your father-in-law and his girlfriend, that's who. You really think they're going to be happy?"

Spike nods and offers his mother a grapefruit section. "It's a pleasure to see them together. But you'll see."

"Sour!" Lucille cries, and Spike has to smile, savoring the thought that there's something in the world they agree on. "But you're delicious," his mother announces. Hands pressing firmly against his ears, she gives him a noisy kiss. "No matter what, to me you'll always be delicious."

Blushing in the intense bright heat of his mother's love, he is luminous.

The dress Shavonne has squeezed herself into for the wedding is made of black Spandex and is shockingly skimpy, revealing far more than Alexander would like to see. His eyes widen, his bad shoulder aches at the sight of her. She is standing at the kitchen table, playing happily with the dancing Coca-Cola can, clapping her hands together in rhythm, snapping her fingers, shouting "Boo!" and "Dance, you!" so that the can sways and shakes at her command. Perched on a chair at Shavonne's side, Deneece watches silently for a while, then goes for the can with both hands, knocking it over and onto the floor.

"No!" Shavonne says, and slaps the baby's wrist, a hard clean crack that goes straight to Alexander's heart. Deneece weeps, outraged, but quiets as soon as Alexander whisks her into his arms. She is wearing a pale pink dress studded with sparkly chips resembling diamonds, and her hair is in cornrows, each tail tied together with a small silver ribbon.

"Don't you ever do that again!" Alexander warns Shavonne. "She's a baby, Shavonne, and we don't hit babies. Not ever."

"We don't?" Shavonne stares at him, surprised and disappointed. "But why can't I hurt her if I want to?"

"You know why," he says. He looks her up and down, shakes his head at her. "And that dress is much too tight."

When the doorbell rings, he is grateful for the opportunity to disappear, and rushes to answer it with Deneece riding his hip. Mrs. Fish, her hair a bouquet of pink curlers in preparation for the wedding, greets him apologetically. "I know it's your wedding day, Mr. Fine, but my blinds just came crashing down and I can't have the whole world staring in at me, can I? Hello, cutie," she says to Deneece. "I love that hairdo on you. And where's the beautiful bride?"

"Doing her makeup," Alexander says. "Or maybe she's still in the shower, I don't know. I don't know."

"Nervous?" Mrs. Fish teases him, flicking his elbow with her fingers. "You look so sweet and handsome in your lovely navy-blue suit, but you seem a little . . . rattled. But that's natural, I'm sure." He follows her into the apartment and goes to work on her blinds, which are surprisingly heavy and full of dust. "I just came back from a memorial service a little while ago," Mrs. Fish tells him. "A dear dear friend of mine and her ashes were sitting in the mortuary for two weeks, waiting for some niece of hers out in San Diego to come and collect them. She was such a dignified lady too, and the thought of her ashes just sitting on a shelf all alone like that with no one watching over them made me heartsick. When my time comes, I hope my son comes to collect me right away. Not that you can force anyone to do right by you, but even so . . ."

"I'm getting married in a couple of hours," Alexander says, coming down from the stepladder and brushing the dust from the sleeves of his jacket. "A joyous occasion. So I don't want to hear about anyone's ashes waiting around for a pickup. Not today, all right?"

Deneece is licking the TV screen with the tip of her tongue and cooing sweetly. "Dirty!" says Alexander. "Dusty! Stop that!"

"I'm not the housekeeper I once was," Mrs. Fish admits. "I suppose I could use a little help in that department. In fact," she says, "it occurs to me that your wife might be interested in helping me out, maybe once or twice a week, something like that?"

"She doesn't do that kind of work anymore," says Alexander, and, snapping the stepladder shut with a deliberately heavy hand, murmurs, "Jesus Christ."

"I hope I haven't offended you," Mrs. Fish says quickly. "Here, let me give you your wedding gift. It's right here in the closet."

Positioning herself directly on top of Alexander's feet,

Deneece grinds the heels of her white patent leather shoes into his polished wing tips. "Want to go home?" he says. "Me too."

"It's something practical," Mrs. Fish says, handing him a box wrapped in paper that appears to be patterned with Liberty Bells or, possibly, wedding bells marred by jagged cracks. "An electric can opener. Please don't tell me you have one already. I dragged myself all the way downtown to Macy's and agonized for a good half hour in the small-appliance department. So for God's sake, please don't tell me I made a mistake."

"Actually . . ."

"It's no problem," says Mrs. Fish, suddenly brightening, sounding pleased. "How about if I just keep it for myself and get you something else?"

"Forget about a gift. There's nothing we need. Really."

"An extra bedroom, maybe."

"Pardon?" says Alexander.

"That big chubby girl who's been staying with you. The one who never smiles at me in the elevator. In fact, she doesn't seem to smile at all."

"She's Ionie's granddaughter."

"Oh," says Mrs. Fish, but clearly she wants more, her whole body leaning forward eagerly for another word or two, anything he might offer her.

"She wasn't feeling well, but she's fine now and she's moving back to Staten Island tomorrow with her aunt and uncle," Alexander says.

"Is she an orphan?"

"No, she's not." Lifting Deneece onto his shoulders, he says, "I really have to go. The caterer should be here any minute."

"Well, tell the chubby girl it wouldn't hurt her to smile every now and then."

"I'll tell her," Alexander says as Deneece pulls on his ears happily, riding high and proud on the long narrow shelf of his shoulders.

• • •

Just before leaving to pick up Leora and Ben on his way to the wedding, Spike puts in an emergency call to Dr. Kling. The answering service promises his call will be returned promptly, and though Spike is skeptical, fifteen minutes later Dr. Kling is on the phone, slightly exasperated but willing to listen.

"It's Saturday night, Spike," he says. "What's the problem?"

"I just wanted to say good-bye, I think."

"We've already said our good-byes. What's wrong?" In the background Spike can hear a woman's voice saying, "Let's *go*, Bern."

"I wanted to hear the sound of your voice one more time," Spike confesses.

"You're going to do fine, Spike, believe me. If I didn't think you could handle it, don't you think I would have encouraged you to stay on?"

"Yes."

"Well, then, there you have it. But listen, I've got theater tickets for tonight. If we miss the overture, my friend here will never forgive me."

Spike digs deep into his pants pocket and comes up with a little cellophane-wrapped package containing a piece of candy-coated gum shaped like a Life Saver. He unwraps the cellophane and blows on the circle, making mournful whistling sounds, an impromptu dirge played on a piece of sticky candy. "Have a good time at the theater," he tells Dr. Kling. "Have a nice life."

"Listen, my friend," says Dr. Kling with a sigh, "you've successfully completed a long course of therapy. You should be proud of yourself. Now, get moving and go reclaim your family."

"Now?"

"What are you waiting around for?"

When he emerges from the bedroom, his mother examines him critically, finding fault with his tie, which could be a little more subdued, she claims, and his shoes, which could use new heels and a more careful polishing. "Other than that, you look beautiful," she says. "Aren't you going to change?" she asks in surprise as he heads for the door.

"Nope."

"Never mind, then. But I'll give you a hundred dollars if you get your hair cut Monday."

Spike laughs and closes the door behind them.

In front of Suzanne's building a man in a sleeveless undershirt sits in the open trunk of his car, smoking a cigarette and drinking coffee while he converses with a friend standing at the curb. The license plate at the back of his beat-up Buick reads "GRIMREPR" and Lucille pokes at Spike excitedly with her elbow. "Do you think it's an omen?" she says.

"Of what?"

"I'm not sure, but I find it very chilling," she says breathlessly, following him up the flight of steps to the vestibule. "Maybe we should warn the bride and groom."

"It's just a license plate," says Spike. "You pay a few dollars extra and they'll print anything you want."

"A dark shadow has fallen across our path," Lucille insists. "Watch and see."

They wait outside Suzanne's apartment for what seems like a long while, and when at last the door swings open, it reveals two adults and a child all on their knees in the narrow hallway, all of them watching a little see-through plastic racing car speed across the floor.

"I'm here to pick up the ring boy and his mother," Spike announces. "May I come in?"

"Watch out for the hamster!" Leora shrieks as the racing car bumps into the refrigerator at the end of the hallway. Suzanne turns the car around carefully and points it in Spike's direction.

"What hamster?" says Spike, and then sees the tiny orange-and-white creature in the revolving wheel that's propelling the race car forward at a good clip. Down on his knees with the rest of them now, he urges the hamster on.

"Excuse me, *children*," Lucille says, hands at her hips. "If any of you happens to think this wedding is going to be delayed by a little mouse, you're sadly mistaken."

"Hamster," Leora says, and rises from the floor to greet her mother-in-law. "Suzanne bought him and all his paraphernalia as a present for Ben. And incidentally, I can't say that missing the ceremony would be the worst thing in the world."

Spike is up in an instant and easing himself and Leora past the refrigerator and into the living room. "There's no reason we can't be at this wedding on time," he says. "And you look great, I might add, except for those big smudges of dust on your knees." Squatting now, brushing them clean, he says, "Let's get a move on."

"What if that ceremony turns out to be the end of me?"

"Well," says Spike, "I promise to bring you back with mouth-to-mouth or whatever it takes."

Leora smiles for a moment, then lets it go. "I dreamed about my mother last night," she tells him. "I was a little girl, maybe four or five, and we were shopping in a department store together. I dived under a rack of silky dresses and hid myself away in there for a long time, loving the feel of all that soft stuff against my arms and legs. When I finally came up for air, my mother was gone—it was as if she had just vanished. I raced around the dress department in a panic, and then the whole floor, calling her name more and more frantically, but no one paid any attention to me. And of course," says Leora, her voice wavering, "I never found her."

"Subtle," says Spike. "There's nothing like being hit with a ton of bricks, is there?" Embracing her, he feels her go limp against him, feels her head heavy against his shoulder.

"I'm a grown-up," Leora weeps, "but that doesn't make it any easier. It's supposed to, but it doesn't. It's like I'll always be a little lost in the world without her."

"You have me," he hears himself say. "You always have me."

"I can't imagine not having Suzanne," says Leora in a whisper, absently wiping her tears away with her wrists. "There's something incredibly comforting about feeling so intimate with another woman, the two of you feeling you know almost everything about each other . . . it's funny, she thinks I know her better than you ever did."

"I *told* you, there was always so much she held back," Spike says, pulling away, undoing the circle of his embrace. "And I'm telling you now, I don't care."

" 'I don't care'?" Leora mimicks. "That's the best you can come up with—'I don't care'?"

"Look what she's doing to us! She's doing it to us again!" says Spike, and smacks his fist against his thigh. "Not you— *her!*"

"O-*kay*," Leora says, looking cowed, her shoulders hunched, palms thrust upward. "I want to come home," she confesses. "I feel so worn down all of a sudden. And soft, like I want to give in."

"You do?" he says, astonished to hear this.

"I think it will be an enormous relief, giving in. And that's what I want—an unburdening. We'll work out the rest of it when we can."

"Are you sure?"

"I just want to come home," Leora says wearily. "I can't focus on the rest right now. It's my mother, my father, Ionie— I'm so full of them, so weighted down by everything I feel."

"I know," he says, "I know," but he himself feels buoyant, as if he might rise above the floor and float past her as he slowly caresses her cheek now, his fingers absorbing its heat.

"Go get your things and let's go."

Making his way to the door, he gathers his son to him, grateful for the way the smooth little legs hook automatically around his waist. "I've missed you too much," he confides.

Ben jerks the snap-on bow tie from his throat and tosses it over Spike's shoulder. "Hate it," he says.

Retrieving the tie from the floor, Suzanne holds it in her palm and regards it wistfully. "Everyone looks so lovely in their wedding finery," she says. She's dressed in cycling shorts and a leotard that show off the sharp points of her bones; her long bare feet are bony too. Without her dark, striking makeup, she looks droopy and in need of sunlight.

"I feel a little like Cinderella tonight," she says, clipping

Ben's tie in place for him, just before he slips down from Spike's legs and out of the room. "Everyone's going to the ball except me." She's so close to Spike he can see a fine turquoise vein pulsing faintly at the corner of one eye, and he nearly reaches out a fingertip to quiet it. He's known her forever, he thinks, and for a moment almost convinces himself that perhaps it is his fate to simply endure her, as he might endure any other exasperating friend of Leora's. But he's fooling himself and knows it; this woman he was once married to is far more than exasperating—standing so near to her, he knows she's a dangerous weight his marriage cannot withstand.

The turquoise vein is still flickering; his fingertip moves on its own and touches the softest fringe of eyelash. "Just a speck," he mumbles. "It's gone now."

"Thanks."

"I don't know what's going on in your life," he says.

"There's nothing going on," says Suzanne. "School is over in a couple of weeks and then I'm off to Morocco and Spain for a month with another teacher in my department. The rest of the summer is just a big blank," she finishes with a shrug.

"That's great!" Spike says, and flashes her a broad, open smile. "I mean, have a great time."

"You love the thought of my being out of the country," she says, testing him. "Admit it."

"I don't want to get into an argument, okay?"

Suzanne shakes her head. "I feel so strongly that I should have been invited to this wedding," she says. "Doesn't it seem to you that I belong there?"

"What? Why?"

"Because you and Leora and Ben and I, we're all connected."

"What is this, an ad for the phone company?" he says, and can hear the swelling, openly sentimental music of a television commercial. He realizes instantly that he has insulted her but still is astounded when Suzanne kicks him between the legs with her bare foot.

"Don't you ridicule *my life!*" she says furiously, raising her foot again in his direction. "I won't permit it."

He watches her rib cage heaving under the thin skin of her leotard, stares at the spots of high color that have appeared on her cheekbones, two crimson stains that unmistakably mark her anger. He is shaken by her passion, by what is so clearly the passion of her life. He had not known. But she has to know that she has gone too far, even disturbing his dreams, a phantom who'd kept her eyes shamelessly upon him at all the wrong moments.

"You're too much for me," he says, but suddenly finds he cannot tell her all the rest. *You imagine me in your bedroom, in your bed, and then blame me for being there?* he can hear her saying, her voice rising in disbelief. *You're blaming* me?

"I'm sorry I kicked you," Suzanne is telling him. "I've never done anything like that in my life. Maybe it's because I'm about to get my period."

He winces at this intimacy. "Maybe it's me," he offers.

"You know, I never apologized properly for leaving you," Suzanne says. "I was so sure of what I was doing that somehow there seemed no need to apologize."

"Apology accepted," he says.

"Too little too late, I guess."

"I don't think about those things anymore. They don't mean anything to me. I've moved on to a new place."

Suzanne stands unsteadily, one foot on top of the other, rocking slightly, without a word. "I love your little family," she murmurs. "You I could live without. It's funny, in a way, isn't it?"

"Hilarious," he says. He imagines her in Morocco, in the shadow of the Rock of Gibraltar, the rock itself and also Suzanne obscured in mist rising from the Mediterranean. Perhaps she is smiling in this distant place, perhaps not. *Can't you fill up your life with something?* he urges her silently. *Anything at all.*

"Remember the day I told you I was leaving you?" she asks, sounding nostalgic, as if she were recalling something lovely and tender from their shared history.

"Not really," he says, and it is true that he no longer remembers with any clarity the shock, the sharp sting of humiliation, the nervous little speech she delivered, her eyes luminous as she spoke of kismet.

"You're moving in the wrong direction," he tells her impatiently.

Automatically, she looks down at her feet. "I'm standing still," she says.

"You're moving backward," he insists, and puts out his hands to stop her.

Ionie's left hand is soaking in a plastic sandwich bag half-filled with milk—therapy for her nails, she explains to Alexander in an irritated tone. "And don't you be laughing at me." Because she had missed out on a real wedding the first time around, she's dressed in a floor-length gown decorated with a spray of seed pearls across the bosom and a lot of lace at the cuffs and neckline. At her wrist is her lucky bracelet—a circle of linked silver cats, each about the size of a half-dollar.

Sitting at her side at the edge of their bed, Alexander listens to the string quartet in the living room warming up with a little Mendelssohn. "I'm not laughing at you," he reassures her. "I just happen to think your nails are perfect the way they are." He fingers her lucky bracelet for a few moments, then cautiously plants a kiss on her damp neck. "Do you love me?"

"Now, what kind of dumbbell question is that?" Ionie snaps, and wiggles her fingers through the milk.

"Just checking," he says. He opens the door a crack and peeks out at Ionie's family sitting on a row of rented folding chairs arranged by the caterers in the living room. He stares at the tops of the heads of Ionie's little nieces and nephews, whom he'd met once before at a barbecue on Staten Island. The adults there were friendly and hospitable, the children noisy and long-limbed in their bathing suits as they ran through the sprinkler that had been set up for them on the front lawn of Ionie's brother's attached town house right off the highway. Now the children are all sitting motionless in their seats, hands folded decorously in their laps, he imagines. He sees a tall woman in a pink turban—Ionie's sister-in-law—moisten a fingertip on each hand with saliva and smooth back the hair of one of the little girls. Raising her eyes, she notices Alexander looking at her, and waves excitedly. He returns her wave, then closes the door and approaches Ionie.

"I saw Rockell out there and all the kids. It's late; we've got to go out there."

"I know it." She raises her hand carefully out of the milk and wipes her fingers with a towel. "Don't know what's wrong with me," she says. "My nails are in real bad shape and my heart's all jumpy, flapping all around in there like a crazy thing."

"Cold feet?"

"No way, baby. It's just like my own true self left me and what I got stuck with is a different me, someone who's too shaky to stand up and walk out the door and see people."

"We can get married right here in the bedroom. You won't have to see anyone except the rabbi if you don't want to."

"I'm not crazy," Ionie says. "I got to get me some aspirin, though. I might be getting a headache pretty soon." When Alexander puts two Bufferin in her palm, she closes her fingers over them and studies the taut shiny skin of her knuckles. "You been thinking about your poor Margot at all?"

"No," he says, then a moment later, "yes. But only that she'd be surprised at how happy . . . at our happiness. Surprised and probably pleased too."

"Oh Lord." Ionie sighs, and her eyes fill with tears. "You going to carry that sadness of your loss with you to your grave. Just like me and my Willie."

Alexander nods. "But most of the time," he says gratefully, "I don't even know it's there."

Tipping back her head, Ionie swallows the Bufferin like a real trouper, without water. "Well, I be fixing to get myself married today," she says. "What about you?"

"Sounds good," he says. Leaning in to kiss her, he hears his mother's voice rising above all the low murmuring in the living room, a voice clear and insistent and a little harsh. "I'm the mother and I ought to know," she announces. "And believe you me, he was always an impossible child."

The living room looks unfamiliar to Alexander as he walks too quickly, swiftly as his heartbeat, up the path between the neat rows of Lucite folding chairs, his arm linked in Ionie's. Out of the corner of his eye he sees Mrs. Fish in a bright yellow dress, and Leora in a black one, Ben twisting around in her lap, his tiny fingers dancing across his father's knee and back again. He hears music from the string quartet, knows it is Mozart but cannot remember its title or even what kind of piece it is, though he chose it himself just last week, after a great deal of thought. "Slow down," someone says in a stage whisper, and he realizes it is Sydney, dapper in a gray suit and red silk tie as he stands up front next to the rabbi, a pale young woman with short feathery hair and a reputation for officiating at mixed marriages without complaint.

The music fades and the rabbi clears her throat; two minutes into her speech she is interrupted by Alexander's mother, who chirps from her wheelchair, "Don't worry—they're just good friends!" Little pockets of shocked laughter erupt everywhere and even the rabbi is smiling. Alexander tightens his grip on Ionie's arm; he can see her shoulders shaking and worries that at any moment her deep warm laugh will take over the room. He wishes he could turn away from her and toward his mother, shoot the old lady a fierce look that would strike her dead in her seat in an instant. But then, inexplicably, the feeling vanishes and he is silently forgiving her, just as Ionie lets loose with a snort of laughter that explodes into something rich and splendid, bending her body nearly in half. "Pardon me," she wheezes, and thumps her feet in their white satin high heels.

"Take all the time you need," the rabbi whispers, still smiling. The words seem to work magic on Ionie; now she is straightening up beside Alexander, slipping her hand in his, full of muted apologies that he silences with a quick nod of his head.

The rabbi clasps her hands in front of her, reveals her bitten-down nails to Alexander. "Occasionally," she says, "these things happen. We lose control—we drink too much, we eat too much, we say too much. We're only human, after all. None of us is perfect. We do the best we can, which brings me to the subject of marriage. For some, marriage is like a prison, for others it is heaven; for most of us, I suspect, it is somewhere in between. The one thing we know for sure is that it's never easy. My own marriage, for example, ended in a terribly bitter divorce just a few months ago. But that's another story. . . ."

Suddenly light-headed, Alexander feels himself swaying slightly. He wonders if he is going to faint, imagines himself keeling over dramatically at the rabbi's little feet. He is no longer listening to her and understands that he is capable at this moment of concentrating on only one thing: keeping himself upright and conscious. The rabbi is extending an arm toward him now, offering a silver cup of wine, which he stares at as though it were some mysterious object whose function he could not guess in a thousand years.

"Sip it," the rabbi says in an urgent whisper.

Obediently Alexander tastes the wine. "Too sweet," he complains.

The rabbi sings a few lines in Hebrew in a lovely soprano. "You look terrible, Mr. Fine," she murmurs afterward. "Like death warmed over."

"Can't you hurry it up, Rabbi," Ionie pleads. "I can see he can't take much more of this." Squeezing Alexander's hand, she says, "Hang in there, hon."

On cue, Ben scoots forward with the rings, which he dumps into the rabbi's open palm. "Bye," he calls loudly, and rushes off, flinging himself back into Leora's lap. Turning to watch him, Alexander sees his daughter's face for the first time. She smiles at him shyly, tentatively, approvingly, he thinks, then busies herself arranging Ben in her lap, dipping her head so that her hair falls over her face, obscuring Alexander's view completely. But he has seen enough.

A gold band gleams on his finger, though he doesn't know

how it got there. He stamps hard on the empty wineglass that is wrapped in a linen napkin and placed at his heel, hears the cries of congratulations rising from the gathering of family and friends as the glass shatters. He kisses Ionie briefly, breathing in the winy scent of her warm breath.

He knows his name and the name of his new bride, but not much else. Dim-witted and slow moving as a dinosaur, his hands and feet icy, he allows Ionie to lead him through the small crowd. People pat him on the back, pump his arm, offer enthusiastic kisses that land awkwardly at the corners of his mouth and eyes. Spike and Leora embrace him at the same moment, sandwiching him so tightly between them that the bony knob of his daughter's shoulder jams painfully into his neck.

Lifting his head away from her, able to breathe more easily, he hears the string quartet playing his favorite song, which stirs him instantly. He looks around for Ionie, who, he sees, is talking to his mother and Venus, holding his mother's hand, pointing downward at her ludicrous silvery shoe, the three of them laughing companionably.

"Ah, the handsome young groom," his mother announces as he steps forward. "I'm told I said something you didn't like."

"True."

"Well, that's too bad. But let me tell you something about me. I'm not very good at censoring myself and that's just the way it is. Ask Venus, she'll tell you."

A waitress dressed like a man, in black pants, gold vest, and a string tie, appears with a round silver tray of hors d'oeuvres. Alexander chooses something in a miniature pastry shell and hands it to his mother. "Enjoy," he says generously.

"Come back here!" Mary cries as he sails off with Ionie. "I want to have a fight with you!"

Navigating through the crowd, threading gracefully in and out of everything in their way—guests holding champagne glasses to their lips and tiny golden cheese soufflés on cocktail napkins, children whizzing around in aimless circles, waiters nodding patiently as people ask, "Is it low cholesterol or just low fat?"—

they arrive at last at the musicians' station. Silently, Alexander admires the cellist's floor-length satin skirt, the way the tips of her shoes peek out coyly from under it, the fluid, synchronized motion of the violinists' bows across their instruments. And the music! Like a child, he could listen to this one song a dozen times over, his pleasure never diminishing.

He circles Ionie's waist with one arm, matches his hips precisely with hers as he takes her hand and raises it to his shoulder. " 'Is-n't it ro-man-tic?' " he sings along with the music in a near-whisper. " 'Mere-ly to be young on such a night as this?' "

He does not wait for an answer, but closes his eyes, intending to lead them both to somewhere they have never been before.